RISE OF THE WORLD EATER

JAMIE LITTLER

PUFFIN

PUFFIN BOOKS

UK | USA | Canada | Ireland | Australia
India | New Zealand | South Africa

Puffin Books is part of the Penguin Random House group of companies
whose addresses can be found at global.penguinrandomhouse.com.

www.penguin.co.uk
www.puffin.co.uk
www.ladybird.co.uk

First published 2021

002

Text design by Janene Spencer
Printed in Great Britain by Clays Ltd, Elcograf S.p.A.

A CIP catalogue record for this book is available from the British Library

ISBN: 978-0-241-35538-1

All correspondence to:
Puffin Books
Penguin Random House Children's
One Embassy Gardens, 8 Viaduct Gardens, London SW11 7BW

For all of you who climbed aboard the Frostheart
and joined me on this adventure

LANDS OF THE ALL-NIGHT
FIRA
SKYBRIDGE
SHADE'S CHASM
FROSTFINGER MOUNTAINS
ENSERA
RUS FLOATING STRONGHOLDS
RIMERIDGE
AURORA'S EMBRACE
PYREFLY
SPIRIT POOLS
BROKEN COAST
DANCING WATERS
SUNREST
SKY FORGE
MURGHUL
N
ICESPIRE
THUDRUK
ASHLANDS
WINTER'S HEART

GLACIA RUINS
VULPIS CARAVAN ROUTE
WORLD'S SPINE MOUNTAINS
SACRED YETI LANDS
AURORA
TEKKO
SKYSHIMMER
SENTINEL'S WATCH
GHOST STONES
ENDLESS FOREST
PINEHAVEN
TWO BROTHERS
EVERSTORM
OSO
THE MAW
THE REND
HORIZON'S EDGE

FRÖST-HEART

FAMILY REUNION

It was an unusual sight indeed.

For the first time in history, the Pathfinders had assembled for war. A vast fleet of sleighs sped across the frozen landscape, led by Commander Ember Stormbreaker, now the most powerful person in the entire Snow Sea. She had vowed to rid the world of the Leviathan menace that plagued all of human-kin, and to fulfil her oath; each vessel under her command was armed to the teeth with powerful ancient weapons from the World Before.

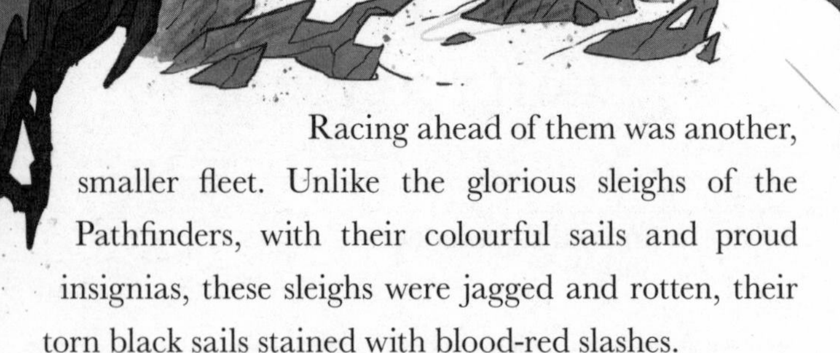

Racing ahead of them was another, smaller fleet. Unlike the glorious sleighs of the Pathfinders, with their colourful sails and proud insignias, these sleighs were jagged and rotten, their torn black sails stained with blood-red slashes.

They were Wraiths, and they had led the Pathfinders on a merry chase to the very ends of the known world. Not that catching the sinister raiders was the Pathfinders' main goal. Their true target – a Leviathan swarm of unfathomable size – had disappeared beneath the snows under the barrage of fire the Pathfinders had unleashed upon them. But the Pathfinder fleet would not give up the chase so easily. Wherever there were Wraiths, Leviathans were sure to be close by.

But perhaps even more strange was the fact that, for the first time in many years, fighting Leviathans

was not the first thing on Stormbreaker's mind. Her focus was entirely on the child she followed into the cargo hold of the sleigh known as the *Frostheart.*

The child, a boy from the far north named Ash, swallowed hard, butterflies circling wildly in his belly. He felt like he was walking through a dream, as though each step he took was on air instead of the solid wood beneath his boots.

Once below, Commander Stormbreaker made to speak, when she noticed someone else had followed them into the dark, creaking hold. It was Lunah, the *Frostheart*'s navigator, who was only a little older than Ash and just so happened to be his best friend.

'Don't mind me, just grabbin' somethin' for the cap'n,' Lunah said, clearly doing nothing of the sort.

For a long moment, Stormbreaker watched the girl pretend to rummage through some crates. The Commander cleared her throat loudly, her cool, steely eye boring into Lunah.

'Know what? I'll come back when yer done,' Lunah said, her face flushing as she rushed back up to the deck.

At last, Ash was alone.

Alone with this woman he barely knew, this famous Leviathan hunter.

His mother.

Ash's thoughts churned and his heart thrummed against his ribs.

He'd imagined this scene countless times. During the lonely years in the Fira Stronghold, throughout his voyage aboard the *Frostheart.* So often it had been his final thought before he drifted off to sleep, a smile creeping on to his face – a thought he'd found comfort in and that had kept him going through it all.

The scene always went the same.

After years of searching, Ash would finally find his parents. His mum and dad would scoop him up into their arms as they cried tears of happiness, squeezing him so close he knew he'd never feel alone again. They would be proud beyond words that he'd journeyed halfway across the world to find them, facing countless dangers that would have daunted even the most experienced Pathfinder, so impressed with the brave boy he'd become.

But now that Ash was standing before his mother – or should that be Ember? Or . . . or Commander Stormbreaker? He wasn't entirely sure what to call her – his imaginings suddenly seemed very childish indeed.

His mother didn't cheer. She didn't reach out for him. She wasn't crying tears of pride or joy. She wasn't even *smiling*!

Should he make the first move? His mother had the reputation of a hardened warrior to uphold: she couldn't be seen *cuddling*. But now that they were alone . . . just *maybe*?

'Mum . . .' Tears stabbed at the backs of his eyes as he moved towards her with his arms open.

She took half a step back.

The movement was small, but to Ash it felt like a slap across his face.

He stopped in his tracks, a lump forming in his throat.

Maybe this is normal, Ash told himself. *Maybe this is just how parents are with their children?*

Stormbreaker's one good eye stared at Ash with an intensity he could barely withstand. Her hands were balled into fists, her already intimidating build made more imposing by her large, rugged cloak. Ash tried to pull his shoulders back in the hope that he'd look bigger, like he really was her son, but he found himself shrinking further into himself under her gaze.

Why is she looking at me like that? Was she angry with him? Frustrated he'd managed to find her? Was she really his mother at all? All Ash knew was that he had to break the unbearable silence.

'I-I'm sorry about the Shrieker . . .' Ash croaked as he nervously tried to tie his fingers into knots. He probably hadn't

made the best first impression arriving on a Leviathan hunter's sleigh riding a Leviathan. 'I-I –'

'So you *are* a Song Weaver?' Stormbreaker asked, the accusation punching Ash in the gut.

He nodded.

Stormbreaker's face shifted, though whether it was from fear, hatred or something else, Ash couldn't tell. 'You took after your father then, in the end.'

The few times Ash had seen Commander Stormbreaker back in the Stronghold of Aurora, she had appeared as hard as stone, but in this moment she looked as fragile as thin ice.

Ash had almost come to terms with what it meant to be a Song Weaver, the few misunderstood and persecuted human-kin who could communicate with Leviathans through their mystical Songs, but seeing his mother's reaction made his stomach clench. His brain flipped through the thousands of questions he'd planned to ask his parents when he finally found them.

Where have you been all this time?

Why did you leave me?

But now that, at long last, he had the chance, words abandoned him.

It wasn't meant to be like this. They were supposed to be laughing and catching up and sharing stories. It wasn't meant to be like this at all!

Stormbreaker broke the silence.

'Why have you come here?'

Ash recoiled. Of all the questions she could've asked, after all the time they'd been apart, that was it? No *how are you*, or *tell me about yourself*, or even a little *I missed you so much.*

Why was he here? Surely it was obvious?

'I-I came to find you,' Ash said in a very small voice.

'You should be with the Fira, where it's safe,' Stormbreaker said, as though he'd disobeyed a clear order. 'I left you there for a reason.'

Safe.

Ash thought back to the way the Fira had shunned him, turned him into an outcast. If it hadn't been for his yeti guardian, Tobu, Ash was sure the Fira would've left him in the wilds for dead.

'They exiled me,' Ash said quietly.

'For being a Song Weaver?' Stormbreaker's expression was unreadable.

Ash nodded. 'You – you never came back. I had no idea where you were, what had happened . . . I thought that maybe you'd left me forever!'

For an instant, Ash thought he caught a flicker of shame somewhere beneath Stormbreaker's ice-cold expression. She stepped closer, reaching her arms out towards him. Her hands hung in the air, flexing with indecision, before she awkwardly patted him on the head.

Ash froze.

His senses burned and his heart cried out at her touch. It wasn't a hug, but it was *something*. It was the closest he'd been to either of his parents since they'd left him all those years ago. He worried that if he moved, even dared to speak, his mother would disappear, and he would be left alone all over again. Stormbreaker smelled of leather and sweat, not quite how he imagined a mother would smell, but it was how *his* mother smelled.

My mother . . . my mother . . . Ash repeated in his head, again and again, as though saying it to himself enough times would make him finally believe it.

'I had to protect you, Ash,' Stormbreaker said, softer than before. 'I knew that as long as there were Leviathans in this world, it wouldn't be safe for you out here. After what happened to your father . . .'

'What *did* happen to him?' Ash blurted, although he already had a pretty good idea. He'd only recently discovered that his father, Ferno, had once been a Wraith – one of the cut-throat Song Weavers obsessed with revenge against the Strongholds for the way Song Weavers had been treated. Ash knew that his father had helped the Wraith leader, Shaard, gather what was needed to release the Devourer, the God-Leviathan that had the power to destroy civilizations. He knew that Shaard had taught Ferno the Devourer's Dark Song, a Song that could force Leviathans to do a Song Weaver's bidding, but which had also begun to slowly eat away at his father's soul. And he knew that with his friend Rook's help, his father had changed, seen the error of his ways, and tried to make things right before he fled far away to escape the Devourer's mind-corrupting Song.

Ash knew all of this, but he wanted to hear it from his mother.

'We lost your father many years ago. The Leviathans *stole* him from us.' She said the word 'stole' with particular ferociousness.

She blames the Leviathans, Ash thought, his heart sinking, *just like all the stupid stories. But Leviathans didn't steal Dad's mind and force him to run away. Only the Devourer's Dark Song can do that. It was Shaard who led my dad into the Devourer's clutches. If anyone's to blame, it's him!*

Ash wanted to tell Stormbreaker the truth, that the Leviathans weren't their enemies, that they had no power to control Song Weavers as all the legends claimed, but as he looked into her glimmering eye his courage failed him.

What if it made her angry? Ash couldn't bear the thought of her not liking him, of not wanting him around.

'On the day we lost him,' Stormbreaker continued,

'when you were still a baby, I made an oath to the fire spirits that I would defeat the Leviathan monsters once and for all. I swore on my life that I would make it a safer world for you to grow up in, a world where we could be happy . . . where we would be free to be a family again.'

A family again . . .? Ash could think of nothing he wanted more.

'Do you . . . do you know where Dad is?'

Stormbreaker turned her head to the side, casting her eye down.

'No,' she replied finally.

Ash nodded. It was the answer he'd expected, but that didn't stop his heart-wrenching disappointment.

'It was Dad who left me a trail to follow,' Ash said. 'It's why I'm here . . .'

Stormbreaker blinked in astonishment. 'Your *father* guided you here?'

'He hid clues in the lullaby he used to Sing to me as a baby,' Ash explained. Stormbreaker was speechless. 'You . . . you didn't know?'

'There is much your father never told me.' She did not say the words kindly.

Ash swallowed, then went on. 'The clues led me to the frost-heart, and then to Solstice, where I was meant to take the frost-heart for safety.'

He'd hoped his incredible journey to the fabled hidden Stronghold where human-kin and Leviathans lived side by side might've impressed Stormbreaker, but if it did, she gave no indication.

'*Frostheart*?' she asked. 'You mean this sleigh?'

'No . . . well, not really – it's what our sleigh is named after. It's the heart of a powerful Leviathan Ancient. It acts like some kind of key to the Devourer's prison.'

'Ferno and Shaard used to speak of the Devourer, the most powerful of all Leviathans. But I thought it was only a legend.'

'Shaard searched the entire world for the frost-heart, and Dad wanted me to keep it away from him. But I . . . I . . .' Ash flushed, his throat tightening. 'I couldn't. Shaard followed us to Solstice. He stole the frost-heart and his Wraiths kidnapped all the Song Weavers who lived there. The Wraiths are forcing them to fight on their side, even though they don't want to!'

Ash paused, not for the first time noticing the similarities between the Wraiths and Pathfinders – how they'd both given the Song Weavers no choice but to obey their orders.

'The Wraiths follow Shaard?' Stormbreaker asked, looking confused. 'Why would such creatures follow him?'

'The Wraiths aren't dark spirits, like everyone believes – they're . . . they're human-kin. Song Weavers.' Ash was ashamed to admit it. People already greatly distrusted Song Weavers, and this awful truth would only reinforce their prejudices. Stormbreaker's eye narrowed and Ash hurried on. 'They've been *turned* by the Devourer's Dark Song and follow Shaard unquestioningly, and they'll force the Solstice prisoners to do the same! Shaard wants to use the frost-heart to unleash the Devourer from its prison. That's where he's heading right now!'

Stormbreaker's gaze grew distant.

'I can't believe I didn't piece it together. It was all there in front of me . . .'

'The frost-heart is calling out to the Leviathans for help,' Ash said.

'And that's why so many Leviathans have gathered together,' Stormbreaker continued. 'To answer the call of this *heart.* We were amazed when we came across the swarm. The fleet had set out to test our new archeoweapons, but never did we imagine we'd come across so many Leviathans at once . . .'

'They're trying to save the frost-heart, and we have to help them,' Ash said. 'If Shaard releases the Devourer, I don't think any of us will be able to stop it.'

Stormbreaker considered his words carefully, her brow creasing at the mention of helping Leviathans.

Ash bit his tongue. He just needed her to believe that Shaard was the real threat; that's what mattered right now. He could show her later that the Leviathans weren't the enemy. Ash half expected her to scoff at him, but instead she gave a curt nod.

'I agree.'

'Y-you do?'

'I don't know much about this Devourer, but I understand Shaard well enough to know whatever he plans will have terrible consequences for the Strongholds, especially if it involves some Leviathan breed we've never seen before. I will put an end to his madness once and for all.'

A cautious smile grew on Ash's face. He barely dared believe it. His mother wanted to help! He had a sudden, overwhelming urge to throw his arms round her. He leaned closer, but Stormbreaker remained still.

'I'm happy I found you,' Ash said, trying to encourage her. 'I missed you so much!'

Stormbreaker seemed taken aback by his words.

'I'm . . . I'm happy to see you too, Ash.' The slight crack in her otherwise firm voice was the only sign she was speaking the truth. 'I just wish our reunion wasn't in the most dangerous part of the world. You being here . . . *complicates* things. And I can't afford any distractions. I need to focus; the fleet deserves that from their commander. They're looking to me to lead us through this.'

Ash stared down at his boots, his belly feeling hollow. He wanted to do his mother proud, not be a nuisance.

'This battle is bigger than any one of us. We are fighting for our very survival, and we must *all* do our part. And that includes you, Ash.'

Light suddenly spilled into the hold as the door to the deck slammed back. Stormbreaker's scruffy first mate stood in the opening.

'Commander,' he said urgently. 'You're needed up top.'

'I'll be right there, Jed,' Stormbreaker said, before turning back to Ash.

She raised her hand again, but still seemed unable to decide what to do with it. Ash willed her to reach out and comfort him.

Without another word, she spun on her heel and headed up top to play her part.

2

THE EDGE OF THE WORLD

These broken southern lands were known as the Rend for a reason.

Stretching far beyond the edges of the map, they were a gnarled, shattered place of colossal craters and crooked canyons so deep, tales said they were bottomless. The entire region looked as though it had been the scene of some extraordinary battle, where forces of unimaginable power had literally torn the world apart. As if in confirmation, countless relic-machines and deadly archeoweapons from the World Before lay scattered across the ice, half hidden and frozen. No wonder the Rend was known as a haunted, cursed place.

It was through this forbidden land that the Wraiths led the Pathfinder fleet for over a week, pushing forward against a blistering blizzard that grew in intensity the further they travelled. The *Frostheart* crew looked out at the mangled terrain in fearful silence. A penetrating wind whipped through their thick furs and bit into their flesh. It was *so* cold in the Rend, even for Ash, who was used to the numbing temperatures of the far north.

It's like we're in the heart of winter itself, he thought as he braced himself against the chill.

'This place is freakin' me out.' Lunah shivered.

'Aye, something sinister haunts this place,' agreed Kob, the *Frostheart*'s squat deckhand, his large moustache bristling with unease. 'I can feel it in my bones.'

'It's that ceaseless racket,' Nuk, the large mursu captain of the *Frostheart,* huffed. 'It's been doing my head in for days!'

'You can hear it too?' Ash asked, surprised.

From the moment they'd entered the Rend, Ash could've sworn he could hear the land itself . . . *Singing.* The strange Song was nothing like he'd ever heard before. It resonated just under the surface of everything. It saturated the air. It danced between the ice and stone, its voice begging the Pathfinders to return the way they'd come.

At first, Ash had thought he was imagining it, this *All-Song,* but Rook, a Song Weaver far more experienced than he was, had confirmed she could hear it too. Not that this made Ash feel much better – Rook could be quite sinister at the best of times.

'Even for us non-Weavers, it's hard to miss an evil cacophony like that!' Nuk said.

'Hey! You think that means the rest of us can Song Weave now too?' Lunah asked, taking a deep breath.

Nuk put a finger on her lips. 'Maybe later, eh, dear?'

'It is not the Song that is evil,' Tobu added, standing protectively behind Ash, his arms folded against his chest. 'It's what's ensnared beneath it.'

Tobu was right. Ash could sense it too, and he suspected it was the reason Rook was hiding in the shadows of the main deck, her hands trembling as frightened whispers rasped from within her dark hood. A sinister presence lurked beneath the unending Song, straining against it. It wasn't a sound, exactly, more like a sensation, a creeping dread that scratched at Ash's mind. He constantly felt like he was being watched, *hunted*, even, the hairs on the back of his neck standing on end. But every time he spun round to see what it was, he found nothing. It was everywhere and nowhere at the same time, a hateful well of malice, radiating a loathing for all the world.

'It's the Devourer,' Ash said with a shudder. 'It's really close now.'

Ash knew the other Song Weavers in the fleet could sense it too. Looking over to his mother's sleigh, the *Kinspear*, running close alongside the *Frostheart*, he saw a group of Song Weavers huddled together at the sleigh's prow. It was the only place the Pathfinders allowed them to be when they weren't being used to power the sleigh's archeoweapons with their Songs. He saw in their eyes the same fear he felt.

'Wax might block it out,' suggested Twinge, the *Frostheart*'s jolly cook. 'I once knew a crew who had to sleep next to a *terrible* snorer, and they all stuffed wax into their ears, just so they could get some sleep. Worked like a charm, I'm told.'

Kailen, the fiercest member of the *Frostheart*'s crew, rolled her eyes. 'That crew was us, and you were the ruddy snorer, you dolt!'

The crew chortled at this, but the laughs were joyless and forced.

'At least we have a fleet-loada' honkin' great weapons to blast whatever nasties are skulkin' around these lands. I'm just glad *she's* on our side.' Lunah dipped her head.

Ash followed her gaze and spotted his mother on the main deck of the *Kinspear*. She was giving orders to her crew, a look of fierce determination etched on to her face. Ash's nerves twitched at the sight of her.

'I still can't believe she's my mum . . .'

She seemed almost otherworldly – so confident and powerful. How could they possibly be related?

'*I* still can't believe she's yer ma,' Kailen said, placing a hand on Ash's shoulder. 'I mean – she's a flippin' legend! And you're . . . well . . . you're Ash!'

'I dunno,' Lunah said, examining Ash. 'If we got you into a bigger cloak and some butt-kickin' poses, I reckon you'd be the spittin' image!'

'You're just fine as you are, poppet,' Nuk assured him, and Ash smiled his thanks. Truth be told, he didn't really know how alike he and his mother might be. They'd barely been able to spend any time together since their first talk in the hold.

She's busy, Ash told himself, trying to stem the hurt in his heart. *We'll get to know each other once this is all over.*

He tried to find solace in the fact that they were fighting for the same thing. She was going to help them stop Shaard.

So why did the look on her face make Ash feel so uneasy?

The next day brought the chase to an end.

The Wraith sleighs had run out of snow.

An enormous glacier blocked the path ahead, a mass of ice so gnarled and broken it appeared like a monster emerging from the swirling blizzard. Cornered, the Wraiths had no choice but to turn and face the Pathfinders, who had fanned out into a wide arrow formation, blocking their escape.

Maybe Nell didn't know the way after all . . . Ash thought hopefully, looking at the trapped Wraith fleet.

Nell, one of the Elders from the Stronghold of Solstice, had been leading Shaard and the Wraiths to the Devourer's hidden prison. Having lost hope that Song Weavers would ever be treated as equals by the

Strongholders, he'd been persuaded by Shaard that they could use the Devourer to topple the rule of the Aurora Council and put Song Weavers in charge.

Stormbreaker and her first mate, Jed, had scrambled across a long boarding plank placed between the *Kinspear* and *Frostheart*, hoping to gather last-minute information from the crew, who knew Shaard better than anyone.

'And which is his sleigh?' Stormbreaker asked, peering through her eyeglass.

'The largest one, surrounded by the others.' Nuk pointed.

'Naturally. Always getting others to do his dirty work.'

'That's where we'll find the frost-heart,' Nuk confirmed. 'The other Wraiths will do all they can to protect it. I suggest we strike for the heart rather than unleashing a full-out assault – send our best sleighs straight for Shaard himself, while distracting the others with our superior numbers.'

'No need for any fancy tactics, Captain Nuk.' Jed chuckled, his long beard tassels fluttering in the wind. 'With our archeoweapons, we can blast 'em all to cinders.'

'I don't doubt it. But let us not forget there are still innocent Solstice folk aboard those sleighs, kidnapped by Shaard. They need our help, not a full broadside.'

'The Song Weavers . . .' Jed swallowed, clearly having forgotten them.

'Of course we'll do all we can to rescue them,' Stormbreaker said to Ash's relief.

'Aye, commander, they'll certainly be useful in our next battle against the wurms,' Jed agreed, darkening Ash's mood instantly.

Most Song Weavers had no desire to be dragged into a deadly war, but as it was only they who could power the deadliest archeoweapons; to aid Stormbreaker's campaign, the Aurora Council had given her the authority to round up all the Song Weavers she could find to serve aboard the fleet, whether they were willing or not.

Even those Song Weavers who had been saved from the Wraiths a few days ago, scared and confused, had been divided between the Pathfinder sleighs to 'do their duty'. It made Ash's blood boil, and the fact that it had been done under his own mother's order made it all the more bitter.

Ash snapped out of his thoughts as the ground gave a sudden tremble. There was an almighty rushing sound, and then an explosion of powdery white snow in front of them.

'Leviathan!' Teya, the *Frostheart*'s lookout, called down from the crow's nest. 'Dead ahead!'

The crew scrambled to the side and gasped. Not just one Leviathan, *thousands* of them! The entire swarm had resurfaced! A wave of serpentine bodies spilled out from beneath the snow, a confusion of whipping tails, scrambling claws and snapping jaws that roared out vicious war Songs. They rushed towards the Wraiths, determined to answer the frost-heart's call and save it from Shaard's clutches.

'They've appeared to protect the Wraiths, just like you said they would!' Jed grinned at Stormbreaker.

'And we *finally* have the firepower to destroy them. After countless centuries of being nothing but prey . . . we have found our moment . . .' Stormbreaker's eye shimmered. 'This is where we defeat the Leviathans *and* the Wraiths once and for all. Prepare to attack, *now*!'

Ash's heart skipped a beat.

'You – you said you were going to stop Shaard – not fight the Leviathans!' he cried before he could stop himself. Both Stormbreaker and Jed gave him a puzzled look.

'Of course we're going to fight the Leviathans,' Stormbreaker said. 'They control the Wraiths. If we destroy them, we stop Shaard. The Leviathans are our true enemy.'

'N-no! They're not!' Ash could barely get his words

out fast enough. 'I mean – they don't have to be! The Leviathans fear the Devourer as much as we do – they're the ones who imprisoned it in the first place! They won't attack us; they only want Shaard!'

Jed chuckled, shaking his head as though he felt sorry for Ash. 'Stop wastin' the Commander's time with yer childish nonsense, kid.'

'It's true – I swear it!' Ash pleaded. 'You don't have to fight them!'

Stormbreaker looked at him, her eye glinting with . . . what? Anger? Worry? Whatever it was, Ash knew it wasn't good. What he was saying went against everything she believed. But if anyone could persuade her on this, surely it would be her own son? Stormbreaker was the one person who could overwhelm the Wraiths and stop Shaard's evil plan to release the Devourer, but only if she wasn't distracted by a battle with the Leviathans.

'They *are* ignorin' us an' chargin' straight for the Wraiths, commander . . .' Kailen pointed out, shielding her eyes against the biting blizzard.

'Whatever it may seem like they're doing, it's a trick,' snapped Stormbreaker. 'The Wraiths and Leviathans work as one. They want us to lower our guard, but the moment we do they'll turn on us.'

'You're wrong!' Ash said, exasperated.

'Ash – be quiet,' Stormbreaker replied. 'You're too young to know what you're talking about.'

Ash paled. Her voice was low, but it held as much power as a roar.

'I must insist you listen to him, commander,' Nuk urged. 'I know it goes against what we Pathfinders have always held true. But we have seen Leviathans act in ways you wouldn't believe.'

'And I insist you remember your place, *captain*, and follow my orders,' Stormbreaker responded.

'Typically a Leviathan swarm will attack a Pathfinder sleigh on sight and rip it to pieces,' Tobu said, his voice calm as always. 'You've gathered the largest fleet of sleighs the world has ever seen, and suddenly they have no interest? Do you not think that strange?'

'It's cos we have 'em on the run!' Jed said, slapping a hand on to one of his biceps. 'They know they can't touch us with our archeoweapons!'

'Doubtful,' Tobu grunted. 'It's because there are bigger things at stake here. Ask yourselves what those stakes might be.'

Ash took a deep breath, trying to muster his courage. 'Shaard *wants* you to fight the Leviathans – it'll give him time to unlock the Devourer's prison!'

Ash did his very best to return Stormbreaker's

gaze, willing her to trust him. The very fate of the world depended on it.

Please, Ash thought. *Please, please, please believe me!*

But there was a hunger in his mother's eye that would only be satisfied by Leviathan blood.

'The *Frostheart* will remain at the back of the fleet,' Stormbreaker commanded curtly. 'You're not to join the battle unless absolutely necessary, do you understand?'

'*What?!*' Kailen cried out, as though she'd just been accused of cowardice. 'But you'll need us! We can fight!'

Stormbreaker's eyes flicked towards Ash, and it dawned on him that she was giving this order to protect *him*. She wanted him out of the way so she could carry on her vengeful crusade without distraction.

'I need the *Frostheart* to guard the sleighs that carry the Solstice elderly and children, who have no place on a battlefield,' Stormbreaker said. 'You'll cover our rear from any surprise attack. It's an honourable, worthy task.'

'So you intend to carry out this foolish attack?' Nuk asked, folding her arms.

'Please, Mum – *please* don't do this!' Ash begged. 'You're making a mistake!'

But Stormbreaker had already turned her back on

him, her large fur cloak fluttering in the wind as she leaped up on to the boarding plank.

'Protect the sleighs, *Frostheart*, and stay out of the fight. That's not a request; it's an *order.*'

A ROCK AND A HARD PLACE

The crew of the *Frostheart* watched helplessly as the rest of the Pathfinder fleet charged forward in tight formation, speeding towards the Leviathans like an arrow.

Caught between two enemies, the Leviathans had no choice but to split their forces. One half continued towards the Wraiths, desperate to stop them from releasing the dreaded Devourer. The other half prepared to weather the Pathfinder charge.

Trapped at the foot of the glacier, the Wraiths began to Sing the Dark Song, their serpentine Song-auras lashing out at the swarm that rushed towards them, taking control of the leading Leviathans to use them as a shield against the rest of the oncoming attackers.

And that's gonna make Mum think the Leviathans really are *allied with the Wraiths*, Ash fretted. *Meanwhile the more we fight each other, the easier it'll be for Shaard to get away!*

At that moment, the Pathfinders unleashed a bombardment of frazzling energy upon the Leviathans, bursts of bright orange light glaring in the billowing snowfall. Leviathans screeched as they were engulfed in roaring balls of flame, rib-rattling booms shaking the *Frostheart*'s timbers.

'*Archeoweapons* . . .' Lunah whispered by Ash's side, flinching with each explosion. Ash reached out for her hand and was relieved that, instead of making fun of

him, she took it gladly and gave it a squeeze. He was frightened, but it gave him a strange sense of strength to know Lunah was too.

The cracks and booms of the archeoweapons were soon joined by a chaotic chorus of blood-curdling shrieks and thunderous bellows as the Leviathans and the Pathfinder fleet smashed together, splinters of wood exploding into the air as sleigh hulls were torn to shreds. Ash could sense the Leviathans' frustration. They wanted to attack the Wraiths, but they knew they had to silence the Pathfinders' archeoweapons or else they'd be annihilated before they got the chance.

'Three armies fighting each other, two of them fighting for the same thing,' said Arla, the crew's elderly healer, shaking her head. 'What a waste.'

'We should be there to catch Shaard,' Kailen said, thumping the side rail with her fist. 'Not sittin' here with our thumbs in our mouths!'

Yallah, the *Frostheart*'s kindly enjineer, nodded in agreement, gripping her bow tighter. Ash shifted uncomfortably, knowing he was the reason the *Frostheart* had been ordered to stay out of the action.

'Interesting that Stormbreaker has such concern for your well-being now, after so many years of being absent,' Tobu murmured to Ash, sensing his troubled thoughts.

Ash hoped Tobu wasn't upset. He didn't want Tobu to think he'd mean any less to him just because he'd found his mother. And Ash had certainly not asked for special treatment, especially knowing how many other Song Weavers were being forced to fight against their will.

The *Frostheart* was one of four Pathfinder sleighs that hadn't taken part in the charge, the others carrying the young and old of Solstice. Their enjins were still, their rigging groaning in the wind with uneasy anticipation.

A Pathfinder sleigh ahead erupted into splinters as

it was torn in two by a screeching Spearwurm.

'Anyone else not in *quite* such a hurry to get involved in *that*?' Kob said.

Ash's belly tied itself into knots, and he clutched his sunstone pendant for luck. He was ashamed to discover he'd felt slightly relieved when Stormbreaker had left the *Frostheart.* The feeling wracked Ash with guilt, and he tried to push it away. He couldn't bear the thought of losing his mother so soon after finding her, but his frustration simmered over the fact that she was stubbornly fighting the wrong enemy. The Leviathans were trying to stop Shaard, just like they were, and if Stormbreaker had put her need for revenge aside for *one second*, the Leviathans and Pathfinders could've overwhelmed the Wraiths by now!

'This is my fault,' Ash said. 'If I'd kept the frostheart safe like I was meant to . . .'

'We'll have none of that, lad,' Kob said. 'That's far too much to put on one person's shoulders. Stormbreaker an' Shaard both know full well what they're doin', an' nothin' you've said or done has made those decisions for 'em. We just have to stop Shaard any way we can.'

'I fear this won't be over until either the Leviathan swarm or Stormbreaker's fleet lie in ruins,' Nuk said sadly. 'If I know Stormbreaker, only one side will leave this battlefield alive . . .'

Ash nearly jumped out of his skin as Rook suddenly appeared at his shoulder.

'*Sense it?*' she hissed into his ear. '*Frost-heart's Song? I cannot hear.*'

Ash took a step away. Back in Solstice, Shaard had revealed that Rook had once been a Wraith. She'd used the Dark Song to force Leviathans to attack the Strongholds. Ash knew she was a changed person now, that she wanted to right the wrongs of her past, but he couldn't help but feel uneasy around his once-trusted friend.

He considered what she said, however, and tried to focus on the call of the frost-heart – the Song he'd come to know so well. If he could find it, he would know exactly where Shaard was amid the chaos of the battle.

Ash pushed his mind past the thunderous clamour of the explosions, the war Songs of the Leviathans and the Dark Song of the Wraiths, focusing his attention on where he'd last seen Shaard's sleigh, but he could find no sign of the heart.

He let his mind circle the area.

Still nothing.

Panic rising, he spun his concentration from here to there, reaching, searching . . .

'I . . . can't hear it,' Ash said to Rook breathlessly.

'*Gone!*' Rook Sang urgently, her crows clicking nervously.

'Be calm, boy. One breath at a time . . .' Tobu said to Ash, sensing his distress.

Ash took a deep breath and continued to focus. And then, suddenly . . . *There!*

He caught the faintest whisper of it, distant and delicate, but unmistakable. The frost-heart was crying out to its Leviathan brethren for help, but they were unable to reach it, thanks to the Wraiths and Pathfinders blocking their path. As Ash centred in on its location, his belly gave a sickening lurch.

'Captain!' he shouted, pointing south-west. 'The frost-heart's not in the battle; it's that way! Shaard must be moving it!'

Nuk squinted in the direction Ash had pointed, but she could make out nothing over the chaos. 'Withering whale wind!' she cursed. 'It's just as we feared – Shaard's using the battle as a distraction to slip away! Teya, Master Podd, do you see anything south-west of here?' she yelled at the sharp-eyed lookout up in the crow's nest and her right-hand vulpis on the bridge.

'I won't lie, captain, I haven't been able to see anything for days in this blizzard,' Master Podd replied from atop a pile of boxes he used to reach the tiller. The crew shared a worried glance.

'Are we *sure* we're all comfortable letting him steer?' Arla asked.

Teya scanned the indicated direction with her spyglass. 'Ice caves! Cut into the glacier!'

'Valkyries curse him!' Nuk said. 'He's skulking away while the rest of his fleet keep us busy out here, none the wiser!'

'He's gonna get away!' Ash cried. 'We have to stop him!'

Without needing to be told, Kob and Kailen raised the warning flags to alert Stormbreaker.

Come on, Mum, Ash prayed, watching in horror as the *Kinspear* blasted its weapons into the thrashing tide of Leviathans. Her sleigh raised its signal flags in response.

'Stormbreaker orders us to ignore him and stay in a rearguard position,' Teya called down, spyglass held to her eye.

No! Ash screamed in his head, his belly twisting. How could she do this? He'd told her that Shaard was the real enemy. Stormbreaker may not have been the mother he'd been imagining all these years, but Ash still wanted to believe she'd do the right thing.

'Not the type to let go once she has the scent of blood, that one,' Nuk murmured, before yelling, 'Scratch that then! Yallah, let's have some power!' The propellers roared to life as Yallah turned the dials on the sunstone enjin. 'Master Podd, guide us south-west, if you'd be so kind!' The little vulpis saluted, pushing hard against the *Frostheart*'s tiller. 'We'll catch that slippery sludgeweed yet!'

'What about Stormbreaker's orders?' Kob asked.

'I'll bake her a cake to say sorry once this is all over! I'm not about to sit back and watch the world end!'

Ash gritted his teeth. At least he could always count on his captain to do the right thing. The *Frostheart* zoomed past the other rearguard sleighs, whose crews eyed the passing sleigh with confusion. Alone, it skirted round the battle, heading towards the closest glacial cave. Enormous icicles jutted in all directions like jagged fangs, the yawning cave mouth delving into deep blue darkness that swallowed the *Frostheart* whole.

INTO DARKNESS

Entering the ice cave was like entering another world. The *Frostheart* drifted slowly through the cavernous tunnel, whose glistening walls could've easily fit three sleighs abreast. Everything was cast in the most vivid blue light Ash had ever seen. From vibrant turquoises where light danced through the fresher ice above, to the deepest, darkest blue-blacks where it hadn't been touched by Mother Sun in centuries.

The noise of the battle outside was now a distant rumble, the cave walls giving an ominous *crack* whenever there was a particularly large explosion. Ash said a prayer to the spirits to keep his mother safe, even though she was the one who'd put herself in unnecessary danger.

'She'll be all right,' Lunah assured him with a

smile. 'Kickin' butt: it's a mum's job, an' ours are preeeetty great at it.'

Ash gave a smile back, though there was little joy in it.

The howling of the storm had turned into an eerie sigh that flowed through the cave like the breath of some colossal beast. The sudden quiet only helped make *another* sound all the clearer. The strange, all-encompassing All-Song of the land resonated throughout the ice. Ash shivered as he tried to imagine what could make a sound that loud and unknowable.

But held back by the All-Song was something even worse. The Devourer's ominous presence steeped the caverns and tunnels in malice. It practically dripped from the walls, like the whispers of a thousand spiteful voices, making the air around them feel all the colder. Tobu stalked the deck with his bow at the ready, while Rook had shrunk into a corner, quivering and mumbling to herself.

'It's gettin' closer . . .' Kailen said, taking a few steps nearer to the rest of the crew. Even the usually unflinching Master Podd was twitching his big ears, his tail fur puffed out. Twinge reached out and wrapped his large tattooed arms round Kailen. 'What do you think you're *doing*?!' she asked.

'I don't like it,' Twinge replied.

Kailen made to push him away, but after a moment she relented. 'Fine. But only cos it's so cold.'

With no sign of Shaard's sleigh, the *Frostheart* continued, further into the eerie cave, until it came to a fork in the tunnel. Yallah shut the enjins down, the sleigh sliding to a gradual stop.

'Which way?' Nuk asked as she climbed down from the bridge.

Lunah and Tobu examined the ice below for any sleigh tracks the Wraiths may have left.

'Looks like they went that way.' Lunah pointed down a tunnel guarded by the icy bones of long-dead Leviathans.

'Bones. A bad omen . . .' Yallah whispered.

'How so?' Nuk asked, joining the crew on the main deck. 'We mursu decorate our floating Strongholds with the most spectacular bones you ever did see, repurposed from the gigantic beasts of the deep. We use them to build our houses, for tools and our jewellery. Not only do they look glorious, but they remind us how short our lives are, of the true, inescapable finality of death, of –' Nuk's eyes suddenly went wide. 'Oooooh, wait, now I see it. Yes, it is rather ominous, isn't it?'

'Bone path it is,' Kailen said, gripping her bow tightly.

'Everybody ready?' Nuk asked.

The crew nodded solemnly – all, that is, except for Rook, who sat trembling, her crows nipping anxiously at her furs.

'Rook?' Ash said gently as he approached. Her hood darted in his direction, her fiery-white pupils, full of fear, only just visible in its shadows.

'*Close. So close,*' she Sang, her voice almost as broken and harsh as when Ash had first met her. '*Devourer's prison here. Too close. Can't fight it. Can't win. Not this time.*'

Her words sent a shiver down Ash's spine.

The prison was here? He'd known they were heading towards it, but he'd kind of hoped they'd capture Shaard before they ever reached such a terrible place.

Ash wasn't sure he had the courage to even *look* at the Devourer.

The glimpses he'd seen in the memory-spheres of the World Before had been nothing short of horrifying, and the thought of seeing it in real life brought bile to the back of his throat. All Ash knew was that the Leviathan Ancients of old, the most powerful that had ever lived, had still not been strong enough to defeat the Devourer, and had been forced to give their lives to imprison it instead.

Will it be trapped in a massive cage? Ash wondered with fear. *Reaching its claws out to get us? Or was it buried beneath this glacier?* Ash's skin crawled as he imagined a giant eyeball watching them through the ice. *Does . . . does it already know we're here? Will it force its Song into my mind until I go mad . . .?*

All of a sudden, Ash had to fight to stop his knees knocking together. He'd thought, or rather *hoped*, that Nell had got lost, but instead he had led Shaard straight to where he needed to go. Ash tried to put on a brave face for Rook.

'Now's our chance to make sure the Devourer never escapes,' he said. 'We can stop Shaard. I *know* we can.'

'Yeah, if fire-boy can do it, so can you, Rook!' Lunah said, lifting up one of Ash's arms. 'I mean, look how noodly his arms are!'

'Erm . . . thanks, I-I *think*?'

Nuk stamped her peg leg against the deck, calling everyone's attention. 'We've been through a lot together, our merry band! We've seen sights that Strongholders would never believe, heard sounds that could raise spirits or chill the bones. We've seen both the great and the bad; *goodness*, we've been at each other's throats enough times!'

The crew chuckled at this.

'We've lost old friends . . .' Nuk continued, casting her eyes down before glancing up at Ash, Tobu and Rook. 'But we've gained wonderful new ones too. Being a Pathfinder is an honour. Together we've saved lives. Together we've done our small bit to make this world a little less gloomy.' Nuk took a moment to gaze at her crew with pride, each of them meeting her eye with steely determination. 'It's been a dangerous life. But it's your bravery that stills my fear and gives me strength. Because you know what? I never once doubted we'd get through the danger. Never doubted that my crew had my back. Never doubted that my brave, brilliant Pathfinders would see me through to laugh, cry and argue another day.'

The crew nodded along, their hearts swelling and shaking off the Devourer's hateful spell, smiling in spite of their fear.

'Hear, hear!' Kob and Arla shouted together.

'We started this run, and we'll see it to the end!' Teya raised her fist.

'There's no other barnacle-heads I'd rather be with.' Lunah grinned.

Even Tobu's mouth was doing the rather unnerving, strained thing it did when he smiled.

Ash laughed, his heart leaping that he'd been lucky enough to find the crew of the *Frostheart*. He held out his hand to Rook, who looked at it as if she didn't recognize what it was.

Ash swallowed hard. 'I'm scared too, but we can do this. As long as we're together.'

Rook's trembling calmed as she considered the words she'd heard. Tentatively she reached out to grasp Ash's hand. He helped her up, and she shook herself free of her fear like a bird rustling its feathers. Her crows called out in triumph.

'We're here together,' Nuk said, looking at Rook with her small friendly eyes, 'and we'll see this through together. Nothing will tear us apart!'

At that very moment, a large pale tentacle wrapped round Nuk's waist. 'Oh, how odd,' she said, looking at it with surprise, before it wrenched her off the deck.

GUARDIANS

'CAPTAIN!' Master Podd cried, leaping up and grabbing Nuk's peg leg. The crew watched aghast as their captain and her right-hand vulpis were pulled through a hole in the cavern ceiling by the strangest creature Ash had ever seen – a huge writhing mass of long, fleshy tentacles that wriggled and squirmed so frantically it was hard to make out the massive wolver-like body they were attached to. He caught sight of six pale eyes above the creature's fang-lined maw.

'A Leviathan!' exclaimed Ash.

'*Guardians!*' Rook Sang. '*Protectors of prison!*'

The Guardian spun round and took off down a passage that tunnelled through the ceiling above the *Frostheart*, far too narrow for a sleigh to pass through.

'AFTER THEM!' Kailen yelled, spinning round

and racing towards the helm, the blurry shapes of Nuk and Master Podd just visible through the ice above.

The propellers roared to life as Yallah pulled down hard on the enjin levers, the *Frostheart* lurching forward in pursuit. The sleigh slid up the high curved tunnel walls as it raced round corners, its timbers groaning ominously under their own weight. The tunnel the Guardian scuttled through criss-crossed above the *Frostheart*, the beast's shadowy form warping and shifting through the ice, but never disappearing from sight.

A gust of freezing air washed over the sleigh as it burst into a vast chasm intersected by numerous naturally formed ice bridges. The Guardian leaped across to a bridge that stretched above the *Frostheart*, dragging Nuk behind it. Master Podd was gnawing on the tentacle that held her, but his tiny fangs couldn't penetrate its rubbery flesh. Nuk squirmed and fought, digging her heel into the ice, but only succeeded in flipping herself over so she was suddenly facing backwards and sliding along the ice on her bottom. She blinked with surprise, before catching sight of the *Frostheart* racing after them below.

'GET ME AWAY FROM THIS OVERSIZED SQUID!'

'Workin' on it!' Lunah shouted back, joining the

others in taking aim at the beast with her bow. But their arrows mostly clacked harmlessly off the ice, the angle too steep to get a clear shot.

'We need to Weave with it,' Ash said to Rook. 'Let it know we're not enemies!'

Rook hesitated. '*Something strange. Not right. Different . . .*'

Ash didn't stop to think. He began to Sing, his Song-aura flowing around him like a whirlwind of starlight. Hoping he could convince the Leviathan to drop the captain, he blasted it forward . . .

And it bounced off the Guardian like water off a mursu's back.

Ash had experienced Leviathans reject his Song before, but he'd never felt such an . . . *absence* as this, a void where a Song should be. The shock snapped him out of his Song-trance, and he stumbled back, gasping.

'What . . .?!'

'*Deaf to Song!*' Rook hissed. '*Prison Guardians! Immune to Dark Song. Immune to Weavers!*'

'Oh . . .' Ash said. 'Oh *no* . . .'

'Ash?!' Lunah asked, her voice strained with worry. ''S the 'viathan gonna play nice or what?'

'It can't hear our Song. We – we can't calm it!' Ash replied.

'Then we'll have to do this the old-fashioned way,'

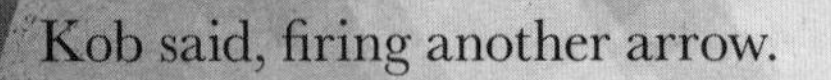

Kob said, firing another arrow.

Suddenly another sound echoed across the huge cavern, growing louder by the second.

'Is that . . . an *enjin*?' Twinge asked.

As if in answer, a huge dark shape tore out of a nearby tunnel, speeding along another ice bridge that ran alongside the *Frostheart*'s, its ragged sails flapping as it fled the reaching tentacles of two other Guardians that chased close behind.

A Wraith sleigh.

For a moment, the two crews could only gaze across the chasm at each other, the maskless Wraiths as shocked at their new company as the Pathfinders. Ash caught sight of Shaard, his vivid turquoise eyes wide with surprise.

Ash heard his heart beat, blood pounding in his ears.

Once.

Twice.

Then . . .

'KILL THEM!' Shaard bellowed, bowstrings thrumming as the two sides began to fire at each other. The *Frostheart* crew took cover from the poisoned arrows that rained down upon them, returning fire as best they could.

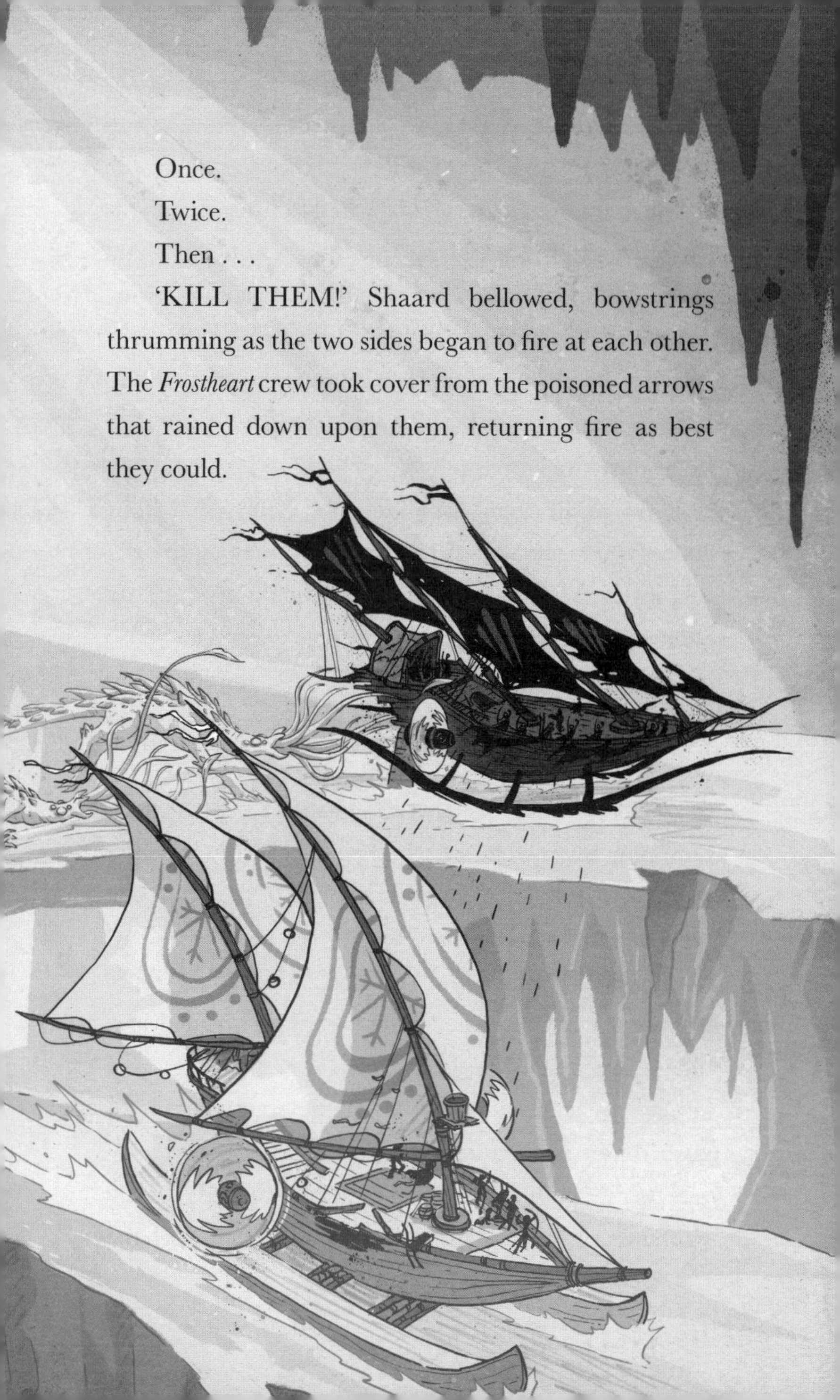

Ash was caught in the middle of the deck, a Wraith taking aim as he desperately dashed for the side rail. A tentacle wrapped round the Wraith just as he fired, his arrow flying wild as he was snatched, screaming, from the deck. Ash skidded behind the sleigh's protective rail, breathing heavily. He tried to take aim at the Wraiths himself, but his arrow bounced off a pillar of ice as they rushed past.

'You're all doing a valiant job,' Nuk yelled from above, where she was still being dragged along the ice. 'But if you *do* find the time, don't forget about your dear old captain up here!'

The ice bridge the Guardian was bounding along was coming to an end, and the Leviathan was preparing to leap across to another. A leap that would take it over the *Frostheart.* Tobu saw this and dashed from his cover. Dropping his bow, he snatched his spear from the sling on his back and knocked an arrow out of the air in one swift motion. He clambered up to the crow's nest, his large powerful limbs making short work of the climb. Despite the arrows whooshing past, he crouched low, his muscles tensed and ready, his eyes narrowed and focused. The moment the Guardian jumped, Tobu pushed himself off and flew up towards it.

Ash's mouth dropped open as he watched. With a swift, precise swing of his spear, Tobu sliced through the tentacle that held Captain Nuk. The Guardian let out a terrible shriek as its blue blood spattered over Tobu's white fur. Tobu dropped his spear and grabbed Nuk in mid-air, before landing on the upper deck with a heavy thud, Captain Nuk safely in his arms. Tobu let out a groan as his legs buckled under her weight.

'You could at least *pretend* to not find it so difficult!' Nuk scolded, just as Master Podd bounced harmlessly off her belly.

Amid the roaring of enjins and Leviathans, a sinister laugh somehow cut through. Ash spun round to see Shaard pointing ahead with wicked glee. Following his gesture, Ash felt his blood turn cold.

Just a few feet ahead, the ice bridge the *Frostheart* was zooming along came to an abrupt end. Waiting beyond the precipice was a swarm of Guardians, their tentacles squirming, salivating jaws open with anticipation.

'Farewell, *Frostheart*!' Shaard cackled as his sleigh vanished into another tunnel.

'Yallah, *full power*!' Nuk ordered, slipping out of Tobu's arms.

Ash was thrown off his feet as the *Frostheart* surged forward. The sleigh shook and rumbled beneath his hands and knees, straining against the sudden speed.

The *Frostheart* hurtled towards the precipice.

'EVERYONE HOLD ON!' Yallah cried.

Ash gripped the side rail, Lunah and Rook braced in front of him, Lunah's hair dancing in the rushing wind.

The *Frostheart* flew off the end of the bridge, soaring over the empty chasm, just above all the tentacles that hungrily grasped for it.

All, that is, but one.

The pale tentacle swept across the deck, dashing Ash, Lunah and Rook overboard.

Ash gasped in horror as he fell beneath the *Frostheart*, which landed with an almighty crunch on another ledge.

He screamed as he found himself falling amid his tumbling friends, the world rushing past in a blue blur. He bounced off a Guardian's rubbery hide, sliding down its slick skin, tumbling and spinning between snatching tentacles and snapping jaws. His backside hit solid ice, pain radiating through his tailbone as he slid down an incredibly steep slope. It was a natural slide created by ice-melt, and tears streamed from his eyes as he shot down it at a tremendous speed, the biting cold air stealing the screams from his lips and leaving him breathless.

Down and down he fell, into the dark unknown.

6

THE PRISON

The glacier spat Ash out like a scrap of unwanted gristle. He flew from the tunnel like an arrow, sliding some distance before coming to an abrupt halt in a large snowdrift, his bum in the air and his legs dangling over his head. He scrambled on to his belly, trying to get his bearings. He was outside again, the glacier walls towering behind him back in the direction he'd come from. He breathed a sigh of relief to see Rook and Lunah had made it out of the glacier too.

'That. Was. UHMAYZING.' Lunah grinned.

'When I became a Pathfinder, I really thought I'd spend more time *on*board a sleigh than *over*board,' Ash groaned.

The trio spun round, readying their weapons, as

a scraping sound came from the tunnel.

Tobu came shooting out of it, skidding deftly along the ice into a standing position.

'Tobu!' Ash cried, startled.

'Tentacle get you too?' Lunah asked.

Tobu raised a brow. 'Of course not. I jumped after you.'

Ash and Lunah blinked in surprise.

'Well, *duuuh*, of course you did! Natural thing to do when starin' down into the snarlin' maws, ent it?' Lunah said, before the smile disappeared from her face. 'I hope the others are OK . . .'

'They've survived worse than that,' Tobu said.

'You could at least *pretend* to care about them!' Lunah snapped, rather uncharacteristically.

Tobu grunted, poking his head above the snowdrift to get a view of their surroundings. They were on the edge of a massive snow plain, entirely encircled within high glacial walls.

'This ent no glacier . . .' Lunah whispered, looking around in confusion. 'This is some kinda crater . . . but . . . but made of *ice*?'

'*The prison!*' Rook hissed, her strange eyes alive with terror.

Ash squinted against the cutting wind that seemed to emanate from the centre of the crater. He saw gigantic pinnacles of ice jutting from the snow and reaching up into the grey sky like the claws of a giant's hand, or the ribs of some colossal beast, but no sign of a cage. The very glacier crater itself sounded like it was Singing, though, the All-Song blasting out of the ice walls, almost overwhelming in its volume. And yet, despite its power, Ash could still not determine what was creating it. It really was the most bizarre thing.

Whatever it was, it Sang a Song of captivity and of protection with such strength and determination Ash felt like he was being pushed back by an unseen force. Despite the defiant Song, the whole area was still heavy with an insidious feeling that made Ash's flesh tingle unpleasantly. The Devourer's evil presence twisted and convulsed in its attempts to escape the All-Song, the invisible battle distorting the very air before their eyes.

'Lovely place, ent it?' Lunah said darkly. 'Surprised people don't come here more often . . .'

'Down!' Tobu snapped, pushing Ash and Lunah into the snow. Before they could ask what he was doing, Shaard's sleigh appeared from a cave mouth in the crater wall. It passed by, moving slowly towards the centre of the plain, before coming to a stop. Ropes were thrown over the sides, and a group of about thirty Wraiths climbed down, their black cloaks stark against the white snow.

'They greatly outnumber us,' Tobu whispered. 'We must be careful and wait for the perfect opportunity to attack.'

'*Wait?!* We don't have *time* to wait!' Lunah hissed.

'If we rush in, we will be killed.'

'So much for the mighty yeti warriors I've heard so much about – s'more like the mighty yeti *cowards*!' Lunah said, her voice rising in anger. 'We can take 'em! My ma could have 'em, one hand behind her back!'

'It is not me I'm worried about,' Tobu snarled. 'I would surely survive, but you, so puny and pathetic, would be crushed into –'

'*Guys!*' Ash hissed, unable to believe they would choose this moment to argue.

Tobu took a deep breath, steadying his temper. 'This place is evil,' he muttered. 'The Devourer's Song is trying to turn us against each other.'

Lunah nodded, wringing her wrists, her cheeks flushing with shame.

'*Shouldn't be here,*' Rook Sang, her bright pupils tiny amid the pitch-black of her eyes. '*Devourer senses me. Reaches for me!*'

Ash took hold of her shaking hands. 'We just need to get the frost-heart back,' he said with a confidence he in no way felt.

'*We should go. Run!*'

'As soon as we get it back, then we can go. Far, far away from here.'

Rook nodded, though it was hard to tell if it was a nod or a shiver. She swallowed hard, the fear never leaving her eyes.

Tobu signalled the others to follow him. Keeping low, they crept towards the Wraiths, using snowdrifts for cover. As they drew closer, they spotted Shaard among the twitching, snarling Wraiths. Rook hissed with hatred, her hands flexing like the talons of her crows. Ash could hear the Song of the frost-heart now, radiating out from a spherical archeomek device Shaard clutched within his hands.

Shaard was obsessed with the World Before, believing the fall of their civilization to be a great loss. He was forever studying the relics he'd found in ancient ruins and the writings that explained how they'd worked. Shaard's workbench aboard the *Frostheart* had been littered with strange archeomek, though Ash wasn't sure he'd seen this

particular artefact before. It was made of a ceramic material, whorled patterns etched on its surface. It was certainly not the same container Ash had used to carry the heart around in.

The frost-heart begged for aid, and Ash wanted nothing more than to help, but even as the thought formed he felt a surge of anger, a hot desire to attack Shaard and the Wraiths and get revenge for everything they'd put him through. But he knew that was the Devourer's aura infecting his mind. He gritted his teeth and waited, just as Tobu had said they should, and Shaard's voice came to them over the wind.

'Where is the prison?' Shaard was saying to Nell, the traitorous Solstice Elder. 'I see no lock or door – nothing!'

Shaard's eyes were wild. His usual composure had faded away, revealing a similar madness to that seen in his followers. Ash was reminded that the Wraiths had once been Song Weavers like him, before the Dark Song of the Devourer had claimed their minds.

'The Devourer is not imprisoned by mere walls or stone,' Nell said in his hoarse voice. The squat man looked even more haggard and aged than Ash remembered, the burden of his decision to help the Wraiths clearly weighing heavily on him.

Good, Ash thought bitterly, remembering how the man had handed all of Solstice over to the Wraiths and their destructive plans. Tobu led the group closer as Nell continued.

'You-you're sure you have what it takes to control the Devourer?' Nell was considering his words carefully, clearly nervous about Shaard's intentions.

Shaard opened his arms wide. 'The Devourer wants to help us. It has *promised* its aid. It will topple Aurora and all those who stand in the way of the Song Weavers and our rightful rule.'

Nell shuffled his feet, apparently still unconvinced.

'Besides, it will be weak after a thousand years

without . . . nourishment. I have the power to command it.' Shaard smiled his distinctive smile, that of a hungry wolver who'd cornered a snow hare. 'I've been preparing for this moment all my life. I know what I'm doing. You have nothing to fear.'

'You will only use it to topple the Council? You know how to imprison it again once this is all done with?' Nell asked.

A flash of impatience darkened Shaard's features as he adjusted his cloak, revealing one of the blades hanging from his belt.

'Trust me.'

Nell nodded, looking as if he did anything but. With that, the Elder cleared his throat and began to Sing. Despite his old age, the man's voice was surprisingly loud and powerful, his Song managing to cut through the booming All-Song.

No, not cutting through it, Ash realized. Weaving *with it*!

Nell's Song-aura whirled into the crater walls, coaxing hundreds of glowing threads out of the ice. The threads combined into Song-auras so immense they flowed towards the centre of the plain like mighty rivers of bright turquoise light.

It was the aura of the All-Song itself.

The Songs spun intricate patterns around each other, as though they were writing words in a language Ash couldn't understand. Nell's Song sounded almost exactly like the All-Song, any difference harmonizing perfectly.

'What shall we do?' Ash asked Tobu.

'We have to act now!' Lunah urged.

Tobu's eyes darted this way and that, considering their options. There weren't many.

Nell changed key, his Song resounding across the crater. Shaard stepped back in wonder as the ground began to quake beneath their feet, the snow parting to reveal that it was no plain they stood on at all but a massive frozen lake. The ice beneath the snow was as black as ink, the disturbing, unnatural sight sending a shiver through Ash's spine.

Entire ice sheets tumbled down from the crater walls in explosive clouds of snow. Ash and Lunah could only shield their heads with their arms, despite what little good it would do. It felt like the world itself was trembling. Rook was muttering to herself, repeating the same sounds over and over like a chant. Only Tobu didn't flinch, his keen eyes watching for any opening, an arrow nocked to his bow.

Nell finally finished his Song and collapsed with exhaustion, his elderly face dripping with sweat despite the harsh chill. As the snow clouds faded, every person on that frozen lake looked awestruck at what had been revealed.

The glacier crater had collapsed, and amid the mass of broken ice stood five gigantic shapes arranged in a circle around the lake. They were the skeletons of Leviathans, frozen bones of ice, each standing the height the crater walls had once risen to, on mighty sleigh-sized legs. Deep within each of their cavernous ribcages glowed huge ice shards, bright and blue. The All-Song's aura radiated out of them in gushing streams of light.

At last, Ash understood where the otherworldly Song was coming from.

'*Hearts . . .*' Rook Sang. '*Just like frost-heart . . .*'

These were the Ancients that had battled the Devourer so long ago and used their Song, and their lives, to imprison it. The All-Song was *their* Song – a Song of such immeasurable power that they Sang it still, beyond death.

And it was the only thing keeping the Devourer confined.

The empty eyes of the Ancients all stared down at the centre of the lake, their Song-auras winding and weaving beneath the ice, threads of blue vivid against the black. A large crevice had cracked open there. A bitter, sickening smell of smoke and blood issued from

it, but this wasn't all that chilled Ash to the core. It was the serpentine tendrils of darkness that snaked their way out from its depths that made his limbs quiver and his heart race.

It was the aura of a dark, hateful Song that Ash knew all too well.

THE KEY

Shaard began to cackle, his laugh uncharacteristically shrill and manic.

'What an honour it is to finally meet you all,' he yelled at the Leviathan Ancients, bowing low with a theatrical sweep of his hand. He spun to face the largest Ancient and lifted the archeomek device that contained the frost-heart. 'I hope you haven't missed this too sorely?'

Ash's breath caught in his throat as he realized it was the only Ancient without a glowing heart.

That's the one the frost-heart belongs to! Ash thought. *The Ancient that has been guiding me this whole time!*

The frost-heart Sang a Song of anguish, crying out at its failure to stop Shaard. Nell flinched at the sound, his growing doubt clear.

Ash's own heart reached out for it. He'd come to see the frost-heart as a comfort in a dangerous, confusing world. It had always seemed to be there for him when he needed guidance, to soothe his fury when the Devourer had attempted to darken his thoughts. To see it mocked was almost too much for Ash to bear.

Chuckling to himself, Shaard strode towards the precipice of the huge chasm and gazed down into its depths. 'At long last . . . I have found you,' he said, as smoke-like tendrils of darkness curled out from it and reached for him longingly.

Hungrily.

'Shaard?' Nell began. 'I-I'm starting to think this is a terrible idea . . .'

Shaard ignored him, twisting the two hemispheres of his archeomek device in opposite directions, the whorled designs etched into its surface flaring with light. Mechanisms within began to click and whir, the contraption vibrating wildly in Shaard's hands. The frost-heart let out a piercing wail, fighting to resist whatever the device was doing to it. But Ash could sense it growing weaker. The All-Song began to sound strange, infected by a strangled, warbling whine that seemed unnatural to Ash's ears.

'*Reversing Song!*' Rook hissed in alarm. '*Frost-heart most powerful heart – binds others together!*'

And she was right. The archeomek was somehow forcing the frost-heart to turn the All-Song backwards, mocking its defiance and strength and warping it into a Song of weakness and defeat.

'*Weakening prison!*' Rook drew a blade from her coat, ready to act.

'We have to stop that machine!' Ash cried out, almost too loud.

'Stay hidden!' Tobu growled under his breath, before leaping to his feet.

Shaard's eyes opened wide as he caught sight of Tobu aiming his bow directly at him.

'*No . . .*' he mouthed, before Tobu's arrow tore the archeomek device from his hand, sending it skidding across the ice. Tobu and Rook wasted no time in bounding over the snowdrift, Ash and Lunah close behind. Nell let out a high-pitched yelp of fear, diving to the ice with his hands over his head.

'STALL THEM!' Shaard yelled, and the Wraiths raised their bows and moved to block their attackers.

Ash ran in a zigzag, his senses flaring with anticipation for the arrows he knew would soon come.

But before the Wraiths could fire, they were suddenly torn from their feet as arrows punctured their sides. The others spun round just as Ash did, to see the *Frostheart* hurtling towards them across the lake.

'YEEEEEESSSS!' Lunah cheered.

Rook used the distraction to dash for the frost-heart, but Shaard got there first. He scooped it up with a swirl of his cloak, a blade slicing outwards from underneath. Rook deflected it with her own, leaping over Shaard's head and slashing at him in turn. They cut at each other, parrying each other's attacks, the clashing of their blades flinging sparks as they fought.

'*MURDERER!*' Rook shrieked.

Lunah charged forward, her dagger aimed at Shaard's side, but then collapsed with a howl as she clutched her head.

'*The Devourer!*' Ash cried, trying to block out the Dark Song that burst from the crevice and rang painfully through his head. Rook's blade clattered to the ice as she fell to her knees, her eyes wide with panic. She made small gurgling sounds as the Devourer focused its attention on her.

'Always weak,' Shaard mocked, kicking her to the floor. 'Always unable to see things through. The

Pathfinders will never accept you. They *hate* you for what you are – for what you've done. You'll never be one of them! And now you've betrayed the Wraiths, your very own people!' He kicked away the blade Rook was desperately reaching for. 'You'll *always* be the outcast, ever the misfit! You will *always* be alone.'

Tears rolled down Rook's pale cheeks as she gasped, the Devourer's Song gripping her heart and making it impossible for her to fight back. But Shaard's focus on Rook allowed Ash to creep up and snatch the archeomek device from his hand.

'NO!' Shaard cried, grasping for Ash as he scurried away, the device vibrating so rapidly it seemed to shift and blur in his hands. The All-Song was now nothing more than a high-pitched screech – its Song-aura pulsating as rapidly as the device, its once vast radiance being forced into a thin line of light.

In the distance, there was a piercing crack. Ash spun to find the source and saw one of the Ancients' hearts had shattered into tiny pieces. A second followed, then a third.

It's destroying them! Ash realized, but before he could think how to stop it, Shaard shoved him hard in the back. Ash ate a mouthful of snow as he hit the ice, sliding dangerously close to the edge of the chasm.

For a moment, he caught a glimpse of the horror that lurked in that dark abyss. Suspended amid a web of tar-like tendrils was a shard about the same size and shape as the frost-heart. But this one was as black as pitch, stealing light from the world instead of illuminating it. A lashing serpentine Song-aura oozed around it, confined within the vibrating sphere of the All-Song that kept it imprisoned.

A wave of nausea rose in Ash as a cold unlike anything he'd ever felt froze his blood. His thoughts became hazy, the inky darkness making him feel like he'd fallen into the night sky and had no way of getting back to earth.

Shaard turned him over and stuck a knee into his belly, pinning him down.

'I searched the entire world for you!' he growled, his furious face so close Ash could smell his sour breath, his hands trying to tear the device from Ash's grasp.

'Don't . . . do this! *Please!*' Ash pleaded through gritted teeth. He held on to the frost-heart with all his strength, writhing and kicking against Shaard's grasping hands, trying to do anything he could to escape him, to *hurt* him.

He hated this man. He hated him *so much.*

'There was a time I would've done anything to have found you. But now?' Shaard finally wrenched the device from Ash. 'Now I can't seem to get rid of you.'

The triumph in Shaard's eyes vanished as he was roughly hoisted up, leaving Ash defeated on the ice. Tobu had Shaard by the neck, lifting him into the air as though he weighed no more than a child. The All-Song was so high-pitched now, it was barely audible, its Song-aura as thin as a bowstring. Tobu looked Shaard in the face, snarling to reveal his large fangs.

'Enough,' Tobu growled. 'I will not allow you to harm the boy. Never again. This ends. *Now.*'

Somehow, even as he desperately tried to prise Tobu's fingers from his neck, Shaard managed to gurgle out a chuckle.

'For once . . . yeti . . . I think you're right . . .'

The whine of the All-Song had reached a crescendo, the archeomek device vibrating so violently it shook itself from Shaard's hand. It seemed to inhale all the air around the lake in a single massive breath and hold on to it for a brief second. And then . . .

BWOOOOM!

Force blasted from the relic, throwing every person on the lake off their feet. Tobu was launched across the snow, Shaard hurtling in the opposite direction. Ash flew over the edge of the ravine, catching hold of the broken precipice just before he fell into the darkness below. He fumbled his way back up, nerves screaming at the thought of falling into that pitiless shadow, just in time to see the remaining heart of the Ancients explode into tiny crystals, leaving only the frost-heart itself, its light pale and flickering within the archeomek device.

But even something as ancient and powerful as the frost-heart couldn't resist the technology of the World Before. With a terrible crack it too shattered, just as Ash felt his own heart had. His world lurched, screaming to a halt. His belly dropped and his head spun.

The frost-heart was gone.

The All-Song was no more.

And the Devourer was free.

THE RETURN

Tar-like sludge burst from the chasm. It reached out in thick strands and slithered across the ice, searching for anything it could grasp. Ash stumbled back, watching in horror as the tendrils crept towards him. They snatched hungrily at Lunah and Rook too, who managed to shuffle themselves backwards and flee. Nell, still trembling on the ground, peeked through his hands with mounting terror at the roiling mass that rose about him.

Shaard laughed hysterically as he picked himself up.

'At long last, I have released you from your prison, just like I promised!' The darkness swelled and surged, apparently considering Shaard with an alien intelligence. 'Now it's time for you to fulfil your end of the bargain. We have work to do!'

Seeming to recognize Shaard as an ally, the tendrils suddenly shot past him towards Nell, wrapping themselves round his limbs and torso. Nell screamed as he was lifted high off the ground.

'TELL IT TO STOP!' he shrieked. 'SHAARD – MAKE IT STOP!'

'But, dear Nell –' Shaard grinned at Nell's horrified expression – 'it's been asleep for a thousand years. Surely you wouldn't deny it breakfast?'

The shadow-slime slithered over Nell like the roots of a tree, enveloping him in a cocoon of sludge. A chill bolted down Ash's spine as Nell's wide, panicked eyes locked on to him.

'Boy,' he squealed urgently, before the slime could cover his mouth. 'The last heart! You must find it! Find the heart!'

But Ash had no idea what Nell was talking about, and could only watch, appalled, as Nell was entirely engulfed by the bubbling mass.

Tobu grabbed Ash's arm, snapping him out of the frightened daze he'd fallen into.

'We have to go. *Now!*'

Ash allowed his guardian to lead him away, all too aware of the darkness growing behind them. Ash ran, his lungs crying out for air and his limbs burning, but

the fear of what lay behind gave him the strength to go on. He focused on getting to the *Frostheart*, where he could see Lunah and Rook already climbing the ropes that had been thrown over the side.

The ice beneath Ash's feet shifted and cracked, making it hard to stay upright. Huge crevices that could've swallowed a sleigh whole yawned open, dangerously close, the ear-piercing cracks of fracturing ice splitting the air. As a cold shadow loomed

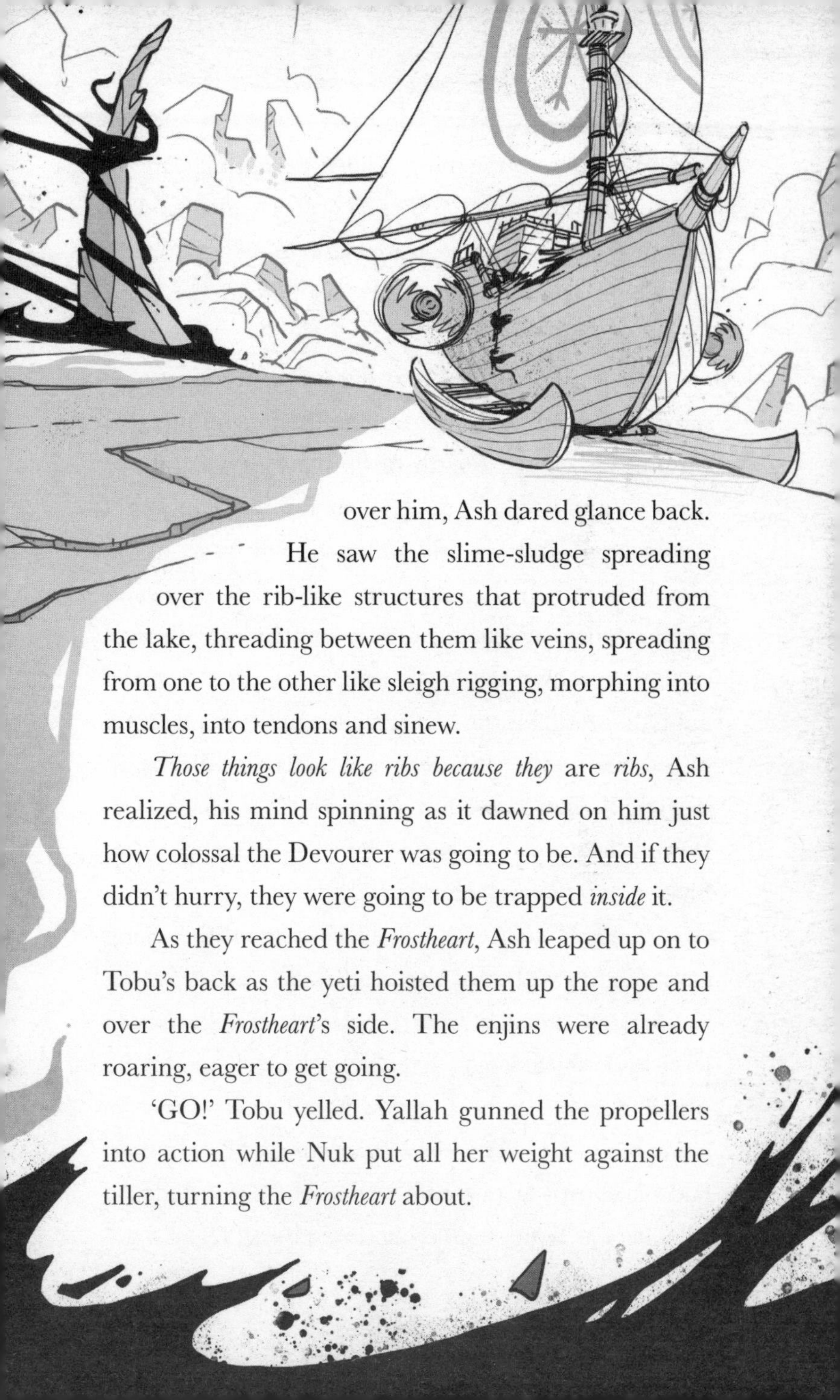

over him, Ash dared glance back.

He saw the slime-sludge spreading over the rib-like structures that protruded from the lake, threading between them like veins, spreading from one to the other like sleigh rigging, morphing into muscles, into tendons and sinew.

Those things look like ribs because they are *ribs*, Ash realized, his mind spinning as it dawned on him just how colossal the Devourer was going to be. And if they didn't hurry, they were going to be trapped *inside* it.

As they reached the *Frostheart*, Ash leaped up on to Tobu's back as the yeti hoisted them up the rope and over the *Frostheart*'s side. The enjins were already roaring, eager to get going.

'GO!' Tobu yelled. Yallah gunned the propellers into action while Nuk put all her weight against the tiller, turning the *Frostheart* about.

'I take it from the mass of horror eruptin' from the snow that things ain't gone too well?' Kailen said as the crew watched the creature begin to take shape.

The Devourer truly gave meaning to the word 'monster'.

The sludge curdled and hardened, forming pale skin that leaked shadows from undulating gill-like slits running down the length of its body. It rose above them on impossibly large segmented limbs, gaunt and sick-looking, and yet still unimaginably vast, like a mountain that had decided to sprout legs and walk. Shadow-auras writhed along its protruding ribcage, endlessly probing the air, searching for prey. It gazed upon the world for the first time in a millennia with six pitiless black eyes sank deep into its serpent-like head, its gigantic fangs bared in a permanent grimace. The Wraith sleigh sped around its feet, tiny in comparison, Shaard a dark speck at its prow.

'Destroy them!' Ash heard Shaard's Song commanding it. *'Do as you promised! Destroy the Pathfinders!'*

Hatred radiated from the Devourer in waves, a force so powerful it felt like a physical attack upon Ash's senses. It looked in the direction of the battle beyond the crater between the Wraiths, Leviathans and Pathfinders, and Sang with grim satisfaction at the bloodshed, the rumble of its Song shuddering through Ash's bones.

'Teya, can you see any way out of here?' Nuk called urgently to the lookout.

Teya shook her head. 'Nothing! The glacier walls have all collapsed. We're totally closed in!'

Now the Devourer turned its attention to the corpses of the Ancients that surrounded it, its gills emitting a raking hiss. Ash could feel its loathing freeze the air around them. Its Song seethed with rage at what the Ancients had done to it, at the fact that it did not get to kill them itself. With a scream that split the sky, it slashed with its massive claws, tearing the giant Ancients to pieces as though they were nothing.

Huge chunks of ice rained down upon the broken lake like a meteorite shower, the *Frostheart* swerving this way and that to avoid being crushed. The Devourer took a terrible delight in the destruction, but nothing that felt like *true* happiness, Ash thought, more like the sinister satisfaction you get by saying something hurtful to a friend in the heat of an argument.

Ash jumped as screaming balls of crackling energy suddenly tore above them, erupting into blooms of roaring fire as they hit the Devourer's hide. Apparently its earth-shaking rage had provoked a reaction from Stormbreaker's fleet.

'They've woken up at last,' Arla grunted.

'Stormbreaker'll show it who's boss!' Kailen said,

thumping her bolt-thrower with her fist. With a shriek, the Devourer smashed through the barrier of debris left by the collapsed glacier, the ground trembling with every step it took towards the Pathfinder fleet. Shaard's sleigh followed close behind, his Song-aura weaving around the Devourer's like two serpents in an embrace.

'Now's our chance!' Nuk shouted, steering the *Frostheart* after it.

'We're gonna *follow* that thing?' Yallah cried.

'Unless you'd rather stay here?'

As the *Frostheart* zoomed through the gap cleared by the Devourer, Ash's breath caught at the sight beyond the crater.

The battlefield was a scene of devastation, with the carcasses of Leviathans and ruined sleighs scattered across the darkened snow. What remained of the Wraith fleet turned to regroup with Shaard.

'All of a sudden, staying here doesn't seem like such a bad idea,' Kob murmured as the *Frostheart* weaved between chunks of ice.

At the sight of their ancient enemy, the Leviathan swarm broke from the Pathfinders and flooded towards the Devourer.

'*TOGETHER!*' they Sang, their blood-red Song-auras rising in resistance. '*DEFEND! FIGHT! DESTROY!*'

Screaming their war Songs, they swarmed over the titan, slashing and biting as it shrieked with fury. The wounds they inflicted bubbled and shifted like boiling tar, reforming with disgusting fluidity.

The Devourer snapped at them as it swept its gigantic claws through the rushing horde. Creatures Ash had once thought of as giants were flung into the air like pebbles kicked by a boot. Despite this, many Leviathans were able to scale its mountainous body, attacking its neck and other vulnerable areas. The Devourer was powerful, but a thousand years of imprisonment had made it sluggish and clumsy. It reared its head back, its mouth opening disturbingly wide, and let out an impossibly loud roar.

Like a tidal wave of sickening shadow, its Song-aura washed over the swarming Leviathans, engulfing them in darkness. The Leviathans dropped like hailstones. The glowing red threads of their Song-auras were torn away from them, twinkling like dancing spirits amid the darkness of the Devourer's Song.

'What – what's it *doing* . . .?' Lunah asked, grabbing Ash's arm.

'I-I don't know . . .' Ash stammered, holding a hand to his mouth.

The Devourer's throat made hideous gulping sounds as it inhaled its dark-aura back into its gullet,

the glowing Song-auras of the Leviathans drawn in with it. The gill-like apertures along the Devourer's body glowed red, the Devourer shivering with the energy it had consumed.

And scattered upon the snow around it lay every Leviathan that had attacked, still and lifeless.

9:

CONTROL

'*Branches above . . .*' Kailen sighed.

'It . . . it killed them *all*.' Kob gasped, the rest of the crew watching in rising, sickening horror.

But still the swarm came.

Gargants rammed into the Devourer's legs while Shriekers dived down from the sky, harrying it with their sharp talons and ear-splitting screams. Ash jolted with surprise as he recognized the scarring on one of the Shrieker's hides and the slight wobble in its glide.

No, it can't be, Ash thought, but his attention was grabbed by the sounds of booming archeoweapons.

Stormbreaker's fleet had formed a solid wall facing the onrushing Devourer, their ancient weapons flaring with blooms of light. As the archeoweapon blasts struck, the bright yellow energy sank deep into the Devourer's flesh, pulsing under its skin as it travelled along its sinuous body and up its long throat. With a mighty belch, the Devourer fired the blasts back at the Pathfinders, sleighs exploding in eruptions of wreckage.

'It's turning our weapons against us,' Kailen gasped out.

As the Devourer closed in on the fleet, Leviathans still swarming over its body, it reared its head back once more.

'Oh no . . .' Lunah said. 'No, no, *no*!'

The Devourer's Song spewed from its jaws, a roiling jet of shadow-fire that engulfed the fleet. Sleighs withered and decayed, ageing centuries before their very eyes. Ash could make out twinkling blue lights floating amid the billowing darkness, before being swallowed up by the Devourer as its dark-aura retreated back down its throat.

More than half the fleet, the mightiest ever assembled in the Snow Sea, the pride of Aurora and the greatest hope for human-kin, lay in utter ruins, reduced to little more than rotting husks.

Ash's mouth had turned bone-dry. Swallowing suddenly proved to be the most difficult of actions.

'*Mum*,' Ash whispered, his heart turning cold, the rest of the crew speechless at what they were witnessing.

'We cannot fight this thing,' Tobu said, even his

usually stone-calm face strained with shock.

'N-no,' Nuk agreed, quiet at first, then louder. 'No. We have to go!'

The Devourer's claws crashed down into the snow dangerously close to the *Frostheart*, its body towering above their mainmast and blocking out Mother Sun. As what remained of the fleet turned to flee, the monster lifted its maw to the sky and roared out another world-trembling Song. Its Song-aura washed over the Leviathan swarm, threads of shadow reaching hungrily for fresh victims.

But this Song was different.

This one, Ash recognized.

This one, Ash had come to *despise.*

The Leviathan swarm cried out in desperation as the Dark Song washed over them, the last action of their own free will. With a barked command from the Devourer, the Leviathans flung themselves off its body, tumbling to the snow in a shower of screeching beasts. Narrowing its eyes towards the fleet, the Devourer growled excitedly. The Leviathan swarm was now under its control.

'*Destroy them!*' Shaard's Song ordered. '*Turn them all to splinters!*'

With another scornful scream, the Devourer commanded the swarm forward. Just like in the puppet shows Ash had enjoyed in some of the Strongholds he'd passed through on the way to Aurora, the Leviathans moved to the Devourer's will as though it was their puppeteer, surging towards the retreating fleet. The Devourer released another blast of its Dark Song at some of the fleeing sleighs. Ash's belly dropped as the shadow-fire loomed over the *Frostheart*, tumbling over the sleigh like a wave.

He heard Rook cry out in distress just as the Dark Song burst into his own head. It reached into his mind, his thoughts shrinking as though touched by frostbite. He could sense other Song Weavers in the fleet wailing in confusion.

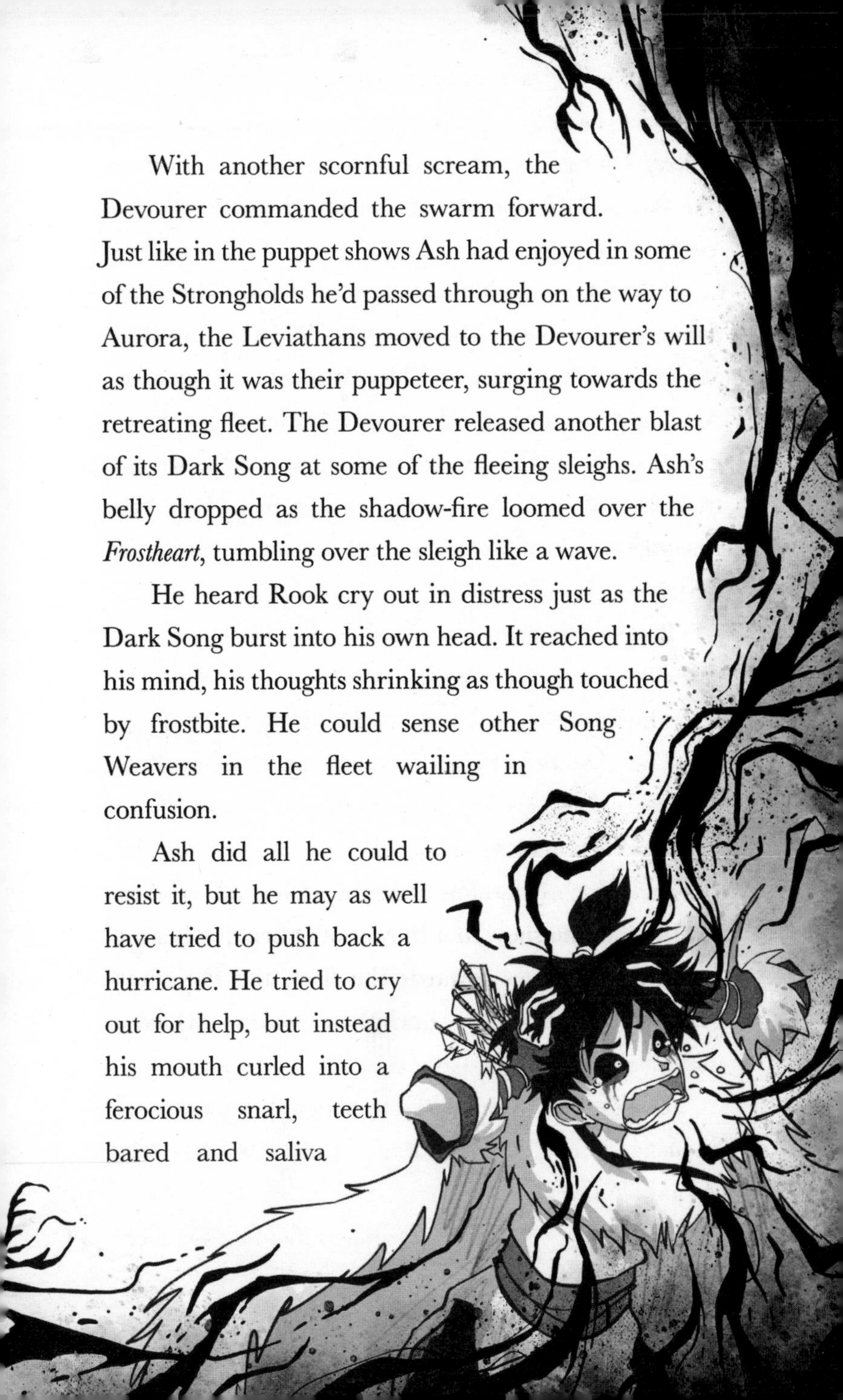

Ash did all he could to resist it, but he may as well have tried to push back a hurricane. He tried to cry out for help, but instead his mouth curled into a ferocious snarl, teeth bared and saliva frothing at his lips, spitting curses full of hate and spite. He felt as if he was seeing the world through a thin sheet of ice, blurry and indistinct, unable to control his actions. The dark-aura was slithering around his skull, erasing everything that made him Ash. He was losing himself, and there was nothing he could do to defend against it.

Is this how the Leviathans feel when Wraiths control them? Ash thought with a shiver. *How they felt when* I *controlled them?*

It was awful.

It was *despicable.*

The *Frostheart* crew turned to face Ash with alarm. Lunah was closest, her eyes wide with shock.

'Ash?' he heard her say, as though from a million leagues away.

And her voice *infuriated* him.

It boiled his blood. It grated in his ears. He couldn't understand how he'd ever been able to bear listening to it. He wanted nothing more than to make it stop.

He saw Kailen, Kob and Twinge staring at him in surprise as he twitched and snarled.

Staring at him with their judgemental eyes, their mocking gazes, so full of disgust at what he was. A Song Weaver . . .

Spirits, he *hated* them. He hated them all so much!

Then get rid of them, a voice, raw as winter, whispered in his skull. *Make them disappear.*

Ash launched himself at Lunah, knocking her to the deck. She pushed him, trying to force him off, but Ash would not let up, clawing and biting as she struggled under his weight. He was dimly aware of something large rushing up behind him but was too furious to care. He felt hands on him, holding him back. His fury mounted, his thoughts and reason refusing to fit into place. He had the strangest sensation that he was falling.

Falling, falling, falling, down into the unforgiving darkness below.

A DREAM

Hate.

All Ash knew as he tumbled through that cold darkness was a consuming, freezing, stabbing hate. He felt he would never escape it, that even trying was pointless. He might as well accept that the world would always be against him. That no one cared about him. Why should he care about anyone else when there was so much hate in the world?

But in that endless darkness Ash caught sight of a light.

It was a glowing thread of white-blue, thin and fragile.

A Song-aura, for sure, but whose? Ash sensed it was not the Song of a human-kin. It was a Leviathan, desperately searching for someone.

But not just anyone. Ash got the distinct feeling it was searching for *him*.

And it felt strangely familiar.

Despite his anger, something in the back of Ash's mind begged him to reach out for the warming light. He extended his own Song-aura, the Leviathan's thread darting eagerly towards it. Their weaving auras bloomed with light, melting the ice that had formed around their thoughts.

'*TOGETHER!*' the Leviathan Sang.

Ash's mind started to clear. He began to feel like himself again. Who was the hateful monster that had replaced him? Ash didn't recognize him one bit.

'*Together*,' Ash Sang back.

Together they grew stronger.

Together they shielded each other from the Devourer's hatred, and pulled themselves free of its grasp.

As one, they rose out of the darkness and back into the light.

'Squawkin' up a right ol' racket tonight, ain't they?'

Ash turned from his vantage point on the western wall of the Fira Stronghold to meet the gaze of the patrolling watchman coming up behind him. 'Might wanna head on home, lad; ya don't wanna be caught up here if the wurms decide to attack.'

'Mmm-hmm.' Ash nodded, getting to his feet as if agreeing to follow the watchman's advice but sitting back down as soon as the guard had passed out of sight.

Ash dangled his legs over the edge of the large wall, digging his heels into the stone to feel a little bit safer. The great drop below made his head spin and his belly lurch, but it was worth it to get this close to the Leviathan Song. Mother Sun was disappearing below the horizon, soaking the once-white world in brilliant oranges and purples.

A bit like my bruises . . . Ash thought, rubbing his aching arm.

It had been a tough day. They'd had spear practice and, of course, Thaw had used the opportunity to 'accidentally' whack Ash as many times as he possibly could.

But up here, Ash could forget all of that. He closed his eyes and took a deep breath, soaking up the Leviathan Song, allowing it to wash over him. He smiled for the first time that day. He couldn't help but feel emotional whenever he heard the Leviathans Sing. Well, as long as it wasn't the violent war Song they used when attacking; that one wasn't *quite* so pleasant.

This Song was different, though. It was one the Leviathans Sang only when they were alone together, human-kin far out of sight. The melody rose high with uplifting wails and dropped down low in mournful howls, as if the Leviathans were searching for something precious they'd had taken from them long ago. It reminded Ash of his parents' lullaby. And he couldn't shake off the crazy idea that if he just listened close enough, he'd be able to understand its meaning . . .

Yeah right, next I'll be hopping over the wall and asking them to hang out. Ash chuckled to himself.

Suddenly something flashed behind Ash's eyes, as though lightning had crackled through his mind.

Something was wrong about this tranquil scene.

He looked down from the wall and the sheer cliff it was built on, a wave of vertigo dragging at him.

Wasn't I falling? Ash thought. *I shouldn't be here . . . this is the past . . . but the others . . . my friends . . .*

The jolt shot through his skull again, this time dark and menacing.

The Devourer.

There was something else there with him. Another Song, another *presence* that came from outside of this place, outside of this time. It wasn't the Devourer and, most importantly, it didn't seem threatening. If anything, Ash got the sense it was protecting him from the Devourer's reach. It was just . . . watching. Watching his memories, *memory-weaving*, just as Ash had once done with Rook.

'*Who – who are you? Why are you here?*' Ash Sang, standing up, his fear of heights forgotten.

'*TO SEE IF I CAN TRUST BOY,*' Sang a Leviathan's voice.

'*T-trust me?*'

'*IS BOY TRUE? OR TRUST-BREAKER? BETRAYER?*'

'*I'm not a trust-breaker!*' Ash insisted, a little taken aback by the accusation, which sounded almost personal.

Again, Ash was struck by how *familiar* the voice was . . .

'*BOY SHARES BOND WITH MY KIN,*' it Sang. 'HEARD OUR SONG.'

'*I . . . I do . . . I always have.*' Ash nodded. '*And it was you who saved me back there, wasn't it? In the Devourer's darkness?*'

'*SAVED EACH OTHER. FORMED SHELL. DEFENCE. UNEXPECTED.*'

So it was true. Their woven Songs had formed some kind of barrier against the Devourer's mind-control. Ash's heart beat faster, his head spinning at the implications of this discovery.

'*Well, thank you,*' Ash Sang. The Leviathan was quiet. '*I mean it. Thank you for coming for me. I felt so . . . alone.*' He shuddered at the memory.

'*MAYBE BOY NOT SO BAD,*' the Leviathan decided.

'*But what we did, the barrier we formed . . . do . . . do you know what this means?*' Ash's Song became quicker and more excited. '*The other Song Weavers . . . they have the same connection to Leviathans that I do. Even if they don't understand it, we all feel it, deep down. We all know that we're not meant to be enemies. We could join forces! We could protect each other from the Devourer and fight back!*'

'*JOIN HUMAN-KIN? BLADE AND FANG? BOW AND CLAW?*' The Leviathan sounded like it was laughing at the idea. '*JOIN BRETHREN KILLERS? KINSLAYER? NEVER!*'

'*Kinslayer? You mean Stormbreaker?*' Ash felt strangely guilty at the mention of her name.

'*STORMBREAKER! FIND STORMBREAKER! KILL STORMBREAKER! EAT STORMBREAKER!*'

'*No!*' Ash cried, louder than he intended. '*Please don't! What she's doing is . . . well, it's . . . she's trying to protect her people!*'

'*KILLS BROTHERS! SISTERS!*'

Ash could understand the Leviathan's anger. He could sense its pain and the overwhelming sorrow at the loss of its loved ones.

'And Leviathans kill human-kin!' Ash Sang. *'There's been enough killing!'*

'HUMANS MUST BE WATCHED. PROTECT WORLD FROM THEIR CURSE.'

Ash shook his head, not sure what the Leviathan was talking about.

'If we keep killing each other, only the Devourer wins.'

The Leviathan huffed, though Ash sensed in its Song that it agreed with him. It too was tiring of the constant fighting.

'JOIN BLADE AND FANG? BOW AND CLAW? PERHAPS . . . PERHAPS . . .'

It appeared to be mulling the idea over.

Suddenly the Fira Stronghold began to fade, the wall Ash knew so well disappearing below his feet, the calming company of the Leviathan's Song dissolving with it, its final words still echoing in his mind . . .

'BROOD MOTHER WILL DECIDE . . .'

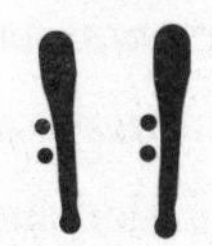

ALL THAT'S LEFT

Ash's eyes fluttered open.

He jolted up, his muscles aching terribly, his ears ringing. A tent canopy swam into focus around him, a fur blanket tangled about his limbs, damp with sweat. He felt warm for the first time since he could remember, almost too warm, his skin feverish. His pulse slowed as he realized it was his own tent, the constant rumble below assuring him the *Frostheart* was still moving.

That's got to be a good sign, Ash thought, though it was hard to take much comfort when his head felt like it had been stuffed full of one of Twinge's sloppy stews.

With a groan and a great deal of effort, he slipped free of his bedding and emerged on to a deserted upper deck, a chill wind whisking past the tents gathered round the humming sunstone enjin. The *Frostheart* cruised in formation with the rest of the Pathfinder fleet. Or, at least, what remained of it.

A trill from above caught Ash's attention, and he looked up into a grey forbidding sky. There, high above the *Frostheart*, a Shrieker was silhouetted against the storm clouds. Ash could almost sense its six eyes looking down upon him as it wobbled slightly in its glide.

'So it *was* you . . .' Ash whispered.

The Leviathan he had just been talking to in his dream was the same one Ash had saved when the Wraiths had forced it to attack Aurora. Since then, they'd formed a kind of *bond*. At least, the Shrieker had followed Ash on his travels, and had even allowed him to ride on its back in an attempt to stop Shaard from stealing the frost-heart.

But during that failed rescue attempt, the scarred Shrieker had become enraged at Stormbreaker for slaying its brethren and had attacked the *Kinspear*. Ash had been forced to use the Dark Song to throw it off the deck, hoping to save the lives of all involved. He flinched with guilt as memories of the Shrieker tumbling through the snow behind the *Kinspear* flashed through his mind. The Shrieker had Song Weaved with Ash; it had helped him, *trusted* him.

And Ash had broken that trust.

High above, the Shrieker gave a meaningful cry, before swooping away into the cloudy gloom.

A word from his dream echoed in Ash's mind.

BETRAYER . . .

'I won't let you down again,' Ash promised under his breath.

There was so much to think about. Who was this *Brood Mother* the Shrieker had mentioned? Ash had never heard of that kind of Leviathan before. It sounded more like a title than a breed, though. If it had the power to decide whether human-kin could be trusted or not, perhaps it was some kind of Leviathan leader?

He just hoped that whatever it was, it was more understanding than his own mother . . .

'*It follows!*'

Ash almost leaped out of his skin as a voice hissed behind him.

'Rook!' he wheezed. 'Don't do that!'

She whisked around him, placing a cold finger to his warm forehead, her black eyes glinting beneath her hood.

'*Resisted Devourer? Resisted control?*'

'W-with the Shrieker's help,' Ash said. 'But it was horrible. Being controlled like that . . . it was . . . it was . . .'

Rook nodded.

She knew all too well, Ash realized. Being under the Devourer's influence had been overwhelming. He couldn't even begin to imagine trying to escape it alone as Rook had done when she'd broken free of the Wraith corruption.

'*Song lives in heart. Do not lose heart to hate. Hold to bond,*' Rook Sang. '*Keep connection. Most powerful defence. Only hope now.*'

'I'll try,' Ash said, gazing in the direction the Shrieker had flown. 'Are . . . are you OK?'

There was something different about Rook. She seemed distant somehow – more feral. Almost like when Ash had first met her.

'*Tired,*' she answered. '*Weak. Frightened.*'

She scurried away before Ash could ask her any more.

Troubled, Ash made his way down the stairs to the main deck. He had to hold back tears when he saw the rest of the crew safe and sound. They were gathered round a large crate that had been turned into a makeshift table, laden with cups, bowls and a steaming flask. They greeted Ash with clear relief.

Everyone was there, except for Master Podd, who was at the helm, steering the sleigh, and Rook, who now sat hunched up on the mainmast with her crows.

And then there was Lunah, who was . . .

'HE LIVES!' Lunah yelled, swinging down from the rigging and jabbing Ash in the side, making him jump so hard he nearly leaped overboard.

'LUNAH!' Ash cried as she hit the deck and gave him the biggest hug, almost squeezing the life out of him. 'Not for long if you keep this up!'

Lunah let go, her face beaming as Tobu strode over carrying a bowl.

'Are you well, boy? You're not hurt?'

'I-I'm fine, I think. Just a bit groggy.'

'Then we all got away lightly.' Tobu nodded, satisfied.

'Speak for yerself – he bent my finger right back!' Lunah said, holding up a swollen, purple digit. Tobu raised an eyebrow. 'It's my pointin' finger, an' it still hurts! How am I s'posed to point?! An' look at the size o' this graze!'

Ash looked at all the cuts and bruises on her skin and swallowed hard.

'Lunah . . . I . . .' His voice broke, the lump in his throat growing.

She placed a good finger on his lips to shush him.

'*Ah-ah-ah!* None o' that, thank you very much, *Ash-the-Very-Apologetic*.'

'What I did . . . I didn't . . . I *never* meant . . .'

Memories of striking and scratching at Lunah flashed into Ash's mind. They made him feel sick.

'It was the Devourer,' Lunah said, poking his nose. 'We all know I woulda kicked yer butt if it'd been just you. Besides, I'm fine. Furball over here pulled you offa me before I could clobber you.' She nodded up at Tobu, who was eyeing Ash carefully.

'I'm so sorry.' Ash sniffed as he looked over to the others, tears stinging his eyes. 'Everyone. I would never want to hurt any of you, ever. What I did was . . . it was terrible.'

'Let's make a deal,' Lunah said, sticking her hand out. 'You gotta promise not to beat yerself up 'bout things you can't control, an' I promise to drop-kick you into the sea if you ever attack me again. Deal?'

She gave Ash a playful wink, and a laugh escaped his tight throat. He took her hand and shook it.

'Deal.'

'I was on my way to check on you,' Tobu said, passing the bowl he carried to Ash. It contained some kind of fish stew, the smell of which made Ash's belly rumble. For the first time since he'd awoken, Ash realized how famished he was. He held the bowl awkwardly to the side as rest of the crew rushed to give him a hug too, no more words needing to be spoken.

They needed the hug as much as Ash did, after what they'd all just been through.

'Come, eat!' Kob said, leading Ash towards the

crate table. Kailen had remained seated the whole time, brooding into her cup, but she kicked a small barrel out for Ash as he approached. He sat and began to eat the stew, thinking that it might've been just about the best thing he'd ever tasted. It was warming and salty, and it filled him with energy and life.

The *Frostheart* crew sat in silence for a long while, taking what comfort they could from each other's company.

'So . . .' Teya said after some time. '*That* didn't go great.'

'As ever, Teya, your keen eye for detail proves invaluable.' Arla chuckled.

'At least we know what to do now,' Lunah said, sitting cross-legged on the table itself. 'And that's to never go anywhere near that flippin' thing ever again!'

'I'll drink to that!' Yallah raised her cup.

'We all escaped with our lives,' Captain Nuk said. 'That's what matters most.'

The others held their cups up to Yallah's.

After a small silence, Ash asked the question that had been burning at the back of his mind since he'd awoken.

'My mum . . . is she . . .?'

'She's fine,' Nuk said. 'Shaken, but whether that's from shock or fury, it's always hard to tell.'

'Yeah, she's got a face made a' stone, like furball here,' Lunah said, patting Tobu's arm.

Ash sighed with relief. 'What *happened* out there?'

Nuk gave Ash one of her sympathetic motherly smiles. 'I'm sorry to say, things went from bad to worse after your *turn*, dear boy. The Devourer took control of the Leviathan swarm and four sleighs' worth of Song Weavers. And what a riotous cacophony of chaos it was!'

'Leviathans tearing apart sleighs,' Teya whispered.

'Song Weavers attackin' Pathfinders, snarlin' an' frothin' like animals,' Kailen added.

Ash flushed with shame. *He* could've ended up like those Song Weavers, had it not been for the Shrieker's help.

'Worry not, boy,' Tobu said. 'As long as I'm here, I will help lift you from the Devourer's darkness.'

Ash smiled his thanks.

'No, seriously, after he pulled you off me, he held you upside down in mid-air till you passed out, it was crazy!' Lunah explained. 'You've been asleep for two days.'

'More than half the fleet was reduced to kindling,' Nuk continued, her eyes distant and troubled. 'The few of us left had no choice but to flee north, the Devourer hot on our tails.'

Ash glanced nervously aft, dread twisting his guts

at the idea of the Devourer being close behind, but the lack of roaring and stomping suggested it wasn't *too* close.

'Valkyries be thanked, it appears to be rather sluggish after such a long slumber,' Nuk went on, 'and we've managed to nab a lead on the beastie. But on a scale of roaring success to crushing defeat, I'm afraid we came out on the tail-between-the-legs end of the spectrum.'

'Where are we going?' Ash asked quietly.

'Aurora,' Kob said. 'Shaard has control of that thing, and we know his greatest desire is to smash the Strongholds' strength and unity. And where better to do that than in Aurora, the centre of it all? That's gotta be where the Devourer is heading.'

'Overthrow the Council, and the Snow Sea is his,' Arla muttered.

'Shaard can *control* that thing?' Ash asked fearfully.

'*Nothing controls Devourer,*' Rook's Song hissed from the mainmast. '*Devourer weak after sleep. Needs strength. Aurora offers best feed.*'

A chill crept up Ash's spine. The greatest Stronghold in the Snow Sea, Aurora was home to countless thousands of people, all going about their lives believing they were safe behind its walls, unaware that a ravenous monster was heading straight for them . . .

Ash looked out at what little was left of the once mighty fleet. Hulls were splintered, runners dented, enjins smoking. The fleet reminded Ash of some poor wounded animal, crawling away to find a place to die.

The *Kinspear* ran alongside them, and the sight of his mother's sleigh made Ash's jaw tighten.

'It didn't have to be this way,' he murmured.

'No one could've predicted what happened . . .' Nuk said.

'Except we did!' Ash snapped. 'We warned her this would happen if she didn't stop Shaard!'

Ever since Shaard had first tricked him into using the Devourer's Dark Song, a seed of anger had festered in Ash's belly. He'd tried hard to push it back, but now that the Devourer was unleashed, he was finding it difficult to control.

The others all knew who 'she' was. They looked like they wanted to defend their commander, but none seemed able to find the right words.

Because they know I'm right, Ash thought bitterly.

'Your mother asked us to let her know when you woke,' Nuk said gently.

'Did she come to see me while I was asleep?'

Ash had to admit it had hurt not to find her at his bedside when he woke. Being there for your children was what mothers were meant to do. Not his, apparently.

'She has a fleet to command, Ash,' Kailen said not unkindly.

Ash nodded, looking down at the empty bowl in his lap.

'Speakin' of which,' Teya said, pointing at the signal flags being hoisted by the *Kinspear.* 'Fresh orders.'

Looming ahead of the fleet was a giant standing stone that rose up into the sky. Others just like it could be seen stretching off into the hazy distance, all in a line as if they were sentries standing guard.

'The Ghost Stones!' Twinge said. Then seeing the confusion on Ash's face, added, 'Standing stones blessed in ages past with protective warding spells. They line the border with the Rend, keeping the rest of the Snow Sea safe from the evils within. Some say they were placed here by giants, or by otherworldly beings who–'

'Whoever put 'em here, let's hope they keep us safe now, eh?' Arla interrupted. 'Cos it looks like we've finally found a place to stop an' lick our wounds . . .'

12

MORAL COMPASS

Nestled in the shadow of the Ghost Stones was an island of ice that floated upon a lake. It was upon this island that the sleighs of the Pathfinder fleet came to a stop and formed a protective circle. Stormbreaker clearly hoped the freezing water they had skated over would protect them from any Leviathan attacks, though not many of the creatures had been spotted since the battle – those under the control of the Devourer were sticking close to their new master, while those who had escaped its Dark Song seemed to have disappeared.

The Pathfinders gathered together on the ice, some speaking in hushed tones, others simply slumping to the ground with exhaustion. Many were injured, wearing red-soaked bandages and slings. As Nuk had once told Ash, at heart, Pathfinders were adventurers trying to help people. They weren't trained warriors, and the Devourer was no ordinary foe. The air was thick with fear.

'The one enemy none of us can defeat is death,' Ash heard a Pathfinder say, 'and that *thing* was death made flesh.'

'Wraiths, I can handle,' another declared. 'Leviathans, perhaps, on a good day an' with a sleigh-loada archeoweapons backin' me up, but that thing? We had the strongest fleet ever assembled on the Snow Sea, an' that thing wiped out *three quarters* of it as if it were brushin' snow off ice!'

Captain Nuk was doing what she did best – boosting morale. As night fell, she passed from sleigh to sleigh, trying to help lift their spirits. Ash hung around with his own crew, keeping one eye on the *Kinspear*, from which his mother had yet to emerge.

The cold, bitter feeling was still stewing inside him, and the sinister drone of the Devourer's Song, now carried on the wind, was doing its best to lure it out.

Breathing deeply, Ash turned his attention to Lunah, who was talking to one of her fellow Drifters.

'Yer sure you won't come? We sure could use ya,' the man said. He wore a cloak embroidered with constellations and his hair, shaved on one side, was festooned with shimmering stars, just like Lunah's. 'Ent

no way the Pathfinders have enough sleighs to defeat that thing without the Convoy's help.'

The Convoy was the Drifter Stronghold but, unlike other Strongholds, which were essentially fortress-cities, the Convoy was a fleet of sleighs that travelled across the snows like a migrating school of fish, never in one place for long.

'Why d'ya need my help?' Lunah asked. 'You got summa the best navigators in the Snow Sea over there!'

She gestured towards a group of Drifters poring over maps and discussing the most likely location of the ever-moving Convoy.

'An' we sure could use one more,' the man replied. 'Some're sayin' the Convoy will be along the Broken Coast right now, tradin' with the mursu, but I reckon with so many Pathfinders gatherin' near Aurora, they might be tempted to drift round Aurora's Embrace . . .'

'The Embrace? The Broken Coast?' Lunah pulled a face. 'My ma woulda read the signs, seen the change in the sky. She'd know somethin' was up and head south to the Ashlands to steer clear. "When the world starts to crash, head to the ash", is what she always says.'

'Ah, y'see!' The man clicked his fingers. 'This is why we need ya! The daughter of the legendary Celeste herself, the greatest explorer in all the land!'

'I ent all that,' Lunah said quietly.

Ash knew how worried Lunah was that she'd never be able to live up to her mother's reputation, and his heart went out to her. He wished he could comfort her, like she always did him, but he didn't want to embarrass her in front of her own people.

'Not what I heard,' the man said. 'Word is it was you found the hidden Stronghold of Solstice! If that ent somethin' for the stories to sing about, I dunno what is!'

'An' look what good it did,' Lunah replied. 'Led the

Wraiths straight to it, an' they kidnapped everyone who lived there.'

The man coughed awkwardly. 'Look, we've all got diff'rent ideas of where the Convoy might be, an' there ent time enough to explore 'em all. Stormbreaker's only lending us two sleighs. We can't be wastin' time scootin' about in the backwards end of nowhere. The Devourer's waitin' fer no one, an' we could use all hands on deck.'

''M sorry.' Lunah shrugged. 'The *Frostheart* needs me too. I can't just up an' leave at a time like this.'

Ash was secretly glad to hear Lunah wasn't going anywhere. He knew she had to leave the *Frostheart* one day if she was to ever finish her Proving, but he didn't want it to be soon. It was selfish, Ash knew, but he wasn't sure he could cope without her.

The Proving was the quest every Drifter child undertook once they came of age. Alone, they headed out into the wilds, using nothing but their navigational skills and the guidance of the stars to find an unexplored part of the map. Charting the uncharted. Only then could they try to find the Convoy and return a true Drifter. That's why so many Pathfinder crews ended up having Drifters for navigators: their skills were second to none and they were raised with a taste for adventure. Though she'd struggled, Lunah had completed all the tasks except for returning to the Convoy, triumphant.

'We're leavin' soon as we're ready,' the man said, turning to go. 'If ya change yer mind, better change it fast.'

'Stars guide yer path,' Lunah said.

'An' may the moon shine on yours, daughter of Celeste.'

Lunah watched him return to the others.

'They'll find them,' Ash said in a rather lame attempt to reassure her.

'I ent so sure.' Lunah looked longingly after the Drifters as they rolled their maps up and headed towards the sleighs that had been lent to them.

Ash recognized that longing. That desperate need to follow the heart. He'd felt it that day the *Frostheart* had roared into the Fira Stronghold. And he knew how much she'd regret this moment if she didn't act.

'If this is something you need to do, Lunah,' Ash began, 'you . . . you should go. We'll be OK.'

They looked over at the crew in time to see Nuk gesture so wildly she accidentally clipped Twinge round the head. He stumbled back and slipped on the ice, taking Teya and Kailen down with him.

'Ent so sure about that either.' Lunah chuckled.

'If anyone can find the Convoy, it's you,' Ash said. 'And it sounds like they might need you more than we do . . .'

'Oi! You tryna get rid of me or somethin'?'

'N-no! It's just – we know how to get to Aurora and . . .' Ash stopped when he saw the smile on Lunah's face. She was messing with him, as per usual. They fell quiet for some time, watching the Drifters climb into their sleighs.

'But what if I *can't* find the Convoy?' Lunah blurted, her voice suddenly full of emotion. 'What if I get it wrong? The fleet would be left without back-up, an' my ma . . . she'd be . . . she'd be *devastated* that I messed up.'

'Just listen to your gut,' Ash reassured her. 'It's always pointed us right before!' Lunah's belly chose that very moment to rumble. 'What if the others go the wrong way and the message doesn't get to the Convoy? You'd never forgive yourself. But you'll make sure that message gets to your mum, I know you will.'

Ash fell quiet while Lunah considered his words, trying to be supportive just by being by her side.

'Helpin' them's the right thing to do, ent it?' Lunah said finally, with a resigned sigh.

Ash closed his eyes, understanding that the moment he'd dreaded had come. The moment he and Lunah had to say goodbye.

'I think it might.'

'Stupid morals. What're they good for?'

Ash laughed, when an idea suddenly seemed to strike Lunah. She unclipped one of the stars from her hair and handed it to Ash. 'Take this. As long as you have it, I'll always be able to find you.'

Ash took it, looking at the piece with reverence. 'R-really?'

'No,' said Lunah. 'It's just an ornament. But least if you have it, you won't forget me. It'll remind you of the promise we made, back before we went into the Everstorm.'

Ash nodded. 'That no matter where we ended up, we'd find each other again.'

'An' I hope you're a man of yer word, Ash the Oath-maker.'

Ash gripped the star, forcing a smile in an attempt to stop his throat from tightening as he caught the starlight glinting off the tears in Lunah's eyes.

'I'll miss you,' he said, choked up, and she pulled him into a tight hug.

'I'll miss ya too, fire-boy.' She let out a strange half-sob, half-laugh. Ash could feel Lunah's tears hot against his neck. When Lunah pulled away, she wiped her eyes and nudged Ash with her shoulder. 'Mums, right? The things they make us do!'

'Right,' Ash said, his own watery eyes darting to the *Kinspear*.

'You *still* not talked to her? This is gettin' silly. You've spoken more to Leviathans than yer own mamma!'

'It's just . . . it's all new, and it's . . . well . . . it's a lot,' Ash finished lamely.

'Pssssh. You jus' need more confidence, tha's all.'

'Confidence?'

'Yeah! Bein' proud, lookin' like you know what yer doin', struttin' yer stuff, y'know?'

'I-I don't know if I do,' Ash said.

Lunah stepped away so she could get a good look at him. She looked him up and down, studying the way he stood, slightly hunched over, holding his arm nervously. She clicked her tongue and shook her head as though she'd just seen a terrible stain on the *Frostheart*'s deck.

'Yeah, I can see that. But, stars above, I'll never know why! You blimmin' Sing to monsters, you've flown through the sky, you've had a duel with the Great Horned One! A Singin' duel, sure, but still! Right then, chin up!' She pulled Ash's chin up, then pushed hard on his shoulders. 'Shoulders back, spine straight!'

'O-OK!' Ash murmured, looking down to make sure he was obeying instructions.

'An' look at me when you talk!'

Ash's eyes shot up.

'Wider! Give me a real stare!' Lunah said.

Ash opened his eyes as wide as he could, his mouth twitching with the strain.

'Tha's more like it! Now show me yer walk!'

Ash shuffled forward, eyes unblinking.

'Bigger strides, throw yer arms back an' forth, like this!' Lunah went into an exaggerated double-bounce walk. Ash did his best to copy her. 'Tha's it! Now strut over to that sleigh and demand to speak with yer ma like it's somethin' you do every flippin' day!'

Ash hesitated. He looked back at his friend and, not for the first time, thought how lucky he'd been to meet her. She'd done so much for him; he didn't even know how to begin to thank her, let alone say goodbye.

Lunah gave him a smile, sharing his feelings. 'Ent no point sayin' goodbye. We've made a promise, remember?'

Ash forced a smile. 'See you later then, I guess?'

'Later. Before that, though, you got some struttin' to do!'

Ash nodded, then started towards the *Kinspear.* Its main deck was crowded with hulking archeoweapons, bolt-throwers, harpoons and a hardened, battle-scarred crew who eyed Ash suspiciously as he approached.

'Don't back down!' Lunah called after him. 'Don't be scared of 'em; they should be scared of *you*! Now go talk to yer mamma!'

Ash strode forward, fuelled by the confidence his friend had in him. As he got closer – shoulders back, arms swinging – he started to feel a bit more positive, even if his unblinking eyes were drying out. Suddenly his mother didn't seem all that scary. It was working! He could do this!

He half turned to give Lunah one last wave, but she had already moved off to say her goodbyes to the rest of the crew. His confidence evaporated instantly.

She was really going.

And without her, what was he but a small, frightened boy?

Ash decided that was a good time to allow himself to blink.

WEAVING HOPE

As Ash reached the *Kinspear*, he passed the fleet's Song Weavers, who'd all been gathered together beneath the sleigh. They were being kept under close watch, the guards encircling them holding their bows at the ready, distrust clear on their faces. The memory of how the Devourer had turned the Song Weavers against them was still raw.

Not many people knew Ash was a Song Weaver himself, and his mother clearly hadn't shared that information. Guilt niggled at him as he realized he'd escaped the same fate simply because of who his mother was.

But what good would admitting the truth do? Ash asked himself. *I can do more out here with my crew . . .*

Half the Weavers hummed a gentle chant together,

weaving a Song of comfort and healing. It was so soothing Ash found himself stepping closer to listen.

It wasn't because he was looking for any excuse to delay seeing his mother again.

No way.

'Wouldn't get too close, kid,' came a gruff voice from behind. It belonged to a burly Pathfinder carrying a large tray. It held bowls of what Ash imagined was some kind of slime dredged up from the bottom of the lake. 'I'm only gettin' near to give 'em their slop. Ent a crowd for normal folk like you or me. All that creepy Singin', spirits know what they're all up to . . .'

Ash clenched his jaw. He was getting *sick* of Song Weavers being treated this way, especially after everything they'd just been through!

'I'm a Song Weaver too!' he snapped, suddenly ashamed that he'd been spared being put under guard while others like him hadn't. He slipped past the Pathfinder and in among the Weavers. The man watched him, then gave a shrug before tossing the tray to the floor, some of the gunk slopping out on to the ice.

'Grub's up,' he announced, striding back the way he'd come.

Ash stood awkwardly in the middle of the crowd. With nobody to direct his anger at, his temper cooled, and he realized he didn't really know what to do with himself. He recognized the weathered faces of the Solstice Elders Loda and Arrus leading the chant. Arrus's wounded leg was bound in a splint. The Solstice Weavers sat in meditative positions, their long white robes draped over their knees like the winding threads of a Song-aura.

The Weavers from the other Strongholds sat silent and sullen, eyes cast down, trying to comprehend the horrors they'd experienced in the Rend. One was watching the Solstice Weavers with mounting agitation.

'How can you Sing at a time like this?' she asked. 'I wish I could block my ears up! All I hear is that cursed *demon's* Song every waking moment and in all the nightmares I have when I sleep!'

'Now is *exactly* the time we should be Singing,' Arrus said, opening his eyes. 'Song Weaving binds us together. It lends us strength and heals the wounds in our souls. Please, join us.'

The woman glared at the Elder. 'It's Singing that got us into this mess in the first place. I would happily never hear another Song in my life.'

'Song Weaving is our *best* defence against the Devourer,' Arrus said. 'Only by weaving our auras together can we hope to shield each other from the Devourer's Song.'

'We saw Wraiths without their masks on,' a man with a large ring through his nose said. 'We saw what they were – human-kin, like us. *They* controlled the Leviathans with their Song. Can't we do the same? Can't we control the Devourer?'

'*Control Devourer?*' hissed a Song from above. The Weavers' eyes shot up, spotting Rook who was perched on the runner of the sleigh next to the *Kinspear.* Her hood was up so that no one could see who – or *what* – she was. '*Sing like Wraiths? Foolish. Dangerous.* Stupid.'

The nose-ring man flinched at the appearance of this ragged, rasping figure.

'I'm just saying, we need to be thinking about these things if we're gonna stand any chance of surviving!'

Unlike the Solstice Weavers, who'd grown up not

having to hide their powers, those from the Strongholds had spent a lifetime concealing their abilities, suppressing their instinct to Sing. Ash had been just like them once. Just as lost, just as confused. They didn't know what it meant to Song Weave. They'd never been taught the incredible things it could achieve, nor the terrible things it was capable of.

'You're right. The Wraiths are Song Weavers, just like us.' Arrus nodded sadly. The Strongholders gasped. 'And, yes, we *could* control the Leviathans like they do. But would you really want to *force* another living creature to do your bidding against their will? You must ask yourself why the Leviathans have become so hostile in recent years.'

'I never wanted to fight them in the first place,' a boy a little older than Ash said.

'I can't see what good killing them does,' added a woman. 'The Leviathans are deadly, sure, but they also Sing Songs of beauty, and sadness, of *love* and *loss* . . .'

'It's true! I've heard them!' said the boy. 'I don't want to harm anything that could feel that way!'

Most of the other Song Weavers mumbled their agreement.

Nose-ring man shifted uncomfortably. 'I . . . don't deny I feel a . . . a *connection* to 'em. But to something as awful as the Devourer . . .'

'The Devourer is not the same as other Leviathans,' Arrus said. 'It's evil – *corrupted*, somehow. And the only way to control Leviathan minds is by using the Devourer's Dark Song – a power borrowed from the same Song that stole the minds of our own people.'

'Will they ever go back to normal?' another Stronghold Weaver asked. 'Those that went . . . *feral* back in the Rend?'

'It's possible to use your Song to rescue someone from the Devourer's control,' Loda said. 'But only if you act fast. Every time you Sing the Devourer's Dark

Song, or every moment spent under its influence, the Devourer consumes a piece of who you are. If you spend long enough under the Devourer's control, it will take your mind, body and spirit entirely.'

'We call them the *Corrupted*,' Arrus finished.

'*Wraiths*,' Rook Sang, leaning down from her railing, the crows around her cawing their displeasure. '*Mindless . . . vicious . . . hateful. Just. Like. Me.*'

Rook's pitch-black eyes glinted within the shadow of her hood, her burning-white pupils piercing through the darkness. The Weavers pulled back in fear.

'What can we do then?' someone else asked.

'We have no hope against that thing!'

'Hope?' Arrus said brightly. 'There's always hope.'

'Sing with us,' said Loda. 'Sing with us, and we'll show you. Together we can be *strong*. United our Songs could be *unbreakable*.'

Slowly the Weavers of the Strongholds moved closer to the Solstice Weavers. Even the man with the nose ring. Even though they had been taken from their homes and forced to fight in Stormbreaker's army, and even though Solstice had been stripped bare of its people and left abandoned, the Song Weavers were coming together. They may have been the outcasts of the Snow Sea, but at least now they were there for each other.

Ash smiled as their Songs began to blend in a

beautiful Song of union and togetherness.

Until a stern voice interrupted.

'There will be no Singing unless I order it.'

Ash looked up to see his mother standing at the top of the *Kinspear*'s gangplank, the epitome of strength and determination. Under the Commander's fierce gaze, the Song Weavers fell silent, eyes cast down so as not to offend any further.

'Ash, come away from there,' Stormbreaker said. 'I must speak with you.'

Ash's blood rushed – cold and bitter.

A MONSTER TALE

Stormbreaker's cabin was small and neat. A table stood in the centre, covered with maps, charts and sketches of all the different types of Leviathan. Words had been roughly scrawled on the pages; notes on the best ways to kill them, Ash assumed. The room was decorated in a Fira style, with flame motifs and triangular symbols dotted around, and many of the weapons that hung from the walls had sunstone charms tied to their hilts or hafts. Ash didn't know why it was a surprise to see them – his mother was a Fira native, just like him. It was just odd to see reminders of his old home so far away. Weirdly it made him feel a little closer to someone who otherwise seemed like a stranger.

'You wanted to see me?' Ash mumbled, avoiding eye contact.

'Sit, please.' Stormbreaker pointed to a stool as she walked behind her table and sat down herself.

Ash did so. He placed his hands between his legs and looked down at them.

'You're unhurt?' she asked. Ash nodded. 'But the Devourer got into your head? Like the others?'

Ash hesitated, then nodded again. He wanted to tell her that a Leviathan had helped him break free, but he couldn't find the words.

Like she'd listen anyway . . .

Stormbreaker laced her fingers, considering him closely. 'You're angry with me.'

Her observation caught Ash off guard. She was right, of course, but he hadn't prepared himself to confront her about it. It had been easier to imagine having a go at her when she wasn't sitting in front of him, her intense glare whittling away his courage.

'I-I just think . . . if you hadn't been so determined to blast the Leviathans, even though they were on our *side*, maybe we would've caught Shaard and stopped all this from happening.'

Stormbreaker stood up suddenly, her stool scraping against the floor, startling Ash. She turned her back on him, clasping her hands behind her large cloak.

'Your father used to argue that there could be peace with the Leviathans.'

Ash's mouth went very dry.

'Can you believe I actually felt sorry for Shaard, the day we found him?' Stormbreaker laughed joylessly. 'It was outside the ruins of Ancients Fall. He was starving – little more than rags and bones – so close to death he looked about ready to give himself up to the spirits. We took him aboard my old sleigh, the *Trailblazer*, and nursed him back to health, fools that we were.'

Ash swallowed, listening intently.

'Still, I was suspicious of him from the start. What had he been doing out there in the middle of nowhere? Where was his Stronghold? How had he survived alone? "I'm an exile" was all he told us, that infuriating grin never once leaving his face.'

Ash's brow twitched. He knew that grin all too well.

'I was softer then. I'd find a way to get the truth out of him now,' Stormbreaker said ominously. 'Shaard said he was searching for a way to save the Snow Sea from its oppressors. I thought he meant the Leviathans, of course. Apparently I was wrong.

'But Ferno lapped it up. Your father was always a people person. He struck up a quick friendship with Shaard, despite my warnings. They were both Song Weavers; they shared a bond that I could never understand –'

'That no one *tries* to understand,' Ash interrupted. Stormbreaker raised a brow questioningly. 'The real bond Song Weavers share is how badly we're treated by everyone else, just cos we can speak to Leviathans. People either hate us or try to *use* us.'

Ash forced himself to hold Stormbreaker's gaze to make his accusation clear.

'You want to be careful, Ash,' Stormbreaker said quietly. 'You're sounding a lot like Shaard. He filled your father's head with hate. As we travelled between Strongholds, he focused Ferno's mind on all the ways Song Weavers were mistreated. Wasn't long before Ferno saw injustice everywhere, even when it didn't really exist.'

'How would *you* know?!' Ash snapped.

Anger flashed across Stormbreaker's face.

'Because I fell in love with a Song Weaver! I wanted to improve the way they were treated too!'

'Well, take a look outside and see how that's going,' Ash said, his face hot. They fell silent, both breathing hard.

'Dad left me a message,' Ash said, once the chilling anger in his belly receded.

'What?' Stormbreaker asked, surprised.

'On the trail he sent me on. He knew he did wrong. He knew he'd been corrupted, but he said he wanted to make things better in the end . . .'

'Then he lied to you,' Stormbreaker said.

'He *didn't*!' Ash insisted, remembering the memory of his father from the message-sphere, and the sincerity it had spoken with.

Stormbreaker shook her head with disappointment. 'When Shaard finally left the *Trailblazer*, he joined a sleigh run by a crew of silent dark-eyed strangers. They weren't Pathfinders, that was for sure, but I didn't think too hard about it at the time – I was just glad he was gone. But something changed in Ferno after that.'

Stormbreaker began to pace behind her desk. 'He grew distant. I saw less and less of him. He'd go on wanderings into the Snow Sea, sometimes for weeks at a time. We still had no idea what the Wraiths were back then, but now I know Ferno had become one of them. As a Pathfinder, Ferno had access to information in Aurora. He was Shaard's man on the inside, passing him voyage plans and trade routes that the Wraiths could use to plot their raids, and information on some ancient relics Shaard needed to bring the Strongholds to their knees.'

'The frost-heart and the archeomek device that destroyed it,' Ash said under his breath.

'I sensed I was losing my friend, my companion, my life-mate . . .' Stormbreaker took a breath. 'At night, he would sneak out and Sing with the Leviathans. When I questioned him, he denied it, of course, but he ended up spending more time with Leviathans than with his own kind!'

'He was trying to connect with them,' Ash explained, remembering what Rook had told him. 'Dad knew the Devourer's Song was getting to him, and so he tried to learn how to use Song Weaving for good, instead of for bad!'

'Who told you this?'

'A . . . a friend,' Ash said, his enthusiasm trailing off.

'What friend?' Stormbreaker eyed him closely.

'It doesn't matter.' He didn't want to think what his mother would do if she found out Rook had been a Wraith too. 'Song Weaving is meant to connect, not control. The Leviathans know this. The Wraiths use the Devourer's Dark Song to control Leviathans and turn them against us. But what you saw was Dad trying to correct his mistakes. He was trying to say sorry to them!'

'The Leviathans ate away your father's mind!' Stormbreaker persisted. 'They turned him against us. I begged Ferno to stop what he was doing. I threatened to go to the Council, to warn the Pathfinders, but the Leviathans had sunk their claws into his mind, and no matter what I said I couldn't stop him. One night, while we were docked at the Ensera Stronghold, he set fire to the *Trailblazer*, stole one of their ulk sleighs and disappeared. He left my crew and me stranded.' She stopped pacing and placed her hands on her table. 'That was the last I saw of him. By the end, your father was gone, and a monster was all that was left behind.'

'You're *wrong*,' Ash insisted. 'That was when he set off to leave the trail for me – to try to clean up the mess he'd made. He . . . he must've burned your sleigh to stop you from following him. He knew he was in danger –

the Wraiths would've been after him for betraying them!'

'When will you get it in your head?!' Stormbreaker snapped. 'The man I loved, the father you once had, is *gone*. Forever!'

Ash recoiled and Stormbreaker took a steadying breath. 'Can't you see that I'm trying to protect you? I'm telling you all this to show you why you can never trust Leviathans. Why there will never be peace between us!'

'You keep saying that Leviathans stole Dad's mind, but they *couldn't*!' Ash said. 'It's the Devourer that steals minds, not the Leviathans!'

'Even if that were true, what makes the Devourer different from all the others?'

Ash's mouth flapped open, unable to find an answer.

'It's a Leviathan,' Stormbreaker said. 'An incredibly powerful one, but a Leviathan all the same.'

'It's different!' Ash said, his jaw clenched with frustration. 'I-I don't know how, but it is!'

'You're young and naive,' Stormbreaker said coldly. 'But you'll learn. I won't lose you to them like I lost your father.'

Ash felt rage swell within him. She was talking down to him like he was some clueless child! How dare she?! He'd seen things she wouldn't believe! Things she *clearly* couldn't understand!

Ash opened his mouth to tell her as much, when there was a sudden commotion outside the door. Banging, crashing and a few shouts.

'Stormbreaker!' came a familiar voice. 'Get out here this instant! We need to have a word!'

A PATHFINDER'S OATH

As the door opened, Ash was greeted by the sight of Stormbreaker's crew trying – and failing – to hold back Captain Nuk. One crew-woman was leaping up in an attempt to put the mursu into a headlock, while another was being dragged along the deck as he tried to get a grip on her peg leg.

'You have . . . to wait . . . your turn!' the first mate, Jed, said through gritted teeth, pulling Nuk's arms back, while Master Podd stood on her shoulders, yanking Jed's plaited beard.

'Captain Nuk,' Stormbreaker said, emerging from her cabin with Ash just behind, 'I hardly heard you arrive.'

'I must insist I speak with you,' Nuk said, shaking herself free and sending her assailants flying. One of

the *Kinspear*'s crew, a scarred vulpis with knotted fur, swished its tail in anger as it stared at Master Podd, who simply folded his arms and pretended not to notice.

'You must address the fleet,' Nuk said. 'You need to reassure them that there's a plan – a way out of this for us! I've been speaking with them, and –'

'I didn't order you to speak to my troops,' Stormbreaker interrupted.

Nuk blinked. 'Well, *someone* had to!'

'I'm perfectly capable of doing it myself,' Stormbreaker said.

'Well, now's as good a time as any.'

Nuk gestured over the side of the sleigh, where all the Pathfinders had crowded together, looking up at them and listening intently. Stormbreaker jerked back, surprised to suddenly have the attention of the entire fleet.

'What're we gonna do?' someone shouted, asking the question all were desperate to have answered.

'We'll return to Aurora to join with the rest of the fleet,' Stormbreaker announced. 'There, we'll regroup and prepare our next attack.'

'You can't expect us to fight that thing again,' yelled another voice to rumbling agreement.

'We should evacuate the Strongholds and flee!' called another.

'Flee? Flee *where*?!'

Stormbreaker strode to the top of the gangplank and raised her hands. The Pathfinders fell silent.

'I understand your concerns. It's clear we're facing an enemy unlike anything we've ever seen before. We were taken by surprise; there's no denying it. But it shows how threatened the Leviathans are by our new weapons. So much so, they've responded by awakening the greatest weapon *they* have. Well, two can play at that game. This isn't over yet, not by a long shot.'

Ash didn't like the way she said that.

'What we all just survived would test the courage of the bravest warriors,' Stormbreaker continued, 'but as Pathfinders we swore an oath to ensure the survival of the Strongholds and their people. We are honour bound to keep our word. And our mission has never been clearer. Aurora is the brightest light in the Snow Sea. A symbol of hope, of all we stand for. Our comrades are there, our friends and loved ones. At its current speed, the Devourer will reach Aurora at the turn of the next moon. We *cannot* leave her defenceless. We *must* beat the Devourer back to her walls, otherwise we are truly lost. The rest of the fleet still awaits us there. And we'll send word to our greatest allies – the mursu!'

She pointed towards a mursu captain, who banged his barrel chest in response.

'The vulpis!' Stormbreaker cried.

A group of the chittering creatures swished their tails with anticipation.

'And, of course, the Drifters of the Convoy!'

A crowd of Drifters cheered from aboard a sleigh, Lunah among them.

Stormbreaker strode down the gangplank and into the crowd, taking a woman's hand in her own.

'Captain Khali,' she said. 'I saw you and your crew

face down a charging Gargant during the battle, just to cover your comrades aboard the *Salvation*.' She took another captain's hand, this one a burly-looking man. 'Captain Nott, the *Bear Claw* continued to fight on against the Wraiths despite having lost one enjin and half her crew.'

'My hair was on fire too,' Captain Nott added, patting his singed head.

'I witnessed countless acts of courage and skill on that battlefield. Even in the jaws of defeat, I saw you risking your lives to protect our people from an enemy determined to see us dead and gone. The foe we face is terrible indeed, but take heart in each other. Courageous Pathfinders we do not lack, and we have already achieved impossible things! Together there is nothing we can't overcome. Aurora's walls have never been breached. We now know what we're up against, and from behind the walls of the greatest fortress in the Snow Sea we'll make our stand. But this time we *will* be prepared! Together we *will* wipe the Leviathan scourge from our world!'

A cheer rose from the crowd, but Ash couldn't help noticing it wasn't nearly as rousing as the one she'd received after her speech back in Aurora, when she'd been made commander. Many Pathfinders still looked frightened and unsure.

'I certainly hope you've a better plan than "Let's just shoot it again, but this time from a wall!"' Nuk called out. 'Did you not see what happened in the Rend? I appreciate you're trying to keep spirits up, but what you're suggesting is madness. The Devourer is quite beyond anything we can hope to go toe to toe against. Your obsession with fighting the Leviathans will be the doom of us all!'

Cries of support rippled through the crowd.

'Something tells me asking them to go away nicely won't cut it, Captain Nuk,' Stormbreaker replied, cool as ice. Some Pathfinders chuckled at this, but many others did not.

'To repeat the same mistake and expect a different result is the definition of foolishness.'

Ash was surprised to see it was Tobu who'd spoken; he rarely meddled in Pathfinder affairs. The crowd shifted uneasily at the reminder of the yeti in their midst. 'We must change our strategy if we hope to succeed.'

'Hear, hear!' someone cheered.

'I agree!' yelled another.

'Our archeoweapons barely *scratched* the Devourer, and you want us to attack it again?' a captain accused.

The atmosphere quickly turned sour, with Nuk and Stormbreaker's supporters hurling insults at each other. Stormbreaker stood silently, her gaze never leaving Nuk. She had a calm smile on her face, but Ash could see anger burning behind that one good eye, a fury that Nuk had dared turn some of her loyal followers against her.

Ash's heart sank. He'd been hoping the Pathfinders would pull together, but it looked like they were falling apart.

The Devourer was winning.

And as if in answer to his thought, a low, distant roar rolled over the plain, the ice beneath their feet trembling. The Devourer's Song drifted in on the wind, infecting the air. It was still far away, but there was no denying it was getting closer.

16

HEART OF THE MATTER

'I won't have you challenge my authority in front of the fleet, Captain Nuk, do you understand?' Stormbreaker said, marching back up the *Kinspear*'s gangplank as the crowd hurried back to their own sleighs, silenced by the cry of the approaching Devourer.

'I cannot stand by and let you lead these brave hearts to their deaths,' Nuk answered.

'Then what *would* you have me do? What is *your* brilliant plan, captain, since you hate mine so much?'

Hearts . . .

A memory flashed into Ash's head. Nell, the Solstice Elder, calling out to him as he died.

The last heart . . . you must find it!

Did he mean another frost-heart? Something that could help them defeat the Devourer?

Ash's heart quickened at the thought. Should he mention it to the others? Nuk and Stormbreaker were still arguing, shooting down each other's suggestions. They were getting nowhere fast. He took a deep breath.

'There . . . there might be another way . . .'

Nuk and Stormbreaker paused to glare at Ash.

He suddenly felt like he really needed a wee.

'Go on, lad,' Nuk encouraged, a smile poking out from behind her tusks.

Ash swallowed. 'Maybe it's nothing, but Elder Nell . . . before the Devourer . . . before it ate him – he said to find the *last heart.* I-I think he was trying to tell me how to stop the Devourer, and maybe this heart is it . . .?'

Ash's voice trailed away at his mother's expression, which was as flinty as a spearhead.

'Who in the *seven underworlds* is Elder Nell?' she demanded.

'Nell was one of us,' called Loda, who was climbing the gangplank, Arrus leaning on a staff behind him.

'Who let you out of your camp?' Jed asked from behind Stormbreaker.

'Nell was an Elder of the Solstice Stronghold,' Loda continued, ignoring Jed, 'and one of the most powerful Song Weavers in the land. He is the one who showed the Wraiths how to release the Devourer from its prison.'

'And why should we trust the word of a traitor?' said Stormbreaker.

'Because, despite his faults, in this he was speaking the truth,' Arrus replied.

Loda snorted. 'Truth might be a bit of a stretch, Arrus . . .'

'It's either real or it's not,' Stormbreaker said impatiently.

'The frozen hearts of Leviathans can take decades, sometimes even centuries, to melt after their deaths. So yes, there must be many so-called *frost-hearts* out there,' Loda started.

'But there are legends of hearts with immeasurable power,' Arrus went on. 'The hearts of the Ancients themselves. They're extinct now but were once the most powerful of all the Leviathans. The frost-heart used to break the Devourer's prison was one such heart and proves the legends to be true. Stories tell of another, equal in power, if not greater, hidden somewhere in the sacred yeti lands . . .'

'But that really is little more than a legend,' Loda argued.

'Many a legend has its roots in fact!' Arrus said. 'I, for one, believe it, and so did Nell, apparently.'

Loda rolled his eyes.

'And what can a frost-heart do to defeat such a monster?' Stormbreaker pressed.

'If the heart's Song still lived within it,' Loda said, 'it *might* be able to weave a new prison for the Devourer, just like the Ancients did in the World Before. But it took five hearts to do that last time. I, for one, cannot believe one would be enough, however powerful.'

Ash's shoulders slumped.

'But that's not the whole story, and you know it, Loda,' Arrus chided. 'While it may not be able to weave a prison on its own, an Ancient's heart could still be used to channel the Songs of others to make them stronger. To *magnify* them, if you will. Then if a powerful enough Song was Sung by enough people, for instance, a prison could still be created.'

Loda sniffed. 'There aren't *nearly* enough Song Weavers in the world to achieve such a thing.'

Arrus shrugged. 'There, I fear you may be correct.'

The words of the Shrieker suddenly echoed through Ash's head.

Join blade and fang? Bow and claw?

Ash felt hope flicker back to life. But the idea of sharing it with the others quickly turned that hope into cold, puke-inducing nerves. But he had to say something. It could change everything!

'What about the Leviathans?'

The others gave him a confused look.

'I-I think they could help,' Ash continued. 'The Devourer nearly stole my mind, like it did all those other Song Weavers, but a Shrieker saved me. I-I know it's hard to believe, but we wove our Songs together, and together were able to break free.'

Stormbreaker's eye gave an involuntary twitch, but Ash pushed on. 'Imagine every Song Weaver and

Leviathan in the Snow Sea joining their Songs together like that. Focused through the heart, our Song might be powerful enough to imprison the Devourer!'

Arrus clapped his hands together. 'Yes! That'd do it! Weaving together, all of us could potentially –'

Stormbreaker pulled Arrus away before he could finish and reached out for Ash. She lifted his chin, turning his face this way and that, as though searching for a wound.

'This Leviathan *spoke* to you?'

Ash nodded, sniffing hard in an attempt to appear confident.

A look of terror so strong crossed Stormbreaker's face, Ash half expected her to scream. Instead, she let out a rasping whisper.

'*I won't let them take you too.*'

Ash was too shocked to speak, and a second later Stormbreaker's iron mask was back in place.

'I will listen to no more nonsense about allying with the Leviathans,' she said. 'People will think you've been corrupted by them, and people's opinion is not something I can defend you against, try as I might.'

'It's hardly nonsense,' Arrus said. 'True, Leviathans can be vengeful, but they're not without mercy. They'll trust those who they feel have proved themselves worthy. Solstice has lived in peace with Leviathans for generations! They don't have to be your enemy. I think the boy might be on to something. Allow us to reach out to them, and –'

'Leviathans are cruel, without exception!' Stormbreaker snarled, her eye burning with fury. 'They hate us with every bone in their wicked bodies. You only believe you had peace with them because they were controlling your minds. There's no reasoning with *monsters.*'

'You're wrong,' Loda said calmly. 'Truth has become blurred by history, and the Leviathans have come to bear the blame for all the Devourer did in the past.'

'You'll have to start trusting us Song Weavers sooner or later,' Arrus added. 'You need our Song to power your archeoweapons and win your war.'

Stormbreaker waved dismissively. 'Any who won't do their duty are free to leave the fleet. That is their choice. I won't stop them.'

Ash gazed out at the frozen wilds that surrounded them,

not so much as a sign of a Stronghold for who-knew-how-many leagues. For anyone to leave the fleet now would be suicide, and his mother knew it.

It was no choice.

It was a threat. And Ash had heard enough.

'We're people too! Song Weavers belong in the Snow Sea just like everyone else!'

'You *are* people.' Stormbreaker nodded. 'People that need protecting. People in danger of being used.'

'But *you're* already using us,' Ash insisted.

'For the good of all!'

Ash growled with frustration. 'Fine. I'll *prove* to you that the Leviathans will fight with us!'

'Such proof doesn't exist,' Stormbreaker retorted.

'But if it did,' Ash insisted, 'would you believe me then?'

'Ash, can't you see you are already in their trap? Ferno was under their control, and he led you to the first frost-heart – which just released the Devourer. If they want you to get this other frost-heart, then they'll somehow use it against us again. This is how they trick you. How they *use* you.'

Ash faltered. He'd seen so much on his journey that showed the Leviathans were more than just evil monsters. He knew it. He could *feel* it. But . . . but what if he *was* wrong? Doubt took root within

Ash's mind, melting away his confidence.

'For once, Commander, listen to your son!' Nuk urged. 'If there's even a chance another frost-heart exists, that it can save lives, isn't that a chance we should take?'

'I will not risk the fate of the world on the word of a child,' Stormbreaker said in tones as unyielding as stone.

Ash shrank as small as he could, his thoughts tumbling.

She doesn't trust me . . .

'We have seen this *child* do incredible things,' Nuk said. 'Each of us aboard the *Frostheart* would stake our lives on his word!'

Ash looked up at Nuk, feeling fierce gratitude for his captain.

'If we can find the frost-heart, and if you'll let the Song Weavers try to make peace with the Leviathans, no one else has to die,' Ash pleaded. '*Please*, I really think this could work, Mum!'

'*Commander*,' Stormbreaker corrected, the word striking Ash like a slap across the face.

'C-Commander,' Ash muttered, tears fighting to break free, though whether they were tears of hurt or anger, he wasn't sure.

'So let me lay this all out, just so I know I'm

followin' . . .' Jed said, jumping into the discussion. 'You're suggestin' we pin all our hopes on some long-lost 'viathan heart – which probably doesn't even exist – hidden in a faraway land – in which human-kin will be killed for so much as lookin' at – just so you Song Weavers can have a good ol' sing-song with the 'viathans?' Jed chuckled. 'Surely yer plan is flawless!'

'I know the sacred yeti lands better than any other,' Tobu said, all eyes turning to him. 'Allow me to lead a crew into the World's Spine Mountains.'

'Aren't you an exile, yeti?' Stormbreaker asked. 'Of course you are; why else would you be here among human-kin, the yeti's most hated enemies? Your people would kill you as swift as they would us for setting foot upon their forbidden lands.'

'I know paths unguarded and routes unwatched,' Tobu replied. 'I will get us to this frost-heart, or at least to one who knows where it is hidden. I will be in and out before the next moon, of that you have my promise.'

'Please, Commander,' Nuk said softly. 'Allow us to take the *Frostheart*. It's just one sleigh. Let us try!'

'No,' Stormbreaker said.

Tobu and Ash groaned, and Arrus shook his head.

'I won't follow you back to Aurora,' Nuk warned. 'I won't lead my crew to certain death.'

'Then you're not fit to be a captain.' Stormbreaker

gestured to her crew. 'Captain Nuk, you're under arrest, for treason against the Council of Aurora.'

Ash and Arrus gasped as the crew grabbed Nuk in numbers even she couldn't resist. Tobu readied his spear and dashed up the gangplank to help. Stormbreaker's followers drew their own blades in response.

'No, Tobu!' Nuk said, shaking her head. 'Don't. It's OK.'

Tobu lowered his spear. Ash gawked, unable to believe what was happening. Stormbreaker addressed him.

'Until we get to Aurora, you will remain aboard the *Kinspear*, where I can protect you.'

Ash's mind jolted. 'A-away from the *Frostheart*? But . . . but it's my home . . . They're my family!'

'*I'm* your family,' Stormbreaker said. She turned to Jed, who tensed in salute. 'The *Frostheart* is yours, Jed, by my order. Fall in line with the fleet and follow the *Kinspear* back to Aurora.'

'Th-thank you!' Jed said, flustered. 'I – this is . . . I didn't expect . . .'

'This is your chance to prove you have what it takes to be a captain,' Stormbreaker said. 'Don't let me down.'

WORKING TOGETHER

Ash felt as heavy as stone, as though each step he took would send him crashing through the *Frostheart*'s gangplank, through the ice and into the dark, freezing waters below. The Devourer's Song snaked through the air, filling Ash's head with thoughts of vengeance. He almost hoped the Devourer *would* destroy Aurora, just to see the look on his mother's face.

Then she'd see.

She'd see how wrong she was, and how right Ash had been all along.

Stormbreaker waited for Ash down on the ice, having allowed him to board the *Frostheart* one last time to collect his things and say goodbye to the crew who'd looked after him for so long. Ash was beginning to think it was a big mistake. Now that he was aboard, he was worried he wouldn't be able to leave without being carried away, kicking and screaming.

Jed, meanwhile, had gathered the *Frostheart* crew together on the main deck for a team talk. There wasn't a smile among them.

'Now, I know you ain't too happy with me takin' over as yer new captain,' Jed said, trying to force a friendly smile. Kailen spat on the deck. 'But I wanna make this changeover as easy as possible. You have my back an' I'll have yours; can we all agree?'

The crew stood in hostile silence.

'Guess they didn't call this sleigh the *Warmheart*, did they?' Jed laughed. 'Look, just cos yer old captain is locked up for treason ain't no reason *we* can't get along now, is it?'

'Don't forget Ash, who you're also taking from us,' said Twinge.

'Now, that's unfair,' Jed said. 'The boy's goin' back to his mother, where he belongs. I'm sure that won't cause any problems, though, will it? It'd be awful if word got back to the Commander that any of you'd been . . . *uncooperative*. Why, poor old Nuk could find herself spendin' the rest of her days in the Aurora dungeons if that were the case . . .'

Master Podd's fur puffed out and Ash watched his friends tremble with anger, his own fists clenched tight.

'But, like I said, I'm sure there'll be no such issues! Ain't that right, friend?' Jed finished, looking at Tobu.

'I am not your friend,' Tobu grumbled.

'Aye, well, we can change that! If we all work together, we're gonna be one big, happy crew. The best on the Snow Sea! You'll learn I'm a fair captain, an' I reckon together we'll do more 'n Nuk ever did for ya. So, are y'all ready to save the world? Who's with me?!'

Jed put his hand out, as if hoping the others would place their hands on top and let out a cheer. Everyone's arms remained firmly folded. 'Waaaaaaaahey!' Jed cheered, lifting his hand alone.

As he did, Ash caught sight of his friends giving each other *a look*. A look that lingered particularly long on Master Podd, who blinked slowly, as if in understanding.

There was something about that look. Something knowing and mischievous.

Something Ash had seen before.

They've got a plan! Ash realized, ducking behind Arla's tent to watch.

'Well, ent no sense in draggin' out the agony, is there?' Kailen shrugged, putting her arm round Jed's shoulders. 'The cap' did wrong, an' she's payin' for it. Fair's fair. Course we'll fall in line, Captain Jed; we got a job to do.'

'Glad to see I've inherited a clever crew.' Jed grinned.

'Before we go, how about a tour of your new sleigh? A good captain knows every speck o' their vessel after all . . .'

'Ain't that the truth!' Jed said, allowing himself to be led into the hold.

The moment the door shut behind them, Master Podd scampered off, while Yallah and Kob rushed to the upper deck, slipping past a confused Ash with little more than a nod. The *Frostheart*'s propellers hummed to life as Yallah fired up the sunstone enjin. Kob climbed up to the bridge, taking hold of the tiller. Tobu leaned on the door to the hold just as Jed began to pound on it from the other side.

'Hello? Hello?! Why's the enjin on? Can anyone hear me?'

Tobu simply folded his arms and dug his heels in.

'Let me out! Let me out right now! That's an order!'

Ash peeked over the side and saw that the enjins had startled Stormbreaker. Arla approached the side rail.

'Where's Captain Jed?' Stormbreaker called.

'Prepping the sleigh, I believe,' Arla answered, perching casually on the side rail as if nothing unusual was happening.

'You're to follow the *Kinspear*,' Stormbreaker shouted over the sound of the enjin. 'We'll lead the way, understood?'

'Aye, I understand that's what you'd like, Commander,' Arla called back.

Stormbreaker looked troubled. Ash watched the strange exchange curiously.

'And my son? Where is he?'

'Gettin' his things; he'll be along soon,' Arla said.

'You'll follow me north. Not to the yeti lands, but to Aurora,' Stormbreaker repeated.

'Aye,' Arla called over her shoulder, smoothing out her robes.

Stormbreaker's eye narrowed. 'Aye, you'll follow my orders?'

'I'm sorry, my hearing ain't what it used to be,' Arla cried, cupping her hand round her ear as the propellers turned faster, whirling up snow in a flurry of white.

'*Arla* . . .' Stormbreaker warned dangerously.

Arla met her gaze, unflinching. Suddenly, as quick as an arrow, Stormbreaker bolted towards the *Frostheart*.

'NOW!' Arla ordered, and Teya grabbed the end of the gangplank.

Without a second thought, Ash rushed down the stairs to help. Together they pulled the gangplank up and over the side rail.

'STOP!' Stormbreaker yelled.

The small spark of guilt Ash felt was quickly doused by his anger at how she'd treated him and his friends. Stormbreaker spun round, her cloak almost tangling in her legs, and raced back to the *Kinspear*, her crew watching in disbelief.

'START THE ENJINS! START THE ENJINS! THEY HAVE MY SON!'

Her crew scrambled to action, the enjineer yanking levers and turning dials. But instead of blasting to life, the enjin let out a piteous choke, and then . . . nothing. The enjineer banged the enjin in confusion, when Master Podd suddenly leaped from beneath it, a sunstone cradled in his arms.

'Stop him!' Ash heard the enjineer shout.

'Atta boy, Podd!' Teya laughed.

The *Kinspear* crew grabbed for the little vulpis, but he ducked and weaved his way through their grasping hands, leaped into the air, bounced off the head of a crewman who had made a dive for him, and landed deftly on the *Kinspear*'s side rail. Bracing himself, he jumped the large gap between the two sleighs. For an instant, Podd's eyes widened as he realized he was going to fall short of the *Frostheart*, but Twinge leaned over the rail and caught him mid-air, swinging him on to the stern deck.

The enjins roared as the *Frostheart* surged forward, Kob steering it through the moored sleighs of the fleet, who looked on in shock. Arla waved to a fuming Stormbreaker, who still stood upon the snow as the *Frostheart* escaped.

'After them!' she ordered the gawking crews of the other sleighs, but whether out of genuine confusion or rebellion, no sleigh gave chase.

The *Frostheart* skimmed across the water, mounting the ice on the other side with a thump. Crows followed, swirling around Rook who sat up on the mast, her ragged cloak billowing in the wind.

'Nobody walks on to *our* sleigh and starts giving us orders 'cept for Captain Nuk!' Teya yelled back at the disappearing fleet. She turned to Ash with an apologetic look. 'Sorry for springin' this on you. Hope you're not mad we stole you away for a bit longer . . .?'

Ash looked back, watching his mother grow smaller and smaller under the shadow of the Ghost Stones. His thoughts were spinning.

After searching for her his whole life and across half the world, who could've guessed that he'd end up running away from her?

'We can always drop you off, if you'd prefer . . .?' Teya suggested.

Ash scanned the horizon. With a pang, he spotted the sails of the sleighs the Drifters had taken, far off in the distance.

Lunah, Ash thought, feeling quite miserable. *She's heading out to do what's right.* Somewhere beyond those sleighs lay the broken prison that had once held the Devourer. He could still hear its malicious Song whispering on the wind, promising more death.

So much destruction. So many wasted lives. And no one but the *Frostheart* crew willing to do anything to stop it.

Could they even hope to defeat something as

powerful as the Devourer? Certainly not without the Ancient's heart.

'This is what I want,' Ash said finally. 'This is the right thing to do.'

Though his nerves were aflutter, he knew he meant it.

Teya smiled, ruffling his messy hair. 'We'll make a Pathfinder of you yet!'

'Next stop – the sacred yeti lands!' Kob called down from the bridge. Tobu, who still leaned on the door to the hold, stared ahead with a grim expression.

Beyond the horizon lay his homeland.

A land forbidden to them all, and yet the one place that might hold the key to their survival.

FALSE-HEART

18

A NEW ORDER

Amid an endless field of white, Ash could see his parents.

They smiled at him, so very proud of their son.

Ash reached out for them.

Their smiles were kind. Loving. But they didn't offer him their hands.

'Mum!' Ash called out, returning their smiles. 'Dad!'

He tried to make his way towards them, but his legs carried him backwards. It was as though he were moving against a powerful, howling wind.

'Mum! Dad! Help me!' Ash cried.

The smiles on his parents' faces grew bigger, but they remained still and offered no help, no shouts of encouragement. The more Ash struggled, the further back he was pushed, before finally his parents turned and began to walk away.

'MUM! DAD!' Ash screamed. 'PLEASE! PLEASE DON'T LEAVE ME!'

But they didn't stop.

They just kept on walking, leaving Ash alone.

Ash woke up with a start. The familiar rumbling of the *Frostheart*'s enjins calmed his racing heart. He sighed, rubbing his sleepy face. Since leaving the Ghost Stones two days before, Ash had tried his best to keep the painful thoughts of his parents out of his head.

Sometimes he succeeded. Sometimes he even began to feel positive again. The *Frostheart* raced forward, and the sense of movement filled Ash with wary hope. Though the path ahead would be difficult, they were doing something to stop the Devourer. Something useful that could save lives.

It made him feel like they had a *chance.*

But then his parents would sneak back into his head. The way his mother had betrayed the *Frostheart* crew, how his father had caused this whole mess in the first place. It left him feeling lost and abandoned, a sensation only worsened by the fact he wouldn't be able to talk to Lunah about it.

He missed her *so* much. How she made him smile,

the way she could find the good in any bad situation. Sure, he could talk to the others, but it was only with Lunah that he felt he could *really* open up. The sleigh felt empty without her. Stars above, the entire *snow plain* did! He missed Nuk too, of course, especially the way she could convince everyone that whatever crazy, dangerous adventure they were embarking on was the right thing to do. He wondered how the old mursu would be coping with imprisonment on Stormbreaker's sleigh.

Ash reached to the side of his bedding and retrieved the star Lunah had left for him. He gave it a squeeze, praying they really would be able to find each other again.

Master Podd guided the *Frostheart* through snow-covered hills that became more rugged with each passing day. A vast mountain range peeked above the horizon, little more than a darker shade of grey against the bleak sky.

The World's Spine Mountains, Tobu had called them. The border of the sacred yeti lands.

On the main deck, Jed was busy yelling at the night-shift crew. Ash couldn't help but feel Lunah had lucked out, not having to hear Jed's constant whining.

'You may have kidnapped me, but that don't mean I ain't still yer captain! You have to do as I say, an' I *order* you to turn this sleigh round and rejoin the fleet!'

'For the last time, we didn't kidnap you.' Yallah waved dismissively. 'We thought you *wanted* us to go after the last frost-heart, and we couldn't find you to check!'

'Tha's cos you'd locked me in the hold!' Jed's face was turning red.

'Ah, the door got jammed, that's all,' Kob said. 'Does that sometimes. Just gotta lift it a little as you push.'

'Have you no honour? No sense o' duty?' Jed fumed. 'The others need us, an' you're drivin' us straight into the jaws of certain death!'

'Ah, the jaws of certain death . . .' Yallah shielded her eyes to look ahead. 'Captain Nuk used to take us there often, and we've always come out the other end perfectly fine.'

Ash grinned but kept quiet as he helped Kob check on the ropes. He glanced up at Rook, who was still perched on the mainmast, silhouetted against the grey morning light. She was still meant to be teaching Ash about Song Weaving, but ever since they'd escaped the fleet, she'd just roosted high above the deck, chanting the same Song over and over under her breath.

'*Danger. Threat. Resist. Protect. Danger. Threat. Resist. Protect.*'

Ash could sense it was a Song of warding, healing and protection. He could also sense a new darkness in her.

It was the same darkness that was in him.

Over the first few days of their journey, Ash had started to convince himself that maybe the Devourer had just been a nightmare. It was easy to feel hopeful racing away from the monster and the aura of dread that surrounded it. But to his growing despair, Ash had come to realize the Devourer's Song had followed them, even all the way out here. Though little louder than a whisper, it was definitely there, bleeding into the air like water soaking into a cloth. As someone who had once allowed the Devourer into her heart, Rook was the most vulnerable to its effects, and Ash understood why she was doing all she could to block it out.

He gulped, saying a silent prayer to the spirits to keep her safe.

'Stormbreaker'll come through for us,' Jed continued. 'She always does. She is a true hero of the Snow Sea.'

'Well, until then, we're just gonna have to act on our own instincts, I'm afraid,' Yallah said, sighing. 'Hey, don't look so scared – they've kept us alive so far!'

'This is mad!' Jed tugged at his hair. 'No human-kin've ever returned from the yeti lands! *Yeti. Hate. Humans.* We'll be dead as soon as they get so much as a whiff of us!'

'I will lead us. The yeti won't even know we're there,' Tobu said.

'An' how do *you* know where this Leviathan heart is hidden?' Jed asked. 'They a common sight around the Yeti Lands or somethin'? Pick 'em off bushes like berries, do ya?'

'We will ask Master Yanpa,' Tobu said, as though it was the most obvious thing ever.

'Ah, Master Yanpa – why didn't you just say that in the first place?' Jed smiled, before gesturing wildly with his arms. 'An' who in the seven underworlds is Master flippin' Yanpa?!'

'A relation of yours, Master Podd?' Twinge called up to the helm. Master Podd looked down from his pile of boxes where he stood to reach the tiller.

'*Master* isn't my name, you know.'

'It's not?!' Twinge looked genuinely shocked.

'It's a title.'

Twinge turned to the others and gestured that his

mind had been blown.

'When we come of age, every yeti must choose a Path,' Tobu explained. 'A way of life we dedicate our entire selves to perfecting. Some, like me, choose the martial Path of the Warden. Others choose the Path of the Artisan – or become Shapers, who build our homes and temples. There are seven Paths in all, and each has a ruling Master. The Masters lead the yeti, much like the Council in Aurora. Master Yanpa is master of the Path of the Listener, those whose sole duty is to untangle the intricate threads of the World Weave and discover the will and Song of our world itself, and all the mysteries that lie hidden within.'

Jed blinked in confusion.

'Best you don't get him started on the World Weave . . .' Kob muttered.

'Master Yanpa is wise beyond all other yeti. If the heart exists, she will know it,' Tobu grunted. 'She is an old friend and will help us.'

Jed dragged his hands down his face as he groaned in exasperation. 'I'm not gonna change yer minds, am I?'

'Only just gettin' that, are you?' Kob said, tying a rope to the side rail.

'This sleigh'll run outta supplies soon enough, though, an' you'll *have* to return to civilization. Yer fates will depend on my word then!' Jed threatened. 'I *could* tell Stormbreaker about yer back-stabbin' mutiny, an' make sure you spend the resta yer lives as outcasts, shunned by Strongholds the world over! Or . . . I could tell her that after our . . . *shaky* start, we managed to achieve somethin' meaningful from this mess. So, what'll it be? Y'all seem determined to drag us on this insane mission, but will you *at least* follow my orders from here on, an' let me get us out of this alive?'

'If it'll make you *shut up*, I'm willin' to try anythin' . . .' Kailen yawned, emerging from her tent.

'Glad to hear it.' Jed put his hands on his hips proudly. 'Onwards then – that way!' he declared, pointing ahead.

The crew rolled their eyes. He was pointing in the direction they were already travelling.

Jed spun on his heel and pointed at Kailen. 'An' I want you to have a look at the hold door. It seems to be gettin' a little stuck.'

'Aye aye, cap'n.' Kailen saluted. 'Right after breakfast.'

Jed eyed her with annoyance as she strutted towards the kitchen. He was about to say something, when he caught sight of Ash, who flinched as Jed's eyes suddenly locked on to him.

'As fer you, kid, I'm gonna need you to move over to the prow.'

'The prow?' Ash asked. 'But Captain Nuk usually has me helping Kob and Kailen with –'

'Aye, the prow. And I'm gonna need you to stay there. Can't be trustin' you to wander about like you ain't a danger to us all. It's for the safety of the crew, you understand.'

Oh. Because I'm a Song Weaver.

As one, the crew paused what they were doing.

'We can only take so much, *captain*,' Kob grunted. 'You start targetin' our own, we're gonna have to put our foot down.'

'On yer *face*,' Kailen muttered.

Ash trembled. Jed was treating him like some wild animal, just like his mother had the other Song Weavers. The Devourer's whispers encouraged the chill growing in his belly. Ash wanted to scream; he wanted to attack Jed, to bite and tear at him and curse his name and – and –

The sound of Tobu's voice broke through the chaos in his mind.

Deep breaths, boy. One step at a time.

Ash inhaled the frozen air. It hurt his throat, but it helped. A little.

'Ash has been with the crew a long time and we've all survived just fine,' Yallah said, flexing her fingers.

'I'm sure there's lots of things you've been doin' wrong, but luckily fer you all I'm here to put things right,' Jed said. 'Off you go, kid, there's a good lad. Kob, you'll be the first to guard him.'

'The boy's fine where he is,' Tobu growled, stepping in front of Ash protectively.

Jed sighed with irritation. 'See, here I thought we'd agreed y'all were gonna start followin' my orders? Let's not forget how difficult I can make yer lives when we return to the Strongholds . . .'

Tobu looked out at the rugged landscape, sniffing the air. 'The nearest Stronghold is Sentinel's Watch, three hundred leagues away. That's a long way to walk alone in the wilds.'

Jed looked confused. 'Why'd anyone try an' walk it?'

'These lands are rough and bumpy,' Tobu explained, stepping closer. 'If he's not careful, a man might find himself . . . thrown overboard. And with the enjins roaring, who knows if we'd even hear his cries for help.'

Tobu came to a stop, towering above Jed.

''S'true, I've heard a' such things happenin'.' Kailen nodded. 'Real tragic.'

Jed looked from Ash to Tobu, doubt eroding his stubborn confidence. His throat moved as he gulped, nodding with understanding.

'Aye, well,' he said finally. 'Perhaps the boy *is* all right where he is. The deck could use some swabbin' after all.'

19

UNWELCOME

A week ago, the World's Spine Mountains had been little more than distant fangs poking above the horizon. Now they soared so high Ash felt dizzy just looking at them, their mighty peaks hidden behind clouds. They were surely the biggest mountains he'd ever seen!

The incredible view proved a welcome distraction to Ash, who'd otherwise been all too aware of Jed's eyes boring into him every step he took. Whenever Ash looked over his shoulder, Jed was sure to be close by, keeping a watch on him.

Far, far to the east, through the icy haze, Ash could make out a gigantic wall. It rose to a great height and stretched for many leagues, blocking any passage into the land beyond the mountains. At its centre, two watchtowers flanked a huge gateway that looked as impenetrable as the mountains themselves. Though Ash had seen some incredible sights since leaving the Fira, the fact that things of this size could be built still took his breath away.

'The Southern Gate,' Tobu explained to the crew as they eyed the defences with apprehension. 'I used to guard the Northern Gate, far from here.'

'I can see why no one's ever been able to penetrate these walls . . .' Kailen murmured, her eyes darting between the enormous bolt-throwers that lined the battlements and the many banners that fluttered in the wind, suggesting that large numbers of yeti warriors stood guard there, too small to see from this distance.

'Hmm,' Tobu said, considering the view. 'It could use some improvements. But fear not. Our path lies elsewhere and is mostly unwatched.'

'*Mostly?*' Jed said nervously.

'Mostly,' Tobu confirmed.

'I mean, would sure be nice to go somewhere new an' not be greeted with arrows pointed at our faces for once,' Kailen said.

'I once heard a story of a group of Pathfinders who went into the Yeti Lands and almost escaped . . .' Twinge started.

'And what happened to them?' Arla asked.

'Well, they didn't make it. No one does. I thought that was obvious.'

Arla blinked. 'I s'pose it was. Good story, Twinge.'

The sight of what they were truly up against chipped away at Ash's shrinking positivity, butterflies whirling unpleasantly in his belly.

This might prove *slightly* more challenging than he'd first imagined . . .

'Are – are you sure this is a good idea?' Ash asked quietly, so only Tobu would hear him. 'You were exiled from here, like we were from the Fira. I know *they* would not be happy to see us again – how will the yeti react to seeing *you*?'

'They will welcome me with open arms.'

Ash looked up in surprise. Tobu's face was a mask, but then the corners of his mouth began to quiver, before curling into the smallest of smiles. It took a second for Ash to realize Tobu was joking.

This is more serious than I thought . . .

'Y-you don't think they'd hurt you, do you?'

Tobu didn't reply for some time, which was answer enough.

'It is not for me to know the future,' he said eventually, shielding his eyes as he watched an eagle gliding high above. 'But I do know one thing . . .'

He took a deep breath of the mountain air and smiled once more. 'It is good to be home.'

After another day's travel, Tobu guided Master Podd to a mountain pass so hidden and narrow, you'd have needed super yeti eyesight to spot it. The steep, mountainous terrain forced the crew to leave the *Frostheart* behind, sheltered beneath a large rocky overhang. Kob and Arla volunteered to watch the sleigh while the others were gone.

'Got a greater chance of wrestling the Devourer to the floor than climbing those mountains,' Arla said, 'an' Kob here ent getting any younger.'

Kob lunged forward, knees cracking, as if to prove the point.

Jed looked about to agree but then recoiled in shock as

Rook leaped down from the mainmast.

'Spirits! I didn't even know there was someone up there! That's not another Weaver, is it?'

'Are you OK?' Ash asked Rook, ignoring Jed, as Rook's crows took wing into the sky.

'*Dark Song follows,*' she answered. '*Must climb mountain. Escape Devourer.*'

The further they'd travelled, the fainter the Devourer's Song had become, but it still reached them, an unmistakable malice tainting the wind. Ash watched Rook crawl away on all fours, frightened he was losing his friend.

The crew climbed overboard cautiously. True to Tobu's word, they saw no sign of the yeti, just a rugged, steep climb ahead of them. But that didn't mean there wasn't terrible danger.

'Anyone else find it a bit . . . *unnerving* that we haven't seen any Leviathans since the Rend?' Teya whispered, testing the snow with her boot as though she half expected a Lurker to burst out and snatch it up.

'I was kind of enjoyin' it,' Kailen said. 'But gotta admit . . . it's gettin' eerie now . . .'

''S'well known yeti an' Leviathans are best mates,' Jed said. 'They're probably plottin' a joint welcomin' party for us.'

'It's well known, is it?' Tobu asked.

'No offence, friend. But you can't deny both the yeti an' wurms hate us, an' the enemy of my enemy an' all that . . .?'

'I am not your friend,' Tobu replied.

'Some believe,' Twinge added, his eyes wide, 'that beyond these mountains lies a magical promised land where Leviathan attacks don't happen.'

'It's why some Pathfinders have tried to break in.' Teya nodded. 'Despite the terrible risks . . .'

'I can't wait to see it!' Twinge said excitedly, to looks of bafflement from the others. 'What?! It's a once-in-a-lifetime opportunity!'

'For the most part, Leviathans live in peace with the yeti, it's true,' Tobu said. 'But it is down to mutual respect, not magic. There's no time for a history lesson. Do you hear anything, boy?'

Ash listened hard for any sign of Leviathan Song.

'No . . . I don't think so.' But then something caught his ear, coming from above. The sky was only a small sliver of grey between the tall cliffs and trees that surrounded them. And despite what Ash had suspected for a moment, there was no sign of a scarred Shrieker, or anything else for that matter.

Ash looked to Rook to see if she could hear anything, but she only chanted under her breath, her hood hiding her face.

'Danger. Threat. Resist. Protect.'

'Let's not hang around then, eh?' Jed said. 'We're on a bit of a deadline. Emphasis on the *dead*, let's not forget. It's only a week until the Devourer gets to Aurora. If we gotta do this, let's get a move on.'

'Quietly then. Follow me. Master Yanpa's temple is on the other side of this mountain,' Tobu said, pointing the way.

'Ah-ah-*ah*!' Jed chided, running in front of Tobu. 'Let's not forget who's in charge here, eh?'

Tobu groaned, allowing Jed to go ahead. He walked with a spring in his step, clearly happy to be leading his own crew at last. Ash watched Jed with a bitter dislike, reminding himself to recommend to Lunah that she add his name to her enemy list. But after the third time Tobu had to correct his course, Jed wordlessly slunk back behind the big yeti, his face red.

The going was tough. They had to climb over large boulders, through deep snowdrifts and over loose, treacherous scree, sheer walls of craggy blue-grey rock towering high either side of them. They walked for hours, the climb growing ever steeper. Ash's legs burned, but he kept on moving. Finding the last frost-heart was the only thing that mattered now. He listened for Leviathan Song, but the only thing he could hear was that faint Song from far above. Although it drifted

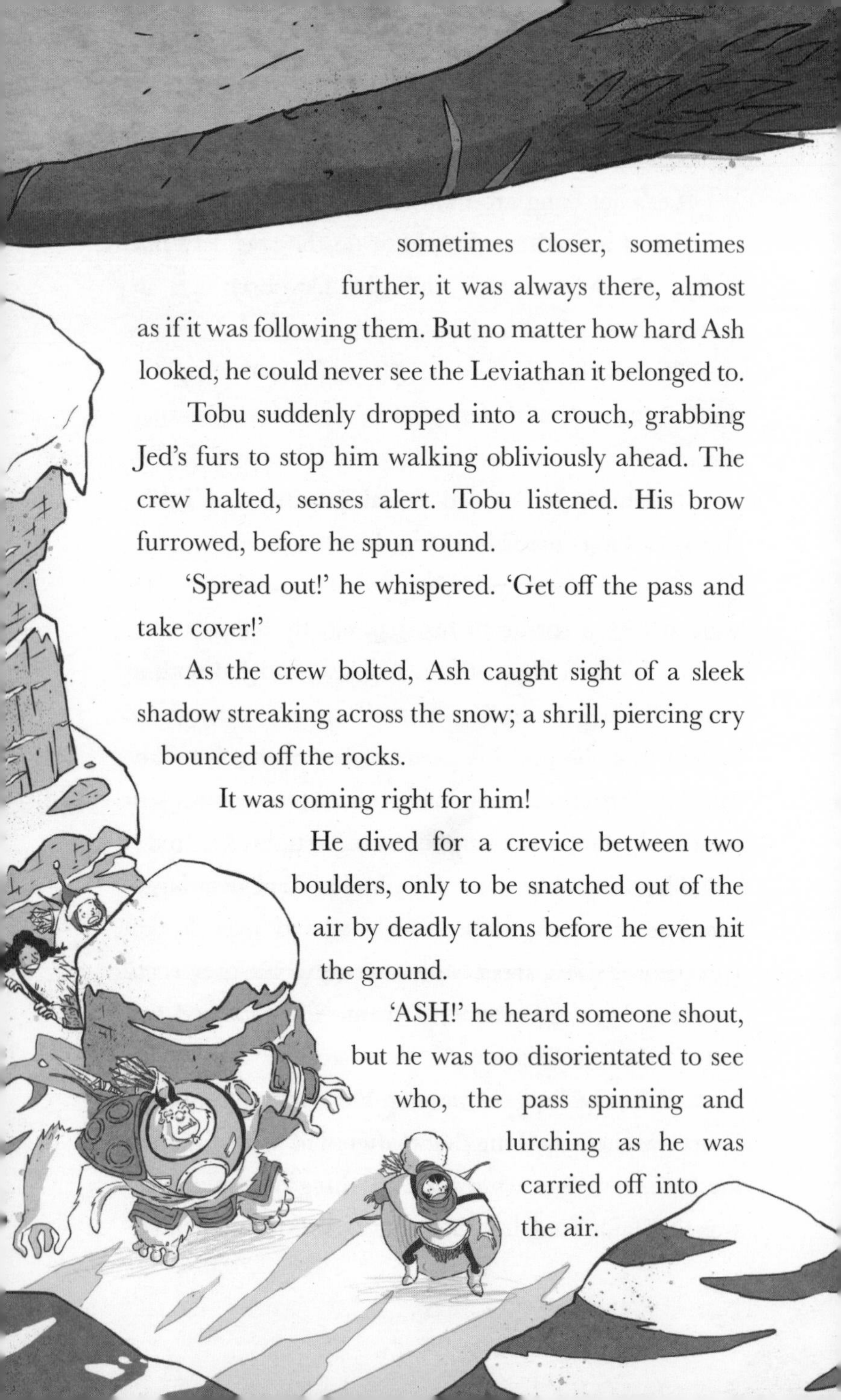

sometimes closer, sometimes further, it was always there, almost as if it was following them. But no matter how hard Ash looked, he could never see the Leviathan it belonged to.

Tobu suddenly dropped into a crouch, grabbing Jed's furs to stop him walking obliviously ahead. The crew halted, senses alert. Tobu listened. His brow furrowed, before he spun round.

'Spread out!' he whispered. 'Get off the pass and take cover!'

As the crew bolted, Ash caught sight of a sleek shadow streaking across the snow; a shrill, piercing cry bounced off the rocks.

It was coming right for him!

He dived for a crevice between two boulders, only to be snatched out of the air by deadly talons before he even hit the ground.

'ASH!' he heard someone shout, but he was too disorientated to see who, the pass spinning and lurching as he was carried off into the air.

The ground fell away at an alarming rate, and bile rushed into Ash's throat. Flailing about like a fish on a line, he struggled to get a look at what had grabbed him.

It was the scarred Shrieker, just as he'd suspected, although he'd certainly not expected this greeting.

'*GOT YOU!*' it Sang.

'*Let me go!*' Ash Sang back, vertigo dragging at his innards as the mountainside whooshed by far below.

And with another piercing cry, the Shrieker obeyed, releasing its grip and allowing Ash to fall.

20

SCRATCH

Ash wanted to scream till his throat went raw, but instead he fell with more of a gurgle, the rushing wind ripping tears from his eyes as he spun and tumbled through the air.

The Shrieker swooped down and caught him just before he splattered against the rocks.

'*BAD BEING THROWN? TUMBLING? NO CONTROL?*'

'*Wh-why are you doing this?!*' Ash whimpered, hanging upside down, cloak flapping over his face.

'*BOY STOLE MY MIND. THREW ME. TUMBLED ME.*'

Ah. Ash had worried this might come back to haunt him – the moment he had used the Dark Song to control the Shrieker on the *Kinspear.*

'I-I'm sorry! I did it so that the Pathfinders wouldn't kill you! I promise!'

'SAVED KIN-KILLERS.'

'The Pathfinders? I didn't want you to hurt them either.'

'WHY?! THEY KILL BROTHERS. SISTERS.'

'I don't want anyone *else to die!'*

The Shrieker's Song wrapped round Ash's, investigating, trying to find the truth. Ash allowed it to Weave with him, trying his best not to look down. His face was lathered with sweat, which was cold against the mountain wind.

With a scream, the Shrieker tossed Ash into the air, spinning him around helplessly before catching him by the shoulders, upright this time. Ash had expected its talons to pierce his flesh, but the Shrieker held him with surprising care.

'WEAVER BOY INTRIGUES BROOD MOTHER. CURIOUS. BUT SHE DOESN'T TRUST. NOT YET. NEED PROOF HUMANS WANT PEACE.'

As delighted as he was to hear that the Leviathans might be willing to make peace, Ash really wished the Shrieker had found another way to tell him. He gritted his teeth, thinking of his mother's bovore-headed stubbornness.

'I-I've been trying to convince my people, but our leader doesn't believe we can have peace! Not yet – we need to convince her!'

'*STORMBREAKER . . .*' The Shrieker growled the name with hatred. '*KILL KINSLAYER. TEAR HER APART. THEN PEACE.*'

'*No!*' Ash cried. '*No more killing!*'

'*WHY PROTECT HER? STORMBREAKER DEAD, PEACE LIVES.*'

'*Because you'll prove her right and the Pathfinders will want revenge! And because . . .*' Ash hesitated, but he knew he couldn't hide the truth while Song Weaving. '*She's my mother!*'

'*MOTHER?!*'

'*Yes. And I know what she's done is bad, but your brothers and sisters have done bad things too! I need to convince her that we can join together against the Devourer. If your Brood Mother is willing to talk, maybe that'll be enough!*'

The Shrieker circled the mountain pass in worrying silence.

'*You don't make peace by killing people!*' Ash tried again.

The Shrieker let out another cry, and then plummeted downwards. Ash gripped on to its ankles with all his might as his friends came into view, looking up in astonishment. The Shrieker opened its membranous wings wide, catching the rising air currents to keep aloft above the Pathfinders. They raised their bows but Ash cried out.

'DON'T! It's a friend! DON'T SHOOT!'

The crew hesitated but lowered their weapons. All except for Jed, who released his bowstring with a thrum. Luckily Tobu grabbed Jed's bow just as he fired, sending his arrow clacking harmlessly among the rocks. Tobu swung the bow round, throwing Jed to the snow.

'What are you doing?!' Jed yelled. 'You blind?! That Leviathan's attackin' us – I order you all to kill it! NOW!'

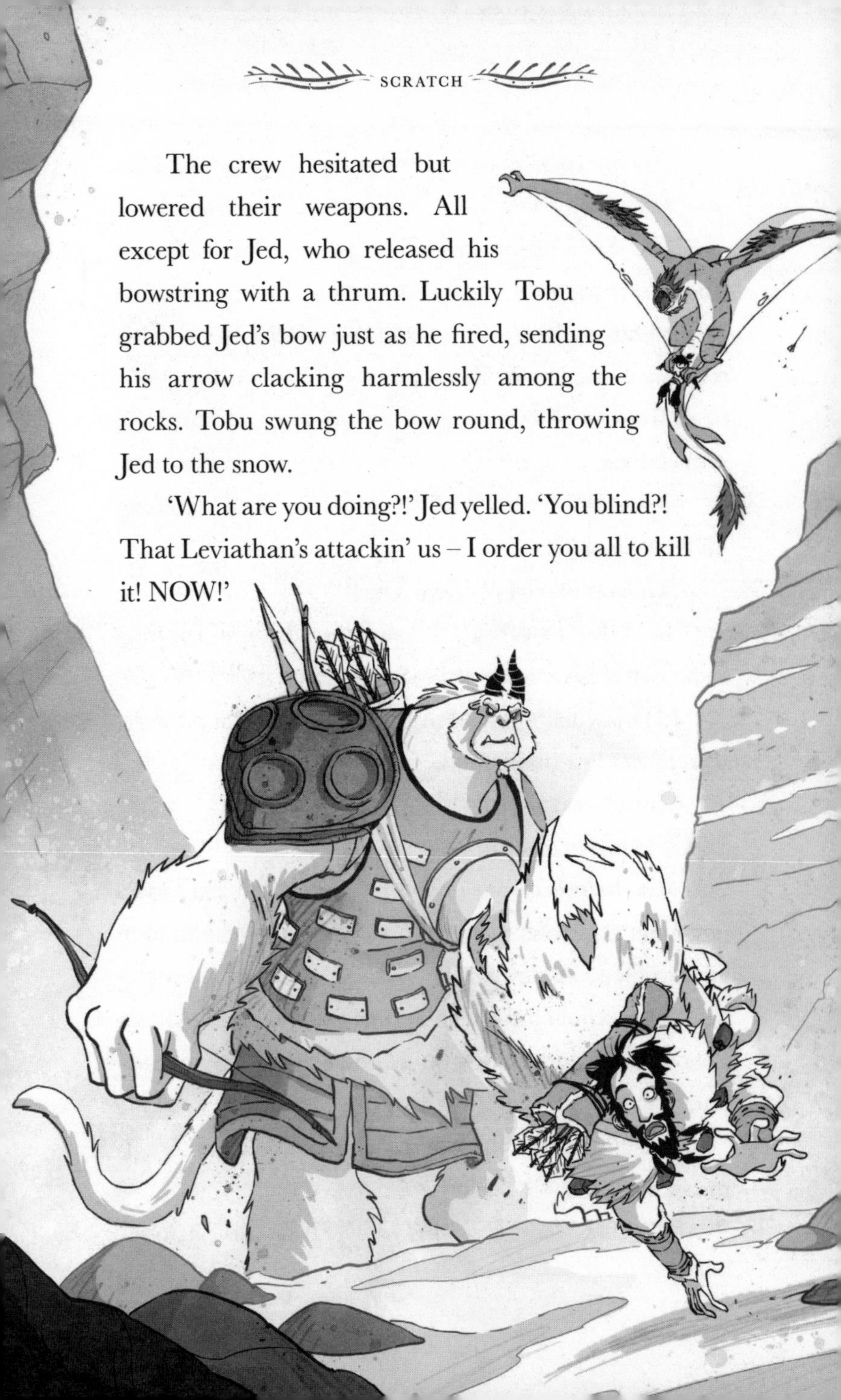

The Shrieker roared in anger.

'It's OK, I promise,' Ash shouted. 'It's a friend!'

The Shrieker suddenly let go of him and Ash tumbled through the deep snow as he hit the ground. His friends rushed over to help, except for Rook, who remained hidden in the shadows. They pulled Ash's head from the snow, the chill wet soaking into his hair and clothes.

'*NOW WE'RE EVEN!*' the Shrieker Sang, landing on a rock above.

'Are you all right?' Teya asked.

'It's OK, it's OK . . .' Ash assured them, spitting snow out of his mouth. 'I kinda deserved it . . .'

Jed's jaw fell open. 'Am I the only one 'round here who hasn't lost their mind?'

Master Podd raised his paw. 'I haven't.'

'There's a flippin' Shrieker Singin' to the kid! Shoot it, before it takes over his mind! He may look harmless now, but soon he'll be frothin' at the mouth an' bitin' our ankles!'

'Why would it use Ash to hurt us when it could just swoop down and munch on us all itself?' Teya pointed out.

Jed blinked at the obvious logic. 'Well, it . . . I mean, it's probably . . . It's goin' to . . . I –'

'*BROOD MOTHER WILL WATCH,*' the Shrieker

Sang to Ash. '*WILL WAIT. SEARCH FOR PROOF HUMANS CAN CHANGE. PROOF HUMANS CAN CARE.*'

'*Where is she?*' Ash Sang back, rising on to still trembling legs. '*How will we show her proof?*'

'*BROOD MOTHER SEES ALL. HEARS KIN SONG. OUR EYES HER EYES. ME. BROTHERS. SISTERS. SEES WHAT WE SEE. HEARS WHAT WE HEAR.*'

A shiver ran down Ash's spine. He was definitely creeped out by the idea of something powerful and unseen watching him through the eyes of all the Leviathans. He suddenly felt very exposed, even though they were hidden within the ravine.

'*SHE WILL JUDGE,*' the Shrieker said rather ominously, before turning to leave.

'Wait!' Ash called out. It stopped, craning its long serpentine neck to look back. '*What . . . what do I call you? Do you have a name?*'

The Shrieker cocked its head, then let out an awful, ear-splitting screech. The crew covered their ears.

'*Wow. It's, um . . . lovely.*'

'*NOT FOR HUMAN TONGUE. GIVE NAME. I CARE NOT.*'

The others looked at Ash questioningly, and so he quickly explained that the Shrieker was hoping to convince the Brood Mother to make peace with humankin, just as Ash had tried to do with Stormbreaker, and that the Shrieker was allowing them to name it.

The crew glanced at each other.

'Is it a boy or a girl?' Twinge asked.

Ash frowned. 'Um, well, it's *clearly* a . . . um . . . a bo–' The Shrieker growled deep in its throat. 'Girl! Clearly a girl!' Ash finished.

'How about Fluffy?' Twinge suggested. The others gave him a withering look. 'What? I think it's nice!'

'Ear Splitter?' Master Podd offered. 'It's got a nice ring to it, and speaks the truth.'

'Chirper is a bit nicer . . .?' Yallah said.

The Shrieker didn't look so keen. Apparently she cared more than she'd first let on.

Ash looked at the Leviathan. She was sleek and streamlined, her flesh dark and rubbery. Purple feathers crested her head and limbs, but there was one feature that stood out above all others.

'*Would Scratch be OK?*' Ash asked, looking at the wounds that covered her body. They were scars inflicted in Aurora, when Ash had first met her.

'*SO BE IT. I CARE NOT,*' she repeated, but Ash noticed her feathers frill up with what might've been pride.

And, thus named, Scratch clawed her way up the cliff face, before gliding off into the air.

'I can't believe this is happenin' to me . . .' Jed groaned, falling back into the snow. 'This crew'll be the end of me. Mark my words: this mountain is where I die.'

'Then do it quietly,' Tobu said, tossing Jed's bow back to him. 'We have made too much noise already.'

21

THE FORBIDDEN LAND

A stone statue of a fierce yeti loomed over the pass; frost gathered about its features like tears of ice. It looked almost alive in its fury.

Lunah would've loved it. Ash suppressed a shiver.

'This marks the border of my ancestral home,' Tobu said softly, touching the stone. 'The statue acts as a warning to all those who would trespass.'

'I'd say it's pretty successful too,' Teya said.

The path passed under its open jaws. The group hesitated, all eyes on Tobu as he looked up into the eyes of the stone yeti.

'I have not set foot in these lands for so long.' He took a slow breath. 'It's time to stop running.'

Tobu strode forward.

The others followed, gazing warily at the fangs

above. Ash half expected the stone teeth to chomp down on them as they passed.

The eerie calm of the mountain disappeared almost as soon as they crossed the border. Mist spilled down from the heights above. The air smelled of tree sap and freshly cut wood. A river of icy water tumbled over icicles the length of spears, weaving between the coniferous trees that clung to the mountainside. The woods were alive with half-seen shapes shifting through the mists, some as large as Tobu, some larger – *much larger* – whose mighty footsteps crunched through the snow. Ash clung as close to Tobu as he could without tripping him up, unnerved by the sudden waking of the mountain.

Tobu moved quickly, tense and alert, the crew following low and silent behind him. Rook moved stealthiest of all, slinking from shadow to shadow, barely seen by even her comrades. Ash couldn't deny her distance upset him. He'd been so thrilled by his progress with Scratch and was desperate to share his excitement with Rook. She was his Song Weaver teacher after all, and he was keen to show her how well he'd learned from her. But she'd only responded with her endless chant.

'*Danger. Threat. Resist. Protect.*'

They heard loud cries ringing out, fierce and

focused. Cautiously peering over a steep ledge, Ash could make out movement in the valley far below. Hundreds, perhaps thousands, of shadows were moving through the landscape like a Spearwurm winding through trees. He gasped as he realized they were yeti warriors, many riding vast armoured beasts, marching down towards their border.

This wasn't just a guard patrol; this was an *army*.

'I thought you said this pass was safe?' Jed hissed with alarm.

'It was,' Tobu answered, watching the march with mounting confusion. 'This isn't normal.'

'The yeti appear to be mustering for battle,' Master Podd said.

'But what battle?' Tobu questioned. 'We yeti never strike the first blow.'

'Might wanna tell them that . . .' Kailen growled, watching the columns of armed warriors with a frown.

'It must be in preparation to defend against the Devourer,' Tobu reasoned.

'They know about it already?' said Twinge.

'The Listeners will have heard its Song in the World Weave.'

'Either way – it can't be safe to use these paths any more,' Yallah said. 'Is there another way?'

'Not without travelling far to the north . . .' Tobu said, eyeing the shifting masses.

'No way! We have no time!' Jed insisted.

Ash's determination deflated. Yallah was right. There was *no way* they could sneak past an army like that. Not even Nuk or Lunah would try something so rash!

Then the sound of marching footsteps came from the path ahead of them. Tobu signalled for everyone to fall back, but it was too late. The approaching warriors were almost upon them, and the path was far too narrow for them to pass by unseen. The crew ducked down, fearing the worst.

Suddenly a piercing shriek split the air. Scratch had landed on an outcrop nearby and was making quite the ruckus. She screeched and lashed out and writhed about as if she'd lost her mind.

'*GO!*' she Sang to Ash, who saw at once that the Shrieker was creating a diversion. With the yeti distracted, the Pathfinders were able to slip by unnoticed, using boulders for cover.

'I'm all for seeing the sights,' Twinge said once they were clear, 'but if I'd known we'd get that close I'd have brought a spare pair of trousers!'

'He's right – that was *too* close,' Jed huffed.

'It was,' Tobu agreed, clearly disappointed in himself.

'We need to find a way off this mountain,' said Teya.

'Once I might've agreed with you. But now . . .?' Tobu said, watching Scratch glide above them, then turning to Ash with a glint in his eye. 'Working together, I believe we can still get to Master Yanpa.'

22

SHAPES IN THE MIST

Tobu knew the mountain well and chose routes he knew the yeti were unlikely to use. Although the routes were longer and harder to climb, they kept the crew hidden from being found . . . or, at least, they did with Scratch's help. The Shrieker was gliding high above the party, keeping a close eye on the ground.

'*YETI*,' she Sang to Ash. '*TWO HUNDRED LEAPS WEST*.'

Ash went to alert Tobu, but he'd already heard them and was taking the group further east to steer clear.

'*YETI. TEN LEAPS UP*,' Scratch trilled.

'More on the cliff ahead,' Ash whispered to Tobu, who nodded, veering away again. Ash couldn't help grinning.

It was *awesome* having a Leviathan ally.

Ash had spent a lifetime fearing the creatures, and to have one actively helping them felt like some kind of dream. Scratch's method of measuring distances in 'leaps' had taken some getting used to, but now Ash felt like a hero from the tales, striding into danger alongside his mighty beast companion. It had helped restore a drop of hope, and, spirits knew, that was in low supply.

Imagine if all the Leviathans and all the Song Weavers managed to join forces like this? Ash thought excitedly. *Maybe we would stand a chance against the Devourer.*

That was what Song Weaving was all about. Forming connections with the world and all the life in it, just as Rook had taught him.

Back when she used to Sing to him at least.

He watched Rook slink ahead. She held on to a tree for support, shaking her head before lurching onwards again. Ash swallowed hard. Despite hoping they'd escape it way up here, the Devourer's spiteful Song still rustled on the breeze.

Just hold on, Rook, Ash willed her. *After everything you've been through, you can't let the Devourer win now. Just hold on a little longer . . .*

Ash could feel Jed watching them both from behind. Ash turned, and Jed's gaze shot up, pretending he'd been looking at Scratch instead. His eyes were alive with mistrust.

Good, Ash thought. *I'm glad he's uncomfortable!*

He wanted Jed to see that Leviathans were so much more than mindless beasts.

Ash huffed, his breath turning into clouds, and pushed on through the snow. The next time he looked back, Jed seemed about to speak when Tobu suddenly dropped and raised a fist. The company instantly followed, crouching behind him on the lip of a ridge.

'What's wrong?' Twinge whispered, trying to spot what had alarmed Tobu.

The yeti said nothing, his eyes narrowing. As the wind shifted the mist, shapes emerged from the gloom. Crouched on either side of the narrow pass sat numerous yeti-sized shapes, each one covered in snow.

'More statues?' Jed whispered, giving Tobu a scornful look. 'Thought you yeti were made a' stronger stuff? Those ain't gonna hurt us!'

'The path is watched,' Tobu said. 'We must find another way.'

Ash hoped Scratch might weigh in, but she'd had to make a landing on the rocks above. The pass remained deathly quiet, rolling wisps of mist the only thing that moved. Annoyance flashed across Jed's face.

'Every second wasted on this mountain is another we're not there for the fleet! We're running out of time!'

He made to get up, but Tobu pulled him back. 'No. You'll be seen. We must go back down.'

Jed's face reddened. 'I'm sick of you all actin' like you can order me around! Treatin' me like I'm some kinda joke! Well, the Commander put her faith in me, and I will *not* let her down! *I'm* the captain here, an' I order you all t'follow me!'

Jed pushed Tobu's hand away and slipped over the ridge.

The others began to rise, but Tobu shook his head. 'Don't.'

Jed strode down the path, bold as a bandihoot. As he passed the statues, even Ash wondered if Tobu had been overcautious.

But then it happened.

A stone arced across the path, hitting Jed right in the head.

He remained standing for a moment, before collapsing in a heap.

Ash's heart skipped a beat as the statues began to rise up, bows in hand. They weren't carvings at all, but yeti who had hidden among the statues with such stillness and patience that snow had settled upon their fur.

Ash stared with wide eyes at the first yeti he'd seen clearly apart from Tobu. He'd always thought of Tobu as a giant, but Ash was impressed to see that these others weren't much smaller, and their armour made them look even bigger. There were only three, but, even so, they appeared to be a formidable force. Their faces were grim, mostly hidden behind frightening mask-like helmets. A female warrior with a braided mane approached Jed and turned him over to inspect his face.

She spoke. 'A human.'

The second warrior, a male, drew a dagger and held it to Jed's throat.

'Wait!' the female said.

The second yeti hesitated. 'I take no pleasure in needlessly ending lives, but we have our orders.'

'He's defenceless,' she said.

The second warrior looked torn. 'If we don't kill him, the Mountain's Ward will – and punish us for disobeying his command.'

Tobu shifted at the warrior's words. The title *Mountain's Ward* sounded familiar to Ash, though he couldn't remember why.

'Better to question him,' the female warrior said. 'Discover why he's here.'

'They're always here for the same reason,' the male grumbled, hoisting Jed's limp body over his shoulder with ease. 'To escape the Snow Sea.'

'Or perhaps the humans have caught wind of our movements and he is a spy?' suggested the female.

'He won't have come alone then,' said the third warrior. 'I will search for the others.'

Even though Tobu had insisted the crew stay off the path so as not to leave obvious tracks, Ash still held his breath. His friends gripped their weapons tighter, Tobu's muscles taut and ready. The female yeti touched the arm of the warrior who was about to set off, pointing upwards with the same hand. The darkening sky looked tortured and wild, the clouds bruised and heavy.

'A storm is coming,' she said. 'We'd better take the megadon and seek shelter.' As if in response, a strong wind blew through the pass. 'The storm will finish the human trespassers for us.'

'And if they find shelter?'

'Then we'll hunt them down in the morning.'

Jed, still hanging like an ulk carcass over the yeti's shoulder, let out a low groan.

'Let us go then,' said the one who carried him. 'See what this spy has to say.'

The warriors turned to leave, taking their captive with them. One paused, turning to look back at the ridge. Ash ducked down, his heart in his throat.

The yeti's nose twitched as he sniffed the air, his eyes narrowed.

The Pathfinders tensed. Tobu nocked an arrow to his bow.

Another gust of wind blew over the mountainside, snowflakes dancing in its wake. The yeti turned and followed his companions out of sight.

The Pathfinders let out a collective breath of relief.

'That *idiot*!' Teya whispered.

'We have to catch them,' Tobu said.

'To save Jed?' Kailen pulled a face. 'I was just about to say *problem solved* . . .'

'We can't alert the Wardens to the fact we're here,' Tobu insisted. 'If they are searching for us, we'll never make it to Master Yanpa.'

'As well as the fact that, despite being a fool, Jed *is* a Pathfinder,' Yallah said. 'He's one of us, like it or not.'

'I wouldn't go *that* far . . .' Teya said. Yallah raised an eyebrow. 'But I *suppose* . . .'

'We must hurry,' Tobu said, leaping over the ridge. 'They are riding a megadon, which we can't hope to catch. Our only chance is to see where they take shelter. We cannot lose sight of them!'

RETURN TO FORM

Staying low and quiet, the Pathfinders followed the yeti at a safe distance. As they emerged from beneath a naturally formed archway of rock, Ash gawped at the sight that welcomed them.

The yeti had thrown Jed on to the back of a mighty beast. It was as large as a Leviathan, its long shaggy belly held low to the ground by powerful legs with clawed paws. The beast's hide was shaggy with coarse white fur, long tusks protruding from its head, which were decorated with colourful cords and bracelets.

'A megadon,' Tobu confirmed.

Following the megadon proved to be a wholly different game to tracking the yeti. It moved incredibly fast for its size, its claws perfectly adapted for clambering over mountainous terrain, allowing it to scramble over rocks and boulders with ease, its strong legs leaping across chasms and death-defying drops as though they were a mere nuisance.

As Tobu had suggested, the best the Pathfinders could hope to do was keep sight of it and see where the yeti took shelter. But as Mother Sun fell, the Ice Crone's breath consumed the mountains.

Stinging snow tore across the slopes upon a terrible fierce wind that howled like some ancient god. The Pathfinders pushed on against the roaring force, unable to see much in the darkness and dizzying dancing ice.

Tobu seemed to have a sense of which direction they had to go in, following his nose rather than his eyes. The others trudged in his footsteps until even he finally stopped.

'We've lost them,' Tobu growled, his voice barely audible above the howling winds.

'We need to get out of this storm,' Yallah panted.

'*Please* . . .' Twinge shivered, hugging himself against the chill.

It was then that Ash heard Scratch's Song. It was distant, muffled by the blizzard and hard to hear, but it was there.

'*HUNDRED LEAPS. AGAINST WIND. FOLLOW SONG.*'

'What is it, boy?' asked Tobu, seeing Ash's face crease with the effort of listening.

'It's Scratch,' Ash replied. 'She's guiding us again. Follow me.'

Ash followed the sound of the Shrieker's Song, the others close behind. Sure enough, not far from where they'd stopped, just beyond some boulders and after a small climb, light appeared through the tumultuous snow.

As the Pathfinders crept closer, they discovered the glow came from a watchtower perched upon a ledge. It looked to Ash like a multi-layered mushroom, its sweeping rooftops covered in skins and furs that billowed in the wind like sleigh sails. The megadon had its own shelter at the foot of the tower, similarly organic in shape.

Ash and his friends took cover behind some rocks as Tobu made his way inside the megadon's shelter. No sound could be heard over the storm. To everyone's relief, Tobu re-emerged, looping a long coil of rope in his hands.

'Tie this round your wrists,' he said, offering it to the others. 'But not so tight that you can't slip free.'

Cupping a hand to his mouth, Tobu howled out a deep call, like some mountain beast, guttural and strange.

He howled three times, then waited, the end of the rope in his other hand. Ash and the crew stood behind him, the rope loosely binding them as instructed.

Light scattered off the whirling snowflakes as a hatch opened in the bottom of the watchtower.

'Whatever happens, do not harm the yeti,' Tobu whispered to the crew. 'Take captives, not lives.'

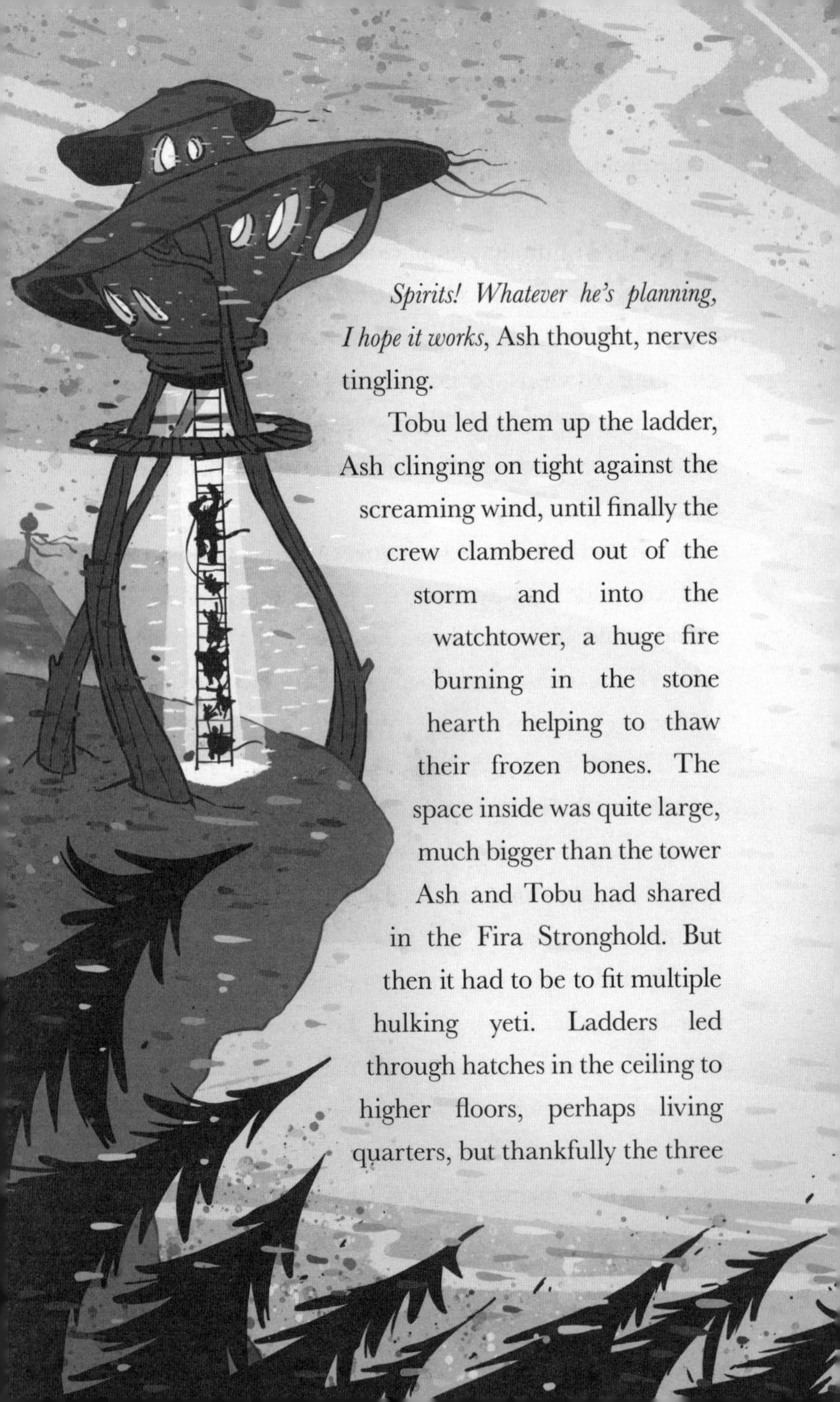

Spirits! Whatever he's planning, I hope it works, Ash thought, nerves tingling.

Tobu led them up the ladder, Ash clinging on tight against the screaming wind, until finally the crew clambered out of the storm and into the watchtower, a huge fire burning in the stone hearth helping to thaw their frozen bones. The space inside was quite large, much bigger than the tower Ash and Tobu had shared in the Fira Stronghold. But then it had to be to fit multiple hulking yeti. Ladders led through hatches in the ceiling to higher floors, perhaps living quarters, but thankfully the three yeti they'd followed appeared to be the only ones stationed at the outpost.

'I found human trespassers,' Tobu announced to the two yeti waiting at the top of the ladder, spears ready in their hands.

The yeti warriors, *Wardens*, Tobu had called them, made space for their new visitors. They'd removed their helmets, and their eyes watched the newcomers closely. The third yeti was seated but tense and alert, his spear leaning on the table beside him. Ash caught sight of Jed, who was tied up and hanging upside down, his eyes wide at the crew's appearance.

'Who are you?' the female yeti demanded of Tobu. 'We've had no word of other Wardens patrolling here?'

The yeti beside her stared at Tobu intently, as though he had an itch he couldn't scratch. Then his eyes suddenly widened.

He recognizes him, Ash realized, his heart pounding. *Quickly, Tobu, quickly!*

'Tobu . . .?' The warrior gasped, looking like he'd seen a ghost.

In a motion almost too swift to follow, Tobu grabbed the heads of the two closest Wardens and cracked them together. With a cry, Twinge charged into them, knocking them off their feet as Ash, Teya and Kailen looped the rope round them.

The third Warden swiftly recovered from his initial shock, and reached for his spear, only to find it kicked out of reach by Master Podd, who had crept under the table.

Tobu rushed towards him, turning aside the punch the yeti threw with a fluid motion. Rook sliced at the yeti's other side with her blades, making a high-pitched keening sound.

'Don't wound them!' Tobu warned, thrusting an elbow towards the Warden's face. The Warden ducked below it just in time, catching Rook's arm in the process. He pulled her back with him as he darted for a window.

'NO!' Tobu yelled. But the yeti dived through the fur cover and fell outside, taking Rook with him. Tobu followed, leaping out without so much as a second glance.

'Tobu!' Ash cried, running to the window.

The Warden faced Tobu in the blizzard below, one arm locked round Rook's neck. Rook snarled, kicked and struggled, her hood pulled back to expose her furious eyes and the black veins that marked her face, vivid and darker than the night itself. No matter how skilled Rook was, she was no match for a yeti's raw strength.

'Why have you come here?' the Warden yelled at Tobu. Ash saw fear in the yeti's eyes. 'The Mountain's Ward will tear you limb from limb!'

'He may try,' Tobu replied.

His confidence clearly shook the warrior, who loosened his grip on Rook just enough for her to bite his arm. The Warden roared in surprise, and Rook slipped out of his grasp. He swung for her, but she rolled behind him, drawing a dagger from his belt as she whirled past. With a shriek she leaped up on to the warrior's back, slashing at him with terrible ferocity, the ring of blade against armour clamouring against the storm. The yeti roared, grasping for her as Rook screamed in fury, teeth exposed. The Warden managed to shake her off, but that didn't end her attack. Rook slashed and stabbed with the dagger, forcing the yeti back. Lines of red appeared on the yeti's white fur, the blade clanging on his armoured gauntlets.

The yeti stumbled in the snow, and suddenly Rook's blade was beneath his chin.

'Don't!' Tobu bellowed, grabbing Rook's wrist before she could plunge the dagger deep.

Rook screamed, her white pupils aflame, all signs of the woman Ash knew lost to hate and anger.

It's the Devourer! Ash thought as he dashed for the ladder. *I have to help her!*

'What's happening?' Kailen asked, but Ash didn't wait to explain, sliding down the ladder two rungs at a time. Rook was bearing down on Tobu now with a frightening ferocity, Tobu parrying her attacks but able to do little else without hurting her.

'ROOK!' Ash cried, rushing towards her. He blasted out his Song-aura, desperate to help her break free of the Devourer's grip, just as Scratch had helped him. Rook's own aura was a writhing living shadow snapping at Ash's as he sought to find the true Rook lost within.

'ENOUGH!' Tobu roared as he caught hold of her blade arm, throwing her to the snow and pinning her down. Despite his strength, she still kicked and spat like a rabid animal.

Ash's aura drove deeper into the Dark Song, forcing its way through the chaotic hate until he found Rook's true aura, a jagged, broken strand struggling within the pulsating murk. As she desperately reached out for Ash's help, the darkness tightened, trying to strangle the life from her Song, but Ash's star-light aura surged forward and coiled tightly round hers. He pulled with all he had, tearing Rook's true Song out of the darkness.

Rook gasped, her flailing limbs suddenly falling limp. She huffed and panted, covered in sweat, looking up at Tobu with a mixture of confusion and hate.

'Enough,' Tobu said again, and for now it seemed it would be.

But surely not for long.

For the Warden had escaped into the stormy night.

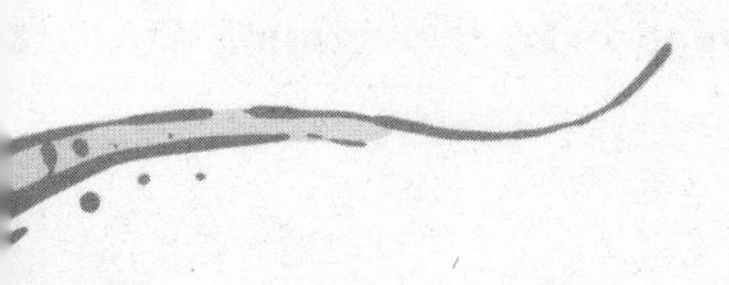

24

CAN'T WIN

'Ooooh no!' Jed cried as Rook rushed back into the watchtower. Teya and Kailen were busy cutting through his bonds. 'No, no, no – I gotta draw the line somewhere! We can't have a Weaver as dangerous as her in here with us!'

Rook slumped into the shadows of a far corner and clutched at her head, her face full of anguish, whispering her Song over and over.

'Danger. Threat. Resist. Protect. Danger. Threat. Resist. Protect.'

'She wasn't herself,' Tobu said, rifling through the watchtower's healing supplies to find something to bind the wounds Rook had inflicted. His horns brushed through colourful cords that dangled from the ceiling. They were tied in intricate patterns, flowing and weaving about each other to make the most beautiful designs.

Everything was large inside the watchtower, the wooden furniture all made for yeti use. Master Podd looked like he'd walked into a giant's home. Sitting at the oversized table with Twinge and Yallah, the vulpis looked positively tiny, the tips of his ears barely poking above the tabletop.

'Exactly!' Jed continued. 'The 'viathans've got into her head! She's dangerous! Listen – what's that she's Singin'? Is she speakin' to 'em now? We don't know!'

'You don't know, so shut up!' Kailen said, cutting through the rope holding Jed up. He hit the floor with a thump. 'She wouldn't have even got into that fight if it weren't fer us having to rescue your sorry behind!'

'The Devourer's taking her heart,' Ash said, his body trembling at the shock of seeing Rook change like that. 'That Song she's Singing protects her. It keeps the Dark Song at bay.'

'Well, it's doin' a marvellous job, ain't it?' Jed said, his remaining binds forcing him to flounder around like a fish. 'Least we know she'll be Singin' a merry tune when she slits our throats while we're sleepin'!'

'You keep this up, Jed, and we'll be forced to take action,' Yallah warned, holding up the gag they'd

removed from his mouth. 'Rook is one of us.'

Jed glared at Yallah from the floor, sizing up the threat.

'People will never trust Song Weavers,' Ash muttered to himself glumly. 'No matter how much we help them . . .'

His words made him the next target for Jed's frown. 'Song Weavers have my sympathy, kid, but it don't stop you from bein' a danger to us all.'

'Only if the Devourer gets into our minds!' The chill feeling stewed in Ash's belly. 'Don't you see – *this* is why we're trying to stop my mum's plan! If she sends the Song Weavers into battle against the Devourer, this is what'll happen to all of us!'

'The Commander knows what she's doing!' Jed declared.

Ash's anger was churning up like a wave now, slithering towards his skull. 'You only see us as . . . as weapons! You don't see us as people!'

He tried to calm himself, to push the anger back down. His eyes darted to Rook. He couldn't end up like that. Not again.

Ash took a deep breath to steady his throbbing temper. 'We never wanted this. We tried our hardest to hide, to not be noticed . . .'

'We must all do our part,' Jed said.

Ash's mother's words. A chill flared through his veins.

'Then you'd better get used to havin' us around!' he snapped.

'OK, time out for you,' Yallah said, shoving the gag back into Jed's mouth, his cries of anger muffled by the cloth.

Ash was fuming. Song Weavers just couldn't win. If they tried to keep to themselves, they were treated with suspicion. If they tried to help, they were treated like tools to be used and then put away out of sight until they were needed again!

Ash was determined to prove to the world what Song Weavers were worth. That people like Jed and his mother had it wrong, and it was *their* fault the world was in the mess it was right now.

Then *they* would know what it was like to be shunned by others.

To be like a Song Weaver.

To be like *him*.

Ash turned his back on Jed, all too aware of the captain's eyes boring into him.

'Besides, I suspect the yeti who escaped presents a greater threat to us than Rook for the time being,' Master Podd pointed out, sipping the tea he'd found brewing on the hearth.

'He'll be forced to take shelter tonight,' Tobu said, dabbing his wounds with a cloth. 'Thankfully, in his eagerness to escape, the Warden left the megadon behind. No one is going anywhere in this storm. But in the morning our cover will be blown. We have no choice but to use the megadon ourselves to get to Master Yanpa faster than word can travel.'

Ash watched Rook as they spoke, wishing he knew how to help her. He clutched the sunstone pendant he wore round his neck, the one his parents had given him before they left the Fira. He knew his father had been as infected by the Devourer as Rook had. But Ash had always hoped he'd managed to escape its hateful poison. Once – or rather *if* – this was all over, Ash had hoped to be able to find him. But that hope was dwindling fast.

Rook had always managed to resist the Devourer's influence where Ferno had failed, and yet the Devourer was now stealing her mind before Ash's very eyes. To escape the Devourer's grasp, Ferno would've had to travel far, far away.

Off the edges of the map.

Over the borders of the known world.

If Ferno had escaped the Devourer's Song, which even now seethed in the air, hundreds of leagues away from the monster itself, he would've had to travel further than Ash could ever hope to follow . . .

Ash shook himself free of his dark thoughts as Tobu finished bandaging his arm and went to stand above the two yeti they'd tied up. Their eyes were cast down with the shame of having been overwhelmed.

'You're a fool to come back here, Tobu,' the female warrior said.

'The Mountain's Ward will kill you,' agreed the male.

It was then that Ash remembered where he'd heard that name before. Mountain's Ward had been the name the people of Aurora had used when they first saw Tobu. They spoke it with fear. Tobu had said it was a name from his past he was happy to forget.

'He won't even know we're here,' Tobu said.

'You have no idea what you're walking into.' The female began to laugh. 'The entire Warden Temple has assembled. The Mountain's Ward has ordered us to march from our lands to reclaim those the humans stole from us.'

For the first time he could recall, Ash saw Tobu look truly stunned.

'Impossible,' he said, gasping.

The female shook her head.

'It is happening, Tobu. The yeti are going to war.'

25

OLD WOUNDS

'Can it be true?' Kailen asked, concerned. 'The yeti plan to invade the Snow Sea?'

'Gods – we're already on our knees without another enemy to contend with,' Yallah said.

'They are simply trying to intimidate us,' Tobu assured them, tying gags round the mouths of the two captives. 'Aggression is not the yeti way. Our Wardens have only ever fought in defence of our lands.'

The rest of the Pathfinders fell silent, watching the two yeti with worry.

With the storm raging outside, the crew sheltered in the tower overnight. Kailen kept watch, just in case the escaped Warden had managed to raise the alarm sooner than they thought. Rook remained in her corner, chanting to herself. Jed sat alone at a window, peeking past the thick fur cover to watch the storm. He'd been warned not to start on the Song Weavers, or he'd get the gag again. The two bound yeti watched the crew with unblinking eyes, sitting straight up and alert, just like the statues they'd been mistaken for earlier. It was certainly unnerving.

The rest of the crew had gathered by the warmth of the hearth, exhausted after the day's climb. Master Podd had fallen asleep, his legs twitching as he let out little barks in his dreams. The others chatted quietly among themselves, telling stories and jokes to try to keep their spirits up.

'You OK, there?' Yallah asked Ash, edging closer. 'You've been very quiet.'

Ash felt his face flush. 'Have I?'

In truth, he'd been desperate to talk to the others, but he'd felt too ashamed. It'd been *his* idea to come looking for the other frost-heart. Because of him, they were all trapped on a mountain of doom surrounded by an army of angry yeti. He was losing hope they would ever survive this trip, let alone be able to stop the Devourer. After seeing what had happened to Rook, Ash doubted anything could defeat it. And what if the Devourer came for *his* mind next? There seemed to be no escape from its Song.

'"It's always after the darkest night that the sun shines brightest",' Yallah said, nodding wisely. 'Y'know who says that?'

Ash shook his head.

'None other than our own Captain Nuk. An' just because she's not here, doesn't mean she isn't right. As long as we're together, we can do this.'

Ash nodded, forcing a smile. Really he just wanted to cry.

We aren't all together, though, are we? he thought. *Not all of us.* How he wished they were. He reached into his furs and pulled out Lunah's star.

'You're not alone, Ash,' Yallah said gently. 'You can always talk to any of us if you need to.'

'I-I know,' Ash said. 'Thank you.'

'If it helps, try to think what Lunah would say at a time like this. Probably something like: "You ent givin' up yet, are you, Ash-the-Slacker-Slug?"'

Ash grinned at that, squeezing the star tight.

'And I hope you haven't!' Yallah pressed.

'I haven't,' Ash said, feeling a bit better already.

As Yallah returned her attention to the others, Ash looked at Tobu beside him. He'd barely said a word all night. It couldn't have been easy for him to return to the yeti lands and fight against his own.

Tobu was gazing at the wooden sculptures he'd carved of his life-mate and son, his mind distracted by painful memories. Ash suspected Tobu had lost his family, but Tobu, not one to waste words, had never said as much, let alone explained what had happened to them.

Yallah had made Ash feel better; perhaps he could do the same for Tobu? After a moment's hesitation, Ash reached out and patted Tobu's knee. Tobu palmed the sculptures and looked up as though waking from a daze. Seeing Ash's concerned expression, Tobu unknitted his brows.

'We've come far, we two, haven't we?' Tobu said.

'All . . . all the way from the furthest north,' Ash agreed.

'Not bad for a pair so badly suited, eh?' A smile crept on to Tobu's face. 'Who'd have thought it, back in my tower at the Fira?'

Ash smiled. 'Not me. I was *so* scared of you.'

'And now you're not?' Tobu leaned towards him playfully, looming over him. 'Well, you should be.'

'Who'd have guessed we'd be on the borders of your home so many moons later?'

'Who indeed? And yet still in a tower.'

They fell quiet again, Tobu opening his palm and gazing longingly at his sculptures.

'You have been through a lot, boy,' Tobu said. 'More than most. And, despite it all, you strive on, trying your best to do the right thing. The honourable thing. You have learned well. I'm supposed to be the teacher, but here I am receiving lessons from you. It seems I, too, must take the difficult path to do what's right.'

Ash blinked, not quite able to believe the words he'd just heard.

He didn't only give me a compliment; he said I've done something better than him!

These truly were the end times.

Ash plucked up his courage.

'Will we find your family here?' he asked, looking at the sculptures in Tobu's hand.

Tobu took a long, deep breath.

'I buried my life-mate far to the north of here.'

'Oh, Tobu, I'm so sorry,' Yallah said.

Tobu looked up in surprise to see the whole crew was listening. His brow creased and his mouth twitched, clearly uncomfortable.

'What was her name?' Twinge asked.

'Perhaps he doesn't wanna talk about it?' Kailen said from the window.

'That's fine, but sometimes it's good to talk about those we've lost,' Yallah said. 'It helps keep their memories alive.'

'Amula,' Tobu said softly. 'Her name was Amula.' He caressed her sculpture gently, his eyes misting over. 'She was . . . kind . . . and strong. She saw the best in everyone . . . and everything. She raised our son to do the same.'

'What happened to them?' Ash said, almost too afraid to ask.

'Amula wasn't a Warden, like me. She followed the Path of the Listener, those that dedicate themselves to listening to the Song of the great World Weave. She had a deep understanding of the connection between every living thing in our world and the threads that bind us. She believed, more than anything, that balance had to be restored to the Weave and to our world. To do that, the Leviathans and yeti would have to make peace with human-kin.'

'Is that really such a bad thought?' Twinge asked.

'To the yeti of the Warden's Path, it is treason.'

'But . . . why?' Ash just couldn't understand why there was so much hate. Everywhere he looked, hate, hate, hate. He *hated* it! 'Why do the yeti hate us so much?'

The other Pathfinders made like they were going to answer but discovered they couldn't.

'It is known.' Yallah chuckled. 'But it's been known for so long we seem to have forgotten why.'

'You said earlier there was no time for a history lesson,' Twinge said, grinning and rocking back and forth. 'There is now. Tell us a tale!'

Tobu considered his words carefully. '*Old wounds scar deep*,' he said finally.

The crew sat silent, waiting for more, but that's all Tobu offered.

'Well, that answers that then,' Teya said, dusting off her hands.

'Answer me this – why is it human-kin hate Leviathans?' Tobu asked.

'Cos they kill us any chance they can get,' Kailen

growled, rubbing at her scarred eye.

Tobu nodded. 'The memories you have of their hostility courses through your veins. Old wounds scar deep, and they are not easily forgiven. It is the same with us yeti. Our memories of war against the human-kin.'

The crew glanced at each other.

'War?' Twinge said.

'The human-kin of old wanted what was not theirs,' Tobu said. 'They wanted the world. And they very nearly took it. They waged war on all the other races – the mursu, the yeti, the Leviathans. Even themselves.'

'Yer sayin' *we* started the war?' Kailen asked in disbelief. 'I don't believe it. Dunno if you've noticed, but human-kin ent all that high up in the pecking order.'

'It doesn't matter what you believe,' Tobu said. 'It is the truth. The yeti of the Chronicler Path take great care to record history. It is written that human-kin used their dark technologies to overpower their enemies where their natural strength could not.'

'You mean – the World Before . . .?' Ash asked. Tobu gave a nod. 'We *did* see all those rusty death machines in the Endless Forest . . . like, *hundreds* of them,' Ash pointed out, stroking his chin as Lunah had taught him to do to seem wise and thoughtful.

'And Stormbreaker *does* have an armada armed to the teeth with powerful archeoweapons,' Yallah added.

'Yeah, but . . .' Kailen trailed off, unable to think of what to say next.

'It is something the yeti have never forgiven, especially those who follow the Warden's Path, who've spent lifetimes guarding our borders from the human-kin desperate to escape the Leviathans. Human-kin wounded the World Weave, shredded the bonds between the races and threw balance into chaos. When the great human civilizations collapsed, the yeti built their walls and retreated from the broken world human-kin left behind. The few human survivors were left to what the yeti believed was a well-deserved fate. Alone, defenceless and at the mercy of the vengeful Leviathans.'

'That's horrible!' Yallah said.

'It is,' Tobu agreed. 'But old wounds scar deep . . .'

'Just one moment,' Teya said, raising a hand. 'How come we've never been taught this? Surely someone would know? The mursu? The vulpis even?'

Master Podd's ears twitched.

'We have excellent memories,' he murmured, eyes still closed, 'but short attention spans.' He was snoring again almost before he had finished his sentence.

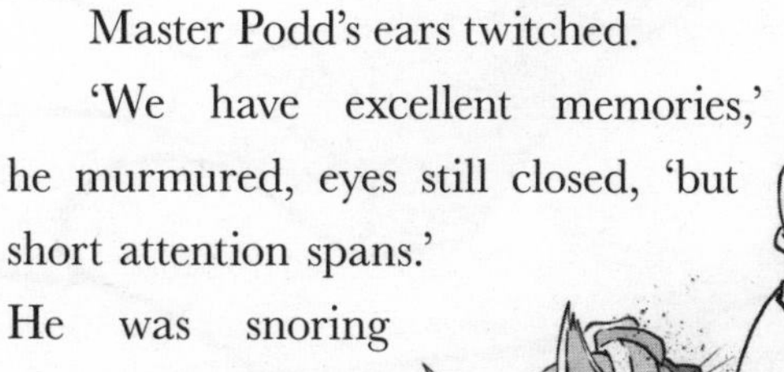

'Perhaps others do know,' Tobu suggested. 'But most human-kin histories were lost with their civilization. It was a thousand years ago, and human-kin have short lives and even shorter memories. But we yeti? The Leviathans? We have long memories indeed.'

The crew fell silent as they soaked in the gravity of Tobu's words.

'And so what happened to Amula?' Ash asked again.

Tobu looked down at the sculpture, before closing his hand over it.

'I didn't listen to her.'

26

FOLLOWING IN THE FOOTSTEPS

The dreams Ash had that night were strange things, as twisting and restless as the storm that raged outside. Most involved the thick, suffocating shadow of the Devourer's Song closing in on Ash and threatening to smother him. Ash tried to flee, but his run was as slow as a crawl. The shadow caught Ash, bearing down on him in a tide of oppressive darkness, and as he screamed, shielding his face from the onslaught, he heard croaking caws and guttural cries.

'Danger!' the voices Sang. *'Threat! Resist! Protect!'*

Daring to peek through his arms, he was astonished to discover the shadow had turned into a flock of crows that raced past in a manic flurry of wings and feathers.

'Danger! Threat! Resist! Protect!'

They were as desperate to escape the Devourer's shadow as he was, the shadow which, to Ash's immense relief, he found still hadn't managed to catch him after all.

The crows moved together as if of one mind, flying out towards the horizon of an endless snow plain. It stretched off as far as the eye could see, the air shimmering with ice. The crows weren't flying aimlessly, however. There, in the snow, Ash spotted a set of tracks. The crows were following the trail someone had walked before.

Ash wasn't sure how, but he somehow knew they were the footprints of his father.

Ash opened his eyes to find Master Podd's face filling his vision. Ash yelped and Master Podd pulled back slightly.

'You Sing in your sleep, you know?'

Even though it was still dark outside, everyone was up and preparing to leave. The world felt very quiet. The wind had stopped howling, and the storm had come to an end.

'We must get to our destination before the Warden warns the others,' Tobu said. He was dressed head to toe in full Warden armour that Ash guessed he'd found in the watchtower, his face half hidden by a grim helmet. He looked even more formidable now, if that were possible, like a mighty warrior from legend.

Ash got up and gathered his things, trying to shake the strange dreams from his head.

'How long were you to keep watch over this place?' Tobu asked the captives, who still sat rigid and tense, eyeing Tobu with hatred. He pulled the gag from the female yeti's mouth so she could answer.

'Our relief will arrive this evening,' the yeti replied, stretching her jaw to loosen it.

'Good. Then they can cut you free,' Tobu said, removing the gag from the second warrior.

'What, yer jus' gonna leave 'em here?' Jed asked. 'I say kill 'em both, leave no witnesses!'

'I do not care what you say,' Tobu growled. 'I will not kill my own people.'

'You'd better listen to the human, Tobu,' the male yeti said. 'You leave us alive, we will hunt you down. The Mountain's Ward will have your head, I swear it.'

The Pathfinders gave Tobu an uneasy glance. He paused, then pulled open the hatch, cold air blowing snowflakes into the watchtower.

'A day is all we need to get this done. Let's go.'

Ash waited for his turn to climb down the ladder, trying to soak up as much warmth as he could before heading back out into the harsh mountain air.

It was then that it hit him.

Rook.

Where was she?

He spun round, searching the corner she'd hidden in. It was empty.

With mounting dread, he ran to the ladder that led to the upper levels, ignoring the calls of the others. He poked his head into the sleeping quarters above.

'Rook? You here?'

Nothing.

Ash slid back down to the alarmed faces of his friends.

'Rook,' Ash said. 'She's gone!'

Her tracks were clear in the fresh snow. Tobu crouched to inspect them, then sniffed the air. They led off into the forest, still dark in the early-morning gloom.

'She left us?' Jed asked.

'I thought that's what you wanted!' Ash snapped, barely able to believe it. Another friend, another person he relied on, taken away from him.

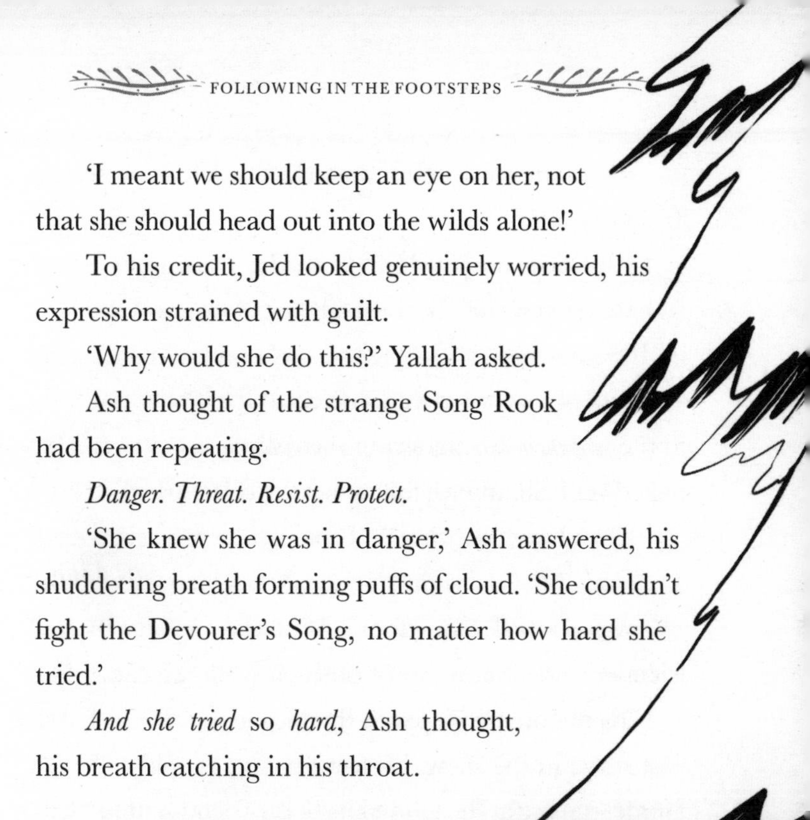

'I meant we should keep an eye on her, not that she should head out into the wilds alone!'

To his credit, Jed looked genuinely worried, his expression strained with guilt.

'Why would she do this?' Yallah asked.

Ash thought of the strange Song Rook had been repeating.

Danger. Threat. Resist. Protect.

'She knew she was in danger,' Ash answered, his shuddering breath forming puffs of cloud. 'She couldn't fight the Devourer's Song, no matter how hard she tried.'

And she tried so *hard*, Ash thought, his breath catching in his throat.

He swallowed, before saying, 'She left to protect us from herself.'

'But how do you hide from the Devourer's Song? Where do you go?' Teya asked, her voice cracking.

'Somewhere it can't reach,' Ash said, remembering the trail of footprints in his dream.

Somewhere only one other person has gone . . .

'Well? Should we follow her?' Kailen asked.

'We have no time,' Tobu said. Ash grimaced, knowing he was right. 'It won't be long before the Wardens come looking for us. With the megadon, speed is on our side, but we must push on while we can.'

As the others prepared the megadon for travel, Ash just stood in the snow, his feet turning as cold as he felt inside, staring at the footprints of the friend he'd just lost.

They were all he had left of her.

For all those years, she'd waited for Ash. Alone and forgotten in the ruins of Skybridge, the crows that haunted its heights her only company. But that hadn't stopped her from trying to do the right thing. She'd been determined to correct her past mistakes and help Ash in any way she could.

But Ash couldn't help her, not when she'd needed him most.

A hand touched his shoulder, pulling him out of his misery.

'She'll be all right,' Tobu said, looking out into the forest. 'She's a survivor.'

For the first time since they'd arrived, the morning light succeeded in burning away the mists, at last revealing to the crew what lay beyond the cold purple mountains. A sea – no, an *ocean* – of lush snow-coated coniferous forest sprawled as far as the eye could see.

Towns and temples jutted from the surrounding vegetation and disappeared into the misty clouds that poured down from the mountains into the verdant valleys. Light glinted off coursing rivers fed by mighty cascading waterfalls. It was almost exactly how Ash had imagined the place when he'd heard the stories, but somehow it was more vivid, more brilliant in its realness.

'*The sacred yeti lands*,' Teya whispered. 'We might be the first outsiders to see it in well over a century!'

'Eh, it's all right, I suppose,' Kailen said.

Ash knew it was a sight to behold, but losing Rook made it hard to appreciate. He fished into his furs and squeezed Lunah's star for comfort. He hoped that she'd managed to find the Convoy. And, more importantly, that she was still alive. Who knew what kind of havoc the Devourer was wreaking while they were here in the mountains? Those he cared about were disappearing faster than he could react, and if it kept up like this, he'd soon be left all alone.

Riding the megadon, the Pathfinders made great headway. Tobu sat at the reins, guiding the beast over the craggy terrain, while most of the others sat in a line behind him, half covered under a huge tanned skin, as if they were just so much cargo. They'd already passed one group of yeti warriors, throwing the skin over themselves just in time. The armour Tobu wore hid his

features, and, thankfully, a polite nod was the only attention they received from the travellers.

They weaved under roots of breathtaking size that had grown around the mountain. Ash couldn't even begin to imagine the size of the trees they must belong to.

'Ent half as big as the ones we have in the Endless Forest,' Kailen remarked, as though it were a competition.

Perhaps she was right, but these forests were certainly more tranquil. It was very strange then, amid all this vibrant life, to discover large areas of dark mouldering foliage, the plant life turning black with decay. Tobu eyed these places with deep concern, his troubled expression revealing that the blight was not normal for these lands.

Chilled by the view, Ash looked up to the sky and found reassurance at the sight of Scratch gliding above them. He was becoming rather attached to the Leviathan. One thing was for sure: they'd never have made it this far without her help.

Jed was also watching Scratch, but with a look of distaste.

'She led us to you, you know,' Ash said. Jed looked at him as though he didn't understand. 'We got lost in the storm trying to find you, but she guided us to the watchtower. It's thanks to her we saved your life.'

'An' why would she do a thing like that?' Jed asked with suspicion.

'I don't know,' Ash admitted, watching her gracefully skim the air currents. 'Maybe because she can see how hard we're trying to save the world?'

Jed didn't answer, just watched Scratch until she swooped out of sight, his look of resentment turning into something more like curiosity.

'Crew, your captain would like to say somethin'!' Jed announced a short time later.

'I'm sure you would,' Teya groaned, the rest of the crew eyeing Jed wearily.

Jed cleared his throat. 'I just wanted to thank y'all for rescuin' me. You didn't have to put yer lives on the line like that –'

'Kinda did, actually, storm an' all . . .' Kailen murmured.

'But you came back fer me anyway,' Jed continued. 'That can't have been easy, considerin' how . . . strained our relationship has been so far. I 'preciate it, is all.' His face turned red as he looked down at his hands.

'Ahhh – you would'a done the same for us, Jed.' Twinge smiled, clapping him on the back.

'*Captain* Jed, please.'

27

ON TOP OF THE WORLD

Up at these heights, Ash found himself breathless, though he couldn't be sure that wasn't because of the dizzying drop just beyond the precipice of the narrow mountain path the crew were following.

'We're here,' Tobu said, pointing to the peak above them and momentarily distracting Ash from his lurching insides. Nestled at the mountain's summit was a village, and the sight made Ash gasp. It was on fire! Although the longer Ash stared at it, the more he realized something wasn't right.

'The flames . . . they're not moving.'

'They're not flames, they're flowers,' Tobu replied.

'Flowers?' Ash repeated. He'd never seen flowers before. They were so bright, they almost glowed in the sunlight.

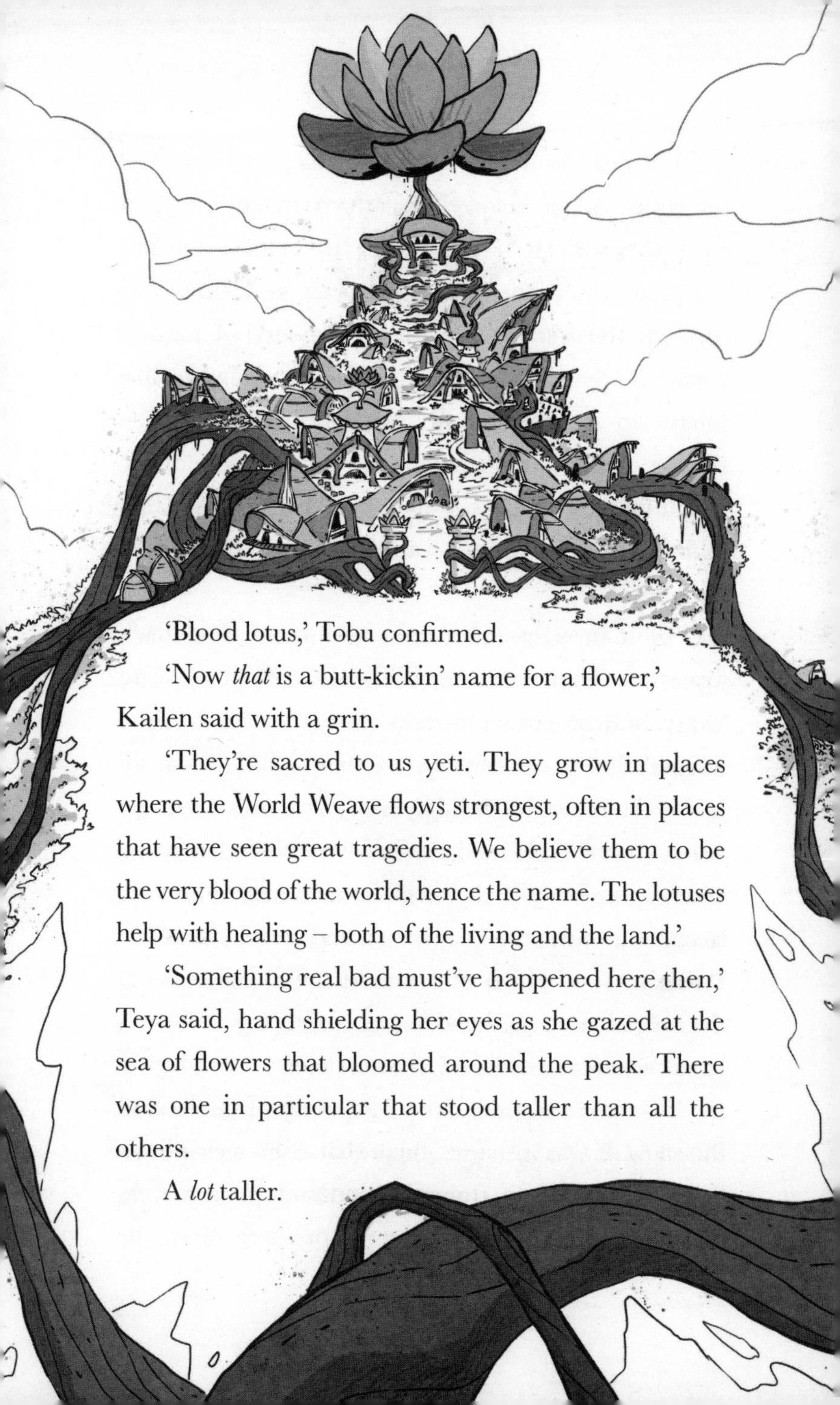

'Blood lotus,' Tobu confirmed.

'Now *that* is a butt-kickin' name for a flower,' Kailen said with a grin.

'They're sacred to us yeti. They grow in places where the World Weave flows strongest, often in places that have seen great tragedies. We believe them to be the very blood of the world, hence the name. The lotuses help with healing – both of the living and the land.'

'Something real bad must've happened here then,' Teya said, hand shielding her eyes as she gazed at the sea of flowers that bloomed around the peak. There was one in particular that stood taller than all the others.

A *lot* taller.

It was a blood lotus so gigantic its petals sheltered the entire village below. It was the source of the giant roots they'd been riding under, the massive tendrils creeping round the mountain peak and threading through the village, creating a network of natural bridges. The village clung to the mountainside like fungus to a tree, an impression heightened by the sloping mushroom-like rooftops of the yeti buildings, which made it seem as if the village had been created with the help of nature, rather than in competition with it.

Tobu brought them to a stop some way down from the village entrance. While the tanned skin had successfully concealed the crew during the climb, Tobu warned that it wouldn't be enough to hide them all under the many watchful eyes of the bustling village. Ash, Master Podd and Kailen were forced to cling beneath the belly of the megadon, covered by its long shaggy fur and secured by a rope tied round its midriff. With the crew hidden as best as he could, Tobu steered the megadon up to the village gates, trying to look as unsuspicious as possible. Crimson flowers flourished in the frost-covered streets, as bright as drops of blood in the snow. It was a shame, then, that Ash's view of this beautiful place was from the underside of a greasy, smelly old megadon. He sweated profusely from the effort of clinging to the beast's belly, his fingers screaming from gripping so tight.

'Boughs above, it stinks down here!' Kailen hissed, screwing her nose up. 'Let's hurry it up, yeah, Tobu?'

'Stay strong,' Tobu murmured under his breath. 'We must not draw attention to ourselves.'

Master Podd made a small squeaking sound as he tried to edge away from something. Ash's face paled at the sight of the megadon unloading a steaming pile of droppings dangerously close to where they hung.

'*Seriously?!*' Kailen whispered.

Holding his breath, Ash tried to focus on the village around him, despite the distracting noises from the megadon's rear end. Along with the smell of megadon farts, the air was filled with the sound of chanting yeti meditating within temples. Between the many feet of yeti going about their daily lives, Ash spotted artisans busy carving ornate sculptures or painting buildings in the most decorative designs and colours. He saw scholars scribbling on parchment and teachers giving young yeti lessons.

Ash tensed at the sight of a group of patrolling Wardens, but their deception seemed to be working, with some even raising their spears at Tobu in greeting. More yeti warriors were training in open courtyards, performing martial exercises in perfect unison.

They really do seem to be preparing for war, Ash thought anxiously.

A paved street ran through the heart of the village and rose steeply towards the large temple that sat proudly at the mountain summit, the giant blood lotus rising from its centre. As they headed up, they passed a small yeti cub who had stopped to watch the megadon pass. Ash's heart skipped a beat as he realized the cub was small enough to see right below the megadon's belly. A moment later, the cub's eyes locked on to his. Ash held his breath, preparing himself for the cub to cry out in alarm. But the cub just looked at him with wide eyes, popping a finger in his mouth. Ash slowly raised his aching arm and gave him a little wave.

The child slowly waved back, curiously watching the megadon continue up the street.

As they approached the temple, Ash could make out the feet of two Wardens guarding the gate, shifting at the sight of such a large beast.

'They won't let the megadon pass into the temple grounds,' Tobu said under his breath.

'Well, we can't exactly hop down and stroll past 'em, can we?' Teya pointed out.

'Hold on there!' called one of the Wardens.

'What're we gonna do? They're gonna catch us!' Jed whispered.

'Try stabbing shins?' Kailen suggested, drawing a short blade.

'Wait,' Tobu said.

'Wait? *Wait?!* That doesn't sound like a plan, that sounds like you're –'

But Jed's complaints were cut off as Tobu cracked the reins and the megadon began to pick up its pace.

'I said stop,' ordered the guard, levelling his spear threateningly.

'I bring urgent news from the Northern Gate. I must speak with Master Yanpa without delay,' Tobu said in a commanding voice, bringing his mount to a halt.

'Who sent you? We've heard nothing about this,' replied the guard.

'Have you no respect for a messenger of the Warden's Path?' Tobu snapped, using his best 'disappointed teacher' voice, one Ash knew well from his training. 'I've been hand-picked by General Neema herself to speak with Master Yanpa on a matter of great urgency, and you're standing in my way!'

The guards' bluster disappeared. At that moment, Ash was glad Tobu could create such confidence-withering tones. And *especially* glad they weren't directed at him for once.

'We . . . er . . . we can't just let you ride –'

'You still wish to delay me?' Tobu boomed, Ash feeling the rumble of his voice even from below the megadon. In response to the sudden sound, the beast began to stomp its mighty legs with unease.

Thump, thump, thump, its clawed paws pounded the path. Suitably intimidated, the guards backed away, the air of command that surrounded Tobu crushing their will to object.

'Let them through!' came an urgent female voice from within the temple grounds. 'Master Yanpa orders it!'

With palpable relief, the guards waved Tobu through the temple gate, and he guided the megadon through the walled courtyard to the back of the temple, safely out of sight.

'Coast is clear,' Tobu said, leaping down from the beast with ease. Ash let go of the greasy fur, his gasp of relief joining a chorus from the others. Kailen cut through the rope and they fell to snow-speckled flagstones.

The crew tensed as a robed female yeti approached them, speaking with the same voice that had ordered the guards to let them pass.

'Easy . . .' she said, opening her arms in greeting. 'Not all yeti are enemies to those who live outside our sacred lands. You are all welcome in the Listeners' Temple, Pathfinders of the Snow Sea. And you too, Tobu of the Warden's Path. Master Yanpa has been expecting you.'

28

MASTER OF THE PATH

The Listener led the group into the large wooden temple and down a long lantern-lit hall.

'Anyone got any idea how this Yanpa knew we were comin'?' Jed whispered to the others. 'We didn't send word ahead!'

'Master Yanpa hears much,' replied the Listener, as they passed other yeti of the Listener Path, each of them bowing their head in welcome.

These yeti seem much friendlier than the Wardens, Ash thought. He allowed himself a smile, hopeful for the first time since seeing the yeti army that, with the Listeners' help, they just *might* succeed in finding the other frost-heart.

They were led into a large courtyard enclosed by the temple buildings. It was here that the breathtakingly

large blood lotus grew, its massive roots forming the very pillars that held the temple up. Its tree-trunk-sized stem was bedecked with twisting threads and strings dyed in lavish colours Ash hadn't even known existed, each swooping down to the rocks and roots in the courtyard below or to the small statues that circled its base, gifts and offerings placed at their feet.

It was utterly stunning – brilliant splashes of colour standing defiant against the dark sky. But despite its beauty, Ash couldn't help but feel uneasy about the patches of mould he noticed below the petals, the same corruption he'd seen in the mountain forests. This disease, or whatever it was, seemed to be spreading across the land.

Sitting alone before the lotus, surrounded by a circle of candles, was a hunched figure, their robes draped over their crossed legs.

'She awaits,' their Listener guide said, motioning towards the figure. The crew approached the plump, ancient-looking yeti. She had gnarled, twisted horns and a staff decorated with charms and trinkets that lay across her lap. Her ragged, greying mane was similarly festooned, bone talismans and runes tied to her fur by brightly coloured strings.

Her eyes were closed, her breathing so slow Ash worried she might be dead.

'So *this* is the mysterious Yanpa we risked our lives to find?' Jed whispered, sounding a bit disappointed.

'Great Master Yanpa, we have come seeking your wisdom,' Tobu said, his voice low. The old yeti didn't stir. 'The world is in great danger, and we need your aid.'

Yanpa remained as still as stone.

'Is she . . . OK?' Twinge asked, looking like he wanted to give her a little poke.

'She is deep in meditation. As Master of the Listener Path, she spends her life listening to the Song of our world, trying to unravel the deepest mysteries of existence itself.'

'So . . . she's not just havin' a snooze?' Kailen said. 'Cos it looks like she's havin' a snooze.'

'There is little Master Yanpa does not hear,' Tobu said. The group waited for her to do something. 'Master Yanpa?' Tobu tried again.

Ash scratched his head, the Pathfinders shuffling impatiently. Tobu cleared his throat. He edged closer, reaching out a hand.

He drew closer.

And closer . . .

Yanpa's eyes snapped open and she gave a shuddering gasp, startling those around her so much even Tobu jumped.

'The World Weave weeps!' she wheezed. 'It cries out in pain!'

Hammering her staff on to the flagstones, she used it to leap to her feet with surprising agility. She shook her head, jingling her many talismans. 'This is dire, this is very, very dire indeed! The *World Eater* has returned. It seeks to consume our world's very soul! It must be stopped. It must be undone, or everything will be lost!'

'Master Yanpa, we . . .' Tobu began.

Yanpa spun round and looked at her visitors as though she'd only just noticed they were there. The Pathfinders withdrew under her beady eyes.

'What are you standing around for? We have work to do!'

'Yes,' Tobu said rather breathlessly. 'We have come to –'

'Yes, yes, I know why you have come!' Yanpa said, shuffling about the roots and blowing out candles.

'Then let us introduce ourselves, oh wise Listener,' Jed announced. 'I am –'

'I know who you all are, Captain Jed of the *Frostheart*,' Yanpa croaked. 'There's no time for this! No time! We must act, we must –' She stopped abruptly as she passed Tobu, slowly turning to face him. She poked him in the belly with her staff.

'Getting soft out there, are you, Tobu?'

Tobu half smiled. 'It is good to see you again, old greyhair.'

'And you too, my friend. The Weave is kind to cross our threads again, though I wish it were under happier circumstances. And I do wish you hadn't made *quite* such a racket on the way up. This mountain used to be so peaceful . . .'

Tobu's face darkened. 'The Wardens . . . they speak of *war*?'

Yanpa nodded. 'The Mountain's Ward, poor fool. Another victim of the World Eater's hate.'

'Victim?' Tobu asked.

'Although his hatred for humans has been stewing for many years, it was only last week that the Mountain's Ward declared the entire Warden Temple would march to reclaim the lands the humans stole from us, or so he describes it. The other Masters have pleaded for peace, but he won't listen to us, Tobu. He is lost to hate.'

'A week ago, he said this?' Tobu asked.

Yanpa nodded gravely. 'Just after the World Eater awoke. Curious timing, wouldn't you say?'

Ash assumed the *World Eater* was the yeti name for the Devourer, the way Yanpa spoke of it.

'The world is unbalanced, and the World Eater feeds on the chaos. Souls filled with anger shine like a beacon, attracting the World Eater's poisonous Song into their hearts, becoming little more than its puppets, used to sow more division and chaos in turn. And we both know the Mountain's Ward has more than his fair share of anger in his heart.'

Tobu was staring at Yanpa in horror.

'Spirits help us . . .' Jed whispered.

'Sounds like we've already failed in our mission then,' Teya said, flinging her head back in exasperation. 'We can't fight on every front! And this Warden Master doesn't sound like the kind of guy you can have a nice chat over tea with.' She put on a voice. '"Oh, hello, great Mountain's Ward! I know you despise human-kin with every fibre of your being, but care for a cheeky truce? Just while we fight off a Leviathan death-god? Won't be long, promise, then we'll get right to your little war!"'

'Which is why time is of the essence,' Yanpa urged, using her staff to nimbly pole-vault across the courtyard, the others doing their best to keep up. 'We've already wasted enough as it is! We must go!'

'Go? Go where?' Jed asked.

'You seek the last heart, don't you? Well, you'll find it in the Cradle. Though what *else* you find there you may not like . . .'

'What's the *Cradle*?' Twinge asked.

'Enough questions!' Yanpa chided. 'Easier if I show you. We shouldn't, no, *cannot* stop for anything!' She suddenly skidded to a stop, the others running into her. '*Except* . . .'

'Except *what*?' a flustered Tobu said.

Yanpa pointed her staff at the lotus and the thousands of colourful cords winding up its stem.

'You said it yourself. There's no time,' Tobu said, his expression soft.

'For love?' Yanpa said. 'It is the one thing we *should* make time for!'

Tobu eyed the hanging threads, hesitant.

'Go on,' Yanpa encouraged. 'It's been too long. Amula will appreciate it.'

Tobu gave a slow nod, unable to meet Yanpa's eyes. The rest of the crew kept their distance as Tobu, almost timidly, approached the great blood lotus.

29

SOULS ENTWINED

'What is this place?' Yallah asked, her voice low.

'The Oath Bloom,' Yanpa replied. 'The pillar of my Path. It is where yeti of all Paths come to profess their love. Whether it be to a life-mate, to family or dear friends, yeti that wish to make a declaration of their love tie a string to the Oath Bloom before twisting it round that of their partner. Just as our souls intertwine within the World Weave.'

Delicately, almost fearfully, Tobu reached out for a pair of red and blue threads that had been twisted round each other, reaching up to the highest parts of the stem. He bowed his head, eyes closed, caressing the threads gently.

'Tobu's and Amula's threads . . .?' Ash whispered.

Yanpa nodded.

'What happened to her?' Ash dared to ask.

Yanpa took a deep breath, delving into memories that were clearly painful.

'To hear this tale, you must first understand what it means for a yeti to commit to a Path. It becomes all they are, all they know. Tobu devoted his life to the Path of the Warden, the way of the warrior. He spent his days learning combat skills, but also all the intolerances that are ingrained in that Path.'

Yanpa shook her head disapprovingly, her talismans jingling. 'All that bicep flexing and strutting. *Pah!* Tobu's son, a wonderful cub named Temu, took after Amula, thank the Weave. Temu's calling was to follow the Path of the Listener, like his mother, and he believed with all his heart that balance would only be restored to the Weave once all the races of the world found peace.

'But Tobu was having none of it. He was furious! He wanted his son to become a warrior, to walk the Path of the Warden and protect those he loved. Tobu *demanded* it. He would not hear Amula's protests.

'Tobu drilled the living snot out of that cub, poor child. Every single day, without fail, at the crack of dawn – training, exercises, combat practice, on and on, harder and harder!'

'Sounds familiar,' Ash mumbled, his muscles

aching at the mere memory of his own training sessions. Ash felt for Temu. Ash may not have had parents growing up, but he'd also been forced to follow in his father's footsteps in a way. Forced to hide who he truly was.

'At night,' Yanpa continued, 'Tobu would tell Temu the stories taught to the Wardens about humans. About the danger they posed, how they could never be trusted again, and how nothing good could ever come from them.'

Ash's insides suddenly felt like water. Tobu couldn't have been like that, could he? Not the Tobu he knew, no way!

'Do not judge Tobu too harshly,' Yanpa warned, almost as if she had heard his thoughts. 'Remember – it was all he knew. Old wounds scar deep, and all that.'

Ash nodded.

'Tobu was trying to change Temu's peaceful nature,' Yanpa continued. 'But the harder he pushed, the stronger Temu's resolve became. Until the day Tobu pushed him too far.'

'What happened?'

Yanpa sighed. 'Temu ran away. He headed to the closest human Stronghold to our borders, hoping to start peace talks. To prove to his father, once and for all, that there was good in humans, that we could live side by side. To prove his father *wrong*.

'The moment Tobu and Amula discovered Temu was missing, they raced after him in pursuit, terrified of what might happen to him. But they were too late. By the time they caught up to him, Temu was already at the Stronghold. Seeing a yeti at their gates, and two more with wild, manic eyes rushing down from the mountains, the humans believed they were under attack. They defended their walls with arrow and stone.'

'They – they killed Temu and Amula?' Ash said.

Yanpa narrowed her eyes, watching Tobu retrieve the small wooden carvings of his family he'd sculpted. With one last look at them, he knelt and placed Amula's sculpture at the foot of the Oath Bloom, his face a mask. At least to all but Ash. He knew his guardian well enough by now to recognize the pain in his eyes.

'Sometimes I think all three of them were lost that day,' Yanpa said. 'Tobu, certainly, is not the same yeti he once was – the stubborn old warrior.'

'I wouldn't be so sure,' Ash said.

'Stubborn, I've no doubt, but no longer full of anger and hate.'

'No,' Ash agreed, knowing it to be true, and glad for it. 'No, he's not.'

'He's changed for the better. And I believe we have you to thank for that, Ash.' Yanpa smiled at him, and

Ash smiled back, a little uneasy with taking credit for something he felt he didn't do. That, and the fact that Yanpa knew his name, which he'd almost certainly not shared . . .

Without a word of warning, Yanpa began to sing. Her voice was gentle and strangely soothing. The song was sad, but hauntingly beautiful. It reminded Ash of the Leviathans' mournful chorus. The words were in the yeti language, which none of the crew understood, but they all stood transfixed, lost to the enchanting sounds as Tobu said his farewells to the memory of Amula.

As the song progressed, though, a sudden shiver ran down Ash's spine. Not because of Yanpa's voice, nice as it was. No, even though he couldn't understand the words, the song had grown into something familiar, something Ash knew as well as his own thoughts.

'That was lovely.' Yallah smiled as Yanpa finished.

Yanpa waved the compliment away. 'You don't have to flatter a tone-deaf old greyhair.'

'Where . . . where did you hear that song?' Ash asked, breathless.

'It's a yeti folk song, older than I am, if you can believe that,' Yanpa said. 'It tells of two lovers torn apart by fate. They spend their lives searching but, alas, are unable to find each other. Both die, their souls returning to the earth. But it is here, at last, after a lifetime apart, that they're reunited. Overjoyed, they dance together into eternity, surrounded by all the twining souls in the great World Weave. For we are all connected, and those that leave us are never truly lost.'

Ash wiped a tear from his eye. 'It . . . it's the same tune as the lullaby my father used to sing to me as a baby . . .'

The Song that led me here. The Song that started all this.

Yanpa gave him a curious look. 'Some songs are as ancient and powerful as the Weave itself. The words may change, as well as the peoples who sing them, but their true meaning remains the same . . .'

The lullaby was *my dad's promise that we'd find each other. That we'd all be together again as a family, no matter what . . .*

Ash's mind raced. Was the lullaby more powerful than he'd realized? Could it still make them a family again?

Suddenly Yanpa's ears pricked up. She swung her staff round, motioning towards some side doors to the temple.

'All of you – hide! *Now!*'

Her eyes were wild and invited no challenge. The Pathfinders rushed through the door, just before four armoured Wardens strode into the courtyard. They held their spears ready, clearly wary of Tobu, even if he was still kneeling.

Listeners gathered around the many temple doors, watching with grim faces. Some rushed past the hiding Pathfinders towards the temple entrance, and Ash caught a glimpse of what lay in the outer courtyard beyond. Dozens of Wardens, perhaps even hundreds. His blood ran cold.

'I'll have no fighting in here, Wardens, you understand me?' Yanpa said. 'This is a place of peace, much like the rest of our land used to be.'

The warriors bowed respectfully, but did not lower their weapons.

'Tobu, Walker of the Exile's Path,' their captain called, his voice harsh and loud. Tobu's eyes remained closed. 'Word reached us of your trespass into our lands, though we didn't want to believe it. Do not make this any harder than it has to be.'

Sweat beaded Ash's face as he watched through a crack in the door, his friends around him, their weapons drawn, their knuckles white.

'Redeem your lost honour. Come peacefully and the Mountain's Ward may yet show mercy and offer you and your human companions a swift death.'

The Wardens had surrounded Tobu now, closing their circle cautiously, spears levelled.

'*My* honour?' Tobu said. 'It is not I who has forgotten what it means to be a Warden. We are defenders, protectors, *peacekeepers.* But now you march to war, unprovoked. You shame our Path.'

To Ash's amazement, Tobu's words seemed to hit a nerve. The Wardens looked troubled, *ashamed* even. It was as if they knew Tobu was right.

'The Mountain's Ward has told us the humans plan to attack us with their new weapons. Our land is in danger!' one Warden replied.

'When did the Wardens abandon logic for lies?' Tobu asked, still with his head lowered. Taking a deep breath, he opened his eyes, and raised his hands in submission. 'Kozun,' he said to the captain. 'I see the Mountain's Ward has given you a promotion since I left.'

Kozun approached Tobu slowly, his eyes alert for any sign of movement.

'Personally, I'd question that decision. It is clear your observation has not improved.'

Kozun's eyes widened as he realized Tobu's tail had wrapped round his spearhead. Tobu yanked the point downwards, the butt cracking into Kozun's jaw. Tobu leaped up and crunched his elbow into Kozun's face, sending him tumbling to the ground like a sack of redroot.

Two of the other Wardens charged. Tobu stomped down on one of the stabbing spears, catching it under his foot and using the momentum to push himself into the air. He grabbed a handful of the colourful cords and brought all his downward motion into a strike, cracking a fist into the face of one Warden and whipping the cords round the other, pulling them tight to restrain her. The remaining Warden launched his spear straight at Tobu, who kicked it out of the air, spinning it back to smack the warrior right in the face.

Before Ash and the crew had even begun to comprehend what was happening, Tobu was rushing towards them.

'CLOSE THE DOORS!' Yanpa yelled, using her staff to bound after Tobu. 'CLOSE THE DOORS!'

The gathered Listeners shouted and pushed the temple doors shut just as Tobu and Yanpa slipped through. Huge timber beams thudded into place, sealing the doors as the mass of Wardens in the outer courtyard began to bang furiously against them.

Yanpa burst out laughing. 'I *am* glad you're back, Tobu, you do make things interesting! Though I wish you'd been a bit more respectful of our holy Oath Bloom.'

'I did what I had to do,' Tobu growled. 'The path-threads of others may have just helped us save the world.'

'You could even say: *love binds us all*,' Twinge said, opening his mouth in an exaggerated smile, as if expecting them all to roar with laughter at his joke.

No one got it.

'That's impressive an' all, but what're we gonna do now?' Kailen asked.

Despite Tobu's small victory, the temple was entirely surrounded.

The Pathfinders were trapped.

30

THE DEPTHS BELOW

Yanpa rushed them all to the front of the busy temple.

'This is it! This is where we die!' Jed cried out, tearing at his hair.

'Jed, do us a favour and shut up,' Kailen growled.

The large hall looked rather out of character compared to the rest of the building. It was made of stone instead of wood, for starters, the masonry engraved with the sweeping circles and whorled patterns common in ruins of the World Before.

'Everyone into the centre!' Yanpa ordered, pointing to just such a circle carved into the centre of the floor. As everyone obeyed, Yanpa bounded over to a wall and twisted a circular relief set within the stonework. She pulled it out, the mechanism making a loud clunking sound.

'We're all gonna die like trapped squinks, instead of bravely on the battlefield, an' fer what? Some stupid heart that doesn't even *exist*?!' Jed continued to complain.

'Please try to calm down,' Master Podd said.

'I can't believe I let y'all talk me into this!' Jed yelled. 'What was I *thinking*? There's no way out of here!'

As he spoke, the floor began to tremble, the Pathfinders stumbling in shock. To their amazement, the stone circle they stood upon began to descend into the floor amid a cloud of dust. Stone ground against stone as unseen mechanisms clunked and ticked.

'What *now*?!' Jed squealed.

'You're never happy, are you?' Yanpa asked, leaping across the hall to join the others as the platform descended into the deep darkness below. 'This, oh mighty whiner, is a way out of here.'

'A mechanical lift?' Yallah said in wonder.

Down, down, down the lift went, into the belly of the mountain. The intense darkness was barely kept at bay by sunstone lights embedded into the walls that flickered to life as the platform passed them. Their wan light stretched the shadows of the company into long twisted things.

Ash shivered, the damp cold somehow having managed to creep under his furs. This cold felt different to that of the icy world above. This was the cold that chilled your blood when you were scared, that ran down your spine when you sensed something bad was about to happen. Tobu drew closer to Ash, like he usually did in these dangerous situations. Ash hesitated, then stepped away, looking at his guardian as though he hardly knew him.

Tobu stared back, confused, and not without a small hint of hurt.

It took every bit of Ash's willpower to not go back to him, especially after the pain Tobu had just relived over his lost family, but he couldn't forget the story

Yanpa had told.

Tobu had once hated human-kin.

What made him any different to those who hated Song Weavers?

Or to Shaard and Ferno, who hated the Strongholders so much they were willing to unleash the Devourer for vengeance?

Or even his own mother and her desperate need to wipe out the Leviathans?

Hatred was everywhere, even in Tobu, and the realization hung over Ash like a storm cloud. In this world of hate Ash had always trusted Tobu to do the right thing.

Apparently that trust had been misplaced.

The image Ash had dreamed up of his perfect parents had already vanished. Now he was losing Tobu too.

'Where are you taking us?' Jed asked after some time.

'To a place of forgotten secrets and ancient memories,' Yanpa said. 'A place that holds the answers you seek.'

Finally, just as Ash began to fear the shadows would engulf them, the lift came to a stop. They were met with the stench of centuries-old dust and stale, forgotten air.

Cautiously the group stepped off the platform. With a rumble, it ascended back up the shaft, returning to the temple hall high above and leaving them on their own.

By some ancient sorcery, lights began to flicker on, illuminating the space yet somehow never enough to chase away the suffocating darkness. They revealed a huge cavernous chamber that stretched off into shadow, archeomek machines of all shapes and sizes strewn around. Some chugged, others clicked and whirred, but most were dead and silent.

The light was reflected in the ripples of a large lake of glacial water that had flooded the cavern ahead. The sound of grinding, shifting metal echoed somewhere far off, as though the place was stirring back to life, as well as a deep steady thrumming, which seemed to vibrate through the walls.

Ash noticed Master Podd's tail swishing excitedly at the sight of so much ancient loot.

Teya whistled, gazing around with her mouth open. 'You could fit an entire Stronghold in here.'

'Maybe even two,' Twinge whispered.

Despite the cavern's size, Ash felt claustrophobia pressing down on him like a terrible weight. The air was thick with the taste of despair and hopelessness.

'This place is evil,' Yallah said, making a sign to her gods.

'It has been under the temple all this time?' Tobu asked.

'The temple was built around the Oath Bloom, which grows from this place, which we call the Cradle,' Yanpa replied. 'There's a reason the blood lotuses bloom so freely on this mountain, and why centuries ago it was chosen as the location for the Listener Temple. The world suffered a grievous, terrible wound here, and the World Weave gathers, desperately trying heal it.'

Despite himself, Ash took a step closer to Tobu.

Massive tubes the size of tree trunks trailed from machines like tentacles, the ground around them black where something awful had once leaked out. Scaffolding and platforms scaled the walls, reaching all the way up to the shadowy ceiling high above, from which metal vices and clamps hung on thick cables like grasping claws. An eerie glow was pulsing on a walkway up there, but they couldn't see what it was from where they stood.

'Look!' Jed said quietly, pointing at a line of archeoweapons in various stages of completion that stood against a nearby wall. 'You think this was some weapon workshop or somethin'?'

'Maybe . . .' Kailen said. 'Hate to think what weapons were large enough to need this kinda space, though . . .'

'Come this way,' Yanpa said.

'Can't you just tell us where we're goin'?' Kailen asked.

'If I did, I'm afraid you wouldn't follow.'

The crew paused, sharing a worried glance.

'Anyway,' Yanpa said, a mischievous smile creeping across her wrinkled face, 'I don't want to ruin the surprise.'

31
THE CRADLE

Many of the corridors had caved in or been flooded with ice-cold water, but the group slowly managed to make their way up to the higher levels.

The higher they rose, the louder the strange repetitive thrumming became.

Ba-thomp.

Ba-thomp.

Ba-thomp.

The chambers they passed through had become little more than mineral caves, thanks to the stalagmites and stalactites that had grown on and around the machinery and control panels.

As they neared the top, Tobu had to ram a stone door that had frozen shut, his weight and strength forcing it open. The large chamber within practically danced with archeomek. Orbs spun and floated, mechanisms rotated and chugged, lights blinked and flared. Master Podd could no longer help himself. He raced to a small archeomek contraption, snatching it up greedily. It fired a beam of energy into the ceiling, debris raining down on to the vulpis.

'How about we all try our very best to not touch anything that could kill us, eh?' Yanpa suggested.

'Sorry,' Master Podd said, carefully placing the archeoweapon back where he'd found it.

'You *sure* you don't like archeomek as much as the rest of the vulpis?' Yallah teased.

Master Podd cleared his throat. 'O-of course not. I have no need for such trinkets.'

His ear gave an involuntary twitch as he backed away. And Ash could've sworn he saw Master Podd pocketing the weapon again when no one was looking.

The thrumming sound was almost overpowering here, each beat thumping through Ash's ribs and through the floor.

Ba-thomp.

Ba-thomp.

Ba-thomp.

Ash followed Tobu closely, scared some archeo-horror might reach out from the shadows and snatch him up as they approached a section of wall that was as smooth and shiny as ice. Light danced upon its surface, shifting and changing into different pictures. Ash blinked, still awed by the ancient magics of the World Before. The pictures were of Leviathans – Lurkers, Hurtlers, Spearwurms, Shriekers, Gargants – they were all there and more besides, types Ash had never seen nor heard of before.

Next to the Leviathan breeds were words written in a language Ash couldn't understand, but sometimes these were accompanied by other pictures. Images of archeoweapons, of war machines and stone giants.

'Whatever the World Before would throw at them during the war,' Tobu said, 'the Leviathans adapted to defend and fight against it, remoulding themselves like clay. Time and again, the human-kin of the World Before were outmatched, despite their advanced technology.'

'Or were they?' Yanpa said ominously. 'Perhaps they decided to do the same?'

'Adapt?' Ash whispered, swallowing hard. It was

the exact word his mother had used when she'd convinced the Aurora Council to form a Pathfinder fleet armed with weapons they barely understood.

'That thumpin's doin' my head in!' Kailen complained. It was starting to do things to Ash too. He felt dizzy, and a little bit sick.

Ba-thomp.

Ba-thomp.

Ba-thomp.

As much as it frightened him, though, Ash suspected he knew what it was.

He approached the sound, careful and slow. It was guarded by a huge stone doorway covered in symbolic etchings.

'The World Weave has guided me to this place before, though I have never been able to pass this door,' Yanpa said. 'It can only be opened by those that once ruled the human kingdoms of the World Before.'

Placing her hands on her hips, she turned to face Ash as though he could solve her problem.

'Right.' Ash nodded wisely, no idea how else to reply.

'I mean, that's sound thinking, Master Yanpa, but the only problem I can see is that they've been dead an' gone for the last thousand years,' Teya said, shrugging. 'Just sayin'.'

'Aha! But their blood lives on,' Yanpa laughed, pointing her staff towards Ash, who shrank back.

'The kid's a king?' Jed asked, pulling a face.

'Song Weavers, my whiney companion! It was Song Weavers who ruled the World Before!'

'You must be joking!' Jed huffed.

'Look at my face,' Yanpa grunted. 'Do I look like one who jokes? Why do you imagine the most important ruins of the World Before are always protected by Song? You think it a coincidence that the most powerful archeoweapons can only be operated by Song Weavers? The rulers of the World Before were unwilling to share the true power of their empire with anyone but themselves.'

Ash cast his gaze down, suddenly feeling terribly ashamed. As though, by being a Song Weaver, he was somehow responsible for their actions.

All that amazing technology, and you don't let people use it because they can't Song Weave? That's . . . that's awful*!*

It was almost like how the Strongholders treated Song Weavers now! Ash told himself that Song Weavers were no longer like that – that they would be happy just to be treated like normal people nowadays – but he knew that wasn't *entirely* true.

No wonder Shaard admired the World Before so much – I bet he'd love the world to go back to those ways. All of human-kin living under the rule of Song Weavers . . .

'Why don't Song Weavers rule us now then?' Jed asked, still doubtful.

'If you stopped yammering for a second, perhaps you'd find out!' Yanpa said. 'The Song Weaver rulers of the World Before built this place and were responsible for what we'll find within. Provided Ash manages to open this blasted door!'

Ash gazed up at the entrance. It looked as solid and impenetrable as you might expect. Inlaid at its centre, though, were three spherical sunstones, long dead and dark. Looking at them made his mind lurch all of a sudden, like he was falling from a great height.

Despite the unpleasant sensation, a Song filled Ash's head as if from thin air. A Song he'd never heard before, but one that he somehow knew was the answer they needed.

'I . . . I think I can open it . . .' Ash said, steadying himself.

Yanpa made room for him.

Taking a deep breath, Ash Sang the Song the sunstones had revealed to him. It was a Song of admission and welcome. His glowing Song-aura encircled the three stones, filling them with bright light once more. With a grinding crack and a shower of ice, the door began to shudder open.

Ash made a small choking sound when he saw what lay beyond.

A long stone walkway, stretching out into the cavernous main hall and over the flood-lake far below. And at the end of the walkway, floating in the air above a rusting archeomek machine . . .

A frost-heart.

But this frost-heart was *huge*, at least twenty times the size of the one Ash had come to know. It was little more than a chunk of heart-shaped ice now, all its inner glow lost. All, that is, except for a small piece in its centre, which still pulsed with a blue light, resonating with each rhythmic beat.

'You came with questions,' Yanpa said, 'and I give you answers.'

'Gods above . . .' Yallah whispered.

'I . . . I . . .' Jed said, his eyes wide in astonishment.

'It's the heart of a Leviathan Ancient,' Ash said breathlessly, recognizing its Song. 'Same as our frost-heart.'

The heart was truly ancient, there was no doubt about that, and had clearly once belonged to a Leviathan of incredible size and power. But unlike the first frost-heart Ash had found, this one's Song was rife with fear and desperation. Ash's skin prickled unpleasantly at its anguish.

'Why's it in this spirits-forsaken place?' Jed said. 'What were they *doing* with it?'

But it was not the Pathfinders who answered, or even Master Yanpa.

The ruins suddenly echoed with the sound of hundreds of voices, a cacophony of noise that chilled the Pathfinders' blood and quickened their hearts.

Growls, howls, shrieks and roars – a thousand Leviathan Songs in chorus.

The Pathfinders reeled in shock, clumping together

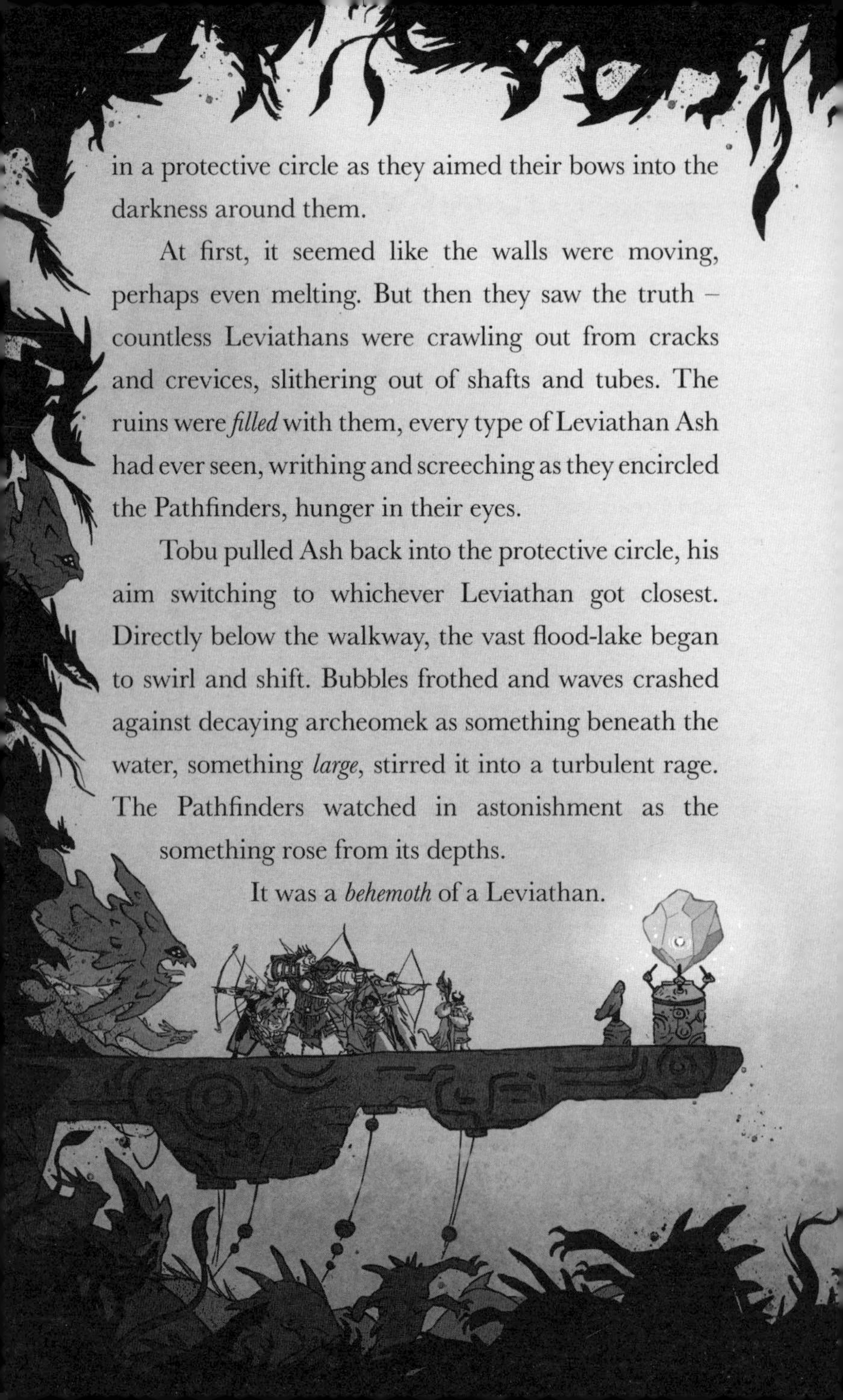

in a protective circle as they aimed their bows into the darkness around them.

At first, it seemed like the walls were moving, perhaps even melting. But then they saw the truth – countless Leviathans were crawling out from cracks and crevices, slithering out of shafts and tubes. The ruins were *filled* with them, every type of Leviathan Ash had ever seen, writhing and screeching as they encircled the Pathfinders, hunger in their eyes.

Tobu pulled Ash back into the protective circle, his aim switching to whichever Leviathan got closest. Directly below the walkway, the vast flood-lake began to swirl and shift. Bubbles frothed and waves crashed against decaying archeomek as something beneath the water, something *large*, stirred it into a turbulent rage. The Pathfinders watched in astonishment as the something rose from its depths.

It was a *behemoth* of a Leviathan.

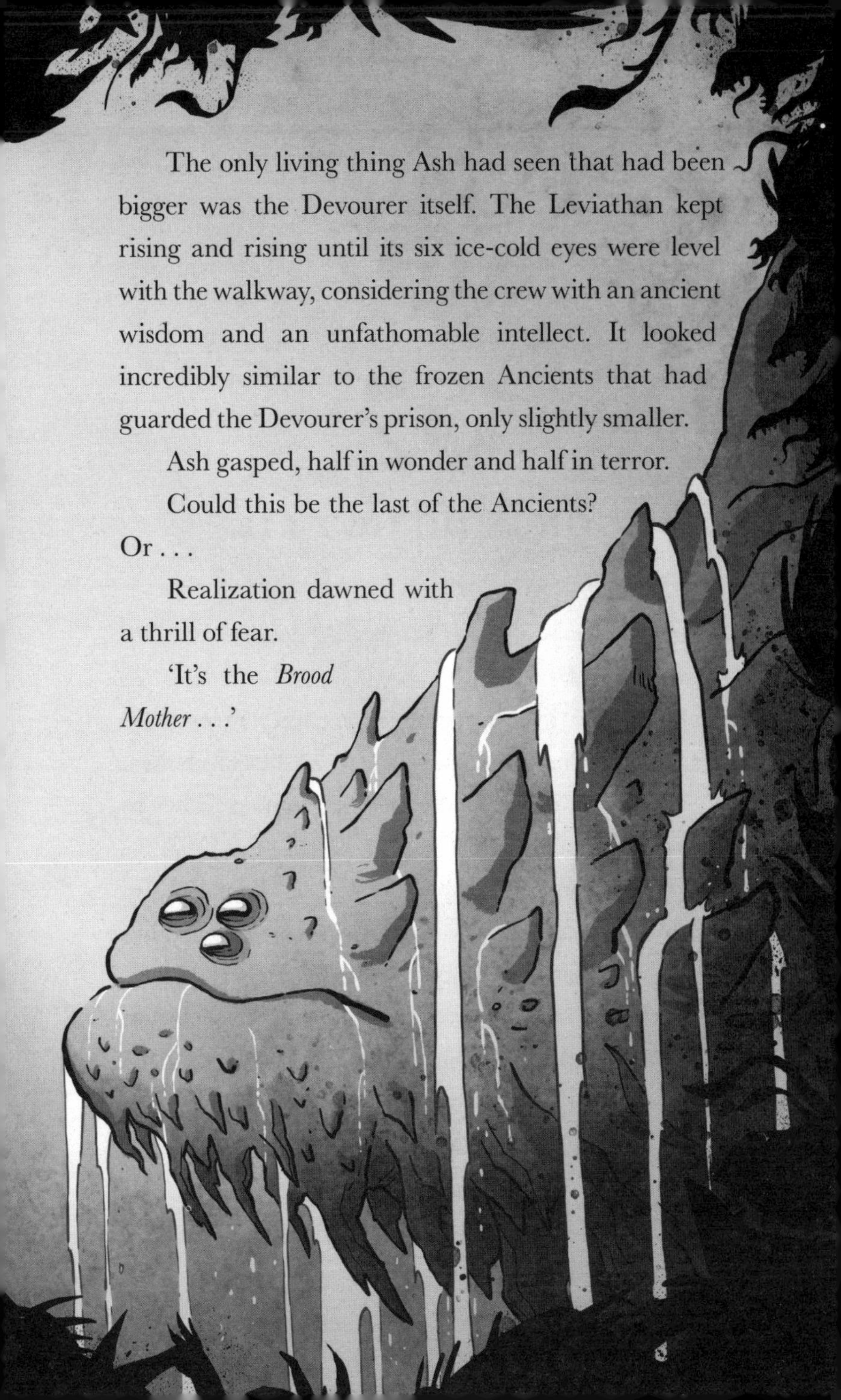

The only living thing Ash had seen that had been bigger was the Devourer itself. The Leviathan kept rising and rising until its six ice-cold eyes were level with the walkway, considering the crew with an ancient wisdom and an unfathomable intellect. It looked incredibly similar to the frozen Ancients that had guarded the Devourer's prison, only slightly smaller.

Ash gasped, half in wonder and half in terror.

Could this be the last of the Ancients?

Or . . .

Realization dawned with a thrill of fear.

'It's the *Brood Mother . . .*'

32

SONGS DO NOT LIE

'What the *heck* is a Brood Mother?!' Kailen asked, her bowstring taut.

'The one I've brought you to see,' Yanpa said calmly. 'A Leviathan as old as the ruins she calls home.'

'You set us up, you old crone!' Jed snarled. 'They're gonna kill us all!'

'Crone?! How dare you? I'm in the prime of my life!' Yanpa snapped. 'If you want *any* hope of defeating the World Eater, *child*, you must speak with her! And I'd recommend lowering your weapons. The Brood Mother is the closest thing to a leader the Leviathans have, and they're very protective of her.'

Ash's hairs stood on end as he looked up at the thousands of eyes staring back at them, glowing and fierce, almost *daring* them to make a move. Gathering his courage, Ash pushed his way out of the circle.

'Boy!' Tobu warned, pulling him back.

'Yanpa's right, we need to speak with her,' Ash insisted, trying to peel his hand away. 'This is something I have to do!'

Tobu didn't loosen his grip, eyeing Ash with worry.

'*Tobu*,' Ash said forcefully. He didn't need his protection. Not from this.

After a moment, Tobu relented.

Ash strode forward, looking up at the mountainous creature before him. Walking proved hard, his legs trembling so much they knocked into each other. As he walked, Ash Sang a Song of peace and friendship, hoping it would be enough to keep him from being squished.

The Brood Mother narrowed her eyes, sniffing Ash's scent, her breath as powerful as a gale, and just as cold. Ash could hear his heart pounding in his head and feel the weight of the responsibility that rested on his shoulders, so much that he barely had energy to be frightened. Under the Brood Mother's gaze, Ash felt incredibly insignificant, like an insect that had landed in the lair of a god.

With a high-pitched cry, a Shrieker launched itself from a ventilation shaft high above, swooping down into the cavern.

Scratch! Ash beamed, the weight on his shoulders lifting somewhat at the sight of his friend . . .

'*HUMAN WHELP, HATCHLING OF KIN-KILLER,*' Scratch announced to her brethren. '*BETRAYER OF TRUST.*'

. . . and the weight came crashing back down.

The Leviathans roared in anger. Ash gulped, wondering if this had been Scratch's over-elaborate plan to claim revenge all along.

'*LEVIATHAN ALLY!*' Scratch then cried, spreading her wings to slow her speed before landing deftly beside Ash. '*BRINGER OF PEACE. ALLIANCE OF BLADE AND BOW, TOOTH AND CLAW!*'

That's a bit better, Ash thought, sweat trickling down his back despite the cold.

'*We have been watching you, human hatchling,*' the Brood Mother Sang, her voice gentle and powerful at once, both elderly and full of life. She Sang more clearly than other Leviathans; or, at least, Ash found her Song easier to understand. '*You are not like others of your kin. We shall not kill you.*'

Ash breathed a sigh of relief. One of the Leviathans sighed with disappointment.

'*But peace?*' she boomed. '*My kin gather to hunt the Cursed One. To protect our world! But humans have shown no will to change. Still full of hate. Still full of violence!*'

The Leviathans let out a deafening bellow that shook the walkway, stone and ice tumbling down from the ceiling and splashing into the flood-lake.

'*Because we're* scared*!*' Ash responded, the calm of his Song-aura trembling into something wilder. '*We've been reacting to* your *violence! You don't think preying on us for a thousand years is enough punishment for the war?* You've *driven humans to this!*'

The Brood Mother roared, sending Ash stumbling back, afraid the cavern might cave in.

'*The darkness lives in you too, hatchling,*' the Brood Mother growled, her aura flaring red for just a second, her Song echoed by another roar from the swarm.

Ash gritted his teeth, recognizing the Dark Song writhing within him, stoked by his frustration. He took a deep breath, clenching his fists till his knuckles turned white.

OK . . . bad start . . .

He wished Rook was with him. She was much better at communicating with Leviathans than he was – he was still so new to this. What if he messed it all up?

Everyone was counting on him, everyone in the entire world!

'*We do not wish to punish humans*,' the Brood Mother continued. '*We defend against them. Past human treachery cannot repeat. We won't allow it!*'

'*But human-kin can't go on like this*,' Ash Sang, his Song-aura calmer – almost pleading. '*Soon there won't be any of us left! Stormbreaker –*'

At the mention of her name, the Leviathans erupted in screams of fury.

'*KINSLAYER! KINSLAYER! KILL HER! KILL! KILL! KILL!*'

'*What Stormbreaker's doing is wrong!*' Ash Sang over the chaos, his throat hoarse. '*But she's only fighting Leviathans because she feels like it's the only option human-kin have left! Your "defence" has done the opposite of what you wanted. History* is *repeating itself!*'

The Brood Mother growled. '*Kinslayer unearthed weapons that threaten Leviathans, but Devourer, World Eater, Cursed One – it threatens us all! Song Weavers released it! Humans – full of hate, full of violence!*'

'*I know!*' Ash's Song-aura turned a deep blue in despair. '*I know. But the Devourer is a Leviathan! It was your kind who unleashed it in the first place to win the war! This is both our faults!*'

Ash knew the argument was weak, and not the

words of a peace talk, but it's all he could think of to say in human-kin's defence.

'US?!'

The Brood Mother reeled back, her voice booming so fiercely Ash fell to the floor. Her aura turned jagged and threatening, her ice-cold eyes focusing on an archeomek device in front of the frost-heart. Ash recognized it as the same type of memory machine he'd used in the Endless Forest to hear his father's message. A stone sphere etched with the voices of the past sat snug and waiting within a hollow in the machine.

'Hear Song,' the Brood Mother urged. *'Discover truth.'*

Ash picked himself up and stumbled over to the device. What did she mean, *truth*? Whatever it was, Ash was positive he wasn't going to like it.

He looked back at his friends for strength. They were still huddled together, watching him with confusion. Of course, they weren't Song Weavers; they couldn't understand what was being said. Well, all except for Yanpa, who somehow seemed to have a firm grasp on what was happening. Jed looked particularly terrified, not used to being surrounded by Leviathans who weren't on the attack. Ash gave them what he hoped was a reassuring nod, though suspected was more of a fearful tremble, and then placed his hand over the small orb on the device.

A voice filled his head.

What message would you like to experience?

It was a female voice, speaking a long-forgotten language, but one Ash understood thanks to the fact he was hearing the Song etched into the sphere.

Songs are soul's voice, Ash remembered Rook had once explained to him. *Can be understood by any who know how to listen.*

Ash was somewhat taken aback – the other message-spheres had never given him any options!

'*Um . . . what . . . what is this place?*' Ash Sang into the sphere, a bit unsure. '*What were they doing with the Ancient's heart?*'

The sphere vibrated under his hand, growing warm to the touch, before a vision flooded Ash's mind.

*

A man and a woman, dressed in the unusual clothing of the World Before, stood on the very walkway Ash was on now.

A vast shape, mountainous in scale, shifted in the centre of the cavern. It moaned in pain, a deep rumble that shook the very foundations of the building. Tubes trailed from machines and stuck deep into its flesh, removing strange liquids from it and pumping stranger liquids in. It wailed a Song of such anguish that Ash could hardly bear it. The man and woman watched the process, grim-faced and intense.

'The transplant was a success?' the man asked, considering the huge frost-heart that floated in the machine, startlingly blue, its glow reflecting brightly off his face.

The woman nodded. 'The Ancient will be rebuilt to our vision. The artificial heart is weaker than we anticipated, however. It will need constant fuel to sustain itself. I recommend we run further tests to find a way to make it more self-sufficient.'

The man waved his hand dismissively. 'Isn't that what we created it for? To feed? To consume? What about the heart's Song? That's the true sign of success.'

The woman took a deep breath. 'The artificial heart will enable us to implant the Song we designed.'

'The Song that will bring this war to a swift and

decisive end.' The man smiled at that. 'It is a perfect weapon, fuelled by violence itself, strengthened by conflict and hate. The Leviathans may adapt to our tactics, but this weapon will evolve into war itself. Fighting it will only make it more determined, wounding it will only make it stronger. Nothing will stand in its way. Nothing will defeat it.'

Although the creature in the cavern was held in place by colossal vices, it managed to turn its incredible weight, and Ash's breath caught as he saw what it was. A Leviathan Ancient – but twisted and changed. It mewed in fear, crying out to its brethren, to anyone who would listen. Crying out for help, for mercy.

But help never came.

How could it, when the creature was hidden so deep behind human-kin borders?

The Ancient seemed to catch Ash's eyes, its giant white orbs desperate. Bile burned his throat as he watched in horror. He wanted desperately to help. But what could he do? He was a thousand years too late.

Slowly the Ancient's Song began to change. A new one was being burned into its false-heart, one of death and fury. A burning pain, a boiling rage, an unquenchable need to take revenge on a world that had wronged it. Its white pleading eyes turned red, its mutated, malformed body strained against its shackles, desperate to cause harm. Ash squeezed his eyes shut, unable to watch any more.

'*What – what is the Devourer's weakness?*' Ash asked the sphere.

The memory-vision blurred and started again.

'It is a perfect weapon,' the man repeated.

'*How do we fight it?*' Ash called out, panic rising. The memory reversed.

'Fighting it will only make it more determined, wounding it will only make it stronger,' the man boasted again.

'*HOW DO WE STOP IT?! THERE HAS TO BE A WAY!*'

Ash was screaming now, desperate. The vision began again, Ash utterly repulsed at the sight of it.

'This weapon will evolve into war itself . . .' the man said, the evil, despicable man. 'Nothing will stand in its way.'

Ash gulped, his throat raw.

'Nothing will defeat it.'

33

BLADE AND FANG

Ash snapped out of the vision, hope draining out of him. His friends had rushed to his side, concern etched on their faces.

'It . . . it was *us*,' Ash said, choked up.

He looked up at his stunned friends and caught Yanpa's eye. She gave him a sympathetic look that suggested she already knew. 'It was human-kin who created the Devourer, in the World Before . . . They captured an Ancient and brought it here where they . . . they *warped* it into something else. Into a *weapon*.'

'*Now you see*,' the Brood Mother rumbled in response to the truth. '*Song Weavers created weapon they could not control, and it destroyed them*.'

The Leviathans had fallen silent, as if in mourning for their fallen Ancient.

Ash tried to answer but found his voice had abandoned him. He swallowed, trying to clear his tightening throat.

'*Since the beginning, my kin wove our threads with the other races, but none so much as with humans,*' the Brood Mother Sang. '*With humans, we wove our Songs, our Souls! But human greed tore Weave in two. They hunted us for our hearts! Used them to feed their machines. Used machines to fight world. Our own friends, our trusted Song brethren!*'

This was all so world-shattering, Ash's mind could barely keep up.

'Humans used Leviathan hearts to *fuel* their machines?' he said, disbelieving.

'The things you call sunstones,' Yanpa said.

'Sunstones . . . are *hearts*?!' Yallah looked appalled. As appalled as Ash felt. He clutched at his sunstone pendant, desperate to hide it.

Yanpa nodded. 'It was when humans began hunting Leviathans for their hearts that the war ignited, a war that consumed the world . . . '

'*My poor kin* . . .' The Brood Mother swayed her head from side to side, indicating the silent Leviathans that surrounded her. Scratch had dipped her head, mewing gently. '*War changed them, changed their Song! Leviathan hearts once burned hot with joy. Now cold hate is all they know. I weep for them. They will never know the warmth of true Song.*'

Her aura was now broken and blue, as thin as morning mist. '*Humans took our trust and crushed it in claws of betrayal. We imprisoned humans in their Strongholds. History* cannot repeat. *But we have failed. The Cursed One is free.*'

The Leviathans howled as one.

Ash stood rooted to the spot, his mouth opening and closing, his head full of nothing but shame and sorrow. He took a step back, wanting to flee, but Scratch nudged him forward with her snout.

It was a small gesture, but one that filled him with

a sudden determination.

'*What human-kin have done, I know it's unforgivable. But . . . I'm asking for your forgiveness anyway. We aren't the same people who did those things, and we want to stop the Devourer as much as you do. Even Stormbreaker – my mother!*'

The Leviathans cried out in disbelief, all except for Scratch, who screamed for them to listen.

'*All this fighting has to end!*' Ash Sang over the noise, his aura weaving round the Brood Mother's pleadingly. '*We have to put the past behind us and join together, otherwise the Devourer eats us all! A wise yeti once told me: "Clinging to a painful past will only poison the present, but the future is still there to be made."*'

Ash sensed Tobu shift behind him.

The Brood Mother made a sound that shook the very mountain around them.

'*We were always stronger together. All the races, standing as one. It is balance. It is natural order.*' The Brood Mother moved closer to the frost-heart, eyeing it with devotion. '*This is our last hope. The Cursed One's true-heart. The only thing that can stop it now. Remind it of the thing it once was. Life still beats within. Its Song, though faded, still pulses. It can focus our Song, make it powerful beyond us.*'

Just like Elder Arrus had said it would, Ash remembered, his heart beating faster.

Maybe there was still a way to stop the Devourer!

'A heart is the source of Song, source of soul,' the Brood Mother explained. *'The Cursed One has a false-heart, shaped by human-kin hands. Its Dark Song is powerful, but its false-heart weak. Must always be feeding on souls to survive. Ever hungry. Ever devouring. Alone, this true-heart will not be enough to stop it. But joining our Songs together . . .?'*

'What Song would we have to Sing?' Ash asked.

'You will know it, just as you know your own Song. It is known to all, deep in our hearts. All Song Weavers, all Leviathans – true-heart will focus our power. Make us strong. Perhaps strong enough to seal Cursed One away once more. Cursed One is weakened from slumber. Will only get stronger. Now is the time. The only time we have.'

'The Song Weavers will help!' Ash's aura leaped, pulsing with energy. Hope was an incredible thing. Fragile but powerful. He Sang of the experiences he'd had, of how all Song Weavers shared the unexplainable connection to the Leviathans. Even though they feared them, Song Weavers knew – *felt* – a bond with the creatures that stretched back through time.

Solstice had already proved that living in peace with Leviathans was possible! Now it was time to go further . . .

The Brood Mother's aura swirled round Ash's.

'I see through eyes of my kin,' she Sang. *'Hear their Songs. I know what you say is true. Song Weavers not twisted by Cursed One's hate, still remember our soul-ties. But what of Kinslayer?'*

'Let me take the true-heart!' Ash begged. *'Stormbreaker will have to believe the truth if I show her this! She'll see we have to stop fighting if we want to survive!'*

'Take true-heart?' The Brood Mother's aura flickered, the Leviathans grumbling. *'I have guarded it for ages past . . .'*

'Without it, my mother will never stop fighting. It is the only thing that will convince her,' Ash Sang.

The Brood Mother was silent for a long moment, then Sang again.

'Very well. Take true-heart. It serves no purpose unless we Sing together as one.'

Ash's pulse quickened. *'So . . . you'll trust us? You'll join fang with blade?'*

'That is up to you. If humans can show a will to change, if humans willing to sacrifice themselves for the good of all, to heal wounds of past and stand together as one, then yes. Perhaps join fangs with blades, claws with bow.'

Ash felt the flame of his hope, so nearly snuffed out, reignite. Just the smallest flame, flickering in the wind, but there all the same.

'But know this,' the Brood Mother thundered. *'Leviathans* are *the world. We shall defend it until our last. Always we will protect world, whether that's* with *you –'* the Brood Mother narrowed her eyes – *'or* from *you.'*

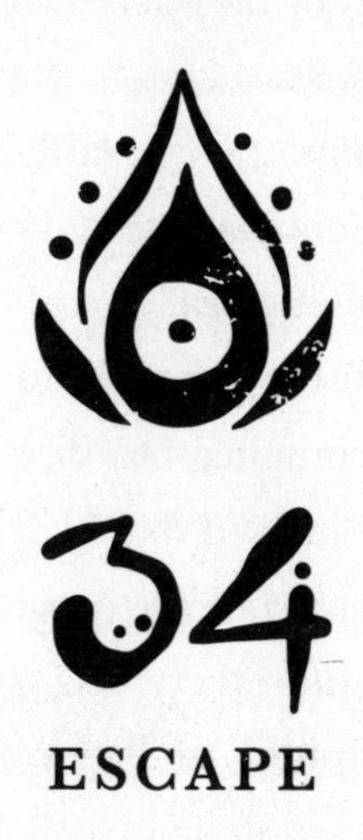

ESCAPE

Tobu's spear made short work of the wall of shimmering icicles that hid the way out. Pale moonlight poured in as he sliced through the frozen spikes, revealing the cold, unforgiving mountainside beyond.

'You mean, this door was here the whole flippin' time?!' Kailen groaned, the memory of their hard climb still fresh in her mind.

Twinge put an arm over her shoulders. 'We're Pathfinders, Kailen. Nothing can be too easy, remember?'

The Cradle had extended into a sprawling network of chambers and tunnels that burrowed through the mountain. Master Yanpa had guided them back to the base of the mountain, far from her temple, which was still surrounded by Wardens.

'We have to hurry,' Teya said, gazing at the sky. 'It'll be the new moon in four days – that's when the Devourer will reach Aurora!'

'If it's true that the Devourer is made stronger by violence, I'm just praying Stormbreaker hasn't been busy *blasting* it,' Yallah said darkly. 'I don't even wanna think what that thing would be capable of *powered up* . . .'

Ash had told the others everything he'd learned from the Brood Mother, and they were struggling as much as he was to comprehend it all. He clutched at the bundle of rags tied to his belt, the chill of the true-heart within biting his hands even through the layers of cloth. With the Brood Mother's permission, the crew had chipped away at the dead ice around it and had retrieved the living heart within.

'This is our best chance to stop the Devourer,' Ash said. 'We have to get it to my mum!'

'You really think it'll work?' Kailen asked.

'If the Pathfinders make peace with the Leviathans and allow them to join their Songs with the Song Weavers, I think so,' Ash said.

It has to . . .

'So all we gotta do is convince *Stormbreaker* to make friends with the *Leviathans*? I think knocking the Devourer out with our fists might be easier,' Yallah said, looking at Jed to see what he had to say about the

Commander he so adored. But Jed's mind was leagues away, still in shock at what they'd just witnessed.

'Why . . . why didn't they attack?' he murmured to himself. 'They had us surrounded! It just . . . it doesn't make sense!'

'Jed,' Yallah said not unsympathetically, 'the sooner you realize this kinda thing happens around Ash *all the time*, the easier it'll be for you.'

The sight of the *Frostheart* brought a smile to each and every one of the crew's faces. There it rested, moored exactly where they'd left it. Even Yanpa grinned, happy she'd managed to lead them to safety.

'Now go, all of you. I have to clear up the mess you made back at my temple.'

'You'll be all right?' Tobu asked.

Yanpa sniffed scornfully. 'The Wardens may be the ones with the spears, but they still fear my tongue.'

'As they should.' Tobu smiled.

The smiles weren't to last, however. The crew called out as they rushed towards the vessel but received no reply. Even more concerning was the fact that the ropes used to board the sleigh hung over the side, something Kob and Arla would never be so careless to allow.

'Kob? Arla?!' Kailen yelled, scaling the rope as fast as she could, Ash and the others right behind.

'Wait!' Tobu called suddenly, his ears pricked, but Ash ignored him, scrambling over the side.

There, alone on the empty deck, sat a yeti warrior.

His eyes were closed in meditation, his muscular back dead straight, his hands resting on the spear that lay flat over his crossed legs. Tobu took a sharp intake of breath as he leaped over the side and saw who was waiting for him.

'Tobu,' the mysterious yeti said, his voice deep as a drumbeat. Opening his eyes, he rose to his full height. The yeti was even larger than Tobu, but where Tobu was the epitome of composure, everything about this yeti radiated violence. His eyes burned with a cold fury, his horns and fangs were wicked and deadly, his fur painted with blood-red tattoos. Even the hairs of his mane looked sharp as blades. 'I'm surprised to see you again.'

Tobu's eyes widened.

'Start the enjin,' he said to the crew, voice strained, as he stepped forward. 'No matter what happens, get the *Frostheart* away from here.'

'T-Tobu . . .?' Ash asked, voice edged with fear.

Kailen, Yallah and Teya backed up towards the upper deck, never turning away from the armoured yeti, who watched them without concern.

The door to the hold suddenly slammed open. Three Wardens emerged, blocking the staircase and throwing Kob and Arla on to the deck.

'There's nowhere to go,' the big yeti said. 'You're surrounded.'

As he spoke, armed Wardens emerged like ghosts from the trees and rocks along the cliffs that overlooked the *Frostheart.*

'There's *hundreds* of them.' Jed gasped, the whites of his eyes glinting in the dim light.

The Pathfinders shrank back into a huddle as their sleigh was encircled. Tobu gritted his teeth, clearly furious he'd walked into a trap.

'Now . . . now look here, friend,' Jed said, raising

his hands, their shakes betraying his nerves. 'We ain't here for a fight. In fact, you caught us just as we were leavin' your, may I say, *lovely* lands . . .'

'Let them go, Temu,' Yanpa demanded, using her staff to vault up on to the deck.

Ash's breath caught in his throat.

Temu? Tobu's son, Temu? It couldn't be – he'd died years ago!

Or . . . or *had* he? Ash thought back to Yanpa's words . . .

Sometimes I think all three of them were lost that day, she had said. *Tobu, certainly, is not the same yeti he once was.*

Had she meant Temu was not the same caring yeti he once was either? The young yeti who believed in peace between yeti and human-kin? Judging from the look of hatred that burned in Temu's eyes, Ash suspected that was a safe guess.

'Master Yanpa,' Temu said with a cruel smile. 'My Wardens searched the entire temple for you. I was beginning to think you'd abandoned us.'

'I'm a busy yeti, Mountain's Ward,' Yanpa replied. '*Someone* has to figure out how to save us all from disaster.'

'And so you'd follow this traitor and turn your back on your own kind?' Temu pointed his spear towards Tobu.

'Traitor!' a Warden shouted, before Yanpa could answer.

'Traitor!' yelled another.

'Traitor! Traitor! Traitor!'

The gathered warriors banged their spears with every chant, over and over again, all eyes on Tobu, fierce and angry.

'TRAITOR! TRAITOR! TRAITOR!'

Ash had seen Tobu shrug off terrible attacks as though they were snow off his back. He'd seen him roar in the face of a Spearwurm without so much as flinching. But every time the word was chanted, Tobu recoiled as though he'd been struck. Ash might have recently discovered some uncomfortable truths about his guardian's past, but this was almost unbearable to watch.

But what could he do for Tobu against such strength and numbers?

'Temu, the humans don't have to be our enemy. You *know* this,' Tobu said. He looked beseechingly at the younger yeti. 'Please . . . my son.'

Temu's jaw twitched.

Although his every tendon had been taut as though straining against a body yearning for carnage, Temu had remained calm.

But Tobu's words snapped something within him.

Temu cracked his neck.

And then he roared like a beast.

35

LIKE FATHER, LIKE SON

'YOU ARE NO FATHER TO ME!' Temu crossed the distance between them in a single leap, taking Tobu by surprise and cracking him under the jaw. 'AND YOU WILL NOT RUN AWAY THIS TIME!'

Tobu stumbled back into Ash and the others, who drew their weapons to defend their friend.

'Don't!' Tobu cried, just as Temu swung his spear.

Tobu ducked under the blade, rolling towards the middle of the deck to take the fight away from the others. He drew his own spear just in time to parry another of Temu's strikes. Each yeti pressed against their spear haft, trying to overpower the other.

'You let Mother *die*!' Temu snarled. 'You let them *kill* her!'

He shifted his weight and shoved Tobu, slashing

his spear after him. Tobu fell back into a defensive position, some white fur sliced from his mane slowly floating down to the deck.

'Temu, come to your senses,' Yanpa demanded. 'This is no way for a Path Master to behave!'

But her voice was drowned out as the Wardens began to bang their spear butts on to the ground as one, the sound shaking Ash's bones.

THRUM. THRUM. THRUM.

The thumps thundered through the valley like its very own heartbeat.

The Pathfinders could only watch the duelling warriors, helpless and aghast.

'What happened that day was an accident,' Tobu cried over the noise. 'There was nothing either of us could've done to save her!'

Temu stalked around Tobu like a predator.

'I refuse to hurt you, Temu,' said Tobu, and to prove the point he stepped down on the butt of his spear and wrenched it upwards, snapping the spearhead from the haft.

'It wasn't enough to run away from your own son – you must dishonour yourself by refusing him a duel as well?' Temu grunted, clutching his own spear tight. 'My father the COWARD!'

He dived forward, Tobu only just parrying his attack with his broken haft. Tobu ducked and dodged, his movements strong and deliberate. Temu, on the other hand, fought with a furious energy, his movements wild and animalistic, his strikes almost too fast to keep track of.

Ash took a shuddering breath, his thoughts whirling with each clack of spear against spear.

Run away? Had Tobu not been exiled, like he'd said?

'You left your people defenceless! Without a Mountain's Ward! Temu roared. 'You abandoned us!

You abandoned *me*!'

'You . . . you *left* him?!' Ash snapped, his voice louder than he'd expected.

Tobu had his back to Ash, but he saw him flinch at the accusation.

A chill anger bloomed in Ash's skull.

'How *could* you?!' Ash tried to rush forward, but the others pulled him back. 'Do you have any idea what it *feels* like to be abandoned by the ones that are meant to take care of you?'

'Even the human whelp sees how you've wronged me,' Temu sneered.

'I was a fool,' Tobu admitted. 'But you were never like me, Temu. You were kind. *Forgiving.* Like your mother. This person I see before me, this is not you, my son.'

'I knew *nothing* back then!' Temu hissed. 'But I have learned the truth, and I suppose I have you to thank for that, Father!'

'I was weak.' Tobu's voice was strained. 'Losing my life-mate was hard enough without having to witness my son become the very thing he had always stood against. I left because I could not bear to watch hatred consume you!'

'Anything I am is what you made me!' Temu growled, cutting down with his spear.

'And it breaks my heart, every waking moment,' Tobu said, dodging out of the way.

But the attack was a feint. Temu dropped into a sweeping kick, taking Tobu off his feet. He smashed his spear butt hard into Tobu's breastplate, bringing a gasp of pain. Tobu rolled aside from another blow, pulling Temu's spear away with his tail and kicking him hard in the shin, using the momentum to push himself into a backwards roll and on to his feet.

But Ash could see Tobu was in trouble. He was tiring, whereas Temu seemed only to be getting started. But what could Ash do? He couldn't fight a yeti!

Does he even deserve your help, whispered a dark voice in Ash's head, *after what he did to his own son? He's no different to your parents. To all those who hate Song Weavers!*

Frozen by indecision, Ash did nothing.

'How far the mighty fall,' Temu growled, cracking Tobu round the back of the head. Tobu stumbled, his breaths ragged.

Ash winced, his mind spinning. Since becoming his guardian, Tobu had been Ash's shield. The one constant in a life full of uncertainties. Always honourable. Always dependable. Always there to stand for what was right in the face of injustice.

Now to learn the truth? That Tobu was just as . . . *flawed* as the rest of them?

Temu jabbed, slashed and lunged, Tobu only just managing to evade the flashing blade, forced back by such furious aggression.

'You were once the Mountain's Ward, our greatest protector,' Temu continued, crunching Tobu in the belly.

Tobu had always seemed as unbending as a mountain. Ash could barely believe he was seeing him being beaten. Through all his whirling anger and confusion, Ash felt a pang in his heart.

'You once defended us from the humans. You once warned us all of their greed and savagery!' Temu whipped his spear butt upwards, Tobu's jaw cracking from the impact. 'But now . . .?' Temu swung around Tobu and kicked him hard in the side, sending him sprawling across the deck. 'Now you scrounge at the humans' feet like some lowly pet! You dishonour me!

You dishonour *all* yeti!'

Clenching his teeth, Tobu struggled up on to his elbows. 'My . . . my only regret is not listening to you both. Amula was right. *You* were right, before hatred clouded your heart!'

'Do *not* say my mother's name,' Temu warned. 'You have no right!'

'I have lived with the human-kin,' Tobu said, loud enough for all the gathered Wardens to hear. 'I have seen first-hand how dangerous the teachings of our Path truly are. Human-kin are no different to us, capable of both terrible cruelty and selfless acts of kindness!'

'Human-*kin*?' Temu laughed without joy. 'They are not *your* kin. *We* are, and you turned your back on us! You truly have been fooled by human trickery. Do you forget how they killed my mother?'

Temu paced, his voice rising with anger. 'Have you forgotten all our lessons, those nights when all you could lecture me about was the savagery of humans? They are weak! They are selfish! They will never change, and they will never be on our side!' He pointed to the *Frostheart* crew. 'And they *shall* be executed for trespassing on our sacred land!'

Ash's heart skipped a beat as the Wardens upon the cliff raised their bows, preparing to unleash a deadly volley upon the Pathfinders.

'Is this what our great Wardens have become?' Tobu bellowed. 'All the races of the world once looked to us as protectors! We were the very definition of honour! But now, while the human-kin risk everything they have to fight the World Eater that threatens us all, the Wardens prepare to strike them while they're down! Like cowards! Like thieves in the dark! *That* is the true dishonour to our people!'

The Wardens hesitated. Just like at the temple, Ash could sense that the aggressive changes Temu had brought to the Warden's Path were not something they all were comfortable with.

'Do not forget what the humans did to us,' Temu insisted. 'Left unchecked, they'll always be a danger to us all!'

Despite their doubts, the voice of their leader stirred many Wardens to action. They were disciplined warriors, oath-bound to follow orders. They raised their bows once more.

'NO!' Tobu roared, scrambling to his feet and dashing to shield his friends.

Temu rammed into Tobu's side, almost toppling him over. With a growl, Tobu locked horns with his son, driving his heels into the deck in a desperate effort to hold him back.

An almighty scream split the night.

Large dark shapes tore down the mountain pass. Ash watched in amazement as a swarm of Shriekers landed on the cliffs in front of the Wardens, blocking their line of sight. The yeti staggered back, confused, the Shriekers poised and ready. Neither side made the first move, unwilling to attack those who had, until then, been old allies.

Temu and Tobu were still horn-locked in a contest of strength. Tobu grunted as his feet began to slip, his legs trembling.

Ash felt sick. What could he do? What *should* he do?!

Tobu had done wrong. He'd allowed hate to get the better of him, just like everyone else in the world.

But there *was* a difference.

While his mother, Shaard and Temu were still obsessed with revenge, Tobu had steered his course away from hatred. He'd overcome it. What made Tobu different to everyone else?

He'd been willing to change.

Ash was snapped out of his thoughts by a terrible crack that echoed off the mountain.

Temu had broken a horn right off Tobu's head.

With a cry of agony, Tobu crashed to the deck, Temu raining his fists down upon him, roaring in blind rage.

'STOP IT!' Ash screamed.

Suddenly thoughts of the Devourer, of the true-heart and his parents didn't seem important. All that mattered was saving Tobu. He charged into Temu's side.

It was like running into a boulder.

Ash was thrown to the ground, his back jolting painfully. Temu spun round, grabbing Ash by the neck and lifting him high off the deck. Ash struggled, his breath stolen, his fingers desperately grasping at Temu's massive hand, but he might as well have been trying to move mountains.

'NO!' Tobu reached out a trembling hand, blood trickling from his jaw. 'Temu, he's just a child!'

Temu's breath was hot against Ash's face. He stared at him in wide-eyed fury – or . . . or was it puzzlement?

'Please don't hurt him,' Ash said, choking.

'You would risk your life for this *traitor*?' Temu asked, spittle flying from his mouth. 'Even knowing what he *did*?'

'He is . . . the only one . . . who looked after me . . .' Ash croaked, throat burning, lungs desperate for air that just would not come. 'He didn't abandon me . . .'

Through his dimming vision, Ash caught sight of Tobu's eyes, wide and glassy and full of fear.

But not fear for his own life.

Fear of losing *him*.

Tears stung Ash's eyes as his face grew hot, his vision turning black.

'I . . . love . . . him . . .' Then Ash gasped, using up the last air he had left.

YETI GUARDIAN

Pain shot through Ash's legs as he hit the deck hard. His eyesight returned in dazzling spots as he coughed and spluttered. Craning his neck, he saw Temu towering above him, staring at Ash in shock.

'You . . . you *care* for him? A *yeti* . . .'

As the ringing in his ears stopped, Ash became aware of Master Yanpa's voice.

'I think you've certainly impressed on us how strong and powerful you are, *Master Temu.* But if you're quite finished strutting about, perhaps we can get to the small matter of the World Eater?'

Ash crawled towards Tobu. He looked hurt. Really hurt.

Apparently for the first time, Temu noticed the Shriekers perched on the cliff, screeching a warning at any yeti who looked like they were about to attack the humans.

'Why have they turned against us?' Temu asked.

'Because they see that we cannot save the world alone,' Yanpa said. 'Have you met the World Eater, by the way? It's the demon currently tearing our world to shreds while we bicker and argue – I do believe you two would get along *famously*.'

'My scouts tell me it was the human Song Weavers who released the World Eater,' Temu growled.

'And it is these human Pathfinders who are trying to stop it! Your scouts also tell you how our forests are withering with rot,' Yanpa said. 'I'm sure you don't mean to accuse the humans of that too?'

Without warning, she hurled her staff at a nearby tree, but rather than bouncing off the tough bark, the staff head sank deep into the trunk with a sickening squelch. The gathered warriors gasped in horror. The tree was black and rotten inside, lines of slime stringing from Yanpa's staff as it fell free.

'The blight has even affected the Oath Bloom itself. The World Eater's Song burrows into the World Weave like a cancer, corrupting all it touches. It is everything we stand against, and it is killing our world, whether you want to admit it or not.'

Temu's eyes widened at the disturbing sight.

'While it lives, nothing else can,' Yanpa continued. 'I'm pleading with you, Temu. Call off this foolish invasion and join forces with the humans. Together we may yet free the world from this evil, and save us all.'

Temu furrowed his brows, clearly wracked with indecision. He turned to his Wardens for support, but found none, instead finding something in their eyes he'd never seen before.

Fear.

'Please remember your mother's words,' Tobu groaned. 'Remember what you used to believe. There is . . . good in the humans, if only we look . . .'

Tobu held out the carving he'd made of Temu – of the kind-hearted son he once knew. Temu blinked at the sight of it, his frown softening.

'They have made mistakes . . . but be careful . . . not to make the same mistakes yourself,' Tobu continued. 'We yeti barely remember why we are even supposed to hate humans. The great war was a thousand years ago. We do not need to keep stoking its flames. Patience . . . peace . . . balance. *That* is the true yeti way.'

Temu clenched his fists. For a terrible moment, Ash feared he was about to strike Tobu a killing blow. Instead, he opened his hands, flexing his blood-stained knuckles.

'Take him away,' he ordered the Wardens, gesturing towards Tobu. Then he turned to Jed, who stared back boldly. 'Leave this place. If you ever return, I will kill you all myself.'

'Tobu,' Ash said, placing a hand on his mentor's bloody fur.

'Go . . .' Tobu coughed, ragged and raw. 'Get the true-heart . . . to your mother . . .'

'I don't want to leave you,' Ash said through burning tears. 'He'll kill you!'

Tobu forced a smile. 'It is . . . no less than I deserve.'

'No!' Ash sobbed, gripping tighter to Tobu's arm.

'Somewhere . . . trapped beneath all that hatred . . . my son still lives. I need . . . to try to reach him.'

Tobu managed to place his own hand on top of Ash's, its familiar leathery texture drawing a shuddering sob from Ash's throat.

'Thank you, boy . . .' Tobu said, squeezing his hand. It was a squeeze of reassurance, of protection.

Of love.

'For what? I couldn't help you, I'm useless!'

'For giving me a second chance.'

The Wardens hoisted Tobu up by his arms, the big yeti hanging limply between them.

'Please *don't*!' Ash begged, reaching out for his guardian. 'Don't take him . . .'

'Don't worry. You don't need me,' Tobu tried to reassure Ash as the Wardens dragged him away. 'If anyone can stop the Devourer . . . it's you.'

Temu looked on, silent, before turning his back and leaping over the side of the sleigh.

Helpless, Ash could only watch through tear-blurred eyes as his loyal guardian was taken away from him.

The yeti he'd once been so afraid of. The yeti he'd once tried to escape from.

The yeti he would do anything to have back.

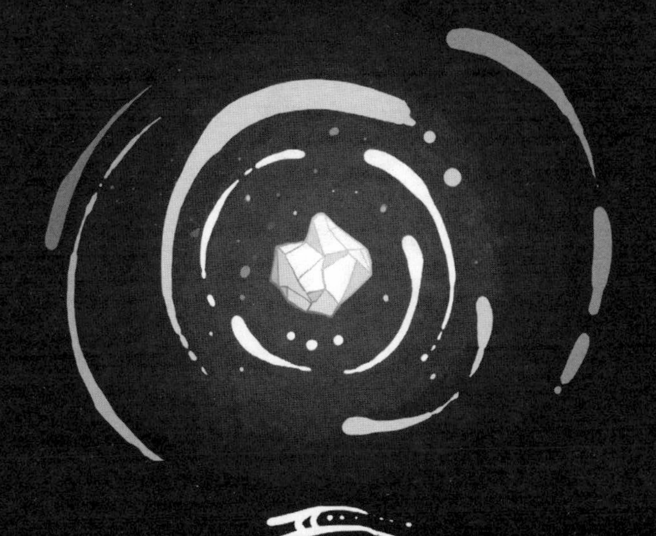

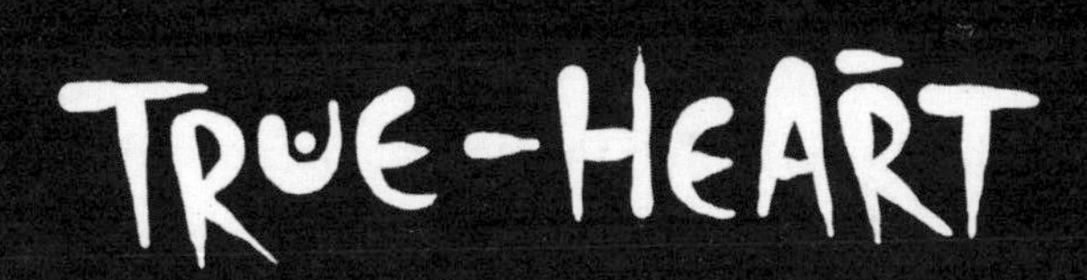
TRUE-HEART

37.

THE NEW MOON

Time was running out.

For three days, the *Frostheart* had torn across the snow plains between the World's Spine Mountains and Aurora, moving with all haste to come to the great Stronghold's aid before the new moon arrived – and with it the Devourer.

Everyone was busy. The *Frostheart* needed to be in the best possible shape for the battle to come, so all hands were on deck. Ash had been tasked with dismantling empty barrels, the wood of which Kailen and Kob were using to mend sleigh damage. He worked alone at the prow of the sleigh, the memory of Tobu being dragged away repeating over and over in his mind.

Despite his injuries, all that had mattered to Tobu

was Ash's safety. He'd offered his life to ensure the *Frostheart* crew could escape.

And they'd left him behind.

Left him to Temu's vengeance. Who knew what he would do to Tobu? Who knew if Tobu was even still alive?

Ash gritted his teeth, a turbulent storm of anger and confusion swirling within his heart. He hadn't felt this lonely since the Fira, and back then the pain of losing real friends had been unknown to him.

The world felt hollow and empty, and he was powerless to change it.

As if mocking Ash's distress, the Devourer's Song rose in volume. It was much louder down here, away from the mountains, and it grew in strength the closer they got to Aurora. It sizzled under the sounds of the world, gnawing away at the spirits of all who heard it.

Putting his hand to his side, Ash felt the radiant chill of the true-heart seeping through its cloth wrappings.

This is our only hope now. It has *to work.*

'All right there, kid?'

Jed's voice snapped Ash out of his gloomy thoughts. The captain sat down beside him, apparently considering his next words carefully.

'Seems I owe you an apology,' he said to Ash's

surprise. 'Turns out that frost-heart thingy was real after all. I was wrong to . . . well, ridicule you, back at the Ghost Stones. You, the crew, even the Leviathans . . . y'all saved our lives. You may have got us into that mess in the first place, but you got us through it, like you said you would. Clear I misjudged y'all, an' I'm sorry fer that.'

Ash prised a nail out of the barrel.

'It's OK,' he said. He wished Jed would go away, but he seemed unsatisfied with Ash's forgiveness. Probably he sensed that Ash hadn't really meant it.

'It's just, all a' this . . .' Jed gestured, his arms wide. 'All I've seen with you folks. It goes against everythin' I've ever known, everythin' I've ever been told . . .'

'"Old wounds scar deep."' Ash felt another stab of hurt as he quoted Tobu.

'Right.'

'It takes some getting used to,' Ash said after some time.

Jed nodded. He looked at Scratch, who lay curled up on the main deck, snoring gently, and shook his head, as if still unable to believe he'd allowed her to come aboard. Scratch was going to act as an ambassador of sorts, to show Stormbreaker that the Leviathans were offering an alliance.

'Well,' Jed said, chuckling, 'this is either gonna

convince everybody, or we'll never be able to set foot in a Stronghold again.'

'That's if there's any Strongholds left after all this,' Ash said quietly. 'And even though we have Scratch *and* the true-heart, I still don't know if Mum will believe us.'

Truth be told, Ash was dreading seeing his mother again. The thought of trying to convince her to side with the Leviathans gave him a headache. There was also the small matter of the crew's disobedience to consider. The last time they'd seen Stormbreaker, they'd been kidnapping her only son. Ash couldn't imagine she'd be *too* happy to see them again.

Jed gave Ash a sideways glance. 'You should give yer mum some credit, kid.'

'She hates Leviathans too much to listen,' Ash murmured.

'The Commander, she's been through the wars. Literally. But she's done it all for the good a' humankin. An' fer that, perhaps she deserves a little trust?'

'You trust her, but what about us Song Weavers?' Ash asked. 'Pathfinders *choose* to fight. Song Weavers have no choice.'

Jed pulled his head back, thinking on that. 'I know she can be . . . *difficult*, but she's had to harden her heart to be strong for the rest of us. She loves the Strongholds, an' would give everythin' to see 'em all survive an' prosper. But that don't mean she don't love you too.'

Ash caught his finger on a splinter.

'We've got the proof she needed. We found the heart. The wurms – sorry, *'viathans* – are willin' to give us a chance. But none a' that matters. She'll listen to us cos *you're* her *son*.'

Ash looked up at that. Jed flashed him a grin.

'An' cos she respects me so darn much, a' course. Take it from someone who knows her better 'n most,' he said, getting to his feet and placing a hand on Ash's shoulder. 'I know it ain't easy, but try givin' her a chance. I'm glad I gave you one.'

Ash blinked as he watched the captain leave.

Had Jed just given him some good advice?

Ash found it hard to get over what his mother had done to him and his friends, but he could hardly preach about forgiveness and understanding if he didn't try to do the same. Temu had crossed borders into enemy lands just to prove his father wrong, and, though well intentioned, it had ended in disaster. Ash had to rise above hate. If any of this were going to work, he had to learn to forgive.

'Oh, and, Ash?' Jed said, turning back. 'People may see you Song Weavers as somethin' to be feared, but after what I've seen you do, I'll always see you first and foremost as a loyal Pathfinder.'

Ash smiled.

Jed gave him a nod, before jumping as Scratch snorted in her sleep.

IN THE NICK OF TIME

Aurora stood as defiant as ever, its gleaming spires rising majestically from behind its massive walls. It truly was the jewel of the Snow Sea, a monument to human-kin's will to survive.

Thankfully the Devourer was nowhere to be seen, though judging from the deep darkness clouding the sky on the southern horizon and the oppressive, soul-crushing Song growing stronger by the minute, it wasn't far away.

As the *Frostheart* approached, Teya spotted a handful of sleighs sitting stationary on the plain before Aurora's outer wall, their enjins silent.

'Carrying supplies for the defence, I reckon,' she reported from the crow's nest.

'So why they just sittin' there, sails flappin' useless

in the wind?' Jed asked, gazing at the unmoving sleighs with concern.

He didn't have to wait long for an answer.

Four Wraith sleighs slipped like shadows from behind some ice hills. Two came from either side, racing to cut off the *Frostheart*'s route to the outer wall's southern gate.

'Leviathans take 'em!' Kailen cursed. 'It's a blockade. They're stoppin' reinforcements gettin' to Aurora!'

'We have to get past 'em,' Kob grunted. 'If the Pathfinders aren't warned not to attack the Devourer, we're all finished!'

'Can we outrun 'em?' Jed called to Yallah, who was already turning dials on the sunstone enjin.

'Haven't got much choice but to try!'

She pulled hard on a lever, the crew bracing themselves as the *Frostheart* surged forward. Snow trailed behind them like plumes of white smoke as they sped towards the gap between the black sleighs.

The gap that was getting smaller by the second.

'We're not gonna make it!' Ash cried. The Wraith sleighs were built for battle and much faster than the *Frostheart*.

Jed slammed his fist against the side rail. 'Everyone, to arms! We're gonna have to fight our way through!

Whatever happens, we *have* to reach Aurora!'

Kob and Kailen rushed to man the bolt-throwers. Ash spun round, expecting to find Tobu's reassuring bulk behind him as he always did. His belly gave a lurch when all he saw was empty space. Doing his best to muster his courage and do his mentor proud, Ash fumbled an arrow on to his bow, hands trembling.

Four sleighs against one? We don't stand a chance!

Scratch growled deep in her throat, desperate to take wing and attack. But she knew as well as Ash that, at the first sight of her, the Wraiths would use the Devourer's Dark Song to steal her mind and turn her against the *Frostheart.*

The *Frostheart* roared past the motionless Pathfinder sleighs and Ash saw, to his horror, their crews dead upon the decks, riddled with black-feathered arrows.

'*Spirits!*' Ash whispered, taking cover to try to avoid a similar fate.

'Steady . . .' Jed warned as the Wraith sleighs drew closer. 'Steady . . .'

Ash swallowed. He tried to think of Tobu instructing him to take deep breaths.

The Wraiths screamed forward, the ghost-like figures aiming their poison-tipped arrows.

'Steady . . . NOW!'

The crew rose to fire.

Only to see the Wraith sleighs make a sudden turn, wheeling round and racing back towards the hills.

'Whuh?' Twinge said.

'This some dirty Wraith trick?' Jed asked. 'I know we're pretty intimidatin' but . . .'

'Don't think it's us they're frightened of,' Kob said just as Teya yelled, 'Sleighs! Right behind us!'

The crew rushed to the stern.

There weren't just *sleighs* behind them. There was an entire *fleet*!

Three gigantic craft trundled along the plain, so large their timbers groaned under their weight, their shadows stretching off into the far distance. Wooden huts and cabins were crammed closely together on multiple tiered levels held up by huge tree-sized supports.

They're like moving Strongholds, Ash thought in wonder.

Around them, a forest of masts rose up to the sky, holding aloft a sea of sails, while huge wind-powered turbines drove the vessels forward. Dozens of battle-sized vessels darted in between the mobile fortresses like fish, each manned by crews of warriors who whooped and cheered as the Wraiths fled.

Ash strained his eyes and recognized the star-embroidered cloaks of the warriors, the way they wore their hair half shaved.

'It's the Drifters!' he cried with joy. 'The Drifters are here!'

The crew cheered, Kailen so relieved she even allowed Twinge to take her by the arms and dance round her in circles. The others waved eagerly to the allies who'd just saved their lives.

Yallah and Kob quickly threw a large canvas cover over Scratch so the sight of her didn't cause panic. She wriggled beneath it, Singing a Song of annoyance.

'*It's just till we get to Aurora*,' Ash reassured her, petting the cloth and trying to encourage her to be still.

One of the smaller Drifter vessels had pulled up close beside the *Frostheart*. A figure stood proud at the side rail, her cloak fluttering in the wind, her hair whipping in front of her face like a hero from legend.

'In trouble again?' she called.

'No more than normal,' Yallah called back, laughing.

The biggest smile spread across Ash's face as his belly did a flip of joy.

He didn't think he'd ever been so happy to see someone in his life. It was Lunah. It was his best friend.

And she'd brought the Convoy with her.

PROOF

Aurora, the most spectacular Stronghold in all the Snow Sea, was built within the hollow mountain of an extinct volcano. It was defended by two mighty walls that surrounded the mountain in huge concentric circles, much like the rings of an archery target, but dozens of leagues apart and over a hundred feet high. Throughout its long history, its walls had never been breached. And as Ash gazed up at the hundreds of archeoweapons bristling atop the stalwart battlements, it was tempting to believe they never would be.

But he had seen what the Devourer could do.

The wall defenders welcomed the Convoy through the southern gate with thunderous applause, as overjoyed as those aboard the sleighs that they'd made it in time to help protect the Stronghold.

And it seemed they weren't the first reinforcements to have arrived.

The vast snow plain between the inner and outer wall was crowded with an army of vessels, even larger than the fleet that had been lost in the Rend. The Convoy fell in line with the Pathfinder fleet, which had been strengthened by the sleighs kept back in Aurora. Next to them was a large force of the clanking, smoke-spewing contraptions of the vulpis. Though they looked rickety, they were heavily armoured and armed to the teeth. Flanking the vulpis was a fleet of hulking sleighs made from a peculiar patchwork of hide armour and bone.

'Who are they?' Ash asked Kob.

'The mursu.' Kob's moustache twitched as he smiled. 'Looks like Stormbreaker's been as good as her word – she's gathered our allies together!'

Not all of them . . . Ash thought, thinking of the Leviathans. *Not yet* . . .

He had to admit, though, the fleet his mother had gathered to defend Aurora was impressive indeed. Though that didn't stop his guts from tying themselves into knots. They now knew the Devourer was strengthened by violence. If this . . . *armada* were to attack it, who knew how powerful it might become?

They had to stop it from happening. And that

meant a tricky conversation with his mother . . .

The *Frostheart* docked next to the *Kinspear* at the long stone wharf that ran along the entire base of the outer wall. The Drifter sleigh that Lunah rode drew up behind.

Lunah disembarked, followed by a man, a woman and two teens who bore a striking resemblance to her. She ran at the *Frostheart* crew full pelt, leaping into a hug that nearly took both Ash and her over the edge of the wharf.

'You're aliiiiiiiive!' she squealed, pulling away to examine Ash closely. 'You've barely changed at all!'

'Well, I mean . . . it's only been three weeks.'

'I guess.' Lunah shrugged. 'Thought you might at least have a bit of a beard by now.'

'But what about you?' Ash asked eagerly. 'Your Proving – is it over?'

'Oh, that ol' thing?' Lunah looked at her nails. 'Set out from the Convoy on my lonesome? Check. Charted a new location on the map? Uh, that's a check. Returned to the Convoy? Yeah, completed that, whatever.' A smile crept on to her face and she suddenly leaped up and down, unable to keep up the act any longer. 'Yer only lookin' at a fully fledged Drifter navigator!'

'Lunah, that's amazing!' Ash laughed, jumping with her.

'Amazin' ent half of it,' said a familiar man, beaming. Ash recognized the Drifter who'd asked Lunah to join the search for the Convoy back at the Ghost Stones. 'Not only did she return to the Convoy, she's the one who found it! The two sleighs Stormbreaker sent out to find it couldn't agree on where to look. One headed north, an' are still up there lookin' fer all we know. But Lunah stuck to her instincts. She knew how our people think better 'n any of us. She knew how to read the signs, the stars, the whole lot. Lo and behold – the Convoy were in the Ashlands, just like she reckoned. A better bit of navigatin' I ent seen.'

The Drifters behind Lunah grinned with pride.

'Tha's my girl!' said a tall friendly-looking man as he scooped Lunah up into a hug.

Lunah's dad, Ash realized. *And this must be her family!*

The world suddenly felt a bit more whole again, a bit more as it was supposed to be. Ash even started to think that, with Lunah there, they might even succeed in stopping the Devourer. But to do that, they had to act fast.

'Touchin' though this is, we gotta move, kid,' Jed said, sweeping past.

'Who's *that*?' Lunah asked, squirming free of her father.

'I wish I could stop and explain,' Ash said, truly meaning it, 'but we need to get to Stormbreaker, fast!'

'But – my folks!' Lunah said, gesturing at the group behind her. 'I gotta introduce you!'

'I really want to, but –' Ash started, just as Scratch let out an anxious hiss from under her canvas cover. The eyes of the Drifters widened at the sound.

'Ah.' Lunah blinked. 'Another one of *those* adventures, huh?'

'You know, run of the mill.'

Master Podd nodded.

'Best be off then, eh?' Lunah suggested.

'Best,' Kailen agreed.

Without wasting another second, the *Frostheart*

crew boarded one of the many creaky wooden lifts for the journey to the top of the wall, some hundred and twenty paces above, Lunah's puzzled family following close behind.

The wall was packed, a large crowd watching with grim faces as huge cranes hauled massive archeoweapons up the battlements. Scattered among the throng of Pathfinders and Aurora Guard stood groups of beefy mursu, tusks gleaming, and their tough leathery skin exposed to the bitter elements. Packs of chittering vulpis hung together at the feet of the crowd, eyeing the archeomek enviously.

The *Frostheart* crew pushed through the press, ignoring the grumbles and complaints that followed them. From up here, you could see a darkness rolling in from the south, twisting and quivering as though it were alive.

Ash knew it was the Devourer. He could sense it.

The crowd could too – the air was thick with fear.

Ash found his mother exactly where he'd expected – in the centre of it all, directing the cranes that lifted the archeoweapons. His legs suddenly felt wobbly and strange, unwilling to take him any closer. Stormbreaker looked anxious, her concern for those she'd sworn to protect clear on her face. Jed was right – she cared for these people.

Ash just wished she would show as much care for him.

'Mum!' he forced himself to call out. 'Mum!'

'Ash?' Stormbreaker said, her eye widening at the sight of him. The crowd cleared a space for the newcomers. 'Jed? Where have you been, what have you –'

'You can't use archeoweapons against the Devourer!'

The words just spilled out. Despite his anxiety, Ash knew telling

Stormbreaker the truth was all that mattered.

'*What?*' Stormbreaker asked in confusion.

'It's true, Commander,' Jed added, the crew backing him up. 'You gotta listen to what he has to say!'

'The Devourer is different to other Leviathans cos it was made by *people*!' Ash explained breathlessly. 'We went to the place it was made. The World Before combined a Leviathan Ancient with powerful archeomek and created something that destroyed them all. It was made just for war. Every time we hurt it, it becomes stronger – that's why the World Before couldn't stop it!'

Jed nodded along to Ash's words. Murmurs rumbled through the crowd like a wave. The *Frostheart* crew glared at those gathered, challenging any doubters. A few did laugh, but most fell deathly silent, looking to Stormbreaker for her response.

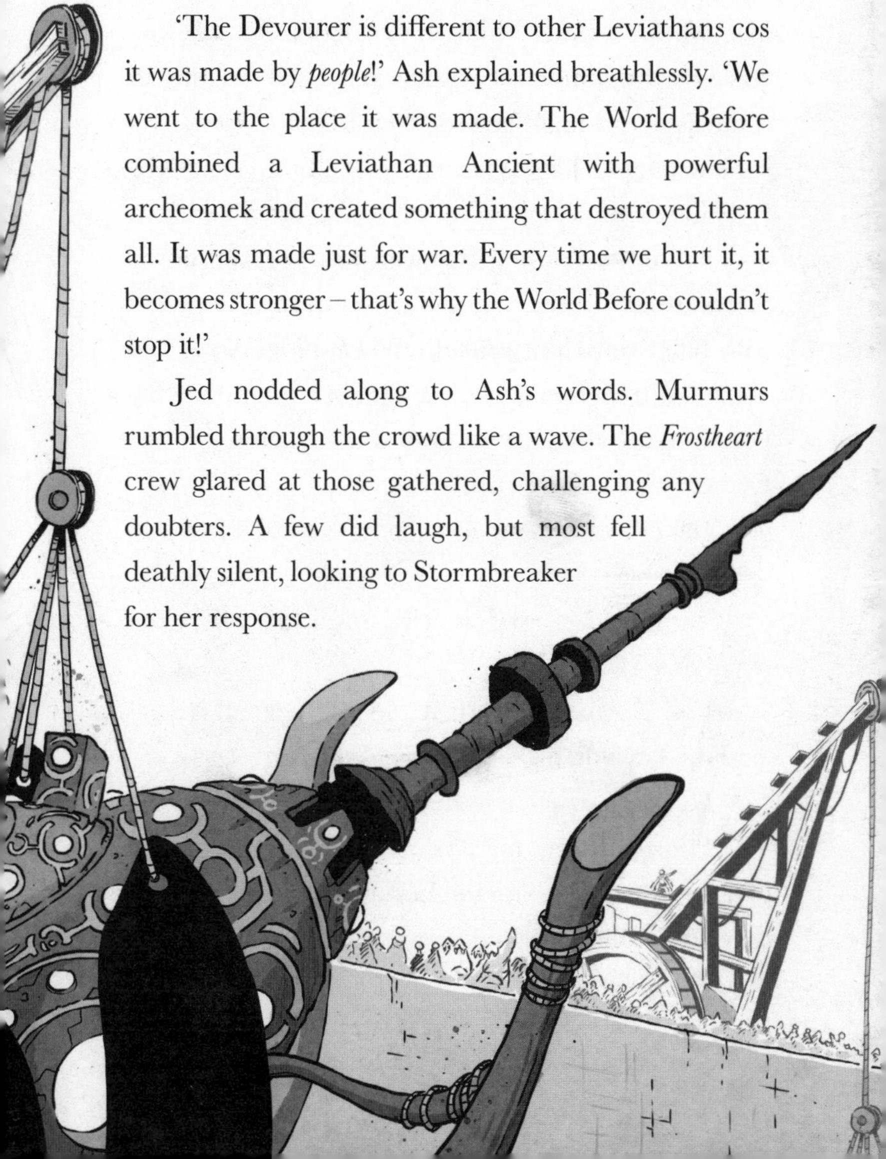

'Childish fantasies,' Stormbreaker said shortly. 'We can't use archeoweapons against the Devourer? What would you have me do instead, *tickle it*?'

'No.' With trembling fingers, Ash untied the bundle hanging from his belt. He peeled away the rags and revealed the true-heart within. It glowed bright and cold, specks of light leaping from it like embers. Ash held it up for all to see.

'This is what's left of the Devourer's original heart, and it's the only thing that can stop it!' He looked Stormbreaker in the eye, trying to imagine Tobu was with him to give him strength. 'What Elder Arrus said about it is true. If enough of us join our Songs with the heart's Song, it'll make us powerful enough to put the Devourer back into its prison!'

The crowd became even more captivated, if that were possible.

Stormbreaker eyed it with suspicion. '*We?* You mean *Song Weavers*?'

'And –' Ash gulped, then added in a small voice – 'and the Leviathans.'

That got a reaction from the crowd.

'Please, listen to me!' Ash cried over the explosion of noise. 'We spoke with the Leviathan leader! She said they'd be willing to stand beside us as long as we don't attack them!'

'I don't have time for this,' Stormbreaker said, signalling to the rest of her crew. 'Get them out of here.'

'Commander, please, you've always trusted me before, an' I'm beggin' you to trust me now,' Jed insisted, lurching forward and grabbing her by the wrist. At first, Stormbreaker looked shocked that Jed had had the nerve to do such a thing, before she tore her wrist from his grasp. Jed gulped. 'I . . . I know it sounds mad – I barely believe it myself – but I saw it with my own eyes. The Leviathans . . . they *helped* us.'

The crowd gasped.

'What if they're right?' a captain asked.

'Everything we threw at the Devourer in the Rend got sent right back at us,' agreed another. 'Every wound healed instantly. We failed to even slow the thing down!'

'Don't believe a word of it!' somebody countered. 'The wurms'll tear you to shreds soon as look at you!'

'When respected, the Leviathans can be a great aid to our fishing,' a particularly large and gnarled-looking mursu announced. 'Chase the fish right into our nets. It is known to the mursu.'

'*Enough!*' Stormbreaker snapped. 'There will be no alliance with the Leviathans! All they want is to see us *dead*.'

'Only because they fear us,' Ash insisted. 'But if we can prove to them they have nothing to fear, they'll change – it's what they do. But we have to do the same. Trusting each other is the only chance we have left!'

Tension rose as Pathfinders argued with each other, tempers flaring and fingers pointing. Ash knew what he was suggesting went against everything they knew, and the Song Weavers were too frightened to back him up.

But the Brood Mother had Sung that she'd give human-kin a chance.

And Songs don't lie.

Closing his eyes, Ash began to Sing.

'Now!'

40

ANOTHER WAY

In a blur of scrabbling claws, Scratch hauled herself over the wall. The squabbling crowd erupted into cries of alarm as they scattered away from the Shrieker, drawing their bows and blades in shock. Vulpis aimed archeoweapons, their trigger fingers itchy, while the mursu hefted large harpoons that could've speared three human-kin at once.

'WAIT!' Ash cried, rushing to shield Scratch with his arms out wide. 'Don't shoot!'

'Get away from there, Ash!' Stormbreaker said, her eye brimming with hatred at the sight of such a creature.

'It's OK,' Ash said soothingly. 'She's on our side.'

'COME HERE, NOW!' His mother's voice was frantic with fear.

Ash flinched but stood his ground. Scratch watched Stormbreaker carefully, her muscles taut and ready.

'*KINSLAYER*,' Scratch growled.

'*Easy* . . .' Ash Sang.

Everything rested on this moment.

They couldn't mess it up.

The *Frostheart* crew rushed to support Ash, shielding Scratch from the arrows aimed at her.

'You *dare* bring this monster here?' Stormbreaker hissed.

'This *monster* saved our lives,' Yallah said.

'On more than one occasion,' Master Podd added.

'You said you'd believe we could have peace if I brought proof. Well, here she is!' Ash said, stroking Scratch's snout. 'See, there's nothing to be scared of. She won't hurt us unless we hurt her.'

The crowd could barely believe what they were seeing. Some looked angry, others confused, but most were in complete awe.

'Show 'em respect, and they'll do the same to you,' the gnarled mursu said with a nod. 'It is known.'

'If we lay down our weapons,' Ash continued, 'and prove that we mean them no harm, they'll help us stop the Devourer!'

Scratch wrapped her tail round Ash as if in confirmation.

The hard edge to Stormbreaker's expression softened.

'Think of Dad,' Ash pleaded, his heart pounding. 'You know he had a connection to the Leviathans – every Song Weaver does!' The gathered Weavers nodded encouragingly. 'He knew there was more to them than meets the eye.'

Scratch made a low purring sound, calm and unthreatening. Stormbreaker lowered her bow a fraction.

Is it working? Ash dared to think. *Is she finally seeing the truth?*

'Please, Mum,' Ash begged. '*Please* believe me . . .'

'Your father . . .' Stormbreaker began, easing the pull on the bowstring. Ash breathed out slowly. Stormbreaker suddenly tensed, and yelled, '. . . was taken from us by these *monsters*!'

She let her arrow fly.

It struck Scratch at the base of her neck, and she reared back with a screech of pain.

Ash's jaw dropped in horror.

Others began to open fire.

'STOP IT!' Ash cried, as the *Frostheart* crew charged into the nearest attackers, forcing them to lower their bows.

'*BETRAYERS!*' Scratch screamed. '*ENEMY!*

KINSLAYER! I'LL KILL HER! I'LL KILL *HER!'*

'Commander, don't!' Jed cried.

Ash tried to wrestle the bow out of Stormbreaker's hand, but she caught hold of his wrist and threw him to the floor. She fired another arrow, then another – each with cold, furious precision.

Ash couldn't breathe. He felt like his heart had stopped.

She's lost, Ash realized. *As lost as Shaard, as . . . as Dad.*

Scratch tumbled over the side of the wall, her blue blood spattering across the stone, and soared away across the plain, her body ravaged with fresh wounds.

'*KILL HER!*' she Sang, her Song-aura red as blood. '*KILL! KILL! KILL!*'

Ash's own blood went cold, the dark chill coiling its serpentine tendrils around his mind. He clenched his trembling fists, trying to resist the anger's call.

'How *could* you?!' he hissed through gritted teeth, tears hot on his face. 'She came in peace! She came to *help*!'

Stormbreaker spun round, her rage replaced by shame as she saw Ash lying where she'd thrown him.

'Ash . . .' she started, reaching to help him up. Ash pulled away from her, shuffling back on his elbows.

'Don't touch me!'

He searched for his friends and saw they'd all been forced on to their knees by the Aurora Guard.

Stormbreaker recovered from her moment of vulnerability. She turned to the crowd, her face hard as stone.

'Surely none of you believed we could let down our defences and allow our ancient enemy to walk over us? Return this '*true-heart*' to the Devourer, which is no doubt exactly what it wants us to do? The Song Weavers can't be trusted, not while the Devourer lives!'

Her words struck Ash like a punch to the gut. Stormbreaker knelt down to face him. 'I'm doing this for your own good, Ash. If there's one thing that's been made clear to me, it's that the Song Weavers are lost to us. Just like your father was, just like Shaard, just like . . .'

'Me,' Ash finished. 'You think *I'm* lost too?'

'It's not your fault,' Stormbreaker said. 'But all these ideas of using a Leviathan's heart to save us were put into Arrus's head *by* the Leviathans. I will not fall into their trap. I will *not* put every life in the Snow Sea in the hands of such people!'

She pulled away, holding the bundle that contained the true-heart.

Another betrayal, Ash raged, anger all but choking him. *Scratch was right – she can't be trusted!*

'We cannot allow the sacrifices of those we've lost to be for nothing!' Stormbreaker announced, standing tall. 'And with the Eclipse, they won't be!'

She gestured at the rune-etched archeoweapon held aloft by the cranes. Ash followed everyone's gaze, looking at the artefacts properly for the first time.

Two of the relics looked like sunstone enjins, though much larger than normal and with appendages extending outwards like ulk antlers. The third, however, looked almost sleigh-like in shape. A huge orb was fixed to its top, pulsing with sickly green energy. Countless sunstones lined the machine's circumference, and from it stretched a long spear-like point. Ash didn't understand what he was looking at, but he knew that whatever it was, it wasn't like the other archeoweapons. It practically hummed with danger.

'The Eclipse is an archeoweapon of unimaginable power,' Stormbreaker explained. 'Everything we've used up until now will seem like child's play compared to this.'

The Pathfinders shifted, visibly unnerved by her words. The mursu looked positively horrified.

'It was never used by the World Before –'

'Probably for good reason!' a voice shouted.

'They never got the chance,' Stormbreaker continued, eyeing the crowd with frustration. 'But if they had, their civilization wouldn't have been destroyed by the Devourer. And now we have it! Our brilliant vulpis allies have helped us to complete its design and its power is now ours to command! After centuries, the Eclipse is finally ready to blast the Leviathans and their Devourer abomination out of existence!'

She paused for the crowd to explode into raucous roars of triumph, as they usually did after her speeches.

But no such applause came.

Aside from a few half-hearted cheers, mostly from Stormbreaker's own crew and the vulpis, the crowd balked.

'What if they're right?' a captain asked, nodding towards Ash and Jed. 'What if the Devourer *is* made more powerful by violence? This would be the worst possible thing we could do.'

The Pathfinders shuffled and murmured.

'They're *not* right,' Stormbreaker insisted, gazing at her people with disbelief. 'They. Are. *Wrong.* I know Leviathans. I've spent a lifetime hunting them! I know what they're capable of, better than anyone here!'

'Hurrah for the Wurmslayer,' someone cheered, and Stormbreaker nodded her thanks.

'*I* am your commander! *I* am the one you chose to lead you! You trusted me then, so trust me now. It's when the night's at its darkest that we must remain strong and stay the course to see the dawn! We are Pathfinders! Vulpis scavengers! Mursu sea-tamers! All of us are here to protect those we love, not cower like frightened children!'

'Commander, listen –' Arla started.

'*Enough!*' Stormbreaker snapped. 'There are *thousands* of people in Aurora depending on us for protection. Countless people across the Snow Sea! The Devourer is coming, and it is up to us to stop it! The

Eclipse is our best and only defence. I ask you all to follow me once more, and we will see victory!'

There were more cheers this time, but most still seemed frightened. Many looked to Ash to see if he had any last words, but he was too angry to speak.

'Now, everyone, back to work!' Stormbreaker ordered. 'We've already wasted enough time!'

As the other Pathfinders returned to their duties, Stormbreaker approached Ash and the *Frostheart* crew.

'I should've locked you all away with Nuk! Call yourselves Pathfinders? You'll turn the entire fleet against me when they need me the most! First you steal my son from me, then you bring our enemy behind our walls?'

'We –' Kailen began, but Stormbreaker struck her across the cheek. The rest of the crew gasped, unable to believe the Commander's behaviour.

'I will *not* have you all getting in the way of the battle to come,' Stormbreaker hissed. 'You're a danger to Aurora and will be imprisoned for your betrayal. As for you, Jed, you're lucky I need you to man the defences. But know that you are on *very* thin ice.'

Jed hung his head in shame, unable to meet anyone's eye. Kailen, on the other hand, glared at Stormbreaker with a snarl, her cheek red. 'To think I once looked up to you.' She spat at Stormbreaker's feet.

'When this is all over, you'll see that I was right,' Stormbreaker said.

'If you use the Eclipse against the Devourer, it really will be all over,' Ash said as a guard forced his arms behind his back.

'When the Leviathans are dead, you'll see that I saved you, Ash – that I freed you from their hateful corruption.'

Ash stared at his mother in cold fury. 'All I ever wanted was for you to be there for me. You said you didn't come back to the Fira because it might have put me in danger. That's a lie. You left me there, all alone, so you could go and fight monsters. It's all you've ever wanted to do, all you care about. You're the real monster.'

Ash could tell he'd hit a nerve.

Good, the darkness in his head said, relishing the pain on her face.

Stormbreaker recognized the hate in his eyes. Her own eye narrowed, and she nodded to the guards.

'Take them away.'

41

TOGETHER AGAIN

Despite Aurora's awe-inspiring splendour, there was no denying that its lowest levels smelled of rotten eggs.

In the bowels of the extinct volcano, deep within caves beneath the docks, each member of the *Frostheart* crew had been placed in a wooden cage and suspended above bubbling pools of the yellow sulphur responsible for such a foul stink.

The only silver lining was that they'd been imprisoned alongside Captain – well, *ex-Captain* – Nuk. She'd been caged in the dungeon the moment the fleet had arrived back from the Ghost Stones.

'Barfing bovores, it's good to see you lot!' she cried as they were locked up. The crew's misery had been sidelined for a moment at the sight of their old captain, everyone eager to swap tales and catch up.

'Surprisingly I've not been doing all that much,' Nuk said. 'I can, however, tell you the *exact* number of stalactites hanging from the ceiling.'

It took considerably longer for the crew to tell their story.

'Valkyries help us, Stormbreaker will prove the death of us all,' Nuk groaned once they'd finished. 'But you found the heart, that's a plus!'

'What good does it do, though?' Ash mumbled. 'Now Stormbreaker has it, and we're stuck in here.'

'Well, I'm proud of you all.' Nuk smiled. 'And I must say, I'm touched by your loyalty! I knew you wouldn't abandon me, though I must admit, I was hoping for a bit more of a rescue . . .'

'Yeah . . . at what point do we admit we've failed our mission again?' Kailen asked, her chin resting in her hand.

'Only when we're in cages hanging precariously over boiling stink-water,' Kob said. 'Oh, wait . . .'

'I'm getting too old for this,' Arla groaned.

'*Shut it!*' snapped the solitary guard watching them from below. He was a large man, but his movements were quick and jumpy, his brow creased with nerves.

'Oh, come on – just one more story,' Twinge said, his round frame practically spilling out of his tiny cage.

'You must be bored to tears hanging around down there!'

'One more word, I'll lower you into the pool.'

A sudden boom shook the cave, dust falling from the ceiling. The guard leaped from his stool, eyes wide. '*Spirits* – was that an archeoweapon?'

'On the outer wall, by the sounds of it,' Kob said. 'Devourer must be in sight.'

The guard nodded, sitting back down hesitantly. He was clearly scared.

They all were.

It didn't help that the Devourer's Song now filled the Stronghold, its hateful madness weighing heavily on all those who heard it, as sickening as the smell of sulphur.

Ash sat with his knees pulled up to his chest, holding the pendant his parents had given him when he'd been born. A gift to remind him that they were always with him, even when they couldn't be there in person.

Ash and his friends had done all they could to try to stop the Devourer. They'd travelled across the world trying to clear up the terrible mess his father had left

behind. They'd tried to protect the first frost-heart and had discovered another one. Ash had even convinced the Leviathans to give human-kin another chance. And with a single action Stormbreaker had thrown it all away.

Ash couldn't get the image of the arrow striking Scratch out of his mind. His belly turned every time he saw it. As they'd been dragged to the prison, Ash had tried reaching out to Scratch with his Song, desperate to see if she was OK, to try to apologize for what had happened. He'd been answered with worrying silence. He wouldn't hear her down here anyway, though that didn't stop him from fearing the worst for his friend.

The Leviathans would never trust human-kin again.

His mother was dangerous; there was no doubt in Ash's mind now. She was making the exact same mistake as the Song Weaver rulers of the past. The Devourer had destroyed an empire advanced far beyond Stormbreaker's wildest dreams. It was strengthened by their hate and violence, made unstoppable by their incredible weapons of war. It was bad enough that Stormbreaker was using those same weapons against the Devourer, but now she was going to use the Eclipse – the deadliest weapon they'd ever created! History was about to repeat itself, and everything would be lost.

Tobu would've stopped her, Ash thought. *He would've snatched that bow right out of her hands and snapped it in half. He would've fought off anyone who tried to stop him, cracking their heads together one by one till there was no one left!*

And how Ash would've loved to see that.

Ash shuddered, both with repulsion and fury. His belly ached, biting anger seeping into his veins, his fingers and toes, his nerves and senses. The Devourer was reaching into his mind, trying to take root, and Ash did all he could to fight it back.

He would *not* end up like his parents. Or like poor Rook, driven almost mad and, in the end, forced to flee off the edge of the world.

Ash studied the pendant, warm in his hand. A sunstone – a piece of some Leviathan's heart, stolen by those of the World Before to fuel their technology.

Even his parents' gift was tainted.

Ash untied the necklace from his neck and removed the sunstone from the cord with frantic motions, before tossing it from his cage into the bubbling pool below.

Ash ground his teeth so hard he feared they might crack.

Reaching into his furs, his hand brushed against the ocarina Tobu had made for him.

So much has been happening, I've not had a chance to play it, Ash thought guiltily.

He swore he'd play it every single day if they somehow survived this.

He searched some more and pulled out the star Lunah had given him. Lunah hadn't been with the crew when they'd disobeyed Stormbreaker's orders, and so she'd escaped imprisonment. Ash gave the star a squeeze, hoping she was OK, before stringing the leather thong of his necklace through a metal loop on the star and tying it back round his neck.

Another boom shook the cavern.

'*Spirits!*' The guard shot up again. 'I'm just gonna . . . see what's happening.' He hurried down the tunnel leading out of the cave.

'We cannot allow mere cages to get in the way of us stopping Stormbreaker's bloodthirsty madness,' Nuk whispered, pulling at her bars.

'I eat cages for breakfast!' Kailen strained, her face turning red with the effort of trying to prise hers open.

'Have you been cooking your own breakfasts?' Twinge asked, offended. '*I've* never cooked us cages . . .'

Yallah swayed back and forth, causing her cage to swing, but not far enough to do any good. 'Urgh, this is hopeless!'

They all jumped as a small explosion sent smoke and rubble flying from the opposite cave wall. The door to Master Podd's cage creaked open, its bindings smoking. In his hand he clutched the strange archeoweapon Ash had caught him nabbing back in the Cradle.

Everyone gawped at him.

He raised an eyebrow. 'What?'

'You . . . you took it?' Kailen laughed.

'I hid it in my tail. Don't judge me.'

'Master Podd, you *genius*!' Nuk laughed just as rushing footsteps echoed down the tunnel. Master Podd pulled his door shut as the guard skidded back into the cave.

'What was that?!' the guard demanded.

'Archeoweapons,' Kob said. He wasn't lying.

The guard nodded, his eyes wide with fear. He sat back down, facing the cave entrance. With the guard's back turned, Master Podd carefully pushed his cage door open again. As quietly as possible, he leaped towards the nearest stalactite, wrapping his arms and legs round it. He jumped to the next one over, and the one after that, until he was safely away from the steaming pools below.

Soundlessly he dropped to the floor behind the guard.

The prisoners watched with bated breath.

Master Podd held up his archeoweapon, and pointed it at the back of the guard's head.

Nuk shook her head vigorously.

Master Podd stroked his chin, then pointed at the blade fastened at the guard's belt.

Nuk shook her head again.

Master Podd looked about the cave, pointed at a large rock and was pleased to see Nuk give him the thumbs up. Grabbing it, Master Podd climbed on to a boulder behind the guard, looming over him.

A bead of sweat trickled down the back of Ash's neck.

Master Podd raised the rock high, preparing to clobber the un-watchful watchman's head.

'Guard!'

The voice came from down the tunnel. Ash caught his breath as the guard rose from his stool, Master Podd frantically ducking for cover.

Two Drifters rushed in, a woman who looked like an adult version of Lunah, and Lunah herself. She gave a sly wink to the crew.

'I've been sent to collect the prisoners for evacuation,' the woman said.

'What?' the guard asked. 'I was told to only release

them if the Devourer breached the inner wall . . .?'

The cave trembled with another boom.

'Whaddya think's happenin', man?!' Lunah cried.

The colour drained from the guard's face. 'I-it's *here*?!'

'Chop-chop, it's time to go!' The woman clapped her hands. 'As many people as we can fit on the Nova sleighs!'

'Those massive Drifter vessels?' the guard asked. 'There's no way everyone will fit on those!'

'Then hurry up before you lose yer space! We'll take care a' these scumbags.'

The man hesitated, wrestling between panic and his orders. The former won.

'Thank you!' he said, running out of the cave. 'Thank you!'

Once the guard was out of earshot, Lunah spun round with her hands on her hips. 'I can't leave you lot fer two minutes without you gettin' in trouble, can I?'

'I was doing OK,' Master Podd said, dropping his rock with a hint of disappointment.

'Let's get you lot outta there then, shall we?' The woman smiled, turning the cranks that lowered the cages.

'The Devourer's not really through the inner wall, is it?' Arla said with a grin.

'It's still on the horizon,' Lunah replied. 'Pathfinders are just blastin' the Leviathans the Wraiths are throwin' at the outer wall to test our defences.'

'I'm going to take a wild stab in the dark that you're Lunah's mother?' Yallah said to the woman.

'Guilty as charged, an' proud of the fact too! I'm Celeste.'

'*The* Celeste – of the Drifter Convoy?' Teya whistled. 'We're talking to a living legend here!'

'That's enough of that,' Celeste laughed. Each cage had now been lowered and Lunah, Celeste and Master Podd cut through the bindings

holding them shut. ''S'me who's honoured to meet all of you. I can't thank y'all enough for takin' care a' this ball of mischief.' Celeste ruffled Lunah's hair, Lunah swatting her away. 'She's told me all about you!'

'She was taking care of us more like,' Nuk said, shaking Celeste's hand once she was free.

'Took good care of all our rations certainly,' Kailen said, stretching her limbs after the cramped space of the cage.

'Introductions can wait,' Lunah said. 'Won't take long before that guard realizes he's been duped. We gotta get outta here!'

'What d'ya say, captain?' Celeste said. 'Shall we go get yer sleigh back?'

Nuk sighed. 'I thought you'd never ask!'

42

SACRIFICE

'Stormbreaker's still at the southern gate,' Celeste explained as they rushed through the deserted docks that circled the base of the city. 'That's where she'll make her stand, hopin' to keep our enemy far from Aurora itself. She plans to destroy the Devourer before it can reach the outer wall, usin' all her archeoweapons to hold it back till the Eclipse is ready to fire.'

The Devourer's Song polluted Aurora, a hateful drone from which there was no escape. Ash was trying his best to block it out, but it seeped continuously through his defences like water through stones. The Song wrung out his courage and replaced it with a maddening despair. The countless people who lived within the mountain milled about the tiered streets, confused and frightened. Some tried to hide in their homes. Others searched to find a place to watch the upcoming battle.

'An' if she can't hold the wall?' Kailen asked Celeste.

'The allied fleet is the last line of defence. That's where Lunah's father and my two eldest are. They're guardin' the inner wall, an' don't plan on lettin' anythin' past.'

'Gods watch over them,' Yallah said.

'Indeed. And my wrath will be swift and terrible if Stormbreaker gets a single scratch on my pup,' Nuk mumbled under her breath, thinking of the *Frostheart.*

A boom shook the Stronghold, sending a flurry of screams into the air. Ash flinched.

'How we gonna get to the outer wall in time?' Teya asked. 'It's too far to walk.'

'My sleigh, the *Meridian.*' Celeste pointed towards the last few sleighs that floated on the canal, each one a Drifter vessel.

'Aren't you needed to evacuate the population if . . . if all goes wrong?' Yallah asked.

A shadow passed over Celeste's face, the fact that she was abandoning her duty not lost on her.

'Ma, if things really go that far south, there'll be no runnin' anyway,' Lunah said, tugging at her sleeve. 'This is it. This is the one chance we get.'

Celeste looked out at all the people on the streets –

parents pulling their children close, lovers holding each other for what might be the last time, friends trying to look brave so that the others might take heart. Smiling, Celeste placed a hand on Lunah's cheek, though her eyes were full of sadness.

'My baby girl, when did you get so grown-up?' She turned to Nuk. 'If my daughter says this is how it's gotta be, I trust her.'

'Then there's no time to waste,' Nuk declared.

They were so eager to get going, they barely noticed Ash hadn't moved.

'You comin', Ash?' Lunah asked.

'I . . . I can't,' he said, lips trembling. The crew looked back at him with surprise. 'I can't do it. It . . . it's too much . . .' He broke down into shuddering sobs.

'Oh, Ash!' Nuk said as the crew gathered around him, faces full of sympathy. 'We're all frightened, but we can do this.'

'*You* can do this!' Ash said through gritted teeth, the Dark Song urging him to lash out. 'But I . . . I've failed every step of the way! What – what am I even *doing* here? I'm just some *kid*! Without you guys, without Tobu and Rook . . .' His voice cracked as he spoke their names. 'I'm *useless*!'

All he wanted to do was run away and hide. He could *never* beat something like the Devourer! Bringing

ancient enemies together to Sing into the true-heart – it all seemed so *stupid* now.

'C'mon, fire-boy,' Lunah said as she reached out, Ash's warm tears splashing on their clasped hands. 'Someone's gotta stand up to yer ma, an' I reckon that someone's *you*. The Fira thought it was madness to leave their walls, but you didn't let that stop you. Were you sacred? Sure! But did you take those steps aboard our sleigh? You bet yer butt you did! An' look where you are now!'

The ground quaked at a terrible roar from outside, and dust rained down on them.

'I mean – that was bad timin', but my point remains. Yer braver than you know.'

'You *are* a kid,' Nuk said, gripping his shoulder. 'But you're also a Song Weaver. A Pathfinder. A friend to the Leviathans!'

'And a member of our crew.' Kailen grinned.

'None of us have to shoulder this alone,' Nuk said. 'We do this together, remember?'

Ash sniffed, then nodded, his friends giving him the strength to fight back against the tendrils of shadow that gripped his heart.

Be calm, said a voice in his head, blocking out the hateful whispers. *One breath at a time* . . .

Ash took Tobu's advice and inhaled deeply.

It helped.

He smiled back at the others, a smile of genuine, heartfelt thanks. It was then that he spotted the bird behind them. A lonesome crow perched on a mooring post. It stared at him, eyes glinting. Strange but not *that* strange.

Until it cawed, that is.

'*Sacrifice!*'

Somehow Ash understood its croak-like Song. The crow cocked its head, then cried out again.

'*Sacrifice!*'

It was just like when he heard the ulk in the Endless Forest with Rook.

Rook!

Ash's heart skipped a beat.

Had Rook sent the crow? Was she trying to get a message to him?

'*Sacrifice!*'

Then it clicked. *Sacrifice* – the Brood Mother's word!

She'd said that if human-kin were willing to show sacrifice for the greater good then the Leviathans would join forces with them. The crow bobbed its head, then took wing. Ash watched it fly up to a bridge that stretched from the streets to an opening in the mountainside.

'Ash? You OK?' Lunah asked.

'You're right . . . we don't have to do this alone,' Ash replied, still gazing up. 'I think Rook is trying to send me a message.'

'Rook? She's long gone, Ash,' Master Podd pointed out.

'I-I know this sounds mad – but you have to trust me on this.' Ash's heart beat faster. 'I think Rook's showing me a way to get the Leviathans back on our side!'

The others shared a worried glance.

'Can we not help?' Nuk asked.

'I think this is something only I can do. Song Weaver stuff. If I can just reach Scratch . . . maybe I can prove myself.'

The others looked utterly lost. 'You're . . . sure?'

Arla asked.

'Don't worry – I'll . . . I'll meet you all on the wall.'

'Without a sleigh?' Kob asked.

'If this goes according to plan, I won't need a sleigh,' Ash assured him.

Lunah had been whispering something to her mother, who nodded in agreement. Lunah gave her a tight hug, and for just a moment looked like the frightened young girl she really was. Then just as quickly she rushed over to Ash, Celeste watching her go with a mix of pride and fear.

'I'm comin' with you.'

'Wh-what?' Ash asked.

'You're gonna ride that Shrieker again, aren't you? An' if you do it one more time without me, I'd have to add you to my enemy list.'

Despite all his fear, his anger, doubt and sorrow, Ash laughed. Secretly he was glad to have the company of his best friend on such an important, dangerous mission.

'Hey!' she said, catching hold of his new pendant. 'My star!'

Ash flushed with embarrassment. Lunah eyed it curiously, then looked Ash in the eyes, strangely moved. 'Suits you.'

*

The cutting wind clawed at Ash.

Plucking up his courage, he dared look over the stone railing that encircled the outdoor terrace jutting out of the side of the mountain.

'Spirits, we're *so* high,' he groaned, pulling back, his head spinning.

'Well, we don't wanna go splat at the bottom *too* fast,' Lunah said, unfazed.

They'd pushed through the anxious crowds of Aurora to its higher levels, following the crow. It was waiting for them when they arrived, its black glassy eyes giving away none of its secrets.

Ash looked to the horizon – *anything* other than looking down. Night was only just being chased away by Mother Sun, although even she was struggling to break through the darkness. At first, Ash thought he could see a black mist stretching across the horizon. But as he looked closer, it proved to be something far more terrifying.

A writhing, clamouring mass of corrupted Leviathans and jagged Wraith sleighs.

And, towering above this ocean of darkness, tormenting all who could hear it with its horrifying Song, was the Devourer itself.

Ash's face paled at the sight of such a *monstrosity*. It looked entirely unnatural, like a nightmare that had crawled into the real world. Its skeletal grin glinted in the morning light, as though it was enjoying the prospect of the carnage to come.

'It's even more horrible than I remember,' Ash whispered. Every instinct told him to flee.

'I dunno,' Lunah said. 'I heard it has a *wonderful* sense of humour.'

But Ash could tell from her wide glassy eyes that she was only joking to avoid being overwhelmed by fear too. It hardly seemed possible, but Ash could've sworn the Devourer had grown even larger since they'd last seen it.

All the souls it's consumed have made it stronger . . .

Ash swallowed.

'Better hurry if we don't wanna miss the show,' Lunah said.

'Right.' Ash took a moment to brace himself. He turned to the crow that had led them here. 'You're sure this is the right place?'

'*Sacrifice*,' it cawed, then nipped at its wing and ruffled its feathers.

'You know yer in trouble when yer plan is based on what a passin' bird tells you to do . . .' Lunah rolled her eyes and pulled herself up on to the railing.

Ash carefully did the same.

He learned two things in that moment.

That his legs had turned to marrow, and apparently

his belly could do the most extraordinary backflips.

Lunah bent over with her hands behind her back. She considered the incredible drop below them, letting out an impressed whistle.

Just watching her gave Ash serious vertigo.

'You still wanna do this?'

'No.' Ash gulped.

'Cos it sounds completely bonkers to me.'

'Yes.'

'But you're still determined?' Lunah asked.

'I am.'

'Thought so.' Lunah grinned. 'So, what now?'

'N-now? Now we *hope*.'

He began to Song Weave, praying Scratch would hear him. She'd followed him everywhere since he'd first come to Aurora all that time ago, but now that he needed her most Ash was worried she'd be nowhere to be found.

She might be too injured to fly, Ash fretted, remembering her blue blood spattered across the wall. *Or maybe – maybe she was so badly hurt she didn't make it . . .*

He swallowed hard, unwilling to even think it.

'Scratch!' Ash Sang as loud as he could, his Song-aura gushing outwards in a vast fountain of light. *'Are you there?'*

No response.

'I'm so sorry! I thought she'd listen to me. But now I know she's as lost as the Corrupted.'

He listened closely, desperate for any sign of Scratch's Song, but all he heard was the howling wind and the hateful droning Dark Song.

'But my mother doesn't speak for all of us. I know there are human-kin who want peace. My friends, the Song Weavers even . . . even some of the Pathfinders. I could see it in their faces, and I know you could too! Don't let Stormbreaker's hate ruin everything we've done. If we fight for it, if we don't give up, we can still stand together! We can still end this!'

Silence.

Ash *really* hoped it was because Scratch was ignoring him, and not because he was just Singing into the wind. Even Lunah was starting to look concerned.

Ash watched the Devourer stalking towards Aurora, tendrils of shadow writhing and whipping about it like smoke caught in a wind.

'*We can't do this alone,*' Ash continued, '*but neither can you. Our only hope is to work together. The Brood Mother said that you'd only join us if we prove that we're willing to sacrifice ourselves for the good of the world. Well, I know you don't trust us, so I'm going to trust you.*'

Ash held out his arms, and Lunah copied him.

'Give us another chance. We're putting our lives in your hands . . . er, claws!'

Ash paused, hoping for an answer that didn't come. He looked at the crow, which just stared at him with its blank eyes.

I hope you're right about this, Ash prayed, his head spinning.

'Spirits, oh spirits, oh spirits . . .' he whispered.

'She'll come, Ash. She always does,' Lunah said. 'Jus' don't think too hard 'bout it!'

Ash braced himself. Lunah was right. Faith in his friends had got him this far. If he didn't act now, he never would. With a last gasp of breath, Ash stepped off the railing.

The mountain tore past in a blur, the icy wind stinging his skin, pulling back his cheeks and exposing his teeth in what he assumed was the most ridiculous face. He spun and he flipped and he tumbled, barely able to tell what was what or which way was which. Just above him, he could've sworn Lunah was *whooping as she fell*, but surely that had to be his imagination?

The fall took far longer than Ash thought it could. Long enough for him to think he'd made a grave mistake. Long enough to wonder why he'd ever imagined

Scratch would care enough to save them. Long enough to scream *Ihatethisihatethisihatethis* in his head a hundred times.

The ground raced towards them.

Ash clenched his eyes shut. This was it. They were going to die.

But then . . .

FWOOSH!

A large shape swooped in from below, catching them both on its back before extending its arms, filling its wings with air.

'Scratch!' Ash gasped, clutching on to her neck with all his strength.

'WAAHOOOOOOOOOOO!' Lunah yelled.

'*FOOL. FOOLISH FOOL! FOOLISH, FOOLISH FOOL!*' Scratch Sang, rising high over the inner wall, the guards below watching in shock. '*SHOULD'VE LET YOU FALL. SHOULD'VE LET YOU SQUISH.*'

Ash laughed, just happy to be alive.

'*I'm starting to think I'm a bit of a fool too,*' he Sang.

'I have *got* to learn how to Song Weave,' Lunah cried, holding her arms out like a bird. 'This *cannot* be the last time I do this!'

43 LAST DEFENCE

From the air, the plain beyond the outer wall convulsed and squirmed. The great swarm of Leviathans that had tried so hard to stop the Devourer from being released was now controlled by their ancient enemy. A mist of dark-aura writhed and twisted from one creature to the next, a cloud of insidious hate forcing its will upon them.

Ushering the swarm forward was the Wraith fleet, which had appeared in its entirety, torn black sails barely distinguishable from the coiling shadow that shrouded them. And looming above them all was the Devourer. Its black pitiless eyes drank in every moment with hungry anticipation. It barked out its Song in terrible blasts, the force of it tearing at the defenders of the wall and stealing courage from even the bravest hearts.

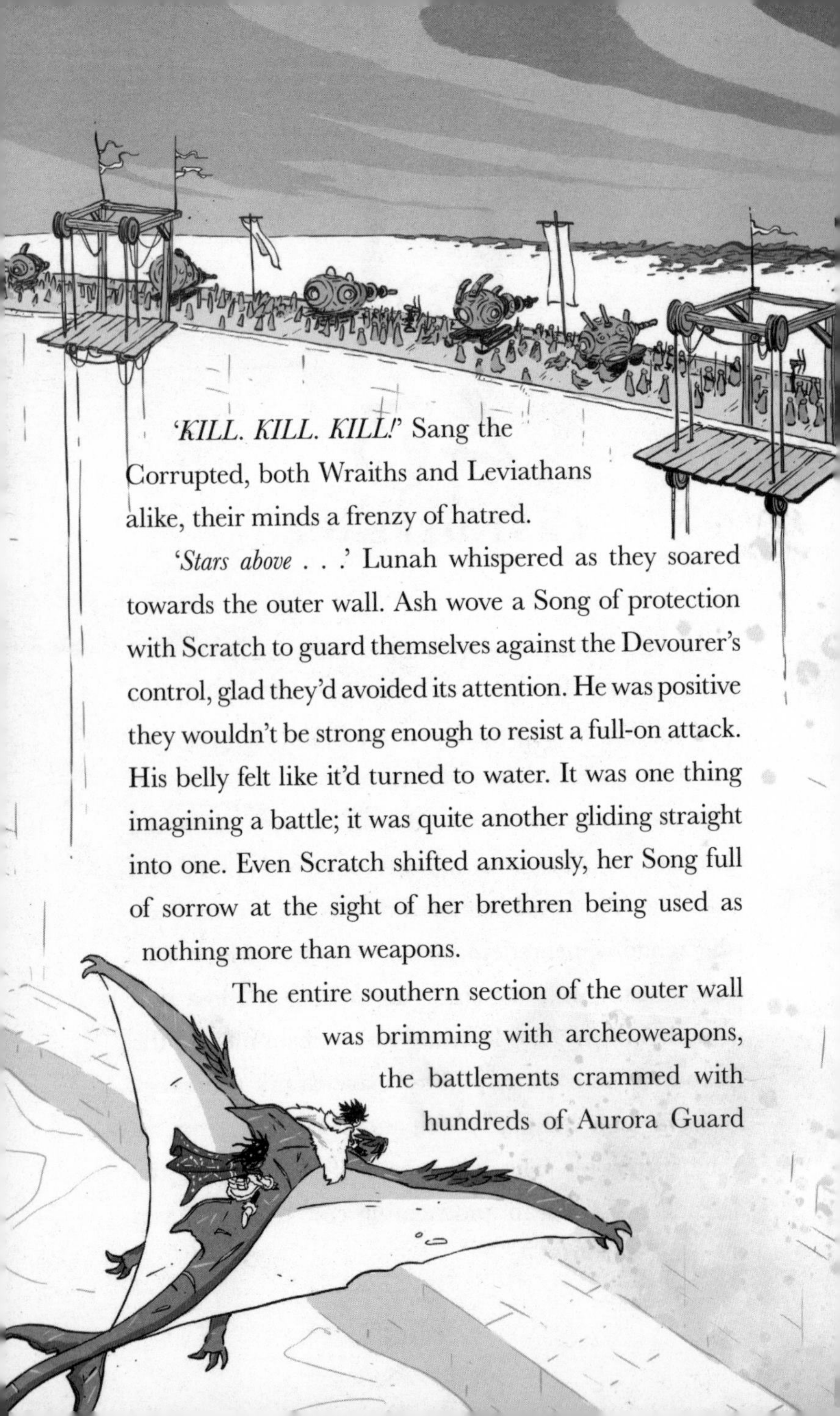

'KILL. KILL. KILL!' Sang the Corrupted, both Wraiths and Leviathans alike, their minds a frenzy of hatred.

'Stars above . . .' Lunah whispered as they soared towards the outer wall. Ash wove a Song of protection with Scratch to guard themselves against the Devourer's control, glad they'd avoided its attention. He was positive they wouldn't be strong enough to resist a full-on attack. His belly felt like it'd turned to water. It was one thing imagining a battle; it was quite another gliding straight into one. Even Scratch shifted anxiously, her Song full of sorrow at the sight of her brethren being used as nothing more than weapons.

The entire southern section of the outer wall was brimming with archeoweapons, the battlements crammed with hundreds of Aurora Guard

and Song Weavers ready to man them. The Eclipse was clearly visible, rising as high as a sleigh and extending from the wall like a giant spear. A sickly green glow radiated from its crackling enjins.

Ash looked down at the fleet below, which had formed a defensive line behind the outer wall. Even with reinforcements, it looked woefully small compared to what they were up against. Aurora itself was now leagues behind them, protected by the inner wall. A wall that had once seemed so impenetrable to Ash, but now appeared flimsy and inadequate indeed. Ash prayed the Brood Mother had taken notice of the sacrifice he and Lunah had been willing to make.

He had no idea how it had been received, or even if the Leviathans would be willing to accept it at all.

All he knew was that Aurora couldn't defeat the Devourer on its own.

But right now he had to focus on stopping Stormbreaker.

And with a resounding boom Aurora unleashed its might.

The line of archeoweapons along the battlements opened fire, the plains trembling with the sound of thunder. A rain of fire tore into the mass of Corrupted, explosions blasting to life in their midst. Song Weavers guided their Song-auras into the sunstones embedded in the ancient weapons, Singing Songs of death and slaughter to fuel them with the power to unleash destruction. The Aurora Guard operated the lesser weapons, firing blast after crackling blast into the enemy.

To Ash's horror, he saw many of the defenders taking aim at the Devourer itself, unintentionally feeding its strength.

'*We have to hurry!*' he urged. Scratch pulled in her wings and straightened her tail, cutting through the air towards the Eclipse as fast as an arrow.

As the blasts burst along the Devourer's hide, the bright yellow energy sank deep into its flesh, pulsing under its skin as the energy travelled along its lithe body and up its long throat. It was almost as if its veins glowed with the light of Mother Sun, strangely beautiful and yet utterly terrifying. With a mighty belch, the Devourer fired the blasts back. The balls of energy screeched towards the wall, erupting into devastating explosions that sent huge chunks of the masonry into the air.

The Devourer shrieked, more with contempt than pain, its wounds bubbling with black goo, sealing and healing themselves. Ash blanched as the smoke cleared, revealing a gaping hole where solid wall had once stood.

And, just like that, Aurora's unbreachable walls had been breached.

'*KILL! KILL! KILL!*' the Corrupted roared in triumph, racing towards the opening. With a blaring of horns, the first half of the allied fleet surged forward to meet them.

It was then that Ash felt a change in the air.

It felt heavier all of a sudden, as though something huge was looming overhead, pressing down on all those below. It was the same fizzy sensation you feel just before a thunderstorm, or when you sense you're being watched.

The pulsating glow around the Eclipse swelled and grew brighter. Green lightning lashed and crackled, coiling round the arms that extended from the enjins.

'*No* . . .' Ash whispered, his heart in his throat. 'She's going to use it!'

With a flash, the bolts leaped up to the giant orb atop the main body of the weapon, dancing in a web of energy. The sound of the Dark Song was replaced by an awful high-pitched whine.

'*KINSLAYER!*' Scratch bellowed. '*WILL DESTROY US ALL!*'

'We have to stop her!' Lunah cried, Scratch swooping towards the wall.

The flickering lightning became more focused, transforming into concentrated beams.

'*I'LL KILL HER! I'LL KILL HER!*' Scratch roared, soaring closer.

'*Don't!*' Ash Sang. '*It's what the Devourer wants! Just help me stop her!*'

Closer they flew, the beams powering the orb atop the Eclipse, now a giant sphere of pulsating green light.

Closer . . .

The high-pitched whine became a scream that hurt Ash's ears.

Closer . . .

. . . but not close enough.

44

ECLIPSED

The Eclipse released a sphere of light with an ear-splitting crack. It surged over the Corrupted horde, tearing up snow in its wake.

'We're too late!' Lunah cried.

'No, no, no, no, no, NO!' Ash wailed.

The Devourer roared defiantly before the sphere struck it dead on.

The world disappeared in a flash of blinding light.

For a moment, all was dead silent.

And then . . .

The largest explosion Ash could ever have imagined tore through the world. The air cracked. The sky shuddered. A towering pillar of intense green light consumed the Devourer, vaporizing the Corrupted closest to it. The pillar erupted towards the sky, the

world turning black against its brightness. Ash, Lunah and Scratch squinted at the spectacle in horrified awe.

And then the shockwave came.

It struck them like a speeding sleigh, the world-shattering boom of the explosion bewildering their senses. Scratch squealed as she swerved and strained against the blast. They spun and they spun, Ash and Lunah clinging on for dear life. Ash thought he was screaming – his throat certainly hurt – but he wasn't sure; he wasn't sure of anything any more except for that blinding, burning, rushing light and the all-consuming roar.

After what felt like an eternity, the shockwave passed.

Scratch wobbled and struggled to gain altitude, panting from her efforts to keep them aloft.

'*Humans. Bring. Death,*' she whimpered in a tiny voice. Ash dared open his eyes and looked breathlessly at the desolation left in the explosion's wake.

An entire part of the world just . . . *gone.*

Erased.

A gigantic flaming crater had appeared where the Devourer once stood, lightning forking around its circumference. The dark sky above had been stained green, sizzling energy pulsing through the clouds and raining down upon the plain as burning hot embers.

To Ash's utter astonishment, the Devourer was still standing within the raging crater, but only just. Its blackened skeleton was exposed, its entire upper half now nothing more than glowing, bubbling goo.

'What . . . what *is* that thing?' Lunah asked. Her voice sounded distant. The blast had near-deafened Ash, and his ears filled with an intense ringing sound. The Devourer pulsed with the same green energy as the Eclipse, its Dark Song leaking out of it in a distressing strangled warble.

'I-it's healing,' Ash said, feeling like there was a stone in his stomach. 'It's using the Eclipse's energy to grow stronger!'

Ash's pulse quickened at the sound of the Eclipse's enjins humming back to life. The glow that radiated from them small for now, but Ash knew it was only a matter of time before they'd be fully powered once more. 'We can't let Stormbreaker fire it again! She'll make the Devourer unstoppable, if she hasn't already!'

The inferno had at least stalled the Corrupted long enough for the allied fleet to form a wall of sleighs to plug the breach. The Wraiths had been forced to slow down and regain control over the Leviathans who were howling in confusion, threatening to break free now that the Devourer's Song had been temporarily weakened.

Scratch drew up close to the Eclipse, the wall

defenders too distracted by the devastation ahead to notice her.

'Look! There!' Lunah pointed towards their friends, who were already confronting the crew of the *Kinspear.* Stormbreaker stood tall and unflinching, bathed in green light, staring with open contempt as Nuk desperately tried to reason with her.

Scratch landed upon the wall with deft precision, and the defenders scattered in shock.

'Tha's right, we ride Leviathans – get used to it!' Lunah shouted as they leaped off Scratch's back.

'I've heard of parents having difficulty disciplining their children,' Stormbreaker said, eerily calm, 'but what exactly do I have to do to get you to stop flying Leviathans at me when I'm trying to save the world?'

Scratch growled, low and deep in her throat, her Song simmering with anger at the sight of Stormbreaker.

'It's the world's survival that's brought us here!' Ash insisted.

The Eclipse was thrumming loudly to their side, the wall vibrating with each pulse of its green glow. Ash recognized the group of five Song Weavers who stood around it, Elders Arrus and Loda among them, all chanting a low dirge to power the machine. 'Please, I'm begging you – don't use it again! You're only making the Devourer stronger!'

'We've blown it halfway to the underworld!' Stormbreaker said. 'One more shot and we'll end that cursed thing once and for all!'

'You think *that's* working?!' Nuk asked, pointing at the seething mass of darkness that was the Devourer.

It had hauled itself from the crater and, with its tendrils still aflame, begun crawling across the snow plain, dragging its regenerating body behind it. The viscous goo plunged over some of the Corrupted, the glow of their souls flickering underneath the darkness as the Devourer consumed them for energy. It even grabbed a Wraith sleigh, the wood withering at its touch, the Wraiths aboard falling dead on the deck while their essence was stolen from them.

It was truly the stuff of nightmares.

Stormbreaker's crew watched, aghast, but their commander didn't flinch.

The tendrils then reached out in wide arcs, bracing the bulk of the gloop as it fell in on itself, forming a mountain of slime. The green lights that pulsated within blinked faster and faster, gathering together in a flare of energy.

'What – what's it doing?' Jed croaked, staggering back in fear.

Like a volcanic eruption, the green energy burst out of the mound in a fountain of searing light.

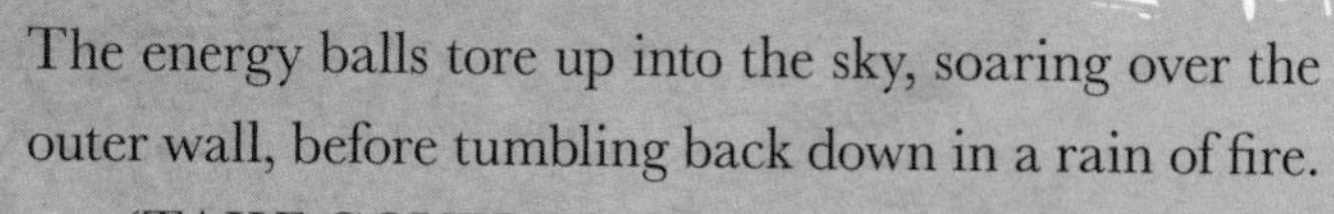

The energy balls tore up into the sky, soaring over the outer wall, before tumbling back down in a rain of fire.

'TAKE COVER!' Stormbreaker yelled, as the first ball struck the allied fleet below.

45
LAST CHANCE

The mighty explosion nearly threw Ash over the wall. He was only saved by the force of another blast, which sent him hurtling back to the stone floor. He covered his head with his arms as explosion after explosion sent terrible shockwaves through his bones. All he could do was wait and hope as the plain was bombarded with a hailstorm of death.

When it finally ended, Ash and the others staggered to their feet. The plain between the inner and outer wall had been devastated by the fireballs, the ground pockmarked by hundreds of large smoking craters. Charred splinters and obliterated fragments were all that remained of the sleighs that had been destroyed. Multiple new breaches had been blown in the outer wall, the smoking rubble hiding the bodies of those who'd stood upon it.

'*Spirits save us*,' a guard behind Ash whispered in horror. The explosions had silenced the Song Weavers, who were just as unnerved as the rest of them.

'Jed, I need the Song Weavers charging the Eclipse,' Stormbreaker ordered. 'We have to end this!'

'Don't!' Ash pleaded. 'You can't!'

'You just saw what it's capable of!' Nuk said, mortified. 'You're not hurting that monster, you're *arming* it!'

'Jed?' Stormbreaker repeated, ignoring Nuk.

'Commander . . . I . . . I think she's right,' Jed stammered, eyes wide, as he watched the Devourer reform one of its front legs.

'I will not ask you again, Jed,' Stormbreaker said dangerously.

'What if it unleashes another blast like that one?' asked a crewman.

'We can't withstand it again!' said a second.

Jed hesitated.

'POWER THE WEAPON!' Stormbreaker screamed.

Jed recoiled.

'Jed . . .' Kailen pleaded. 'Deep down, you know the right thing to do.'

Jed turned to face Stormbreaker.

'No.'

'I'm sorry?' Stormbreaker looked more surprised than angry.

'I won't do it. I won't risk our own, not any more.'

Stormbreaker blinked. 'Then stand aside and allow someone who's actually willing to do their duty!'

She waited for a volunteer from her crew to step forward, but none moved. Their faces were grim, unable to recognize the captain they'd once followed without question. Stormbreaker looked genuinely shocked, not used to such disobedience.

'Mutiny, is it?' she asked quietly.

Suddenly the sound of battle erupted below them, stealing their attention. The Corrupted were pouring through the breaches in the wall like an avalanche. The first wave of the fleet had been scattered, fighting against the tide with bows and bolt-throwers, most of their archeoweapons having been stripped for the defence of the wall.

At the bellowed orders of their captains, the mursu launched volley after volley of piercing harpoons into the writhing mass. Vulpis scampered around makeshift catapults that propelled impressive heaps of heavy scrap into the enemy, while the Drifters flung liquid-filled orbs from slings, which exploded into bright flowers of flame on impact. But still the Corrupted kept coming, and the fleet was soon in danger of being overwhelmed.

Lunah gasped, holding her hand to her mouth. 'Please, please, please may my family not be down there . . .'

Ash grimaced. He knew lives were being lost, but the thought that it could be Lunah's own family made it startlingly real. The Song Weavers around the Eclipse fell back in dismay, unable to watch the carnage.

Ash was suddenly struck with an idea.

'Song Weavers!' he yelled. 'We can stop this! With the Devourer's Song weakened, we can rescue the

Corrupted from its control and bring them back to our side!'

Ash knew it was possible: he'd rescued those Lurkers himself from Shaard back at the Isolai Stronghold.

'You're right, boy!' Loda nodded eagerly.

'You'll do no such thing!' Stormbreaker snapped, but before anyone could argue a voice broke through the din of battle.

Ash ran to the outer side of the wall, his skin crawling as he recognized whose voice it was. There, standing proudly aboard his battle sleigh beside the onrushing swarm, was Shaard.

'*Song Weavers!*' Shaard Sang, somehow using the Devourer's Song to project his own across the battlefield. '*Hold your fire! I have a proposition for you.*'

The Dark Song lowered down to a drone, the Corrupted ceasing their vicious attack to allow Shaard to make his offer. The Pathfinder fleet fell back, regrouping for whatever might come next. The battlefield fell eerily calm, as all but the weakest of the archeoweapons needed Song Weavers to activate them.

'Don't listen to him!' Stormbreaker yelled at the Song Weavers around her, unable to understand the words of Shaard's Song herself. 'Whatever he's saying, it's *lies*!'

'*Surely you can see now how hopeless it is to stand against us?*' Shaard boomed, running along his sleigh's bow sprit and clinging on to the front sail. He swung an arm out gleefully, his cloak floating in the wind. '*Surely you can see the power at my command? Not even Stormbreaker's most powerful weapon can stop us! Soon Aurora will fall!*'

The Song Weavers shrank back at the sight of the bulbous pulsating mess that was the Devourer, which was regaining shape with every second.

'*But you don't need to die,*' Shaard continued. '*We are one and the same! Our fight is with the Strongholders, the Pathfinders and all those who treat Song Weavers like dirt! Join us, my brothers and sisters, and take your revenge!*'

'Don't listen to him!' Ash shouted, but his voice was stolen by the wind. He doubted anyone but those closest to him heard.

'Ash! Join your Song with ours!' Elder Loda called. Arrus and Loda Sang a Song of connecting, threading their auras together.

'Don't you dare, Ash!' Stormbreaker warned. 'Fire up our weapons so we can blast that scumbag to pieces!'

Ash ignored her, joining his Song with the Elders'. Together they helped project Ash's voice further.

'*He doesn't care about you!*' Ash Sang, shocked by the strangeness of hearing his voice so loud. '*He's just scared that you're the only ones that can stand in his way!*'

Shaard's gleeful grin wavered as he heard Ash.

'*Why would you listen to this child – a boy who wishes to be a Pathfinder, a boy who would do anything they say just to be accepted by them? He's their* puppet!'

'*Joining with the Leviathans is the only way we can stop the Devourer*,' Ash continued. '*But we have to show them that we can rise above hate and stand together as one!*'

The Song Weavers were far from convinced. They added their voices to the ever-growing web of Song-auras that spread across the wall, lending each other the strength to be heard. Ash sensed the guards around him backing away, nocking arrows to their bows in fear at all the sudden Song Weaving.

'*None of us stand a chance against the Devourer*,' someone Sang.

'*We do with the Leviathans*,' Ash insisted. '*Sing with me, and we can save them from the Devourer's control!*'

'*Why lower yourselves to such levels?*' Shaard asked, the dark-aura clawing over the wall like spider legs. '*Song Weavers once ruled the World! People and Leviathans trembled at our feet! We were unstoppable!*' Shaard clenched his fist. '*We should take our rightful place as rulers of this world!*'

'*The Wraith's right! Why* should *we help the Strongholders?*' someone else Sang. '*They hate us!*'

Ash was about to answer, but memories of growing up with the Fira flooded his mind. The nasty whispers and wicked rumours they made up about him, and the way he'd been turned into an outcast. He thought of the way the Song Weavers had been treated by the Pathfinders, how they'd been forced from their homes to fight in a war of his mother's making. His own mother, who didn't trust him because of what he was.

Ash swallowed.

He could hear the Song of the Wraiths swelling in volume, drawing inspiration from their leader.

How did Shaard do it? Ash knew their minds were lost to the Devourer's corruption, but *they* had chosen to start on that journey; there must have been a moment when Shaard had convinced them to open their souls to it.

He gives them something to fight for, Ash realized. *Even if it's nothing more than the promise of revenge.*

Lunah laid a hand on Ash's shoulder, sensing his distress.

'Shaard only knows how to hate,' Lunah said. 'He ent got nothin' on all of us.'

Ash's resolve hardened. *We need to be the exact* opposite *of Shaard.*

'*Our ancestors* did *once rule the world!*' Ash Sang. '*They ruled it with fear and hatred, keeping others down to hold on to their power. But that's all that's left of them!*' Ash pointed to the mass of squirming slime that was the

Devourer, pulsing livid green to the beat of its own corrupted false-heart. '*It destroyed them and left us to live in a world that hates Song Weavers for what our ancestors did! And so we hate the world back, which makes them hate us even more. It goes on and on and on until hate destroys us all over again!*'

The Devourer was nearly regrown now, its gills crackling with the green lightning of the Eclipse, as its head bubbled and reshaped itself. The Song Weavers stared at the monstrosity, realizing the truth in Ash's words.

'*But we're* not *our ancestors! And we're not Pathfinders either! We're Song Weavers, and we don't have to follow in any of their footsteps! We can break this cycle! All human-kin, Song Weaver or not, have to come together. Us, the Leviathans, the mursu, the vulpis – everyone in this world has to stand up to this hate!*'

The Song Weavers looked at those in the fleet below, who had fought so bravely to protect the Strongholds. Those who were *still* fighting for them. Their fate, the fate of them all, hung in the balance. And judging from the frightened looks in the Pathfinders' eyes, they knew it too.

Once again, after hundreds of years, Song Weavers held power in their hands.

'Can't you see?' Stormbreaker cried to those

around her. 'They're plotting against us! The Weavers are lost to us!'

'Yer the one who's lost, Ember,' Jed said. 'We would've followed you to the ends of the world, but *this*? Yer obsession has blinded you!'

'*No one* will see clearly until we rid the world of Leviathans! I won't have my life decided by minions of the wurms!' She rushed up to the Song Weavers around the Eclipse. 'All of you, power the weapon, now! That's an order!'

Loda calmly met Stormbreaker's wild gaze.

'We will not.'

Stormbreaker drew her bow, pointing the arrow straight at his face. 'POWER THE WEAPON!'

The other Song Weavers recoiled in shock. Loda looked back at them reassuringly, then glanced at Jed, then Ash.

'Abandoning the Eclipse is exactly what the Leviathans want us to do!' growled Stormbreaker, her bowstring quivering. 'They know it'll be the end of them, and so they've convinced you to sabotage us!'

'The Song Weavers have done everything you've ever asked of them, Ember,' Nuk said. 'They've put themselves in danger many times, while getting nothing in return.'

Stormbreaker's crew nodded in agreement, Ash watching them all with rising hope.

'Why are they Singing with the Wraiths then, if not to turn against us?' Stormbreaker hissed, never taking her eye from Loda.

'Shaard's offering to spare their lives if they'll join him,' Ash said.

'We should be showin' 'em we've got their backs, not threatenin' them!' Jed insisted.

'POWER THE WEAPON!' Stormbreaker screamed at Loda. A vein popped on the side of her head. Her fingers trembled, her eye bloodshot.

'No,' he said.

Stormbreaker fired.

But the arrow missed.

Jed had dived into her side, sending her shot flying wide. The Song Weavers watched in astonishment as the rest of the *Kinspear* crew jumped to his aid, wrestling Stormbreaker to the ground.

'*Without you, the Pathfinders are nothing!*' Shaard's voice boomed. '*This is your one chance to rise above them, as is your right!*'

With Stormbreaker now pinned to the floor, her crew looked round to see what the Song Weavers would decide. The crews in the fleet below gazed up, eyes full of fear, pleading with the Song Weavers not to leave them at the Devourer's mercy. Though they hadn't understood the Songs, they understood well enough the decision the Song Weavers were being asked to make.

And the Song Weavers had made it.

At last, after generations of being mistrusted, they were needed.

For once, they weren't being used or told – they were being *asked.*

Their Songs grew hot as fire with pride and determination.

'*We'll fight because we choose to!*' a Weaver Sang.

'*We'll fight to protect, not to destroy!*' Sang another.

'*We'll fight to prove who we really are!*'

'We'll fight to show that we're more than they think we are!' Ash Sang with them, joy threatening to bubble out of him in a fountain of sobs.

'Now let's free those Leviathans!' he cried out loud.

'YES!' Lunah whooped. 'GO KICK DEVOURER BUTT!'

And standing together, Singing as one, the Song Weavers blasted their Song-auras at the Corrupted swarm, tearing apart the Dark Song that held them captive.

46

PUSHING BACK

Brilliant blue Song-aura cascaded over the wall, crashing into the dark-aura with a deep, resonant hum. Though the Corrupted resisted, the Song Weavers managed to wrestle the Leviathans at the forefront of the swarm free from the Devourer's control. With their minds returned to them, the Leviathans turned back and added their own voices in a desperate effort to rescue their brethren.

'*BROTHERS! SISTERS! NEED HELP!*' Scratch howled, bounding forward and taking wing in an effort to help in the struggle. One by one, those souls that could still be saved were pulled from the hatred that had consumed them and joined those who opposed the Devourer.

The Wraiths fought fiercely to retake control, but

the Song Weavers and Leviathans wove a Song of protection, threading their auras together, forming a protective barrier that grew stronger with every thread.

It was a marvel to behold, but there was no time for that. The Devourer had nearly reformed and the largest bulk of the Corrupted swarm was still fast approaching.

'What now?' Teya asked.

'We have to get the true-heart and all who can Song Weave as close to the Devourer as we can,' Arrus said. 'Only then can we imprison it once more!'

'But the Leviathans . . . there aren't nearly enough!' Ash said.

'I know . . .' Arrus's face darkened. He placed a firm hand on Ash's shoulder. 'But we have to try.'

At the command of raised signal flags, the second wave of the fleet raced to the walls. All the Song Weavers had been loaded up on to the rickety lifts and sent down to the wharfs below to board the sleighs. At no point did they stop Singing, each continually weaving the shield of protection to keep the Dark Song at bay.

'Knew you had some backbone in there somewhere,' Kailen said, punching Jed in the shoulder.

'Yeah, well, I just hope yer plan works an' y'all don't make me look stupid.'

'Don't reckon you need any help in that department.' Yallah smiled.

'Yeah, yeah, I ent cut out for this captain lark, I get it,' Jed said.

'And what does that mean?' Nuk asked, one eyebrow raised.

'The *Frostheart*,' Jed said, looking up at the sleigh that had so briefly been his. 'She needs someone who knows what they're doin' at the helm. Ent nobody knows what they're doin' better'n you, *captain*.'

'My – my pup . . .' Nuk said, a tear welling up in her eye. 'I get my pup back . . .' For a moment, it looked as though she was about to break down. The crew edged towards her to check if she was OK. 'YOU HEARD THE MAN!' Nuk suddenly roared. 'The *Frostheart* is ours again and we've got a beastie to cage!'

'Aye aye, cap'n!' the *Frostheart* crew cried at once, rushing to their stations, wide grins on their faces.

'Oh, and, Jed?' Nuk called after him as he headed to take command of the *Kinspear*. 'I don't think you're as ill-suited to be a captain as you might think.'

He dipped his head in thanks. 'Now if you'll excuse me, all this excitement has given me an overwhelmin' desire to puke.'

As the rest of the crew made ready, Kob hastily tied Stormbreaker to the mainmast. As the sleigh rumbled to life, Ash approached his mother slowly.

'You'd betray me like this?' she said, her accusatory voice hurting more than Ash had expected. 'Your own mother?'

Ash untied the bundle from her belt.

'I-I'm sorry . . .' he whispered, stepping back, the chill true-heart in his hands once again. He looked up to see Captain Nuk up on the bridge, Master Podd at her side. Lovingly she took hold of the tiller.

'Back where we belong, captain,' Master Podd said.

Nuk grinned, her tusks gleaming.

'Isn't that the truth, Master Podd?'

47.

THROUGH THE BREACH

'*Forward!*' the *Kinspear* signalled to the entire fleet as it pushed off from the wharf.

Energy surged through Ash as he stood at the prow of the *Frostheart*, Singing his lungs out beside the other Weavers who'd come aboard. A path to the Devourer needed to be cleared, and they would do it by freeing as many of the Corrupted as they could.

The Pathfinders who'd been defending the breach watched in amazement as the very Leviathans who, until moments ago, had been trying to tear them to pieces now fell in line with the fleet, protecting its flanks from the Corrupted as the sleighs sallied out through the breach.

At Ash's side, the true-heart Sang eagerly, desperate to be returned to its body and defeat the dark heart that had stolen it.

But the Devourer waited for them beyond the wall. It had fully reformed and faced them with a ravenous grin, the veins under its hardened skin pulsing with green light. With a mind-numbing screech, it skittered forward with frightening speed, unnaturally fast for something so enormous.

The Eclipse, Ash thought. *It really has made it stronger!*

The Devourer tore through sleighs and Leviathans alike, not caring which side they were on, just so long as there was destruction. Tendrils of gooey darkness writhed like tentacles along its sides, crashing through sails and masts, ripping them to shreds. It screamed out its Dark Song, a soul-shuddering cacophony that hungered for the minds of those who dared oppose it. The Song Weavers and freed Leviathans staggering back as one as the Song struck like a physical blow.

It was terrible.

It was all-consuming.

The Song surged through Ash's body, an ice-cold fire stabbing through every one of his nerves. He struggled against it, feeling the Song Weavers around him suffering the same agony. A scream of fury pierced his head, forcing his knees to buckle and his eyes to squint as the hateful cry echoed around his skull.

But Ash kept on Singing.

All the Song Weavers did.

And somehow the combined strength of their protective shield managed to hold back the Devourer's influence.

But only just.

Ash knew they couldn't withstand it for long. Enraged, the Devourer forced the Corrupted forward.

The freed Leviathans desperately tried to rescue their brethren, but the Devourer wove its own barrier around those it controlled, a wall of shadow no Song could break through.

'Wraiths, starboard side!' Kailen yelled, just as the Corrupted swarm crashed into the fleet. The *Frostheart* was punctured by a hailstorm of black-feathered arrows. Its crew and the Aurora Guard who'd come aboard took cover and returned fire, poisoned arrows raining down upon them. Some of the Guard were hit, and Arla rushed from one wounded to the next, doing her best to patch them up.

'Would everyone please stop getting shot – I only have two hands!'

'Right – COME GET SOME!' Kailen yelled, firing the starboard bolt-thrower at a black sleigh, Twinge huffing and puffing as he kept the weapon reloaded. The bolts tore through the rotting timbers in explosive showers of splinters, the Wraiths hissing and frothing with anger. A group of Drifters raced past on snowboards, the riders guiding large kites that caught the wind and propelled them forward with surprising speed and grace.

'Ice Cutters!' Lunah yelled with pride.

The riders bent their knees and shifted their boards up and off the snow, their kites lifting them high into the air. As they soared over the Wraiths, they threw down incendiary orbs.

A wave of heat blasted over the deck, the black sleigh bursting into flame. Ash turned away from it, only to see a Pathfinder sleigh being torn to shreds by corrupted Hurtlers and Lurkers who had swarmed over its deck.

'We have to keep Singing or the barrier will weaken!' Loda said to Ash and the Song Weavers around him, who had taken cover, their eyes full of fear.

Ash rose, just in time to be showered with snow as a Gargant snapped a corrupted Spearwurm right out

of the air, a second before it would have struck the *Frostheart*. The sleigh listed sharply as a wave of snow from the Gargant's wake rushed in, timbers groaning under the strain.

Suddenly a shadow loomed over the *Frostheart*. Ash looked up in horror to see the Devourer passing over them. Its incredible size blocked out the sky, its colossal feet thumping into the ground with earth-shattering force, one claw entirely crushing a Pathfinder sleigh.

Shaard's sleigh rushed after it.

For just a moment, Ash caught sight of Shaard himself, locking on to those wild turquoise eyes with his own. Shaard gestured at the monstrosity he'd unleashed upon the world, the death-god whose searing green eyes were focused on Aurora and the abundance of frightened defenceless souls within. Shaard's smile could not have been more full of self-satisfaction if he'd tried.

'It's pushing past the defences!' Kob warned.

'Well, we can't be having that now, can we?' Nuk called out, preparing to turn the sleigh.

'We can't follow,' Teya shouted, firing another bolt at a Wraith sleigh that had rammed a mursu craft. 'If we turn our backs to the swarm, we'll be overrun!'

And she was right.

A dreadful *CRACK* split the air, Ash watched helplessly as the Devourer smashed through the outer wall as though it hadn't even been there. The Eclipse tumbled amid the falling debris and was crushed under the weight of the falling masonry.

But while Shaard's sleigh followed the Devourer, the Corrupted held their ground, ensuring the Leviathans and allies couldn't give chase. Aurora was alone.

'Come back here, you oversized snot-lump!' Lunah yelled after the Devourer.

'Er . . . guys?' Twinge said, looking off to the east. 'We . . . we might have another problem . . .'

The sound of a horn called out across the plain.

The crew whipped round to see what else could possibly be going wrong.

Emerging from the snow hills was a long impenetrable line of armoured megadons stretching far out across the plain. Each was ridden by heavily armoured yeti warriors. Those guiding the loping beasts carried lengthy spears, while those who sat behind reached for arrows in their quivers.

'No!' Ash said with a gasp as, through the chaos of the battle, he caught sight of Temu at the head of the line. He was dressed in his full battle glory and mounted upon the largest megadon in the army. It was true. The Mountain's Ward had emptied the sacred yeti lands of its warriors and led them to crush their ancient enemy.

Temu lifted his spear, his terrible war cry clear even at this distance. The Wardens roared in return, a battle howl that chilled the blood of human-kin on the plain. Another horn blared from the yeti lines, encouraging the megadons to pick up their pace as they began to charge towards the battle.

'There's . . . so many of them.' Nuk gasped.

Ash went numb.

Tobu, he thought desperately. *What's Temu done with Tobu?!*

'You're being outflanked!' came Stormbreaker's voice from the mainmast. 'You have to use the archeoweapons.'

But even if the Pathfinders had wanted to, they would never make it back up the walls in time, and the Eclipse was buried beneath tons of rubble.

The ground trembled. Even the Leviathans and Corrupted twisted their heads to see what was approaching.

We can't survive this, Ash realized with mounting panic. *We can't win against the yeti too!*

'Brace for impact!' Nuk ordered. Ash gripped the railing, steadying his feet against the deck.

'Aim for the legs!' Kailen shouted. 'It's the least armoured part!'

The Wardens angled their spears and aimed their

bows. The plain echoed with the thunder of their stampeding might, the yeti themselves stone-silent and focused. A silence that ended with an almighty *CRASH* as the yeti veered sharply away from the allies and smashed straight into the Corrupted.

They carved through the swarm like a sleigh runner through snow, spears slicing into flesh as the megadons' monstrous tusks tore through Wraith vessels and threw entire Leviathans out of the way.

'They're . . . they're not attacking us!' Kailen said.

'They're *helpin'* us!' Lunah leaped up and punched the air. 'The fuzzy grumps are helpin' us!'

The allies let out a roaring cheer as the yeti smashed through a Wraith sleigh, firing their arrows with deadly accuracy. Ash gawped at the strength of the yeti charge, gripping the side rail as a small smile spread across his face.

Temu led the charge, but another warrior rode at his side, a warrior who matched Temu in ferocity and skill.

A yeti warrior with one horn.

The warrior caught sight of Ash and raised his spear high. Ash gasped out a laugh, tears blurring his vision. He leaped with joy, waving his hand.

The warrior was hidden beneath heavy armour, his face shielded by a masked helmet, but there was no question in Ash's mind. Tobu was alive, and he'd ridden to the rescue. He was keeping Ash safe, just as he always did.

Ash and Tobu held each other's gaze for a second, until Corrupted burst out of the snow into the centre of the yeti charge, showering megadons and yeti with the ice, and Ash lost sight of Tobu in the heat of the battle.

'The yeti will hold them,' Teya called to Nuk, who was already pulling hard on the tiller. 'We're good to go, go, go!'

'Kob! Raise the flags!' Nuk bellowed as the sleigh turned in a wide arc. 'Signal the fleet to follow. Aurora needs our help!'

THE FIGHT FOR AURORA

The fleet tore across the snow plain in an arrow formation, leaving the raging battle behind them. Enjins roared, Yallah pushing the *Frostheart* to its absolute limit.

They had no time to spare.

'Eh, I reckon we could give it a bit more . . .' Lunah joked, bracing herself against the *Frostheart*'s speed.

Fuelled by the Eclipse, the Devourer had already breached the inner wall eight leagues ahead and reached the mountain of Aurora itself. With a terrible cry, it tore its claws into the stone, shredding the rock and causing the towers and palaces that had once stood so proudly upon Aurora's side to collapse in clouds of dust. Shaard's sleigh flitted about its feet like an excited pup.

The Aurora Guard on the outdoor terraces fired everything they had at their attacker – arrows, stones, even the few archeoweapons that remained – but nothing had the slightest effect. With a shriek of irritation, the Devourer slashed its claws through the terraces, the guards disappearing amid the cascading ruins. The beast had torn a gaping wound in the mountain, and it peeked within, its long tongue slithering hungrily. Ash swore he could hear the screams coming from inside.

'Gods . . .' Yallah said, her eyes wide.

The world was already drowning in the Devourer's spiteful Song, and if they didn't stop it now, it would consume everyone within Aurora with a single blast of its deathly aura.

'If you'd let me use the Eclipse, it would be dead by now . . .' Stormbreaker said softly.

Ash felt a chill at his side. The true-heart. He untied the wrappings that hung from his belt, unveiling the glowing heart within. It pulsed with a vibrant energy, more alive than he'd ever seen it. It was as if it knew its time had come, that the corrupted shell of its body was close.

With this, there's still hope, Ash thought. *If only we can get there fast enough!*

The fleet sped forward, but they just weren't going to make it in time.

'Spirits, no . . .' Ash whispered, unable to watch.

The Devourer reared back its head, its jaws gaping wide as it prepared to unleash its essence-stealing aura.

And the ground erupted at its feet.

It shrieked in shock as the snow exploded into vast clouds, rumbling and convulsing as though it were collapsing in on itself. For a moment, Ash thought the volcano had come to life again. That was, until a gigantic shape burst from beneath.

Ash's breath caught in his throat.

It was the Brood Mother.

With a vengeful cry she clawed the Devourer across its snout, dragging it down to the snow with a shattering crunch. The fleet watched in awe as a flood of Leviathans followed the Brood Mother from the depths, leaping and climbing to her aid. Ash could barely believe what he was seeing. Hundreds of them – no, *thousands* – more than Ash had ever seen in his life. They screamed their war Songs, rising from the snow to surround the Devourer.

'They came,' Ash whispered, barely daring to speak the words. 'They *actually* came!'

The Leviathans had seen the people of the Snow Sea come together for the first time since the World Before. They'd seen that human-kin were willing to sacrifice themselves for the greater good.

And now they'd come to stand alongside them.

'Mummy's home!' Yallah cheered, as Ash released the breath he'd been holding.

The Devourer lunged for the Brood Mother. The two behemoths bit and tore at each other with enough force to shatter Strongholds, each strike as loud as a thunderclap. With the Brood Mother keeping the Devourer occupied, her kin formed a huge circle around them. They began to Sing, their blue auras weaving together. From the Brood Mother's own throat thrummed a deep sound, one that grew in strength despite her exertions.

The Devourer's jaws opened unnaturally wide as it prepared another attack, but the Brood Mother blasted her own powerful Song-aura just as dark fire spewed from the Devourer's mouth, the bright blue light forcing the darkness back down the Devourer's gullet and causing it to stagger in shock.

'*Now*,' Ash heard her Sing, her voice filling the minds of all the Song Weavers. '*Now is the time to imprison the Cursed One. We must banish it from our world.*'

With a dreadful shriek, the Devourer bit into the

Brood Mother's neck, blue blood spattering across the snow. She was clearly outmatched, but she'd done what she'd needed to do – keep their enemy busy long enough for the Song Weavers to arrive. Led by the *Frostheart*, the sleighs cut their enjins, pulling in behind the circle of Leviathans.

Ash held the true-heart above his head, the Song deep within its core suddenly bursting out in ripples of light.

Its Song was pained and full of regret. Regret for what had become of it, regret for what it had been forced to do by the World Before, but burning with a fierce determination to put an end to it once and for all. The Devourer seemed to sense it, its eyes darting towards the *Frostheart* with primal fury – and perhaps just a tiny flicker of fear.

Every single Song Weaver in the fleet began to join their Songs with the Leviathans, their weaving auras gathering round the true-heart. The Brood Mother struggled free of the Devourer's jaws and, with a roar that shook Aurora, her voice boomed out across the snows. Her Song-aura, as swift and mighty as a raging river, joined the others. The true-heart gathered the threads of all the different voices, weaving them together in a ring of light round the Devourer. The Pathfinders could only watch the scene with open-mouthed astonishment, the Weave so powerful even they could see its radiant light.

The Wraiths aboard Shaard's sleigh tried to counter the Song with their own, but they were overpowered by their enemies' determination to see the Devourer defeated forever.

'*Together!*' the Brood Mother Sang. '*Together we end this!*'

It was a Song of power, of strength. It was a Song that set light to the hearts of all who stood against the Devourer's corruption.

Ash felt like he was on fire.

But it was a fire of unity and defiance.

Lunah cheered and punched her fist into her palm. 'KICK ITS BUTT!'

Nuk removed her hat and held it to her chest. Even Kailen had a tear in her eye.

Ash Sang with everything he had, until his throat was raw, and even then he didn't stop, the true-heart's power radiating in his grasp. A coat of frost glistened on his hands, creeping down his arms and burning his flesh, but he wouldn't give up; he wouldn't let it drop.

'Ash! Don't!' Stormbreaker shouted, disrupting his focus. 'This is what they want! You're falling right into the Leviathans' trap!'

Ash did his best to ignore her.

The snow plain glowed blue under the thousands of Song-aura threads dancing together in an ocean of light, joining and twisting and forming a net around the screeching Devourer.

It roared and bellowed, calling out to its Corrupted for help, but the yeti were still keeping them busy. It thrashed and squirmed in desperation, but its movements were becoming slow and sluggish. The Eclipse may have strengthened it, but clearly not enough.

The Devourer's Song grew weaker.

Its seething hate, once a force that could level armies, was reduced to a bubbling groan.

'*This . . . this can't be happening!*' Ash heard Shaard Sing. He could see him, a ragged shape on the prow of his sleigh. '*You're invincible!*'

Shaard's Song was wracked with doubt and confusion. The dark, wispy tendrils of the Devourer's aura reached out for Shaard, seeking his help. Shaard gripped the rigging of the forward sail and stretched out his hand.

'*I'm here! What do you need?*' he Sang urgently. '*How can I help you?*'

The shadow-wisps coiled round Shaard's hand, and then suddenly tightened, snatching him forward. Even at this distance, Ash saw his eyes widen with alarm, his bright pupils shining in the dim light.

'*What?!*' Shaard tried to resist. But the tendrils crawled up his arm and pulled him towards the now writhing mass of shadow. '*No! What are you doing?!*' Shaard's Song was full of panic, all sign of triumph gone. '*Stop it! I command you!*'

Shaard tried to Weave his aura round the Devourer's, tried to take control of it as he had done to so many Leviathans before.

But this was one Leviathan Shaard had never had control of.

Shaard began to scream as the darkness wrapped round his body, washed over the sleigh and took hold of

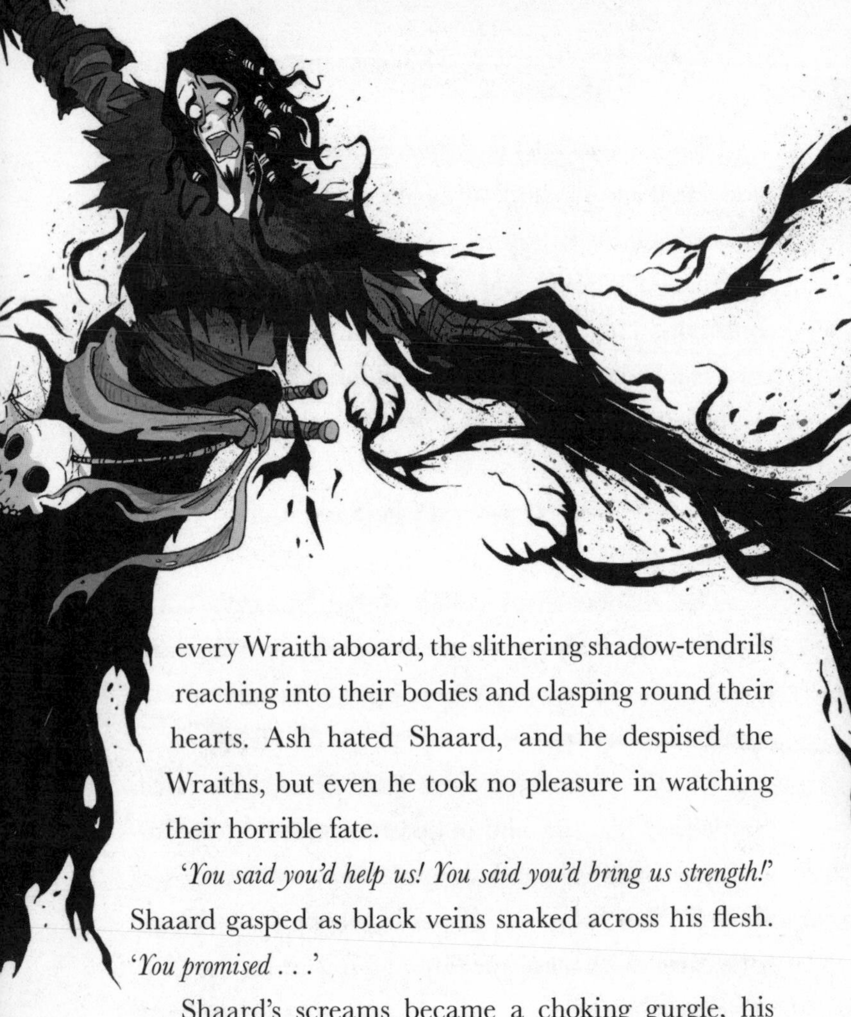

every Wraith aboard, the slithering shadow-tendrils reaching into their bodies and clasping round their hearts. Ash hated Shaard, and he despised the Wraiths, but even he took no pleasure in watching their horrible fate.

'You said you'd help us! You said you'd bring us strength!' Shaard gasped as black veins snaked across his flesh. *'You promised . . .'*

Shaard's screams became a choking gurgle, his vivid turquoise eyes turning as black and lifeless as night.

Ash watched in horror as the tendrils retreated from the bodies of the Wraiths, the flickering, fading light of their Songs ripped out of them.

Shaard's body slumped to the floor.

49

VICTORY

The Devourer had consumed its own servants' life-essence in a last desperate attempt to strengthen itself against the binding Song.

But even that was not enough.

'*It's working!*' the Song Weavers Sang. '*We're winning!*'

'*BLADE AND CLAW*,' the Leviathans Sang. '*BOW AND FANG!*'

'*Just a little more*,' the Brood Mother encouraged. '*Almost there!*'

Together they'd managed to achieve what the World Before had not been able to.

'Enemies, starboard side!' Teya shouted.

A group of corrupted Leviathans had broken free from the yeti and were charging straight for the fleet.

'Please, Ash, stop helping them!' Ember pleaded.

'Stop listening to the Leviathans' Song!'

She still thinks I'm under their control, Ash thought, hurt that she had so little trust in him, even after all she'd seen.

'Remember who you are! You're a good person!'

How would you know? You know nothing about me! You were never there!

Ash swallowed hard, his Song breaking, a cold, gnawing sensation building in the pit of his stomach.

'You're my son,' Stormbreaker said, her voice choked with emotion. 'I know you would never want to hurt anybody. Please – stop this! Don't follow in your father's footsteps!'

You're wrong! You don't know what you're talking about!

But what if she's right*?* a cold, quiet voice whispered in Ash's mind. *What if you* are *being used?*

The gnawing cold in his belly got worse. His Song-aura wavered, and he strained to correct it.

A tear ran down his mother's cheek.

'The Leviathans have won. First Ferno . . . now you. They've taken everything from me. I was so close . . . so close to ending this . . .'

I have to see this through – I can't be distracted, Ash told himself, as a pain deep inside flared to life at her words.

And then what? asked the cold voice. *What do you think will happen if you have victory today? Do you think your mother will truly accept what you are? Do you think* anyone *will?*

Stormbreaker took a shuddering breath. 'Every single day since you were born, I prayed to the spirits. I prayed for them to spare you from this fate.'

They've seen what you're capable of now, the cold hateful voice whispered. *They will be even more scared of you than they were before . . .*

No! Ash tried to block out the words, but his mother carried on. How he wished she would stop, how he wished she wasn't there at all.

'I prayed you would take after me, and not your father . . .'

Ash's throat tightened, choking off his Song. He staggered round to face his mother, tears blurring his vision.

'W-what do you mean?' he stammered, an angry, bitter chill rising up his throat.

'I wanted you to be normal – to live a happy, normal life. Not to be a . . . a Leviathan's *plaything*.'

'But this – this is who I am!' Ash said. 'Who I've always been! I am a Song Weaver!'

'And I wish . . .' His mother took a deep breath. 'I wish, more than anything, that you weren't.'

Ash fell to his knees, tears streaming down his flushed cheeks.

'Mum . . .' He stared at her, his heart breaking in two.

Even your mother wishes you were someone else . . .

A terrible cold gripped his body. The gnawing, hateful cold he'd tried so hard to suppress since that first moment he'd used the Dark Song in Shade's Chasm.

'I wish I'd never found you!' Ash screamed. 'I wish you'd stayed lost forever!'

His mother looked hurt, and Ash was glad.

Tendrils of bitter darkness flashed through his mind, stealing away his self-control. He could feel the true-heart in his hand, its Song pulsing through him.

Suddenly he couldn't stand the sound of it.

It sounded happy – *satisfied* that victory was almost in its grasp. Well, why should it be so happy when Ash was so miserable? Why should it have a happy ending if Ash could not? Why should anyone?

Ash despised the way it needed him, depended on him to hold it aloft so it could imprison a creature that was only trying to take revenge on the world that had turned it into the monster it was.

He couldn't bear to touch it.

Ash's Song-aura warped into writhing tentacles of shadow, which burrowed into the true-heart, infecting

the Song that was being focused within.

Ash didn't care. He wanted to see the binding Song destroyed. All it would take was a crack, a little chink in the armour, just enough for the Devourer to break free, and . . .

With a pulse of force that rattled through the sleigh masts, the binding Song was broken.

The Song Weavers staggered back with a gasp.

The Brood Mother and Leviathans cried out in pain as the Devourer rose up, its Dark Song rising, like a victorious laugh.

Ash stood on the *Frostheart*'s deck, his entire body shivering, his breath misting in front of his frightened eyes.

With a roar, the Devourer struck the Brood Mother, slamming her into the ground, tearing at her with its claws. The Leviathan swarm screeched in panic and charged, biting and slashing and tearing at its flesh.

But they were no match for the Devourer.

Not now.

The ground quaked with its every movement, the sky darkened, the air splintered. Ash saw as if in slow motion his friends rushing around, terror on their faces, the other sleighs of the fleet turning as fast as possible, the Leviathans fighting with everything they had to save the Brood Mother.

With a terrible cracking sound, like the world was tearing apart, the *Frostheart*'s hull burst open, its timbers splintering to pieces.

Ash flew through the air, just like the rest of the crew.

Air burst from his lungs as he hit the snow, and saw how the Devourer's claw had ripped the *Frostheart* in two.

A shadow fell over him, and he found the Devourer itself looking down at him. Its green eyes were full of malice, hungry for vengeance. Ash stared back into those eyes and knew he would never feel joy or happiness again.

And then it Sang. It unleashed a bellow unlike anything Ash had ever heard. It shook the very roots of the world and flooded the minds of every soul within it. Ash watched, horrified, as Leviathans, Pathfinders and Song Weavers alike collapsed to the ground.

Nothing could escape it. It pulled in everything, its shadow-tendrils reaching down into the core of the world itself, ready to consume it all.

ALONE

Ash felt like his spirit had been ripped out of his body and thrown into a river.

No, an *ocean.*

A bottomless ocean, as deep and vast as the sky itself, but as bright and glimmering as fresh ice. Countless threads of light danced around each other like snowflakes in a blizzard.

Song-auras, Ash realized.

There were so many.

Wolvers, ulks, birds, fish.

Mursu, vulpis, Leviathans and people.

Millions, billions, trillions of Songs, of spirits, of *existences.*

Every single Song that ever was and had ever been weaved about each other in a tapestry Ash could barely begin to understand. He was at the mercy of its flow, pulled along by the powerful current.

Is this . . . the World Weave? Ash said. Sang? *Thought?* He didn't really know how things worked in this place, this World-soul, this centre of everything.

It was a wondrous place; his skin felt like it was being warmed by Mother Sun herself. He felt safe and protected.

He felt like he was home.

So it was with horror that he saw the shining threads darken, the Devourer's shadow-aura bleeding through the Weave, smothering the warming light and reducing all to a cold darkness.

It's devouring the World Weave, Ash realized. *It's consuming everything!*

And everyone.

And Ash was powerless to stop it.

He floated there as the endless black void enveloped him.

All the hope and warmth of the World Weave was gone, replaced by the cold hard hatred of the Devourer. The Devourer was everywhere. It was everything.

All the Songs of the world were silenced, all the dancing threads pulled apart, to be consumed as the Devourer pleased.

In that emptiness, that constant, deafening silence, entirely absent of Song or life, Ash was alone.

He shivered. He hated being alone.

With a pang of sadness, Ash thought of the *Frostheart*. His home. He remembered seeing it for the first time, the thrilling excitement that had flooded through him at the sight of its glorious red sails and its huge archeomek propellers. It seemed like a thing from another world, a world he would never get to be a part of. He remembered the way it had called to him, the way it had promised so much.

Adventure.

Excitement.

And most importantly . . . hope.

Hope that he could escape his lonely life with the Fira. Hope that he'd be able find his long-lost parents. Hope that he would finally never have to be alone again.

Saving the sleigh from the Hurtlers had been the best decision Ash had ever made.

Which is why it hurt so much that it was gone. Smashed to pieces and left broken on the frozen snow, the crew scattered like the splintered timbers. The happy family he'd dreamed of finding didn't exist. Even though he'd travelled across the world to find his parents, he was still as alone as the day they had left him.

And he would remain alone as everything came to an end.

As he floated in the frigid, lifeless void, Ash did what he always did when he felt lonely.

He began to Sing.

He Sang the first thing that came to him, just desperate to hear something. He wasn't surprised to find it was his lullaby. He Sang quietly, or maybe that was just what the Devourer's darkness did to sound.

He Sang the sad melody, finding comfort in it despite its sorrowful tune. Tears ran down his cheeks as the words left his mouth, as familiar to him as breathing.

It might've been a sad Song, but it stirred the embers of hope within him. It was a Song about the promise of finding those that you cared about the most, about being reunited with those that you love.

And it was most likely for that reason that the Devourer stirred, its Song-aura shifting, darker shades of shadow slithering through the endless dark. It couldn't let hope survive, not while it devoured the world.

Ash Sang on, knowing that if he stopped, those he loved would be lost to him forever.

The *Frostheart* crew. All gone now.

And it's my fault . . .

His mother had been right. The Strongholders were right to fear Song Weavers. He'd been a danger to every person he knew.

If he hadn't got so angry, if he hadn't let his mother's words affect him like that . . .

I couldn't control my hate . . . I let the Devourer into my head!

What have I done?

The darkness was still shifting, coiling around him to strangle his Song into nothingness. But as Ash opened his eyes, he saw glinting lights in the distance. Small dots of white, bright against the black, like stars.

Like a constellation to guide him.

He tried to move towards them, his Song-aura trailing behind him. But no matter how hard he tried, he couldn't seem to get any closer. Ash was near to giving up, sensing the Devourer constricting around him. But then he noticed that as he Sang, the stars pulsed in time with his words. Ash Sang louder, and the stars grew brighter. Encouraged, he Sang louder still.

The Devourer became angry, the darkness around Ash growing deeper. Ash felt his voice failing him. He held his last note, before his Song, the last thing he had left in the world, was stolen from him.

He clenched his eyes shut as the Devourer's grip tightened, about to snuff him out like a candle flame.

'I made an oath,' said a voice, gruff and serious.

Ash blinked, looking past the slithering aura of the Devourer to find that one of the stars had disappeared.

'I promised to keep you safe, and I don't intend to fail now.'

Ash spun round and saw that the missing star was right beside him, although it wasn't a star at all. It was a thread of light, a glowing Song-aura.

Tobu . . .

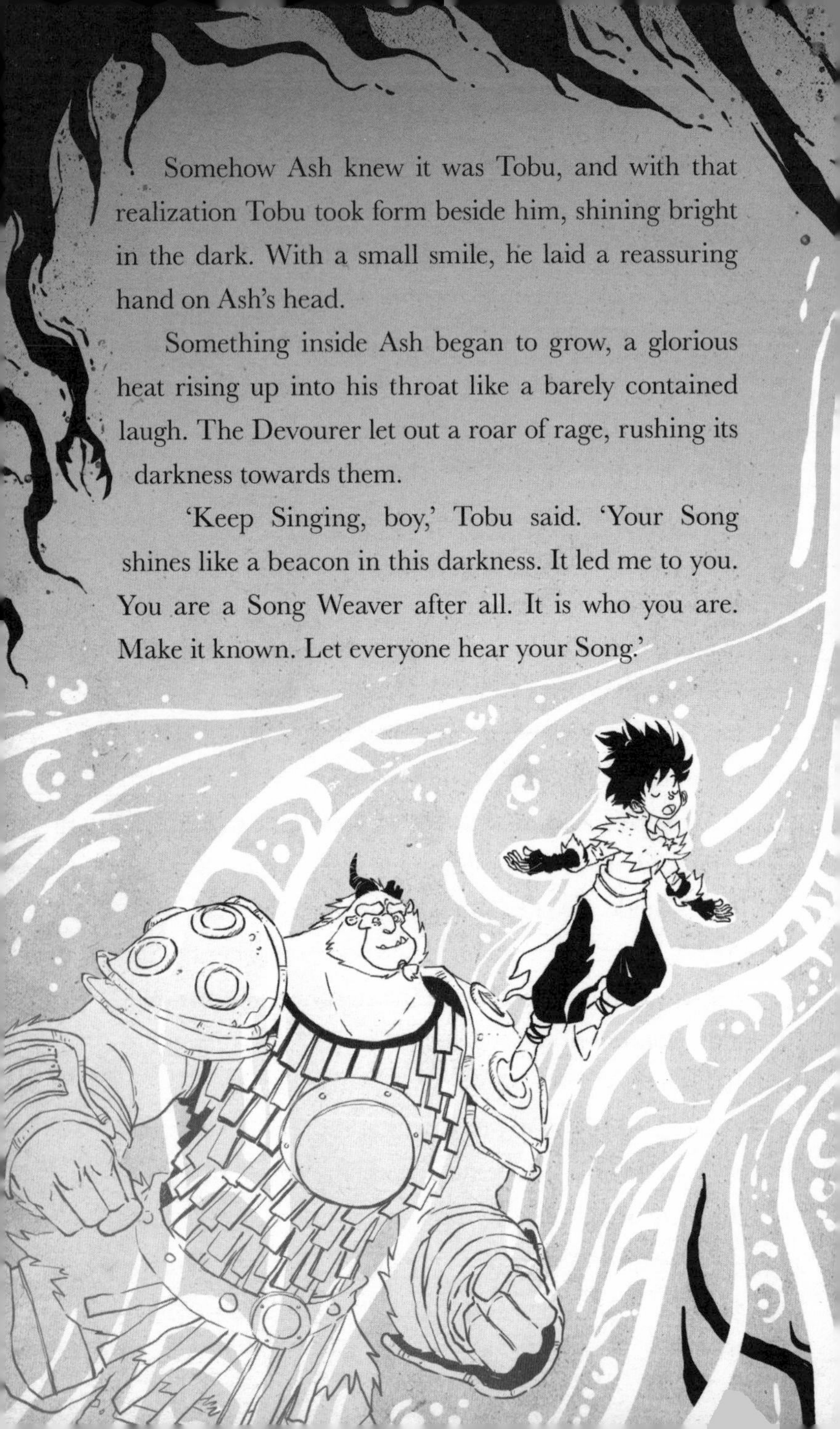

Somehow Ash knew it was Tobu, and with that realization Tobu took form beside him, shining bright in the dark. With a small smile, he laid a reassuring hand on Ash's head.

Something inside Ash began to grow, a glorious heat rising up into his throat like a barely contained laugh. The Devourer let out a roar of rage, rushing its darkness towards them.

'Keep Singing, boy,' Tobu said. 'Your Song shines like a beacon in this darkness. It led me to you. You are a Song Weaver after all. It is who you are. Make it known. Let everyone hear your Song.'

Ash's heart leaped at Tobu's words, his body filled with a brilliant, burning joy. It flared bright, shielding him from the encroaching tendrils of shadow. Ash's Song broke free of the Devourer's grasp, bursting from him like an explosion.

He Sang louder than ever, watching in amazement as another star rushed towards them.

'Hey, don't forget about me!' the star Sang. 'We promised that if we ever got separated, we'd find each other again. I ent gonna break my promise either!'

Ash laughed through his tears. It was Lunah. She grinned as she gleamed into life at his other side, giving him a friendly thump on the shoulder.

'Look at this place.' Lunah whistled as she gazed out at the World Weave. 'Ent us who should be scared, though. The Devourer's made it to the top of my enemy list, an' that ent a place anyone wants to be!'

The Devourer's shadow-tendrils snapped and bit at Ash, but Ash was too quick, his Song strengthened by his friends, who ducked and weaved around his own aura, soaring through the darkness like a comet.

The shadow-aura gathered in a rising wave, trying to block Ash's path, and so he Sang harder still.

As if in response, numerous lights blinked to life, swooping and clawing at the Devourer, cawing out in defiance.

Crows, Ash realized, shooting over the wave.

'*Enough running! Enough hiding!*' Rook cried, her aura burning bright, her Song almost healed and whole again. '*We all deserve a second chance! Together we can stop the Devourer!*'

She wound her Song-aura, no longer black but a vivid blue, round the darkness of the monster that had tormented her for so long, giving Ash time to dodge its attacks.

'As capable as you are, I fear you won't be gettin' very far without some good leadership, as Master Podd would not mind telling you!'

A moment later, the Song-aura of Captain Nuk was whooshing around them, closely followed by a smaller one at its side.

'Indeed, captain,' said Master Podd.

'And what about us?' said another of the stars. 'You're gonna need a crew to back you up, ent ya?'

Ash's Song burned hotter as Kailen appeared, quickly followed by the rest of the crew, even those that had been lost.

'None better that I can see!' Teya said.

'Not that ye can see that far in this nasty sludge,' Arla commented.

'Doesn't matter how dark it is, we're in this together,' said Kob.

'All the way,' agreed Yallah.

'Till the end.' Yorri smiled.

'It's going to make one heck of a story!' Twinge laughed.

The auras of those that had always been there for Ash, those that had accepted him for exactly who he was, wove together, strengthening Ash's radiance, his light growing brighter and brighter.

Other lights burst into life, more and more, as numerous and beautiful as stars in the sky. Their Songs resounded across the void, bright and powerful. Every mursu, vulpis, yeti and human-kin responded to Ash's lullaby, his call to arms. So many voices, so many lives, all standing up to the Devourer, who bellowed with unbridled fury that anyone could dare defy it. But instead of getting lost in the sound, Ash drew strength from it. It emboldened him and his resolve to fight back.

Ash's aura surged forward. It struck the shadow-aura with a blinding glare, the darkness exploding into hundreds of strands, each snapping with jaws of hate. Ash and his friends ducked and weaved, but they couldn't keep fighting forever. They would grow weaker, while the Devourer would only grow stronger.

We'll stop fighting then, Ash thought, aware for the first time that he still held the true-heart in his hands. *There's been enough fighting for a thousand years!*

And so he began to weave his aura *with* the Dark Song instead of against it. When it rushed towards him, he looped around it. When it slashed at him, he danced beneath its jaws. As it tried to strangle the light from his Song, Ash weaved in and out, forming beautiful, intricate patterns.

'You're doing it!' Lunah cried.

'Keep going!' Tobu agreed.

It seemed to be working. The Devourer was becoming desperate. It screamed and shrieked, until Ash could barely focus on where he needed to go.

But just as the Devourer was about to close in on him, its cries were answered with another deafening roar. Ash gasped as countless more lights burned into existence, almost blinding in their brilliance.

'JOINING FANG AND CLAW WITH BOW AND SPEAR!' Scratch's Song shrilled.

Leviathans swarmed around the Devourer,

each of their auras illuminating it with brilliant light.

'Thank you!' Ash Sang through his lullaby. *'Thank you!'*

At long last, everyone was standing together against their enemy, fighting for the one world they all shared.

A heart is the source of Song. The Brood Mother's voice echoed in Ash's head, filling his mind with clarity.

'A heart . . .' Ash repeated, understanding what he had to do.

The Devourer does *have a weakness – its false-heart!*

Ash dashed forward, speeding along the Dark Song, following it to its source. The Dark Song tried to close in on him again, but this time he had his friends behind him.

No, not his friends. His *family*.

Tobu, Lunah, Nuk and the *Frostheart* crew.

He didn't need to search for any other family, for his real one had already found him.

He wasn't alone. Not any more.

He'd reached the centre, the source of the Devourer's Song.

He'd reached its heart.

And everything went white.

THE HEART

Where am I?

Ash opened his eyes and found himself on an ice plain.

It was piercingly cold, the type of chill that cuts through the thickest of furs as though they weren't even there at all. The ice stretched off in every direction as far as the eye could see, featureless and unbroken. Empty except for a child, a young boy with scruffy black hair, standing just ahead. As Ash approached, he heard the boy sobbing gently.

'Hello?' Ash said.

The boy spun round, startled. He had the most piercing turquoise eyes, shining wet with tears. Ash felt like he recognized him but couldn't understand why a child would be alone in this place.

'H-hello?' The boy sniffed. He clutched something close to his chest.

'Are you OK?' Ash asked.

'They . . .' The boy shuddered, unable to hold back fresh tears. 'They – they don't want me.'

'Who doesn't?' Ash said, looking out across the empty plain.

'My . . . my Stronghold. They – they caught me Singing to the *Levy – Levy-ah-thians* . . . They said I was bad.'

'You're a Song Weaver,' Ash said, more a statement than a question. The boy looked frightened at the name, his eyes darting guiltily about. 'It's OK,' Ash reassured him. 'I'm a Song Weaver too.'

'Y-you are?'

Ash nodded, smiling. 'I'm Ash. I can talk to Leviathans, just like you!'

'Does that mean you're . . . bad too?'

'Song Weavers aren't bad. I-I mean, they don't have to be. They can be good or bad, just like everyone else. I'm sure you're one of the good ones.'

The boy looked shocked, his turquoise eyes gleaming.

'You . . . think I'm good?'

'Of course!' Ash nodded.

The boy gave him a small smile.

'Where is your Stronghold? Can I take you back?' Ash asked. 'Even though you can Song Weave, it's dangerous to be out on the snows.'

'They won't let me.' The boy's smile disappeared, his lips trembling. 'They said I'm never allowed back again.'

'But . . . they can't leave you out here!' Ash was shocked. The boy couldn't have been much older than five winters. Tears rolled down the boy's cheeks, Ash actually worried they might freeze in the biting cold.

'My friend said that *they're* the ones who're bad,' the boy said bitterly. 'My friend said it's *them* who should be hurting, not me.'

'And who's your friend?' Ash asked, his belly twisting at the boy's words.

The boy seemed reluctant to say more, as though he hid a terrible secret. He watched Ash closely, those eyes so bright, so . . . familiar.

Shaard, Ash realized. Though clearly not the Shaard Ash knew.

Apparently the boy Shaard found Ash trustworthy, because he brought his hands away from his chest and revealed what he was hiding within them. A small heart-shaped crystal, black as flint. Wisps of shadow rose from it like steam, curling and coiling round the boy's fingers.

Ash swallowed. He didn't want to alarm the child. 'That's pretty . . . Where did you find it?'

'It found me! It's my only friend. It's the only one who likes me.'

'You have to be careful with that,' Ash said. 'It can be dangerous.'

The ends of the wisps grew into serpentine heads, snapping at Ash as he came closer. They whispered to Shaard, who held it away from Ash protectively.

'It says it needs me. It's all weak. It says that without me, it would die.' Shaard started to cry again, his chest heaving with every sob. 'I-I don't want it to die!'

The Devourer's false-heart is weak, Ash remembered. *It needs souls to keep it alive. And Shaard . . . Shaard was the last soul it consumed. It's using Shaard's spirit as a last defence*, Ash realized in horror.

He stepped back, raising his hands in a calming gesture. 'No one has to die! I was just hoping to have a look, but you hold on to it!'

'It's my friend,' Shaard insisted. 'I-I just don't want to be alone.'

The fear and loneliness in his voice were so raw and fierce it hurt Ash's own heart. He felt like he was looking at a reflection of himself, and wanted nothing more than to hold the child and try to reassure him that it would all be OK.

'I used to be all alone too,' Ash said gently. 'But then I found my family. We just need to find you yours.'

'They're gone. I lost my mummy and daddy,' Shaard said, full of sadness.

'I lost my mum and dad too,' Ash said. 'But then I found another family. One that loved me for what I am. We need to find you something like that. How does that sound?'

Ash held out his hand for Shaard to take, but the boy didn't move. He looked as though he longed to, but the shadow-wisps snarled at him warningly. He gazed at the black heart, a look of fear on his face.

'This . . . this is my family,' he said sharply.

'No,' Ash said. 'It only wants to take from you. Your family wouldn't do that. They wouldn't want you to be scared.'

'Why . . . why is it so angry?' the boy asked, looking like he wanted to drop the heart, but was too afraid of the consequences.

'Because . . . because once it was treated very badly. It had all its love stolen away.'

'It's sad?'

'I think so.' Ash nodded. They were quiet for some time, watching the serpent-wisps writhe around the blackened husk.

'How can I help it?' the boy said. 'I want to make it not sad.'

'Let it go,' Ash said quietly.

'But . . . won't I be alone then?'

'You're not alone,' Ash said. 'I'm here with you. And, look, I have this!'

Ash held out the true-heart. Shaard's eyes shone at the sight of it. 'This one is kind. It doesn't tell you what to do. We can swap, if you'd like.'

Shaard looked desperate to take it, but the false-heart hissed and spat.

'The world is full of people who will help you,' Ash said with a smile, 'who will take care of you, who will love you. You just have to give them a chance. But as long as you hold on to that heart, it won't let you see all the love that's out there waiting for you. It will make you angry. It will make you hate them. And then you truly will be alone.'

The boy looked frightened. He held the false-heart out, hand trembling.

Ash edged forward, and slowly held out the true-heart.

'Don't worry. We can do it together.'

The boy looked glad about that. He took a long, deep breath, then looked away, handing the false-heart to Ash with his eyes shut. Gently Ash took it and put the true-heart in Shaard's palm. The false-heart was ice-cold in Ash's hand, its serpentine wisps snapping threateningly. Ash would once have found them frightening, but now?

So much hate, so much death and destruction.

What a sad thing it was.

Without a soul to protect it, Ash closed his hand round it.

Shadowy vapour threaded through his fingers, drifting into the air with what sounded like a long, tired sigh. Ash opened his hand. There was nothing but dust left in his palm.

Trembling, Shaard opened his eyes again, and smiled when he saw the true-heart's warm glow.

He let out another breath, but this time of relief, rather than fear.

'That's better.' He grinned.

'Yes?'

Shaard nodded. 'But your one? It's gone?'

'It's OK,' Ash said. 'We set it free.'

'It won't be sad any more?'

'It won't.' Ash smiled.

Sunlight suddenly streamed out from behind the frozen clouds, filling the bleak grey world with wondrous light. Ash and Shaard looked at it together.

It was the most beautiful thing Ash had ever seen. He closed his eyes, and let it thaw his frozen face.

'I'm tired of being cold,' Shaard said with a little shiver, 'but it's warm over there. It . . . it feels like a new home.'

He walked towards the light that gleamed in the distance, like Mother Sun rising above the horizon. Ash began to follow, but then heard something jingle at his neck. He took hold of the star pendant that hung there.

'*Lunah* . . .' Ash whispered. This place had formed an icy shell around his memories, but the sunlight was melting it away.

He'd made a promise. A promise to find her again, no matter where he ended up.

'It's OK,' Shaard said, noticing Ash's hesitation. 'I can go on my own from here.'

'Are – are you sure?'

'Mm-hm. You said you had a family, and it would be mean to take you away from them.'

'You won't feel lonely?' Ash asked. The boy shook his head.

'I have this!' He held up the true-heart. 'I can already hear it Singing. It's happy!'

The boy trotted off across the ice, towards the light. Ash watched him with a smile, surprised to feel a tear trickling down his cheek.

'Thank you for your help!' Shaard called back, turning to look at Ash with those bright turquoise eyes one last time. 'I'll see you, Ash!'

'I'll see you,' Ash said, waving back.

He stood there for some time, watching the boy walk away into the light.

52

THE PRICE TO PAY

The Devourer's Song came to an abrupt end.

It reared its head back, choking with ice-cracking grunts, its eyes wide with alarm. It tried to roar, it tried to shriek and cry out, but it couldn't make a sound.

Its heart was gone, and, with it, its Song as well.

Lunah came to consciousness, rubbing her head and trying to recall what had just happened. Her head felt thick and full, as though it had been stuffed with fog.

She started, looking up in terrified awe at the monster that towered as high as a mountain above her. It writhed and twisted in dismay, its frantic movements slowing and becoming sluggish. Lunah shuffled back as fast as she could, trying to get out of the way of the squirming black gloop that fell from it like fat from a roasting ulk, sizzling on the snow. Its skin turned deathly pale as frost crawled over its withering flesh, consuming the Devourer from the inside out. Its jaws opened wide as it let out a silent scream as frost engulfed its head, the violent green of its frantically darting eyes draining to a cold, frozen white.

Before long even they didn't move.

The Devourer had become a mountain of ice, standing almost as tall as Aurora itself.

The snow plains fell silent. The entire world seemed to take a breath, as if unsure what had just happened, or how to react.

Wind howled across the snow and ruffled through sleigh sails.

The warriors of the fleet began to awaken, each of them as groggy and confused as Lunah had been.

Someone let out a cry. Quiet and small, compared to the deafening chaos of what had come before. It was a cry of happiness, pure as a bell chime.

There was another shout, then another.

As the truth dawned on them – the wonderful, incredible, *unbelievable* truth – the allies erupted into a victorious cheer. They leaped up and down. They hugged each other. They smiled, they laughed, they wept.

Cheers could be heard from within Aurora, those inside daring to hope that the danger had passed.

They had survived.

Somehow they had survived.

The Devourer had been destroyed.

The Leviathans roared up at the dark sky. They'd gathered around the body of the Brood Mother, who had fallen from her wounds. Their Songs were strained with sorrow at the loss of their leader, their auras weaving up and around the titanic mass of ice tenderly. But for the first time in a thousand years, they didn't Sing only of mourning but also of hope.

The yeti army roared in triumph from outside the walls, the Corrupted's will to fight lost with their master.

Lunah staggered to her feet and stumbled through the wreckage of the sleigh she had loved so much, trying not to think about the *Frostheart*'s demise. There would be time to be sad later.

She needed to find the others. Her crew. Her family.

Her heart leaped when she saw them, huddled together beside the ruined hull. But the relief she felt at finding her friends alive was short-lived.

One of the crew had not got up.

Ember Stormbreaker, once the most powerful war leader in all the Snow Sea, now sat on the ground, her son resting on her knees, his head cradled in her arms.

She was weeping.

'Oh no, oh no no no . . .' Lunah muttered as she ran over to them, the rest of the crew making space for her, their faces creased with sadness.

Ash's limbs were limp, his eyes closed. Ember touched her forehead to Ash's, her tears falling into his messy black hair.

'My boy, my boy . . .' She choked through her tears.

Lunah began to cry, Nuk pulling her in close, Yallah placing a hand on Lunah's shoulder.

Lunah could barely think. How could this have happened?

Ember wailed like a wild animal, her cry full of pain.

'Wake up!' she sobbed, running her hands through Ash's hair. 'Wake up! Please, Ash, your mother's here. She's here, and she needs you to wake up!'

She brought her head back down to his, clutching him tight as she rocked back and forth. The *Frostheart* crew bowed their heads as the fleet continued to cheer around them, unaware of this one terrible loss amid such a joyous victory.

Ember only stirred when she became aware of many large shapes heading towards her. She stiffened, looking up with her good eye as the Leviathans approached. There were many, but one in particular clawed forward, approaching Ash's unmoving body.

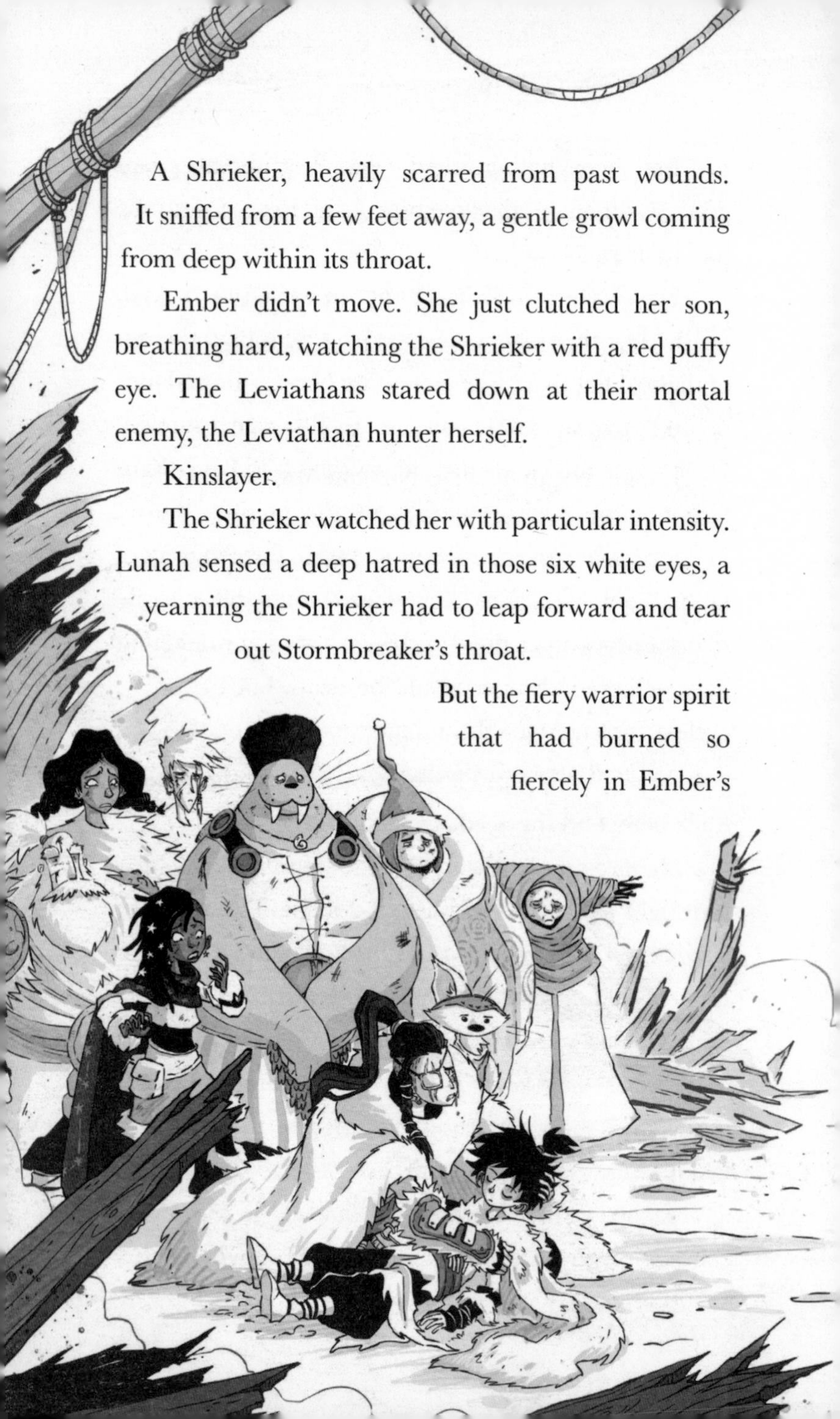

A Shrieker, heavily scarred from past wounds. It sniffed from a few feet away, a gentle growl coming from deep within its throat.

Ember didn't move. She just clutched her son, breathing hard, watching the Shrieker with a red puffy eye. The Leviathans stared down at their mortal enemy, the Leviathan hunter herself.

Kinslayer.

The Shrieker watched her with particular intensity. Lunah sensed a deep hatred in those six white eyes, a yearning the Shrieker had to leap forward and tear out Stormbreaker's throat.

But the fiery warrior spirit that had burned so fiercely in Ember's eye had been extinguished. The Stormbreaker was gone, and now all that remained was Ember. And she had no fight left in her.

Lunah saw something change in Ember then. As if, for the first time, she saw what Ash had shown the rest of them. That there was something besides animal fury behind those six cold glassy eyes. Intelligence. Emotion. Deep anger, of course – there always was with Leviathans – but a great sadness too. All the terrible history Leviathans and human-kin had shared, the centuries of killing and hate. The Leviathans could have easily struck Ember down there and then, but what would that have achieved? Ember would be dead, but the cycle of violence would continue.

Ash had wanted to bring that cycle to an end.

The Leviathans understood that as well as Lunah did. And they wanted to respect it.

For the first time in her vengeance-fuelled life, Ember saw what her life-mate and son had tried to tell her.

That the Leviathans were not monsters.

That they were so much more.

The scarred Shrieker lowered its eyes to Ash, its tail dipping in sorrow. It looked back at Ember, as if acknowledging the price she'd already had to pay for her actions.

And with that the Leviathans turned from the human-kin and vanished beneath the snow.

EPILOGUE

Three Years Later

Lunah strode through the busy Aurora docks, a spring in her step.

The Council Moot had been incredibly exciting. She hadn't really paid too much attention to what was being said (more stuff about the Great Thaw and new trade routes and building roads linking the Embrace, and yadda yadda yadda); she'd just been over the moon to see Captain – wait, *Councillor* – Nuk up there on the *Wayfinder*'s enjin, taking her new position upon the Council.

Where she flippin' belongs, Lunah thought with a smile. She'd been told off by the other councillors for being a distraction during the meeting. All she'd been doing was trying to give Nuk the ol' thumbs up.

Sure, she'd been leaping up and down like a Spearwurm, wildly throwing her arms around all over the place, but how else would she have got Nuk's attention?

Nuk had looked very serious while they were telling Lunah off, and Lunah had worried that the new responsibilities had changed her. But then she caught Nuk sneaking her a knowing wink, that old, mischievous grin creeping on to the mursu's face.

She was the same as ever.

Aurora's Embrace was in for some change, though. Good change. And woe betide anyone who messed with things now that Nuk was in charge.

Lunah pushed through the crowd and arrived at the wharf she needed. She put her hands on her hips, admiring her vessel.

The *Frostheart II.*

It wasn't the most original name, granted. *Frosthearts* had been suggested by the crew, as had the *Heart-Song.* Lunah had wanted to go with the *Frost-fart*, herself, but had been outvoted.

When no clear decision can be made, why fix what isn't broken?

Frostheart II it was.

Lunah liked the name. It had legacy. It had meaning – so much meaning – to each and every

person that served aboard. Besides, it had been built using the *Frostheart*'s salvaged sunstone enjin, so the vessels were related.

Kinda like the Frostheart*'s baby*, Lunah thought.

It was a smaller sleigh than its namesake, but nippier too, and Lunah loved it.

'Preparations are complete, captain,' Master Podd said, appearing at her side and making Lunah jump. He had a habit of doing that.

'Excellent work, Master Podd!' she replied in the most Nuk-ish voice she could muster. She strode up the gangplank, Master Podd following close behind, his paws clasped behind his back.

'How's the ol' cap'n doin'?' Kailen asked as she spotted Lunah.

'Crackin' heads an' takin' names.' Lunah grinned. 'Same old, really.'

'I'd have it no other way,' said Kob.

'How's she soundin', enjineer?' Lunah called to the upper deck, where Yallah poked her head round the sunstone enjin, her face smudged with oil.

'Purring like a Gargant, captain!'

'All supplies an' rations in order?' she asked as Tobu passed by, carrying what looked like three times his weight in crates. He gave a curt nod.

'Aye aye, cap'n!' Twinge beamed, sitting atop the

stack. 'Got some lovely redroot for this trip, learned some delicious-sounding recipes from a travelling group of Rimeridge merchants. Apparently the trick is to hide the flavour with herbs and spices. What they recommended was –'

'Lovely stuff!' Lunah said, trying to avoid one of Twinge's long stories. She wanted them to leave *before* the Great Thaw melted all the ice.

Arla gave Lunah a wave from her healing tents on the upper deck.

How old must she be now? Lunah wondered, waving back. *Seventy winters? A hundred and twenty-five?* The crew was too scared to ask, though all were happy she was still there to fix 'em up.

'How's it lookin', Teya?' Lunah shouted up to the lookout in the crow's nest.

'A few other sleighs on the move, cap'n,' Teya called down. 'But clear enough to leave when you give the order!'

'Nice,' Lunah said to herself.

She was eager to get going. It was a long way to the Fira Stronghold, and the sooner they left, the better. They couldn't go just yet, though. There was still one crew member missing.

Lunah leaped up to a line of rigging that hung low from the mast, pulling herself up into a sitting position.

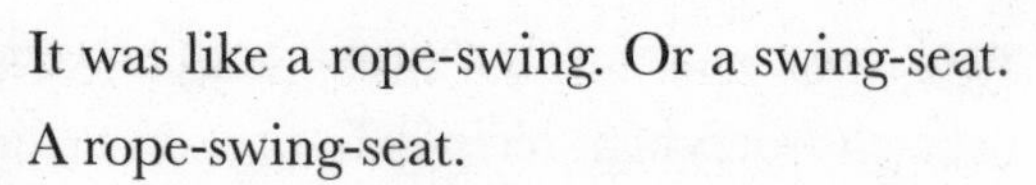

It was like a rope-swing. Or a swing-seat. A rope-swing-seat.

She rocked to and fro, looking out into the bustling crowds.

He wasn't usually late.

Lunah guessed his mum was probably keeping him busy. She'd been reluctant to let him go on the last few runs.

She'd rather have him stickin' round Aurora, Lunah thought, *where it's safe.* But his mother knew as well as Lunah that he wouldn't be able to grow roots in a Stronghold, not having had a taste of true freedom.

Once a Pathfinder, always a Pathfinder.

Lunah looked up at one of the openings in the mountain wall high above the Stronghold. Just visible beyond its rim she could spy the top of the Devourer's frozen head. It had changed shape over the years, the ice slowly melting with the coming of the Great Thaw, but it was still mind-bogglingly large. A truly awesome sight, and one that could still put a chill in one's heart.

A reminder of just how close they'd all come to the end.

Hard to believe that was three years ago, Lunah thought.

And, even after all that time, no one really knew what stopped the Devourer in the end.

Some argued it was the Leviathans and their Brood Mother.

Others insisted it was the Eclipse that did it in.

But all those that had been there during the Battle of Aurora still had the strange dreams. Of an endless dark. A terrible sense of loss and defeat. And yet, amid all the hopelessness, the Song. A Song that brought everyone together, a shining light to guide everyone out of the despair to freedom. But whenever anyone, Lunah included, tried to recall any more details, the images would fade, just like a dream dissolving in your first waking moments.

All anyone really knew was that victory couldn't have been achieved without the Song Weavers, and for that Lunah couldn't be happier. Just so long as the stories remembered the *Frostheart's* part in it all too. And how cool she'd looked riding a Shrieker. That would be sweet.

Song Weavers were in high demand among Pathfinders these days. The Leviathans had gone very quiet since the Battle of Aurora (though the crew had regularly spotted a lone Shrieker up in the skies during their voyages, apparently keeping a protective eye on the *Frostheart II*, a slight wobble in its glide). But out in the wilds sightings of Corrupted were still being reported, souls too far gone to have broken free of the Devourer, even after its death. It never hurt to have someone who could speak 'viathan, just in case.

'Old wounds scar deep,' Lunah whispered to herself. She spotted a crow perched upon the *Frostheart II*'s mainmast. It was staring at her with its fathomless black eyes.

Creepy thing, Lunah thought with a smile. *Kinda reminds me of Rook.*

Lunah had heard rumours that Rook had travelled far, far away, in search of an old long-lost friend. She wondered if she'd managed to find them. Wherever Rook was, she hoped she was happy.

The crow cried out, as if replying to Lunah's thoughts. It then ruffled its feathers and took wing, flying out into the light of an opening in the mountain. Lunah watched it go, then dropped down from the rigging, feeling impatient. She'd just resigned herself to having to go and look for her missing crewman herself when she spotted him.

His unmistakable messy black hair was still tied up in a small flame-shaped ponytail. His movements were still shy and nervous, despite all he'd seen and done. He looked up apologetically, hefting the large bag slung over his shoulder, jingling his star amulet.

'Yeah, you'd better hurry!' she called out to him, a

huge grin on her face. 'You'd a' thought spendin' three weeks in a coma woulda been enough lazin' about to last a lifetime!'

He returned her smile, weaving through the crowd towards the *Frostheart II*, whose enjins roared to life, ready for departure.

'Nearly left without you,' Lunah said. 'An' then you woulda had to walk all the way to the Fira, an' what kinda heroic return would that a' been?'

She was teasing, of course. She would've waited for as long as he needed.

He was her best friend after all.

And what was a Pathfinder crew without its Song Weaver?

ACKNOWLEDGMENTS

And so the *Frostheart* reaches its journey's end, but what a journey it's been! I feel incredibly fortunate to have taken part in this voyage, this passion project, not least because of all the brilliant people I've had the pleasure to meet and work with along the way. Here are thanks to just a few of those who made this adventure possible.

Endless gratitude to my fantastic agent Jodie Hodges and team at United Agents – Emily Talbot, Molly Jamieson and Jane Willis. You are the navigators who are yet to steer me wrong.

To all those at the wonderful home I have found at Puffin. I honestly couldn't imagine having a more passionate, caring and down-right courageous crew to run these dangerous paths with. To my first mates, my brilliant editors – Naomi Colthurst, Maggie Rosenthal and Ben Horlsen. Editors are nothing short of wizards, and this series is as much yours as it is mine. It simply would not be what it is without all your considered, tireless work. I'm especially thankful for all the times you somehow managed to calm my manic panics of self-doubt, how with such patience and good humour you allowed me to chew your ears off for countless hours as I meandered down every possible thread of the story, while kindly filling the plot holes I left in my wake.

Mountains of thanks to my flawless designers Ben Hughes and Janene Spencer. As an illustrator, this series has been an absolute dream project, and this was all thanks to the trust, ideas and endless care you poured into these books. Every time you sent me the finished layouts, I already knew they'd look insane without even having to open the file.

To Stephanie Barrett, Rebecca Blevins, Shreeta Shah, Jennie Roman and all who helped proofread and copy-edit my books. Your attention to detail helped make the Snow Sea feel like a real place.

For the number of times you've saved me from certain embarrassment alone, you have my eternal gratitude.

I couldn't have asked for the Frostheart series to look any cooler and to feel any more special, and this is largely thanks to the brilliant production team at Puffin. I still can't get over the die-cut covers and how well the ink sits on the pages within, and that's not even to speak of the spredges. Oh man – those *spredges*!

It's all well and good putting all this time and effort into making these books, but it's for nothing if no one reads them. So thank the spirits I've had such a fantastic team of publicists and marketers behind me, whose brilliant ideas, captivating campaigns and rousing calls from the crow's nest have got these books into so many readers' hands. Extra rations for Catherine Alport, Kat Baker, Evelyn Opoku-Agyeman, Lucie Sharpe, Roz Hutchison, Sophia Smith and Phoebe Williams (we will take this series on the road again!). This sleigh would never have left port without you all.

Big thanks to Joshua McGuire for lending his voice to the audiobook versions of *Frostheart*, and bringing the characters to such vivid life.

I'd also like to thank all the schools and festivals who've invited me to do events with them. You have all given me such warm welcomes and watched with such rapt attention that you have helped turn this nervous Strongholder into a (somewhat) brave Pathfinder, keen to travel the lands and spread the word!

A big thank you to all my publishers overseas who have shown the Frostheart series as much love in their translations as it was created with.

I want to say a very special thank you to Florentyna Martin at Waterstones and Gavin Hetherington of the Book Keeper Stronghold (and also How to Train Your Gavin fame). I am so lucky and honoured to have received your endless kindness and support. The Weavers will Sing your names for years to come! To all the passionate booksellers, inspiring librarians, heroic teachers, admirable reviewers, bloggers, tweeters, grammers and booktubers. I have felt so embraced by your wonderful respective communities and it never fails to humble me.

Of course, these books wouldn't exist without the support of my amazing family, friends and fellow creators. Karl Newson, Erika Meza, Chloe Douglass, Pedro Douglass-Kirk, David O'Connell, Alex Milway, Sarah McIntyre, Gary Northfield, Samantha Meredith, Steve Wood, Louie Stowell, Steve Lenton, the Hamertons, and, of course, Fran, Lorna and all my wonderful St Albans lot (you know who you are). Having written this book in the midst of a global pandemic has shown me just how important, helpful and inspiring friends truly are.

My mum and dad, who thankfully didn't disappear into the wilds but instead have always been there, encouraging me every step of the way. My brother Paul and my sister Nicole for always having my back.

And, perhaps most importantly, Laura Ellen Anderson. If there was one gleaming guiding star in the night sky, it would be you.

As much as I've gone on here, these thanks barely scratch the surface. There are simply too many names to list, and names I will undoubtedly kick myself for not including. But please know to any who have supported me, read my books, tweeted about them and let me know you or your children have enjoyed them, you have my utmost gratitude and have turned this frosty heart into a thing of warmth and sunlight.

May your paths be clear, the snows be still, and the stars guide your way.